'Funny and witty, a great read that gives us a look into the workings of the male mind' *The Sun*

'A well-crafted tale of when love goes wrong and love goes right – witty, astute but tender too' Freya North

'Frighteningly funny and sometimes just plain frightening . . . the most realistic perspective on the average man's world view most women will get without hanging around in a locker room' Chris Manby

'Delightfully shallow and self-obsessed – that's the male psyche for you' *Elle*

'An amusing insight into the minds of men' *Daily Express*

'A warm, open and damn funny book' *Lads Mag*

'Both hilarious and touching' *Best*

'Hilarious' *Cosmopolitan*

'Funny and sweet, this is a quirky glimpse into the mind of a bloke' *Woman*

Matt Dunn is the author of five previous novels, including the bestselling *The Ex-Boyfriend's Handbook*, which was shortlisted for both the Romantic Novel of the Year Award and the Melissa Nathan Award for Comedy Romance. He's also written about life, love, and relationships for various publications including *The Times*, *Guardian*, *Cosmopolitan*, *Company*, *Glamour*, *Elle*, and the *Sun*.

Matt was born in Margate, but escaped to Spain to write his first novel, in-between working as a newspaper columnist and playing a lot of tennis. Previously he has been a professional lifeguard, fitness-equipment salesman and an I.T. head-hunter, but he prefers writing for a living, so please buy his other books.

Visit the author at www.mattdunn.co.uk

By the same author

Best Man
The Ex-Boyfriend's Handbook
From Here to Paternity
Ex-Girlfriends United
The Good Bride Guide

The Accidental Proposal

MATT DUNN

SIMON &
SCHUSTER

London · New York · Sydney · Toronto

A CBS COMPANY

First published in Great Britain by Simon & Schuster UK Ltd, 2011
A CBS COMPANY

3 5 7 9 10 8 6 4

Simon & Schuster UK Ltd
1st Floor,
222 Gray's Inn Road
London WC1X 8HB

www.simonandschuster.co.uk

Simon & Schuster Australia
Sydney

A CIP catalogue record for this book
is available from the British Library

ISBN 978-1-84739-524-5

Typeset by M Rules
Printed and bound in Great Britain by
CPI Cox & Wyman, Reading, Berkshire RG1 8EX

For Kate Lyall Grant

Sunday, 5 April

9.08 p.m.

'I'm sorry, Edward.' Dan frowns, then places his beer bottle carefully on the bar in front of him. 'What's "re-dancing"?'

'No, Daniel,' I say, as if explaining something to a five-year-old – a tactic I have to employ surprisingly often where Dan's concerned. 'I said, "some Scottish country dancing". Not . . . Well, not what you thought, anyway.'

'Oh. Right.' He grins, sheepishly. 'Sorry.'

As is customary every Sunday evening, Dan and I are sitting at the bar of our favourite Brighton pub, the Admiral Jim. I'm telling him about the wedding that my girlfriend Sam and I went to yesterday, while nervously waiting for the right moment to mention one that he might be invited to – and as my best man – but, as is usual whenever I try to steer the conversation away from the superficial world that Dan inhabits, he's not making it easy for me.

'So.' I take a deep breath. 'Weddings, eh?'

'Tell me about them.' Dan pokes the wedge of lime further down the neck of his bottle with his index finger. 'In fact, why anyone wants to get married is beyond me.'

'There are a lot of things that are beyond you, Dan. Fidelity, an IQ score in double figures . . .'

Dan removes his finger from the bottle and sucks the lime juice off it, childishly sticking the finger next to it up at me at the same time. 'I mean, for one thing, getting married increases your chances of splitting up, doesn't it?'

I put my pint of lager down and swivel on my stool to face him. 'I realize I might regret saying this, but I'm going to have to ask you to explain that one.'

'Simple,' says Dan, although I presume he's referring to his forthcoming explanation rather than me. 'What's the current divorce rate?'

'I dunno.'

'Well I do, mister eye-queue. Two out of three. Which, percentage-wise, is . . .'

I let him struggle with the maths for a moment, then put him out of his misery. 'Sixty-six and two thirds.'

'Exactly,' he says, taking a swift gulp of beer. 'And it's going up.'

'Partly due to the amount of married women who throw themselves at you, no doubt.'

He opens his mouth to challenge me, then realizes he doesn't have a leg to stand on, so instead, just makes the 'what can you do?' face. Dan, it has to be said, is ridiculously good-looking; although at a shade under six feet tall he's slightly shorter than he'd like. Everything else about him – from his uncommonly white teeth, gym-honed physique, the tan he keeps topped up at Tan-Fastic on the High Street, and his immaculately styled and highlighted (although he denies the last bit) hair – evidently combines to make him what I believe is known as a 'babe-magnet'. In fact, on the odd occasion he and I have been out clubbing, I've seen women so keen to sleep with him that they literally trample over each other – and me – like it's the first day of the sales.

'Whereas,' he continues, 'with you and Sam, all the while you're girlfriend and boyfriend, you've only got two options: either you stay together, or you don't, right?'

'Ri-ight. So?'

'So that means there's a fifty per cent chance of you splitting up. Or not.'

'I'm not sure that's quite . . .'

'Which is less than if you get married,' he concludes, gesturing towards me with his beer bottle, then dabbing at the spot of beer he's just splashed down the front of the ironically vintage 'sex and drugs and sausage rolls' T-shirt he's wearing under his leather jacket. 'Proves my point.'

'There's a point in all of that?'

'Obviously,' says Dan, as if I'm the slow one, 'that it's better not to get married if you want to stay together.'

For a moment, I consider trying to explain exactly where his theory falls down, but realize the pub's due to close in three hours. Besides, there's something more important I need to talk to him about.

'Well, that's a shame. Particularly where Sam and I are concerned.'

'Why?'

I grin guiltily at him. 'Why do you think?'

As I wait for the grey mush that passes for Dan's brain to process what I've just said, it's hard to read his expression, although that's probably due to the fact that even though we've been sitting here for the best part of half an hour, he's still wearing the cap and sunglasses disguise he hardly ever leaves home without nowadays. Dan's a bit of a celebrity, having made his name as the presenter of the housewives' and students' favourite daytime antiques programme *Where There's a Will* and, up until recently, playing the part of Wayne Kerr in *Close Encounters*, ITV5's popular soap opera set in a cul-de-sac here in Brighton. At the moment, however, he's 'resting', although it's something of an enforced rest, having been sacked as Wayne after a disastrous appearance on *Children in Need* where he was asked – live – what he liked most in a woman, and he replied 'my penis'.

'You're joking, Edward,' he says, after the best part of a minute.

'I've never been more serious. Both about what I'm saying, and, you know, Sam.'

Dan removes his cap slowly, followed by his Ray-

Bans, but for once doesn't automatically check his hair-style in the reflection of the lenses. 'You've asked Sam to marry you?'

'Well . . .' I shift uncomfortably on my seat, wondering whether I should tell him the actual story, but he doesn't give me a chance.

'She's not pregnant, is she?'

'No, Dan, she's not pregnant.'

'And what did she say?'

'Well, *yes*, of course.'

Dan frowns. '"Yes", of course? Or "yes of course"?'

'What does it matter? The important word is yes.'

'Not necessarily,' says Dan, gravely. 'The "of course" part might suggest that she's doing it out of some mis-placed sense of duty, whereas . . .' He stops talking and scowls at me, possibly because I'm repeating the words 'la, la, la' over and over again with my fingers stuck in my ears. 'Very mature, Edward,' he says, when I've eventually finished.

'Stop over-analysing everything and just congratulate me, will you?'

Dan shrugs. 'Well, congratulations,' he says, picking up his bottle of beer again and clinking it against my pint glass. 'Blimey – you're engaged. To be *married*.'

'I guess so,' I say, conscious that I'm grinning like an idiot. 'I can hardly believe it.'

'*You* can hardly believe it?' Dan shakes his head. 'I mean, you marrying Sam. It's like . . .' He struggles to think of an example. 'Two years ago, you were at the bottom of the second division. And now . . . you've won the European Cup. Talk about a result.'

For a minute I don't know what to say to that. I suppose it's a back-handed compliment, given how unfit, unhealthy, untrendy and evidently unattractive I was back then, which led to Jane, my girlfriend of ten years, dumping me, and telling me to sort myself out. I decided to take her advice, and so started taking Dan's, by losing the weight. Stopping the smoking. Swapping the John Smith's for Paul Smith. And by finding out what women wanted (although initially, I found out what it wasn't – me). And while I might not exactly be in Dan's league, nowadays I could probably pass for his taller, dark-haired, slightly less trendy and athletic cousin in the right light – which Dan would say would be semi-darkness.

'Thanks. I think.'

'So, come on.' He nudges me, causing me to spill some beer on my jeans. 'What was it like? I mean, how did it feel? When you asked her.'

'None of your business.'

'Why not?'

'It's embarrassing.'

Dan starts poking me in the ribs. 'Come on. You can tell me. Your oldest friend.'

'Get off!'

'Okay. I'll get it out of her instead,' he says, reaching for the latest of his regularly upgraded iPhones that he's positioned in full view on the bar in front of him.

'Don't you dare.'

'Well, at least tell me how you did it. Were you nervous?'

'Not really.'

'Not really?' Dan narrows his eyes. 'The man who has zero confidence with women proposed *just like that*, and without the slightest doubt that she might say no?'

'Well . . .' I clear my throat, worrying that I might have dug myself a bit of a hole. 'To tell you the truth, we just, you know, *decided*.'

Dan stares at me, waiting for the rest of the story. 'And that was it?' he says, when I don't expand.

'What do you mean, "that was it"?'

'You didn't get down on one knee? Do all the big romantic stuff?'

'Er . . . not exactly.'

'Why not?'

I feel myself start to blush. 'Because I hadn't really prepared anything. I mean, I would have, if I'd thought about it. But sometimes you've got to strike while the iron's hot, haven't you? See an opportunity and go for it. Like you're always telling me – you snooze, you lose. Nice guys finish last, and all that.'

'Which is a philosophy I subscribe to,' says Dan, leaning over and nudging me again. 'Particularly in bed. Where I'm a really nice guy, if you know what I mean.'

'I get it, Dan. Although I wish I didn't.'

Dan grins, then takes another gulp of lager. 'Hold on,' he says, eyeing me suspiciously. 'Something doesn't ring true here.'

'What are you talking about?'

'Well, how long have you been planning this?'

I shrug. 'I don't know. I mean, "planning" is such a strong word, isn't it? Although I suppose I've been thinking about it for a while.'

'And yet this is the first time I've heard anything about it.'

I sigh. 'Dan, I don't tell you everything I'm intending to do where me and women are concerned.'

'Which is probably why it's taken you thirty-one years to get one to agree to marry you.' He shakes his head. 'But if you've been intending to do it for so long . . .'

'Yes?'

'Why didn't you do it properly?'

I puff air out of my cheeks. 'Well, what does "properly" mean, really? Surely the important thing was that she said yes.'

'Or "Yes of course" . . .' Dan stares at me for a moment, then a smile creeps across his face. 'She asked you, didn't she?'

'No, of course not. How could you say such a thing?'

'Because it's the truth. Come on. Admit it.'

'No!'

'"No", as in you're not going to admit it, which means she did, or "no" as in you're not going to tell me?' He leans back smugly on his stool. 'Which probably means the same thing.'

'Shut up, Dan. It's none of your business. And why are you so interested anyway?'

'It's just that . . .' He starts picking absent-mindedly at a loose thread on his jacket. 'Well, I doubt I'll get married myself. Particularly given the way things are going with my love life.'

'What do you mean? I thought you were still having to fight them off?'

'Of course I am.' He grins. 'This is Brighton. There are women on every corner. Although some of those are prostitutes . . .' He clears his throat. 'Anyway, my point is, why tie myself down with just the one? Which is why I'm interested to experience it through your eyes. You know – like a vicar.'

It takes me a few seconds to work out what he's talking about. '*Vicariously*, Dan.'

He suddenly looks a little sad. 'That's what I meant. But seriously, as fun as this lifestyle of mine is, I can't really see myself ever meeting the future Mrs Dan Davis this way.'

'Well, that's because you generally have to go out with someone more than the once – you know, have what's called a relationship – before you can think about marrying them.'

'That's easy for you to say, mister smug shacked-up,' he says, his bottom lip trembling a little. 'But I have to face the fact that I might never get to experience true love, like you and Sam obviously have. So the thought of someone caring enough about me to ask me if I'd marry them is, well, it makes me . . .' He stops talking, sniffs loudly, then stares off into the distance, lifting up a hand to rub his eye. 'Especially since my one chance of happiness seems to have found someone else.'

'Huh?'

Dan leans heavily against the bar. '*Polly*, you muppet.'

'Ah. Of course,' I say, immediately feeling sorry for him. Polly is Dan's significant ex; the girl he dated for a while after he left college, although when his TV career took off, so did she. I've always hoped the two of them might get back together, and he even thought about it last year, but a rare moment of selflessness given the fact that she had a boyfriend – or more likely, the fear that if he did, it might have to be for ever – meant that it didn't happen. Even so, he still refers to her as 'the one that got away' – although sometimes I think she's had a lucky escape. 'I forgot you still felt that way. Yes, you're right. Sam did ask me, and . . .'

'I knew it!' Dan sits bolt upright and slaps one palm loudly on his thigh. 'Just like I knew those acting lessons would come in handy. You should have seen your face.' He grabs me by the shoulder and shakes me gleefully. 'Admit it. You were about to hand me a tissue, weren't you?'

'You bastard.'

'Sam asked you to marry her,' he says, in an annoying little sing-song voice. 'Ho ho. I bet you thought you were going to get something else when she knelt down in front of you.'

'Dan, it wasn't like that. She didn't kneel down in front of me. And do you have to bring sex into everything?'

'If I can, yes.'

'Well, just don't tell anyone, okay?'

Dan shrugs. 'Discreet is my middle name.'

'Only if 'in' is your first.'

'Edward, I'm offended. Give me an example of a time I've dropped you in it?'

I stroke my chin thoughtfully. 'Well . . .'

'You see, you can't come up with any.'

'I'm having more of a problem choosing just the one.'

Dan laughs, then drains the rest of his beer and slams his bottle noisily down on the bar. 'Anyway, however it happened, this calls for champagne.'

'There's no need for . . .'

'Of course there is. It's not every day that your best friend gets engaged, is it?'

'I suppose not,' I say, then sit there, waiting for Dan to order a bottle, but instead, he starts patting his jacket pockets like a parachutist desperately trying to locate his rip-cord.

As his expression changes to one of helplessness, I sigh. In the twelve or so years I've known him, and despite the fact that his last TV job paid around five times my annual salary, I could probably count the number of times he's bought me a drink on the fingers of one hand — even if I'd lost most of those fingers to frostbite. It's not that he's stingy; more that Dan changes his outfit so often before leaving the house — even when he's just coming for a drink with me — that his wallet doesn't always manage to accompany him.

I wave towards the other end of the bar in an attempt to attract the attention of Wendy, the Admiral Jim's pretty in a dark-haired boyish-figured Meg-Ryan-in-*You've-Got-Mail* kind of way manager. She's just come back to work after having a baby with her boyfriend, Andy, and is evidently suffering from the late nights and early mornings, as she looks as though she's doing her best not to nod off.

'Edward,' she says, ignoring Dan as usual as she walks over to where we're sitting. Wendy's not Dan's biggest fan, although that's due to his rather ungentlemanly attitude towards the women he dates rather than the quality of his television work. 'What can I get you?'

'A bottle of cham—'

'Your *finest* champagne, please,' interrupts Dan, before jabbing a thumb in my direction. 'Edward's buying.'

Wendy raises both eyebrows. 'I'll just dust one off,' she says, reaching into the fridge behind her and producing a bottle of Moët, then heading off to retrieve a couple of flutes from the shelf at the other end of the bar. 'What are you celebrating? Dan finally reaching puberty?'

'No, Wendy,' sighs Dan, sliding his empty beer bottle along the bar towards her like a cowboy in a saloon. 'We just thought it'd make a nice change from this piss-flavoured stuff you sell branded as lager.'

'Yes, well, there's a reason yours tastes like that,' says Wendy, flicking her eyes towards the ladies.

'I've just got engaged,' I say quickly, trying to defuse the situation.

'To Sam,' adds Dan, a little unnecessarily.

Wendy rolls her eyes at him, then breaks into a grin. 'Congratulations, Edward,' she says, leaning over the bar to give me a hug. 'That's a surprise.'

'Not as much of a surprise as it was for Edward,' whispers Dan.

'Pardon?'

'Nothing, Wendy,' I say, a little embarrassed. 'And thanks.'

'You're welcome,' she says, peeling the foil off the top of the champagne bottle. 'So have you set a date?'

'No. Well, not yet. I mean, it all happened so quickly.'

'Funny,' says Wendy. 'That's exactly what my flatmate said after she slept with Dan.'

'Ha, ha, ha,' says Dan, eyeing her warily. 'Not.'

I kick him lightly on the shin. 'Join us for a glass?'

'I can't,' she says, looking at the bottle longingly as she levers the cork out with her thumbs. 'I'm breast feeding.'

'Really?' Dan stares pointedly at Wendy's less-than-bountiful cleavage, and for a moment I'm worried he's going to let slip that he refers to her as 'the pirate' on account of her sunken chest. 'The poor little mite must be starving.'

As he swivels back round to face me, chuckling to himself, Wendy smiles sweetly, then fires the champagne cork expertly at the side of his head, causing him to yelp in pain. 'Well, congratulations again, Edward,' she says, filling up the two glasses. 'To both of you. That's you and Sam, I mean,' she adds for Dan's benefit, before heading back to the other end of the bar.

'You might have told me to duck,' he says, scowling at her, while rubbing the spot where the cork's hit him.

'You're right. I might have – if I didn't think you deserved it.'

'So come on,' he says, picking his glass up, clinking it against mine, then downing the contents in one go. 'How did she ask you?'

I stare at Dan for a moment, then decide I've got nothing to lose by telling him. 'Well, it was yesterday evening, and we'd had a nice day at the wedding, not to mention a few drinks, and we were in bed discussing it, and . . .'

'You were in bed with Sam and *talking*?'

I ignore his wide-eyed interruption. 'And – I don't know – maybe we were caught up in the moment, but all of a sudden, she asked me if I wanted to get married, and before I knew it, I'd said yes. End of story.'

As I take a mouthful of champagne, the colour suddenly drains from Dan's face. 'Hang on,' he says, 'what were her exact words?'

'I can't really remember. "Do you want to get married?" or something like that. You know what my memory's like when I've had a few.'

Dan folds his arms. 'So, let me get this straight. You were both a bit drunk, and at some random point in the evening, she said, "Do you want to get married?" and you took it as a proposal, rather than a question?'

'Well, obviously, yes,' I say, struggling to work out what the difference is.

'She didn't get down on one knee, or say, "Will you marry me?" like most people do. And like you tried to have me believe you did earlier?'

'Well, no, but . . .'

'And you didn't think that she might have been asking *generally*?'

I get a sudden uncomfortable feeling in my stomach. 'Generally?'

'Yup. Like . . .' Dan's face scrunches up in concentration as he tries to come up with an example. 'If you were talking about America, say, and she'd said to you, "Do you want to visit America?" Well, the obvious answer is, "Yes, one day." Unless you're actually standing in the travel agent's, you can't possibly think she's suggesting the two of you go together there and then.'

'That's rubbish.'

'Really?'

'Yes, really. She was clearly asking me.'

'Doesn't sound that clear to me.' Dan snorts.

'Yes, well, you weren't there, were you?' I say, putting my glass down angrily. 'And besides, the only way to make anything clear to you is to spell it out. With very short words. And in very big letters.'

Dan holds his hands up. 'Okay, okay. Keep what's left of your hair on. I just want to make sure you didn't get hold of the wrong end of the stick. After all, it wouldn't be the first time.'

'This wasn't like that, thank you very much,' I say,

glaring at him. Dan is referring to an incident last year, where Sam and I were on holiday in Majorca, and we'd had an argument, and she'd asked me to leave. Turned out she'd been referring to the room, whereas I thought she'd meant the island, and we almost split up because of it.

'You're sure it wasn't?'

'Yes I'm sure.' I take a mouthful of champagne. 'Unlike you, I learn from my mistakes.'

'There are no mistakes,' says Dan, putting on a bad American accent. 'Only experiences.'

I stare up at the ceiling. 'In that case, it's certainly been an experience telling you about it.'

He grins, then helps himself to a refill. 'So, where were we? Oh yes. She'd said, "Do you want to get married?" And you said?'

I think carefully. 'Well, *yes*.'

'And you're sure she wasn't talking hypothetically?'

'Of course.'

'How?'

It's a good question, and I stifle a burp as I think about it. 'By her reaction, for one thing. When I said yes, I mean.'

'She wasn't sick, then? Didn't faint, or show you that she had her fingers crossed all the time and didn't mean it?'

'Very funny, Dan. No – she . . . she just said, "Good", then gave me a kiss and went to sleep.'

'Was that all?'

'What do you mean, was that all? Like I said, we'd had a bit to drink, it was late, and she was obviously tired. We both were.'

'Yeah, right.' He makes a face as he refills his glass. 'That's exactly how I'd react if I'd proposed to someone and they'd said yes. By falling asleep. Unless . . .'

'Unless what?'

'Unless she realized she'd made a mistake − or rather, *you* had − and was just pretending to be asleep while she worked out what to do next. Lord knows, it probably wouldn't be the first time a woman's had to pretend in bed with you.'

'Dan, for the last time, it wasn't a mistake. On either of our parts.'

He shrugs, then holds the bottle of Moët out towards me. 'Well, as long as you're positive?'

'I am,' I say, nodding at Dan's offer of a top-up, while trying to ignore the feeling of doubt that's starting to creep over me.

'Fine.' Dan pours some champagne into my glass, then puts the bottle down. 'And you don't feel . . . No. Never mind.'

'Never mind what?'

'Nothing.' He picks his glass up, then holds it to the light and peers intently into it, as if fascinated by the bubbles. 'Forget about it.'

'No, come on. You were going to ask me if I felt something.'

'Well . . .' Dan glances at me out of the corner of his

eye. 'Emasculated. Seeing as she's the one who did the proposing.'

'No I don't,' I say, although the correct answer is probably, Well, I didn't.

'Because it's the man's responsibility, isn't it?' he continues. 'You know, you're making this huge gesture to her, giving her the biggest thing you can, and she's taken that opportunity away from you. Although if it were me, she'd already have had the biggest thing I . . .'

'Dan, please.' I shake my head at him. 'Besides, it's the noughties.'

He sniggers, like he does every time I mention that word, since I made the mistake of telling him it was how Jane and I used to refer to sex.

'So?'

'So women have equal status now.'

'Huh. To you, maybe,' snorts Dan.

'Piss off,' I say, although I'm a little impressed that Dan's managed to be chauvinistic and insult me at the same time. 'Besides, it's better, isn't it?'

He frowns. 'How'd you work that one out?'

'Because it *is* against the norm. So if Sam did propose . . .'

Dan smirks into his glass. 'If being the operative word.'

'If Sam did propose, then it means she's had to make a special effort. Which means she must think *I'm* pretty special. And doesn't want to lose me.'

He mimes sticking his fingers down his throat, then looks at me earnestly. 'You'd better check, though.'

'What? Why?'

Dan puts his glass down. 'Think about it. The relationship's fine, right? You're getting along just great as you are, no reason to change the status quo, and suddenly, one of you accidentally proposes to the other one.'

'No one proposes accidentally, Dan.'

'Just hear me out. Say she did. Say the words just . . . slipped out. And before she can go, "I'm sorry, that wasn't what I meant," you've already said yes. She sees how excited you are by it. How flattered. So how on earth does she get back from there without doing some serious damage?'

'That's rubbish,' I say, although not quite as confidently as before.

'No it isn't,' insists Dan. 'You can't retract that sort of thing, because if you do, then you don't just revert to before, where getting married was, although unspoken, on the cards, but instead, you're actually saying you *don't* want to marry the other person. Cue all sorts of other issues, and you're splitting up a few weeks later. Hence the reason she probably kept schtum.'

'Thanks a lot.'

Dan makes a face. 'Don't shoot the messenger. I've been very careful not to propose to anyone over the last few years, so I know what I'm talking about.'

I put my glass down on the bar and turn to face him. 'So you're saying that Sam proposed to me by accident, and then immediately realized that she couldn't back out of it?'

Dan nods. 'Yup.'

'But why would she want me to think we're engaged if we're not?'

'Maybe so she can draw the engagement out, until something else gives her an excuse to get out of it. Has she mentioned it again today?'

'Well, no, but . . .'

'There you go, then.'

'If you let me finish, I was going to say that I haven't really seen her. She's been out with Madeleine all day.'

Dan looks up sharply. 'Who?'

'Madeleine? Sam's best friend?'

'And why have I never met her?'

I sigh. 'Why do you think?'

'Fair enough.' Dan grins, and picks the bottle up again. 'But you've got to agree that sounds pretty suspicious.'

'What's suspicious about it?'

'Well, for one thing, if I'd just got engaged, I would-n't be out celebrating with you.'

'Thanks very much,' I say, fighting the urge to snatch the champagne back from him.

'You know what I mean.'

I stare at him for a few seconds, hoping he's misread the situation, but unfortunately, if Dan ever got asked to do *Celebrity Mastermind*, 'women' would be his special-ist subject. 'So how *can* I check?' I say eventually, trying to keep the panic out of my voice.

'Well, the most obvious thing would be to call her bluff.'

'And how do I do that?'

Dan leans over and punches me on the shoulder, which I guess is meant to be reassuring, but only ends up giving me a dead arm. 'S'easy. Get her to the front of a church, have a vicar ask her if she wants to go through with it. If she says "I do" then you're home and dry.'

'As opposed to high and dry. In front of everybody. And that's assuming she turns up.'

'Well, you can't just come out and ask her, can you?'

'Why not? What's wrong with saying, "Sam, you know yesterday, when you proposed to me, were you being serious?"'

Dan looks at me as if I'm stupid. 'Because what's she going to do? Say "actually, no", and hope the two of you can just laugh it off? Besides, if you want a direct answer from a woman then you can never ask her a direct question. It's the way their minds are wired.'

'Dan, will you please stop generalizing. Especially where women are concerned.'

'But it's true.'

'No it isn't. That's like saying that everyone who's Japanese knows karate.'

'Okay, okay.' He leans in to me, then lowers his voice. 'Although that, funnily enough, *is* true. I mean, there's no proof, but it's a fact.'

'Whatever. But I can hardly wait until I've got Sam at the front of the church to find out whether she was actually proposing to me, can I?'

Dan turns and peers towards the other end of the bar,

where Wendy is making herself a double espresso, stifling a yawn as she does so. 'Believe it or not, flatso over there has actually hit on the perfect solution.'

'What do you mean?'

'It's simple,' he says. 'If you can get Sam to set a date, and it's some time this century, then that'll prove she's serious. I mean, that's the whole point of being engaged, isn't it? So you can get married.'

As Dan sips his champagne smugly, I have to concede that it's not such a bad plan, and not only because – thanks to him – I'm now a little worried that I *have* misread the situation, but also because of my existing insecurities where Sam and I are concerned. Maybe it's the legacy of being dumped so dramatically by Jane a couple of years ago, but there's a part of me that's mystified – almost on a daily basis – that someone like Sam wants to go out with someone like me, so if I do get her to set a date, then perhaps that feeling will stop too. But at the same time, I realize that there's another reason why I should push for it. Because I love her. And if it *is* true, and she *did* actually propose, then I can't wait to be married to her.

I glance at my watch, wondering whether I should go home and do it now, but it's late, and Sam will probably be getting ready for bed. I'll just have to wait until the morning. Which means that for tonight at least, I might as well enjoy being engaged.

I drain my glass in a couple of gulps, then pick up the bottle of Moët and help myself to a refill. 'You know, you're cleverer than you look.'

'I am, aren't I?' says Dan, holding his glass out for a toast, without realizing what he's just said. 'Here's to the big day. Hopefully.'

'To the big day,' I say, and then suddenly, something else occurs to me. 'Actually, Dan, strike that. When I say you're cleverer than you look . . .'

'Fuck off.'

'No – I mean, you're a genius!'

'I am?'

'Yes; the big day. I might have missed out on the chance to make a grand gesture by proposing to her first . . .'

'Assuming that she did, of course, actually propose to you.'

'. . . but at least I can make it up to her. By giving her what every woman wants.'

Dan frowns. 'Me?'

'No. A great big wedding!'

Dan breaks into a broad smile, then clinks his glass loudly against mine. 'Now that, Edward, sounds like a plan.'

Monday, 6 April

6.51 a.m.
I'm woken up by the sound of the bedroom door shutting — Sam getting ready to put another victim — sorry, *client* — through their paces, probably. She works (for herself) as a personal trainer, mainly using the seven-mile (and I only know the distance because she's made me run the length of it enough times) stretch of Brighton and Hove seafront to train her clients. Most weekdays, she'll be up and out before I've even stirred and, despite the fact that we've been living together for the best part of a year, I still haven't quite managed to get used to her crack-of-dawn starts, or the fact that whenever she tells me she fancies an early night, that's exactly what she means.

I'm feeling a little sick, although that's probably more down to the amount of alcohol I consumed last night — having decided to stay in the pub until I was sure Sam would be asleep — than my nervousness at asking her to set a date when I get up. And, anyway, as I've been telling myself all night, I shouldn't be nervous; despite what Dan said, we are already engaged — at least, I'm pretty sure we are, having replayed the proposal over and over in my mind. So setting a date is simply the next step. Even though right now it feels like a pretty huge one.

I mean, some people might get engaged simply to take the relationship to another level, but for me, it's definitely the preliminary stage to getting married, and if Sam feels that way too – and I've no reason to think she doesn't; after all, we're already living together – then what's the point of dragging it out? And while the one thing Dan's right about is that I do now wish I'd asked her first, I'm also really flattered she asked me.

With Jane, even though we were together for nearly ten years, marriage was just something we didn't discuss, maybe because I thought we'd just drift along together until it happened. And while what *actually* happened was that I let myself go, got fat, smoked too much, stopped caring about my appearance, and therefore (according to Jane) stopped caring about her, so she dumped me, I have my suspicions that an additional contributory factor in the dumping might have been because I didn't ever get down on one knee in front of her.

The funny thing is, when I think about it now, Jane and I getting married wouldn't really have meant anything. It would have just been the next thing to do, as if because we'd been together for so long why not just go ahead and make it legal – and where's the romance in that? Because by then, the proposal isn't such a big deal whoever does it, the wedding is greeted with a lot of 'about time too' jokey comments, and then the next day, we'd have gone back to being exactly who we were beforehand, except I'd have a large hangover, she'd have my surname, and we'd both have a few too many toasters. Nothing would really have been different, so what would have been the point?

Whereas with Sam, it *will* be different. Her becoming my wife is a step forward – for both of us. And it's not just me saying 'hands off' to every other man; it's because I want to take the relationship to another level, maybe even start a family. More importantly, I want Sam to know I love her, and that I'm committed to building a future with her. Our future.

I glance at the alarm clock on the bedside table, then jump out of bed and stride purposefully towards the bathroom, conscious that I need to catch Sam before she heads out to work. Because as far as I'm concerned, that future can't start soon enough.

7.21 a.m.
By the time I get out of the shower, I've changed my mind as to my tactics. While I'm still planning to ask Sam to set a date, I'm only going to do that when *she* brings up the whole engagement thing, which she's bound to, especially as she must have told Madeleine all about it yesterday, just like I did Dan. That way, I won't have to raise it out of the blue and risk being shot down. And this plan is doubly good, mainly because I still haven't managed to work out *how* to raise it.

When I walk into the kitchen, she's standing by the

window, dressed in one of her usual figure-hugging tracksuits, and snacking on a packet of rice cakes. Sam certainly practises what she preaches, and expects her clients – past *and* present – to as well, which is why I'm hoping the half a litre of mouthwash I've just gargled with will mask the smell of the packet of sour cream and onion Pringles I ate from my secret stash when I got home last night. Not that I'm a client any more, although that is how Sam and I met; when I'd hired her to help me get back in shape so I could (misguidedly, according to Dan) try to win Jane back. Little did I know at the time that the emphasis with Sam would shift from the 'training' to the 'personal' as our sessions progressed. But I'm extremely pleased it did.

'Morning, gorgeous,' she says, standing on tiptoe to kiss me.

'You talkin' to me?' I say, doing what I think is my best Robert De Niro in *Taxi Driver* impression, although when I listen to myself, it sounds more like I've got a heavy cold.

'I don't see anyone else here.'

'Well, in that case, good morning.'

I smile down at her. Of the two of us, Sam's the gorgeous one: short, almost boyish dark hair that on her looks anything but, a cute upturned nose, and the kind of dark brown eyes I could gaze into for the rest of my life – which is kind of fortunate, given recent developments. I kiss her again, and she wrinkles her nose at what I can only guess is a whiff of crisp breath.

'I didn't hear you come in last night.'

'I did,' I say. 'Honest.'

'Relax, Edward. I didn't mean it like that. Did you have a nice time?'

'Er . . .' Yes and no is the obvious answer, but it suddenly seems ridiculous to me that the 'no' part should be to do with the doubts that Dan managed to instil in me. 'Okay, I guess.'

She holds the rice cakes out towards me. 'How was Dan?'

'Oh. You know. Same old Dan,' I say, waving the packet away. I've tried Sam's healthy snacks before, and quite frankly, the plastic lid from last night's tube of Pringles probably has more flavour.

Sam rolls her eyes, then helps herself to another rice cake. 'It can't be easy for him,' she says, walking over to the sink and pouring herself a glass of water. 'To hear news like that, I mean.'

Aha! There it is. My 'in'. Sam must mean the news of our engagement. I almost have to stop myself from doing a celebratory dance in the middle of the kitchen, although I feel a little guilty at the same time. Because of course it can't have been easy for Dan to hear about Sam and me getting married, particularly when he's feeling so low from his recent sacking . . . Ah.

'You mean the *Close Encounters* stuff?'

Sam nods. 'Poor thing. What's he going to do?'

Damn. 'He didn't really mention it, to be honest.'

'What did the two of you talk about?'

'Talk about?' I shrug dismissively, wondering whether she's fishing to see whether I've said anything to Dan at all, although I'm growing increasingly conscious that she hasn't referred to our being engaged even once. And short of me just coming right out with it, I don't know how to, even if I dress it up in a funny 'You know, Dan thinks . . .' kind of way. It just seems so, well, preposterous that I have to ask her if I got the wrong end of the stick. Plus, what will I do if she says I did? 'You know. The usual.'

'You mean his favourite subject. Himself,' she says, downing her water quickly.

'No, we . . .' I look up at the clock on the kitchen wall, conscious that time's running out. This morning, at least. 'Listen, Sam. I was wondering . . .'

'Wondering what?'

I click the kettle on, then follow her into the front room. 'Well, I wanted to ask you something.'

Sam glances at her watch. 'Is it a quick one? I've got to meet a client by the pier in five minutes.'

'Er . . .' I don't know what to say. I suppose it is a quick one – it doesn't take long to say 'yes' or 'no', after all – but I've got a feeling it's going to take more than five minutes for me to get round to asking the question. 'No, that's okay. It can wait till this evening.'

'Well, if you're sure,' says Sam, kissing me quickly, then heading for the front door.

That's the problem, I want to say, as I watch her go. *I'm not.*

8.51 a.m.

I'm walking into work, feeling a little, well, flat. But I have to stay positive – after all, while Sam didn't actually refer to us being engaged earlier, she didn't mention the fact that we weren't. I have to take that as a good sign.

As I turn the corner into Ship Street, where Staff-IT, the IT recruitment consultancy I work for is situated, a voice I haven't heard for the best part of twelve months makes me jump.

'G'*issue*?'

I look up to see Billy, Ship Street's one-time *Big Issue* seller, grinning at me – although whether you can still grin when you've lost most of your front teeth is debatable.

'Jesus, Billy, you scared me. Where have you been?'

'Where haven't I been?' he says, gruffly.

'I thought you must have moved,' I say, then realize that's probably not the most sympathetic observation to make to a homeless person.

'Nah,' says Billy, picking up a can of Special Brew from behind his rucksack and taking a quick swig. 'I've been on me holidays.'

'For a year?'

'I've got a flexible employer,' says Billy, nodding towards the dog-eared magazine he's holding. 'You all right then, Ed?'

'Not bad,' I say, pleased that he's remembered my name. Normally he can't even remember his.

'And how's that gorgeous girlfriend of yours?'

I'm impressed – unless he means Jane, of course. But then again, he'd have to be very drunk to mix the two of them up, and while judging by the number of empty beer cans I can see in the vicinity, that's certainly a possibility, Billy actually knows Sam – she's bought *Big Issues* from him often enough – whereas Jane used to cross the street to avoid him.

'Good. Great, actually. In fact . . .' I take a deep breath, hoping that the more I say it, the more likely it is to be true. 'We're getting married.'

For a moment, Billy just stares at me, and then his face darkens. 'Whatcha want to go and do that for?'

'What?' I say, slightly taken aback.

'Up the duff, is she?'

'No, Billy. Sam's not pregnant.'

He scratches his head. 'So why, then?'

'Well, because we love each other, and . . .'

'Christ.' Billy rolls his eyes. 'If you're that desperate to give your house away, why not give it to someone like me who really needs it?'

'What have you got against marriage, Billy?'

'What d'you think I'm doing out here selling these magazines?' He drains the rest of his Special Brew. 'It's not because I'm after a career as a newsagent.'

I know Billy was married once, to some girl who needed a visa, or something. Though it sounds like it was his Visa card she was more interested in.

'So, you being on the streets is because of a woman?'

Billy shakes his head, then produces another can of

Special Brew from his rucksack and cracks it open. 'Nope. Because of the drinking.'

'Oh, sorry. I thought . . .'

'But the drinking's because of a woman.'

'Your wife?'

'Ex-wife,' snaps Billy. 'Take my advice. Hold on to your freedom as long as you can.'

For a moment, I feel like trying to explain to him that freedom's the last thing I want. But then again, someone who's made the lifestyle choices Billy has probably has a completely different definition of what 'freedom' actually is.

'But surely it's all about finding the right woman?'

'Of course it is, Ed. Of course it is. But that's like saying all you have to do is buy the right lottery ticket and you'll win the jackpot.' He gestures towards me with his can, spilling a couple of drops on my shoes. 'Women are the root of all evil, you know.'

'I thought that was money?'

'That too,' says Billy, holding out a magazine for me to buy. 'And speaking of the devil . . .'

9.58 a.m.

I'm sitting in my office, browsing through the morning suit section of the Moss Bros website, and wondering whether Dan and I will look ridiculous in top hats, when there's a gruff voice from the doorway.

'Morning,' grumbles Natasha, though given the miserable look on her face, that should be spelled with a 'u' after the 'o'. Unusually for her, she's in before ten, and even more unusually, she doesn't appear to be hung over.

I sit up guiltily. Natasha founded the company, and while now we're supposedly equal partners in the business since she promoted me last year, she often acts as if she's forgotten that fact. To be honest, most of the time, I'm too scared of her moods to remind her.

'What are you doing here?' I say, hurriedly clicking on the 'close window' button, although all that does is reveal the travel-agency website I'd been looking at previously while wondering where to take Sam on honeymoon.

Natasha scowls at me, then stomps over to the coat rack and throws her jacket on one of the hooks. 'I work here, remember?'

I open my mouth to respond, then close it again. Natasha's definition of 'work' is somewhat different to mine, although I suppose using your cleavage and long blonde hair to attract new clients could loosely be described as 'marketing'. Luckily, given the not inconsiderable fee we earn each time a candidate accepts a job, she doesn't need to do a lot. Of work, I mean. Not clients.

I glance at my watch, then tap it a couple of times to make sure it hasn't stopped. 'Yes, but . . .'

Natasha gives me a look that suggests I'd be better off shutting up. 'What are you doing?' she asks, walking over to my desk and peering at my monitor.

'I'm, er . . . Nothing,' I say, nervously. I've decided not to tell Natasha about my good news just yet. She's not the biggest fan of marriage, particularly since most of her boyfriends are already in one with someone else.

'Doesn't look like nothing to me.' Natasha taps the picture of a tropical island on my screen with a scarily lacquered fingernail. 'Going somewhere nice?'

'Just on honey . . . I mean, holiday. With Sam.'

'Haven't you just been on one?' She tuts, no doubt not looking forward to the prospect of having to do some actual recruitment work if I'm away.

'That was a year ago. To Spain.'

'Oh yes. Where you and Sam almost split up. And you're risking it again?'

'Yes, well, as I told you, that was a simple misunderstanding.'

Natasha arches one impeccably plucked eyebrow, then nudges my chair with her hip, hard enough to send me rolling across to the other side of the room. 'As in Sam misunderstood why you'd been seeing your ex girlfriend behind her back?'

'No. Well, yes, but it wasn't anything like that,' I say, walking my chair back towards my desk with a series of dainty steps. 'I hadn't been *seeing* her. Jane just . . . I mean, yes, I saw her, but not in the sense that you see your, er . . .' I stop talking. When Natasha's in a mood like this, there's no reasoning with her.

'So where are you thinking of going?' she says, peering closely at my computer screen. 'The Maldives? Isn't that a bit . . . Hold on – honeymoon suite?' Natasha grabs the desk lamp, switches it on, and angles the beam into my face. 'Have you got something to tell me, Edward?'

'Er . . .' I haven't felt this uncomfortable with Natasha since the time I decided not to tell her about Jane dumping me. And now, as then, I cave in after about five seconds. 'Sam and I are getting married.'

For a moment, Natasha looks stunned. 'What on earth do the two of you want to do that for?' she says, only slightly less gruffly than Billy earlier.

'Er, because we love each other?' I say, only this time, as if I'm guessing at the answer. 'And because we want to spend the rest of our lives together.' *And because I don't want anyone else to steal her*, I feel like adding. 'Besides, what's wrong with wanting to get married?'

As soon as I say this, I realize I might have asked the wrong person. But fortunately, Natasha seems more surprised that someone's agreed to marry *me*, rather than at the fact that we've simply decided to get married.

'Let me get this straight,' says Natasha, incredulously. 'You asked her to marry you, and she said yes?'

'Well, not exactly,' I reply, feeling a little put out at Natasha's tone, while trying to ignore the feeling of déjà vu. 'In actual fact, it was me who said yes.'

'Pardon?'

'Sam asked me.'

'Really?'

'Yes, really.'

'Is she pregnant?'

'No!'

'Are you dying?'

Only of embarrassment. 'I don't think so. Why?'

'I can't think of a single other reason a woman would propose.' Natasha looks at her watch. 'It's not a leap year, is it?'

'No, but . . .'

'And you're not rich.'

'Not on what you pay me I'm not.'

Natasha laughs. 'Okay. Fair point. But you've really got no idea why she asked you?'

'Because she loves me, perhaps?' I suggest, crossly.

'No, I meant why *she* asked. Not why she asked – well – *you.*'

'Er . . . Maybe Sam's the traditional type. Wants to be married before she starts a family. That sort of thing.'

Natasha rests a hand on my shoulder. 'You're sure she's not pregnant?'

'No,' I say, shrugging her off. 'I mean, yes.'

'How do you know?'

'Because, well, I'd know. Wouldn't I?'

Natasha raises both eyebrows this time. 'And you're sure she actually did. You know, *ask* you. To marry her.'

'Don't you start.'

'What?'

'Nothing. Yes, I'm sure,' I say, feeling less and less so by the minute.

'You don't think you better check?'

I look up at her crossly. 'Natasha!'

'Sorry.' She smiles down at me. 'I suppose I'm just

being over-cautious, Edward. I mean, as long as she's got a ring on her finger, then you've got nothing to . . .' Natasha stops mid-sentence, as it's obvious even to me that I've gone deathly pale. 'Don't tell me you haven't?'

'It only happened on Saturday night, and I kind of thought that seeing as she proposed to me, then . . .'

'You expected Sam to go out and buy her own engagement ring?'

Bollocks. How could I have been so stupid? 'Well, no, but . . .' I slump back in my chair. The truth is, I don't know what I expected. Sam proposing did catch me off guard. And so I didn't – and don't – have a clue what to do in the circumstances.

'You better do something about that, and fast,' warns Natasha. 'Otherwise you might find yourself disengaged.'

'Sure,' I say, sitting up sharply and grabbing my keyboard. 'I'll get right on it.'

I type the words 'Argos' and 'engagement rings' into Google, but when Natasha sees what I'm doing, she makes a mock-horror face, although on closer inspection, there's not a lot of 'mock' about it.

'Edward, are you determined to sabotage this?'

'Huh?'

She nods towards my computer screen. 'Please don't tell me you're looking for an engagement ring there.'

'What's wrong with Argos?'

Natasha sighs loudly, then walks over to her desk. 'Tell you what. You can have one of my old ones if you like.'

'Your old ones?' Natasha has been engaged about four

times since I've known her. Trouble was, all of those times were to men who were already married, a fact that Natasha was the last person to discover. The last, that was, until she stormed round and told their wives.

'You're joking?'

'Nope.' She fishes around in her top drawer, then produces what looks like a selection of jewellery boxes, before walking back across the room and placing them on top of the pile of CVs in my in-tray. 'Here you go. Help yourself.'

I pick up the first box and open the lid to be blinded by the biggest diamond I've ever seen. 'This must have cost a fortune.'

Natasha shrugs. 'He could afford it. Although not the subsequent divorce, unfortunately, which is why he ended up back with his wife, and I ended up with this.'

I stare at the ring for a few moments before snapping the box shut. 'It's very kind of you, but I couldn't possibly take it.'

'Why not?'

I don't like to point out it's because I think it might be jinxed. 'Well, because it's bad luck. Probably. Besides, I want to choose one for Sam. Myself.'

'Then choose one of these,' she says, flipping open the other boxes in turn and showing them to me like a game-show hostess.

'No, I mean a new one.'

Natasha sighs again. 'You're not going to find a ring in Argos. Not one she'll thank you for, anyway. We women are picky when it comes to this kind of thing. Particularly when we're going to have to wear it for the rest of our lives. And if you want my advice, don't surprise her, unless you're really going to go to town.'

'So where do you suggest I get one from?'

'Like I said. Go to town.' She taps the lid of one of the other boxes, where the Tiffany's logo is clearly visible. 'There's only one place a woman wants her engagement ring to come from, and that's here.'

'Tiffany's? But aren't they rather . . .' I want to say 'expensive', but I don't mean that in the 'I'm too tight' sense. It's more that Sam just isn't extravagant.

'Expensive?' Natasha snaps shut the assorted ring boxes, then gathers them up and dumps them unceremoniously back into her desk drawer. 'Trust me, Edward. It'll be the best money you ever spend.'

As she sits back down at her desk and switches on her computer, it occurs to me that a trip to Tiffany's isn't a bad idea at all. It'll certainly make me feel a bit more secure knowing Sam's actually wearing an engagement ring, and not because it's a badge to say 'keep off', or a symbol to the rest of the (male) world that she's taken, but because it'll prove she's committed to the wedding, and more importantly, committed to me. Plus, doing it this way will give *me* the chance to do the whole traditional down-on-one-knee thing, and actually — hopefully — hear Sam say 'yes', and that way, there'll be no doubt in my mind. Even if she is having a few second thoughts, or feels a little bit disgruntled that she had to do the asking, maybe an expensive ring and a traditional proposal might just reassure her. And then the small matter of setting a date should be a formality.

And as Natasha says, if I do decide to go to town as far as the ring's concerned, then I am going to have to surprise Sam. Because knowing her, if we went to Tiffany's together, as soon as we got there she'd come over all sensible and refuse to let me buy her anything, telling me we could spend the money on something more, well, practical. Which is ironic, because I can't think of a more practical investment than something that guarantees me Sam for the rest of my life.

While I'm pretty sure I can guess the kind of ring I need to buy – after all, most of the ones Natasha's shown me look about the same, with a rock the size of Gibraltar on them – I recognize I could do with some help from someone who's impressed by sparkly, expensive things, and who loves spending money – especially mine. Which is why, once I've checked with Natasha that I can have the rest of the day off, I get straight on the phone to Dan.

11.21 a.m.
We're on the Brighton to London train; Dan preferring not to drive the Tango-orange Porsche that he owns as it's raining and – according to him – there's no point having a convertible if you're not going to drive it with the roof down.

As usual, despite the weather, Dan's wearing his

sunglasses-and-cap combination, although seeing as we're the only people who (on Dan's insistence) have paid extra to travel first class and therefore the only people in the whole carriage, he might as well be naked for all the attention he's getting.

'So,' he says, once he's flagged down the buffet trolley and ordered us both a cappuccino. 'You've checked with her, then?'

'Well, no. Not exactly. I mean, I didn't get the chance. But I will this evening.'

'And you're prepared to bet several thousand pounds that her answer's going to be the one you want?'

'What do you mean?'

'Well, that's what this ring is going to cost you.'

I swallow hard and stare into my cappuccino, although given the way the froth already seems to have evaporated, leaving a chocolate-coloured slick on the surface, I'd have a strong case for the trades descriptions people. 'Surely not *several*?'

Dan removes his sunglasses, though only for long enough to ensure I can see him roll his eyes. 'You've never been to Tiffany's before, have you, Ed?'

'So?' I shrug dismissively, and try to appear more nonchalant than I'm feeling. 'I've never asked anyone to marry me before. Which reminds me. Seeing as I *am* getting married, I need to ask you something.'

'I'd ask Sam something first, if I were you.'

'Be serious for a moment,' I say, as the train pulls into East Croydon. 'This is important.'

Dan sighs. 'Not the birds and bees conversation again, Ed?' he says, staring intently at a couple of girls on the platform in the hope they'll recognize him. 'Why don't I just lend you one of my videos, and . . .'

'No, not that,' I say, quickly. I've seen Dan's DVD collection, and apart from his rather extensive collection of top-shelf Danish porn, he's also got a little sideline in filming himself with his girlfriends – and not while they're having a picnic on the beach, if you know what I mean. 'I just wanted to say . . . I mean, well, I'm obviously planning to do the whole all-singing, all-dancing big church/top hats/marquee-on-the-lawn-type thing, so on the day, will you . . .' For some reason, I'm feeling quite emotional, and the words catch in my throat, which I find worrying. If I can't get this out, I'm going to be a wreck trying to propose to Sam tonight. 'You're the best man, obviously.'

Dan grins. 'Well, compared to you, that goes without saying. What was it you wanted to ask me?'

'No, I mean will you be *my* best man? At the wedding.'

'Oh. Right.' He shrugs dismissively. 'Suppose so.'

'That doesn't sound very enthusiastic.'

He takes his cap off, and puts it on the table. 'It's hardly a surprise.'

'Yes, but . . . It's still an honour, isn't it? I mean, out of all my close male friends, you're the one I've chosen.'

'*All* your close male friends?' snorts Dan. 'And that would be who, exactly?'

'Well, there's . . .'

'Exactly. Me. Unless you count Billy Big Issue, that is. Anyway, it's not an honour. In fact, it's a bit of a chore, isn't it? I mean, it's kind of a distraction from my principal job of chatting up the bridesmaids.'

'Dan, stop thinking about yourself for one moment, please. And besides, Mister Popular, how many of your other friends have asked you to be their best man?'

'That's not the point,' huffs Dan. 'Besides, they were probably worried I'd try and sleep with their wives. Or that I already had. Which was true, in some cases. So if you don't mind, I think I'll pass.'

For a moment, I can't believe what I'm hearing. I'd always kind of thought that in the – admittedly unlikely – event of Dan getting married, I'd be his best man, and that he'd obviously assume the opposite was true. But for some reason, he doesn't seem keen at all.

'Go on,' I say, desperately. 'It'll be fun.'

'Fun? How will it be fun, exactly?'

'You get to make a speech.'

'I do that every day, mate. Or at least, I did. And got paid for it.'

'The drink will be free.'

'I'm a celebrity. I don't have to pay for it that often anyway.'

'And . . . You get to wear a suit. You know you look good in a suit.'

Dan thinks for a moment. 'I do, don't I?'

'Plus, there'll be women there. And like you said, bridesmaids.'

'Over the age of sixteen? Although not too much over.'

'I'll book some specially.'

'Great,' says Dan. 'Because the best man gets to sleep with them. It's the law.'

'So, you'll do it?'

Dan gets up out of his seat, leans across the table, and spreads his arms out wide, although it takes me a couple of seconds to realize he's waiting to give me a hug. 'Of course I'll do it, you muppet. I was just yanking your chain.'

'Thanks, mate,' I say, as he picks me up off the ground, then drops me awkwardly as the conductor gives us a funny look.

'And it will be fun,' he says, a little red in the face, though whether that's from the effort of lifting me up or being seen hugging another man in public, it's hard to tell. 'Especially the stag night. Hey, maybe we can sell the pictures to one of the glossies. You know, "Dan Davis Attends Celebrity Wedding", that sort of thing. Might help my profile a little.'

'Dan, it's hardly a celebrity wedding.'

'I'll be there, so yes it will be.'

'Well, maybe, but I don't think Sam would . . .'

'At least let me try. I've got some contacts at *Hello!*.'

I sigh, and decide to let Dan indulge his little fantasy – for now. 'Okay.'

'Them too. Good idea. And maybe *Heat*. I've always wanted to be in *Heat*.'

'Dan, you're always in heat. And if I can just remind you of something. This is Sam's big day. Not yours.'

'Sam's big day,' says Dan, staring dreamily out of the window, then sitting up with a start as another train thunders past in the other direction. 'Got it.'

But by the look on his face, he's thinking the complete opposite.

12.03 p.m.
Even from the taxi, Tiffany's looks expensive. On Dan's advice, I've phoned the credit-card company from the train to maximize my Visa-card limit, but given that there are no prices visible on the very sparkly items I can see through the double-thickness plate-glass window, I'm worried it might not be enough.

'Excellent.' Dan rubs his hands together. 'Retail opportunity ahead.'

'Are you sure this is the right place? I mean, it looks . . .'

'I hope you're not going to say "pricey"?' Dan smirks. 'Or isn't Sam worth it?'

'Of course she is,' I reply, quickly. 'I was going to say, er, closed.'

Dan makes the 'yeah, right' face. 'You wish. Come on,' he says, handing a tenner to the cab driver. 'Nothing says "I love you" like something in a Tiffany's box.'

'And do they sell just the boxes?' I say, wondering whether an Argos ring would fit inside one.

'What do you think?' says Dan, jumping out of the cab without waiting for my answer.

I follow Dan reluctantly towards the shop, where a liveried security guard ushers us through the heavy glass doors with a brisk, 'Afternoon, gentlemen.' We head on inside, nearly sinking out of view into the thick pile carpet, and, as the doors click shut behind us, we're met by one of the impeccably dressed assistants, who looks us up and down, as if sizing up our spending ability. Immediately I feel scruffy, although I'm already in my best Paul Smith suit. What he makes of Dan's low-slung jeans and 'Give Peas A Chance' T-shirt, it's hard to tell.

'What can I help you with?'

I open my mouth to reply, but can't seem to get any words out. Instead, Dan clears his throat. 'The restaurant, please.'

The assistant frowns. 'Restaurant?'

'That's right,' says Dan. 'We're here for breakfast. You know, at *Tiffany's*.'

As Dan elbows me in a did-you-see-what-I-did-there? kind of way, the assistant smiles mirthlessly. 'Very good, sir. In fact, I've never heard that one before.'

'Really?' Dan raises both eyebrows. 'I'm surprised. No, we're actually after engagement rings.'

'Second floor,' says the assistant, nodding towards the lift, before walking off to attend to what I'm sure he hopes are some proper customers.

'Thanks,' I say – or rather *croak* – after him, resisting

the temptation to add 'my good man', before following Dan into the lift and up to the second floor.

When the doors open and I catch sight of the array of diamonds on offer, for a moment, I don't want to leave the safety of the lift, but Dan physically pushes me out so I've got no choice. We walk over to an expensively stocked glass-topped cabinet, where a man wearing the kind of white gloves normally sported by snooker referees seems to be polishing a non-existent mark on the upper surface.

'Gentlemen?' he says eventually, having given the glass a couple of extra wipes for good measure.

Dan puts an arm round my shoulder and gives me a supportive squeeze, no doubt a little concerned at how pale I've gone. 'He,' he says, 'needs an engagement ring.'

The assistant looks at me briefly, and then smiles at Dan. 'Well,' he says, nodding down at the cabinet in front of him, 'you've come to the right place.'

Dan grins back at him. 'And none of your cheap crap, either. This is for someone really special.'

The assistant studies me for a second or two, perhaps trying to work out how I've managed to get someone really special. 'Just walk this way,' he says, leading us over towards another – even more expensive-looking – cabinet in the corner. 'What sort of budget did you have in mind?'

'I dunno.' Dan looks across at me. 'Edward?'

I puff air nervously out of my cheeks. 'What's, um, usual?'

'Well,' says the assistant, 'without wishing to be indiscreet, three times a gentleman's monthly salary is usually the thing.'

By the looks of the rings in the cabinet, they might be three times my *yearly* salary. 'Okay. How much is that one?' I say, pointing to an understated silver ring with a number of diamonds set into it, although I make the mistake of touching the glass, which leaves a large fingerprint.

'An excellent choice,' says the assistant, without answering my question. 'Did sir wish to try it on?'

Dan winks at me. 'Perhaps later.'

As Dan sniggers, I dig him in the ribs. 'He means the ring, stupid. And, er, what good would that do?'

'Why, to see if it fits, of course,' says the assistant, wiping at the smear on the glass.

'I already know what size I need,' I say, having sneaked home earlier to measure a ring Sam bought from one of the hippy stalls on the seafront.

'Don't you want to see how it looks in situ?' says the assistant, patiently.

'Inside you?' says Dan.

I shush him, then shrug, and hold my hand out. 'Okay.'

The assistant reaches into the cabinet and hands the ring to me, but I'm not quite sure what I'm supposed to do next. 'Er . . .'

'What's the matter?'

'I'm not quite sure where, I mean, which is my, you know . . .'

'Ring finger?' Dan sniggers again. 'Left hand, next to the little finger.'

'How on earth do you know that?'

He grins. 'I didn't get where I am today without being able to spot whether someone's married or not.'

I resist the temptation to ask Dan exactly where he is today, then slip the ring on. But when I hold it up to the light, it looks a little . . . dull.

'What do you think?' I say to Dan, who seems to be studying his reflection in one of the taller cabinets.

'Okay, I suppose.' He shrugs. 'I'd prefer something a bit more showy. But then again, it's not for me, is it?'

'That's helpful, Dan.' I turn back to the assistant, because sadly, Dan's right; it is just okay. 'Have you got any with' – I swallow hard, wondering what the effect on my wallet is going to be – '*bigger* diamonds? Perhaps even, you know, sticking out.'

'Well, yes. Of course,' says the assistant, haughtily, 'but they're for our female customers, traditionally.'

'Your female customers?' I repeat, more than a little confused.

'Yes,' continues the assistant. 'We find that these men-gagement rings are usually more practical if they're a little less showy.'

'*Men*gagement? You thought . . . No. It's not for . . .' As the assistant's face reddens, but not as much as Dan's, I start to laugh. 'It's for my fiancée. And she's a *girl*.'

'It can be hard to tell sometimes,' stutters the assistant.

'Not for me, it isn't,' says Dan, gruffly. 'Christ, Edward.

First of all when we bought your bloody car, and now . . .' He shakes his head in disbelief. 'Why does this keep happening? I mean, do I *look* gay to you?'

'Dan, two incidences in two years is hardly evidence that it "keeps happening".'

'It's two more than I'd like.'

'And besides, what does "look gay" actually mean?' I say, pulling the ring off my finger, panicking for a moment when I have a job getting it past my knuckle. 'Although you are very well turned out, so—'

'So nothing!' snaps Dan. 'Unless, of course, it's you.'

I'm just about to respond appropriately when the assistant clears his throat. 'I'm sorry,' he says, taking the ring from me and setting it back down in the cabinet. 'I just assumed that when you said "he" needs an engagement ring . . .'

'Don't be ridiculous,' snorts Dan, more than a little embarrassed himself. 'I'm the best man.'

The assistant turns back to me, and I think I can detect a look of sympathy on his face. 'And do you know what kind of thing your fiancée likes?'

'Gay-looking men, evidently,' says Dan.

The assistant sighs. 'In terms of *jewellery*.'

'I think so. Although she doesn't wear a lot.'

'Or jewellery,' says Dan.

The assistant ignores him. 'And you're happy to choose it? Without her, I mean?'

The truth is, no, I'm not. At least, not a hundred per cent. Not because I don't trust my own judgement, but it's just that I'd prefer Sam to be involved in a decision as big as this, because I want her to be involved with every big decision I take from now on. And besides, it's a huge commitment too, and not just financially. It's something she's got to be happy with, and look at for the rest of her life – a bit like me, I suppose. But I also understand that sometimes, doing things for her – and without her – is important too.

I take a deep breath. 'Yes,' I say, then point to a ring on the top shelf of the cabinet with the sparkliest diamond I've ever seen. 'In fact, I'd like that one. How much is it?'

12.14 p.m.

I'm sitting in an armchair in the corner of the shop, vaguely aware of a clicking noise coming from somewhere in front of me, and when the room eventually swims into view, the first thing I see is a concerned-looking Dan snapping his fingers underneath my nose.

'What happened?'

'You fainted.'

'What?'

Dan jabs a thumb over towards the centre of the shop, where the assistant is watching us anxiously. 'When he told you the price of the ring. Lucky for you this carpet's so thick or you might have done yourself an injury.'

I try and stand up, but my legs are still a little wobbly, so I lean heavily against Dan's outstretched arm instead. 'Ah. And how much was it?'

He nods towards the chair. 'You better sit down again.'

I feel suddenly woozy, so do as I'm told. 'When exactly did I pass out?'

'*Faint*, you mean?' Dan grins, then looks at his watch. 'About five minutes ago.'

'No, I mean before or after I bought the ring?'

'Before,' says Dan.

I breathe a sigh of relief, which catches in my throat when I notice the Tiffany's bag that Dan's clutching. 'So, er, what's that?'

Dan reaches inside, and produces a ring box. 'I bought it for you.'

'Dan, I . . .' For a moment, I don't know what to say. 'You shouldn't have.'

'With your credit card, dummy. Seeing as I know your PIN.'

'I was right the first time. You shouldn't have. And how do you know my PIN?'

'It's your date of birth.'

'Christ, Dan. The one time you actually remember my birthday . . .' I shake my head. 'So tell me. How much did I end up spending? Or rather, did you end up spending. Of my money.'

He shrugs. 'Only about eight.'

My jaw drops. 'Please tell me that's hundred.'

'I could tell you that,' he says, sheepishly. 'But it's not what it'll say on your next Visa bill. Besides, the one next to it cost ten. So count yourself lucky.'

'Eight thousand pounds?' I try to get up again, but Dan pushes me back down into the chair.

'Relax. You wanted to make a statement. Now you have.'

I take the box from him and open it up. It's certainly a beautiful ring, although the statement it seems to be making is that I'll have to sell my car to pay for it.

'Yes, but . . . eight thousand pounds?'

'Trust me,' he continues, echoing Natasha almost word for word. 'It'll be the best money you ever spend.'

And as I put the ring carefully back in the bag, I can only hope that he's right.

1.15 p.m.

We're pulling out of Victoria – which is a phrase Dan always sniggers at – and, given my precious cargo, for once I'm actually pleased Dan's made me pay extra to be in first class, because we're safely away from the usual collection of druggies and hoodies who tend to use the London to Brighton line as their daily commute from dole office to dealer. Even so, I'm clutching the Tiffany's bag as tightly as I can.

'Cheapskate,' says Dan, for about the millionth time. 'I still think you should have gone for the ten-grand one.'

'Well, I thought I'd leave it for you. So you can get it for Polly.'

'Fuck off,' says Dan. 'That chapter of my life is over and done with. And the only way I'll get my hands on anything of Tiffany's is if Tiffany is an actual girl.'

I reach into my jacket pocket and hand over a smaller

box. 'So you won't be wanting these cuff links I bought you. As a best-man gift.'

Dan opens the box slowly, beaming at me when he sees what's inside. 'These must have set you back a bit.'

I shrug. 'In for a penny, in for a pound. Well, eight thousand of them.'

Dan looks at me sheepishly, then snaps the box shut and hands it back to me. 'Got time for lunch when we get back?'

'Nope. Sorry.'

'I thought you had the rest of the day off? Don't tell me you're going back to the office?'

'Yes, Dan,' I say. 'Seeing as thanks to your wonderful gesture I'm suddenly eight grand in debt.'

'Ah. Good point,' he says, guiltily. 'After work, then?'

'I can't,' I say, holding the Tiffany's bag up reverentially. 'I've got to get this ring where it belongs.'

Dan grins, then leans back in his seat and pulls his cap down over his eyes. 'Good luck with that, Frodo,' he says.

6.05 p.m.

I'm walking home from the office after a (fortunately) busy afternoon, anxiously hiding the Tiffany's bag under my jacket. Not that I think I'm going to get mugged, but more because I'm intending to propose – for the first and, hopefully, only time in my life – the moment I walk in through the front door, and therefore need to be ready to whip it out. So to speak.

I shouldn't be nervous, of course. Natasha's given her

approval of the ring, if not the salary increase I've asked for to help pay for it, and besides, as I keep telling myself – although I'm the only one who seems to actually believe it – Sam's already proposed to me.

Even so, there's a fluttering in my stomach, possibly because I realize there's so much riding on her answer. And though it's probably mostly Dan's fault I'm feeling this way, it does also occur to me that this is Sam's chance to back out if she's having second thoughts, and if she does . . . well, I suppose it's the right thing – for both of us. At least I've got the receipt for the ring. Though not, I realize as I reach the flat, for the emotional investment I've made.

Of course, the way I'm feeling could be due to excitement, too. While I'm sure a lot of men get coerced into proposing, or only ask because they've run out of excuses not to, there's something special about asking – or being asked by – someone you really *want* to be with. When Sam first brought the subject up, I didn't even have to think about my answer. I just have to hope it'll be the same for her when it's me doing the asking.

I push the front door open quietly, then check to see the coast is clear before walking into the flat. By the sounds coming from the bathroom, Sam's having a shower, which is perfect, so I hurriedly remove the ring box from the Tiffany's bag, then pace nervously up and down the hallway until I hear the water stop.

After a moment's panic, when I can't decide which

knee I should get down on, necessitating a quick rehearsal in front of the hall mirror to see which one looks best (although, surprise, surprise, it's pretty much of a muchness), I take up my position outside the bathroom door. Only trouble is, I've forgotten how long women take between getting out of the shower and actually exiting the bathroom, so by the time Sam emerges through the doorway, a towel around her midriff, my knee is starting to hurt, and I'm beginning to wonder if I'll be able to get up without assistance.

'Edward! What are you doing?' she says. 'You made me jump.'

'Sam . . .' I look up at her as she adjusts the smaller turban-like towel on her head. Unfortunately, this has the effect of lifting the other towel up above her waist, meaning that I'm now staring directly into her groin. 'I, er . . .'

'Sorry.' Sam adjusts the towel and kneels down next to me. 'Have you lost your contact lens again? Do you want me to help you look?'

'No. Nothing like that,' I say, feeling suddenly awkward that she's now at the same level as me. 'Could you just stand back up, please?'

'Er . . . okay.' Sam frowns at me, but does as she's told, perhaps wondering whether I've spent the afternoon at the Admiral Jim.

'Great. Thanks.' I hold the Tiffany's box out towards her, trying to stop my hand from shaking, before realizing I've forgotten to open it. 'Hang on.'

I flip the lid open, and for a moment, Sam just stares at me. Then, after what seems like an eternity, she takes the box from my hand.

'But . . .'

'It's just, well, we didn't do it properly. The other day, I mean. So I thought I'd better . . .' I break off, mid sentence, desperate to rock back on my heels to give my knee a rest. 'Will you marry me?'

'I . . .' Sam's eyes suddenly fill with tears, which I'm hoping is a positive emotional response – or even a reaction to the conditioner she's got in her hair – rather than from disappointment at either the box's contents or those four little words. 'You shouldn't have.'

For a moment, an element of doubt creeps into my mind. *Why* shouldn't I have? Is it because she doesn't want to marry me? Or has Sam sensed that my proposal is less 'ring from Tiffany's', and more 'ring of desperation'? But fortunately, the feeling doesn't last that long, as Sam sniffs loudly, then smiles down at me.

'It's beautiful,' she says, slipping the ring onto her finger. 'And it fits!'

'Lucky guess.'

'But . . . Tiffany's?' Sam gazes at the ring, then holds her hand up to the hall light to admire the sparkle. 'It must have cost a fortune.'

'Yes, well.' I don't know what to say. Especially since it did.

'Oh, Edward . . .' Sam stops talking, then does that shaking her hands in the air thing women do which always looks as if they're attempting to dry their nail varnish, whereas in reality they're trying to stop themselves from crying.

'So, is that a yes, then?' I ask, hauling myself back onto my feet, trying hard to resist the impulse to rub my knee.

Sam doesn't say anything, but just drops her towel, takes me by the hand, and leads me into the bedroom. And while my first thought is that I really ought to give Dan a call and tell him my good news, for the moment, I think that can probably wait.

Tuesday, 7 April

8.33 a.m.

Sam's not taken the ring off since she slipped it onto her finger in the hallway last night, and despite the fact that I've got a rather nasty scratch in an embarrassing place where she caught me with the diamond while we were, er, celebrating, it's a small price to pay for the feeling of relief it's given me. The fact that we're engaged, I mean.

Even though it's early, and despite that fact that Dan's unemployed and therefore might not actually be up yet, I've popped round on the way to work to tell him the good news. Once I've finished my breathless explanation – almost before he's had a chance to get dressed – he frowns.

'So, she didn't actually say yes?' he says, pulling on a white T-shirt with 'I ♥ ME' printed on the front.

'No, Dan. But she didn't say no either. Which is probably more important, if you think about it.'

Dan gives me a pitying look as he puts the kettle on. 'You idiot,' he says. 'Your one big chance to find out for sure – which might I remind you cost you eight grand – and you blow it. Did she say anything else?'

'Well, no. But she cried.'

'She cried?'

'Yes, but in a good way.'

'How does anyone cry in a good way? People cry at bad news usually.' He shakes his head slowly. 'I hope you've still got the receipt?'

'Dan!'

He sighs loudly. 'So come on, then. What happened next?'

'Next?'

'After she *didn't* say yes.'

'Well, we – you know – had sex.'

'Lucky bastard.' Dan gives me a tight-lipped smile. 'What kind?'

'What kind of what?'

'Sex. Apart from the most expensive you ever had, of course.'

'Huh? You mean missionary, or whether she was on top?'

'No, Edward – although thanks for the imagery. I mean, was it your normal run-of-the-mill shag, or thank-you sex, or make-up sex, or shut-up sex, or . . .'

'Shut-up sex? What on earth is that?'

'You know. When you're trying to avoid one of those awkward conversations, so you make sure she's otherwise engaged.' He grins. 'After all, she can't talk with her mouth full.'

'It was just, well, sex. There doesn't always have to be an agenda.'

Dan opens his mouth as if to say something, then evidently thinks better of it. 'Okay. But think about it. You did the big proposal, handed over a diamond that would guarantee you the shag of your life – which by the looks of you this morning, you got – and yet she still didn't actually, say yes.'

'Yes, but what about actions speaking louder than words, and all that?'

'What actions did she do, specifically?'

'None of your business.'

Dan walks over to the refrigerator and removes an expensive-looking jar of coffee. 'Why can't you do a single thing properly? Have I taught you nothing?'

'Hopefully not, no. The important thing is, we're officially engaged now. She's wearing the ring. So it makes me feel better, you know? After all, she'd hardly have it on—'

'Unless she was just having *you* on.'

'Dan!'

'Sorry, Ed. If you're sure . . .'

'I am.'

'Good,' he says, spooning coffee into the cafetière. 'So when's the big day?'

'Well, we didn't actually get around to setting a date.'

Dan stops, mid-spoon. 'Don't you think you'd better?'

'Okay, okay. It'll be the first thing I do this evening.'

'Good.'

As he grabs a couple of clean mugs from the dish-washer, I hold my hand up. 'Actually, Dan, I don't think I've got time for a coffee.'

'What? This isn't for you?'

'Who's it for?'

As I wait for him to answer, there's the sound of someone clearing their throat from the bedroom door-way, and I look round to see a short blonde girl with just-out-of-bed hair standing there. She's wearing – appropriately – a T-shirt with 'Love Is Blonde' written on the front, which I recognize as one from Dan's collection. And nothing else.

'Aren't you going to introduce me?' says the girl.

'Er, yes, sorry,' says Dan. 'This is Edward.'

'No,' says the girl, after an uncomfortable silence. 'I mean, introduce *me*.'

As Dan stands there awkwardly, I realize the reason he doesn't is probably because he can't remember her name.

And as I make my way out through his front door, a smile on my face, the girl isn't far behind me. Not surprisingly, she doesn't have one on hers.

10.19 a.m.

I'm sitting in my office, safe in the knowledge that since Natasha's just phoned to say that she'll be in in five minutes I've easily got an hour or two to myself, and I'm reading the engagement announcements in the *Argus*, wondering how to word Sam's and mine, when a knock on the door makes me jump. Assuming it's Natasha and that she's early, I hurriedly hide the paper in my desk, then leap up to answer it, banging my kneecap on the edge of my drawer as I do so.

Cursing to myself, I limp across the office, realizing that if it was Natasha, she certainly wouldn't knock, but when I open the door, it's the one person I want to see less than my boss.

'Hello, Edward.'

Jane smiles, then leans in to kiss me on the cheek, and I'm so stunned I don't have the time to pull away. I haven't seen her for a few months, and almost don't recognize her; she's had her hair cut short, dyed almost copper in colour, and is wearing a pair of those 'statement' glasses, although they look more like those 3-D ones you get at the cinema, and the statement they seem to be making is 'I'm a public danger', as the corner of the white plastic frame nearly takes my eye out.

'W-what are you doing here?' I stammer. The last time Jane turned up unannounced like this, it almost led to Sam and I splitting up.

'Nice to see you too,' she says, looking a little hurt.

'Sorry.'

We stand there awkwardly for a moment until Jane clears her throat. 'Are you going to ask me in?'

'Well, Natasha's going to be here in a moment,' I say. Which isn't strictly untrue, depending on your definition of how long a moment is.

'Great,' says Jane. 'In that case, you can let me buy you a coffee.'

For a minute, I think about telling Jane that Natasha won't be pleased if she comes in and finds the office unattended, but the alternative is that I have to spend time with her here, with no witnesses. And while I might not want to risk upsetting Natasha, seeing as that's actually the lesser of two evils, I agree.

10.34 a.m.
We're sitting in Megabite, the internet café on the corner of Ship Street, and I've made sure we've got a table as close to the window as possible, in case Sam walks past. And while this may sound strange, it's actually because if she does, then I want her to spot us – or rather, the last thing I want is for Sam to think we're hiding from her. Not that I think she doesn't trust me, but last time I saw Jane, I ended up getting myself into trouble by not telling Sam about it. And what a mistake that nearly turned out to be.

'I tried our flat,' says Jane, offering me a piece of her flapjack, then making a surprised face when I turn it down.

'What? When?' I say, not really wanting to ask why.

'Last night. I just happened to be passing. Thought you might fancy a drink. But someone else answered the door.'

Immediately, I'm suspicious. Jane doesn't 'just happen' to do anything. And while her motivation may have been completely above board, I can't help but doubt it.

'It's not *our* flat any more, Jane,' I say, and while my next thought is to inform her that it stopped being her flat when she moved out without telling me, I remind myself that I should be past all that. Especially now. 'I mean, it's rented out. And I've moved . . .' I stop short of saying 'in with Sam', and then realize I'm being silly. While I don't want to rub it in her face, at some point Jane will have to hear I'm getting married. And while, actually, I'd rather she didn't hear it from me, I don't think, with her sitting across the table from me like this, I've got much choice. Besides, starting off by telling her Sam and I have moved in together might well soften the blow. Then again, knowing Jane, it might provoke one. She always had a good right hook.

'Oh yes?' Jane picks her steaming latte up, then puts it back down on the table when she realizes it's too hot to drink. 'Anywhere nice?' she asks, taking a large bite out of the flapjack.

I take a deep breath. 'In with Sam, actually.'

Jane flinches slightly, but doesn't lose her composure. 'And how is that going?'

I try and detect any maliciousness in her voice, but I can't hear any, although maybe that's because it's difficult to be malicious when your mouth's clogged up with a mixture of oats and syrup. 'Good, thanks,' I say, then decide that it's now or never. But before I get the chance, Jane beats me to it.

'Living together, eh?' she says, before taking another bite. 'You'll be telling me you're getting married next.'

'Well . . .' I blow on my coffee, and try to look as innocent as I can. 'Funny you should say that . . .'

But what happens next suggests that it's not funny at all because Jane's mouth falls open, affording me a rather unpleasant view of some half-chewed flapjack.

'What?'

'We're – Sam and I, I mean – well, we are. Getting – you know – *married.*'

I make a jokey-horror face in an attempt to lessen the impact, but it doesn't seem to work, because instead of congratulating me, Jane swallows the mouthful of flapjack with what looks like the greatest of efforts, then starts to emit a low, wailing sound.

Although it takes me a while, I realize she's crying. And even though I've seen her turn on the waterworks in the past as easily as opening a tap, from what I can tell, these tears are for real. Her shoulders are heaving, and after a minute or so, there's even what looks like snot coming out of her nose.

I look frantically round the coffee shop, noticing to my horror that people are watching – probably *due* to the low wailing sound Jane's making, which is actually getting less and less low by the second. I don't know what to do. I can't hug her, partly because I don't think it would be appropriate, but also because I've just had my suit dry-cleaned, and the last thing I want is a snot stain on the shoulder.

Cursing the fact that I don't have any tissues on me, I stand up quickly, and – trying to avoid the black stares from the assembled coffee-drinkers, who probably assume I'm abandoning her – make my way over towards the counter and grab a handful of napkins before hurrying back.

'Here,' I say, handing over the wedge of tissues.

Jane looks at the contents of my hand, then up at me, and starts crying even more loudly and, for a moment, I can't work out whether it's because the napkins have some sort of emotional significance. 'What's the matter?' I say, even though in retrospect it's probably the stupidest question I could have come up with.

After what seems like an eternity, and after working her way through a large number of napkins, Jane manages to pull herself together.

'I'm just so happy for you,' she says, blowing her nose loudly.

'Oh. Right,' I say, wondering whether *yeah, right* might be more accurate.

She looks up at me, and tries to force a smile. 'She's not pregnant, is she?'

'No!' I say, a little annoyed that everyone thinks that's the only reason Sam would want to marry me.

'Oh,' she sniffs. 'Have you set a date yet?'

'Yes,' I say, perhaps a little too quickly. 'I mean, no. Not yet.'

'It's all right, Edward,' says Jane, dabbing at her eyes with the last of the napkins. 'I'm hardly going to crash the church and shout "It should have been me." Although, of course, it should have.'

'Actually, Sam asked me,' I say, maybe because I think that'll make her feel better, although the look on her face suggests it's had the opposite effect. 'And anyway,' I add, sitting back down, and hoping I won't have to make another serviette run, 'for the millionth time, you dumped *me*, remember. So you can hardly sit here feeling all hard done by.'

Jane stares at me for a moment or two, then nods her head vigorously, which catapults a drop of snot dangerously close to my coffee mug. 'Sorry, Edward, you're right. As long as you ignore the fact that we went out with each other for ten years, during which time I waited for you to pop the question, and then when you didn't and I dumped you for your own good and to give you a kick up the backside to maybe do something about it, you sorted yourself out, lost all that weight, got a proper haircut, and then went off and shacked up with the first girl who showed any interest . . .' She pauses for breath. 'No, I shouldn't be feeling hard done by at all. In fact, congratulations.' Jane stands up suddenly, and holds out a hand for me to shake. 'I'm sure you'll both be very happy together.'

'But . . .'

As I stare at her outstretched palm, Jane leans over and grabs my hand. 'Goodbye, Edward,' she says, pumping it up and down theatrically, before shoving her chair out of the way and storming off towards the door.

I sit there, a little stunned. To be honest, there's a big part of me that wants her to go, but there's another part of me that doesn't want her to go like this. Reluctantly, I stand up.

'Jane,' I call after her. 'Wait.'

She stops by the doorway, then turns round 'What?'

'Come back. Sit down. Please. At least finish your coffee.'

For the first time, Jane seems to be aware that other people are watching. She hesitates for a moment, then walks calmly back towards the table, picks up her mug, and downs the contents in one go. It's a pretty impressive feat, firstly because the mug's full, and secondly, because it'll still be too hot to drink. As she starts crying again – which admittedly could be due to her having just burnt her throat – I put an arm round her, and ease her back down into her chair, to a smattering of applause from the room.

'I'm sorry, Edward,' she says, eventually. 'It was just a bit of a shock, that's all. And I know it's my fault, and you probably still hate me . . .'

I'm not too stupid to realize that's my cue. 'I don't hate you, Jane. I'd still like us to be friends.'

'I'd like that too,' she sniffs. 'It's just . . .' She stops talking, and looks up at me with her tear-stained eyes. Her mascara's run, making her look like one of the Goths that hang around outside Churchill Square Shopping Centre. 'I feel I'm being left on the shelf.'

'That's ridiculous. You're only . . .' I stop myself before

I blurt out her age because I'm worried about getting it wrong. 'I mean, you're still young. And quite a catch.'

'No I'm not,' she says, though not with a great deal of conviction. 'Even Dan's likely to get married before me – and he doesn't even want to. And I *love* weddings.'

And maybe it's the fear that Jane will start crying again, but I don't know what comes over me, and I can't stop myself from blurting it out.

'In that case, you should come.'

'What?'

'To the wedding. You should come.'

'Really?'

'Why not? After all, there'll be lots of people there you know, and besides, you and Sam got off on the wrong foot last time. Although, to be fair, that's because you were trying to kick Sam with yours.'

'Yes. I'm sorry about that.' Jane half smiles. 'Are you sure?'

'Of course I'm sure.'

'And Sam won't mind?' she says, a little brighter now.

'Not at all,' I say, although I'm pretty sure of the complete opposite. 'She'll be delighted.'

Jane takes a deep breath, then wipes her nose on her sleeve, smudging her lipstick in the process, and making her look less like a Goth and more like the Joker from *Batman*.

'Well, okay then,' she says, as if she's doing us both a huge favour. 'After all, the two of you would never have met if it hadn't been for me.'

7.13 p.m.

It doesn't take long for me to cheer myself up again, mainly thanks to the selection of wedding magazines I buy Sam from the newsagent's on the corner, then spend the rest of the morning browsing excitedly through myself. Even if Jane does come to the wedding, it's hardly going to spoil my and Sam's big day, and in fact we probably won't even notice her, given everything else that (according to the magazines, at least) will be going on around us. And while there seems to be an awful lot to organize if we're going to have the kind of wedding I'm imagining, I still want to get married as soon as possible. Which is why I need to get Sam to agree to a date. And soon.

The afternoon passes all too slowly, thanks to the series of interviews I've got scheduled, and I almost shove the last candidate out of the door in my rush to get home to Sam. She's sitting at the kitchen table when I get back to the flat, and as I dump the pile of wedding magazines on the chair next to her, she looks at them suspiciously.

'What are all these for?'

'Well,' I say, once I've eventually got my breath back from carrying the heavy bundle home. 'I was thinking. We should, you know, do it.'

'Here? On the kitchen table?' Sam widens her eyes at me. 'Steady on, Edward.'

'Be serious, Sam. I mean, what about a date?'

She pats me on the hand. 'That's sweet of you, Edward,

but you don't have to keep asking me out on dates. I mean, we've been together for eighteen months, and we're engaged now.'

'A date for the wedding.'

'Oh,' says Sam. 'Sorry. Right. Well, er . . .'

'Because I was thinking sooner rather than later. You know, why wait?'

'Well, because I might meet someone better, and . . .' Sam catches sight of my expression, then grins at me. 'I'm joking, Edward.'

I reach into my pocket and remove my mobile phone, then click on the calendar option. 'So when would work for you?' I say, rather formally.

'What's the rush?'

'The rush is . . .' I can't tell her there's no actual rush, it's just that I'm so relieved we're actually engaged now that I don't want to risk her changing her mind. But I might as well be honest. Sort of. 'The rush is that I just want to be married to you.'

Sam leans across the kitchen table and picks up her diary. 'That's lovely, sweetie. But these things take a bit of time.'

'Why?'

'Well, we've got to make sure my mum and dad can make it, for one thing.'

'Do they have to?' I'm scared of Sam's dad, who's got a little too much of the East End gangster about him for my liking, particularly when you consider his early retirement to Spain and the shotgun he keeps above the fireplace in his villa. At least I haven't had to ask him for his daughter's hand, given the fact that Sam proposed to me first, because I'm not sure which of my body parts he'd have wanted in return. 'I mean, I forgot they had to. Come from Spain, I mean.'

Sam picks the pile of magazines up from the chair next to her and puts them on the table, then indicates that I should sit down. 'And they'll need a bit of notice; they've got to arrange their flights, after all.'

'Which is why we should at least decide on a date,' I say, obediently sitting down next to her, 'so they can go ahead and book them. Plus, we've got things to book too. Have you thought about which church, for example?'

Sam frowns at me. 'Which church?'

'I mean, I don't even know what team you support.'

'What team?'

'You know. Catholics, or the old Church of England.'

'Which one are you?'

I shrug. 'The one where you get the wine and the little snack.'

Sam laughs. 'You make it sound like a tapas bar.'

'Because we ought to go ahead and check. Make sure they're free on the day. Meet the vicar. That sort of thing.'

'Ah.' Sam swivels round on her chair to face me. 'I actually thought we might go for something a bit more low key, you know? I'm not particularly religious, and all that church stuff, well, it's a bit hypocritical if you don't actually *believe*, isn't it?'

'Is it?'

'Well, yes. I'd be making all these promises in front of someone I'm not sure actually exists. And there's all that ceremonial stuff too . . .' She takes my hand. 'Surely the important thing is we *get* married? Not *how* we get married.'

For some reason, I'm a little disappointed. I'd always kind of assumed that when I got married, I'd do it the traditional way, in a church with everything that goes with it. And yet Sam seems to be quite happy to go for the registry-office option, which to me is about as romantic as signing a contract to buy a house.

'Yes, but don't you think that sometimes it's for other people too?' I say, hoping Sam will think I mean family and friends, though I really mean me.

She gives my hand a squeeze. 'Edward, as far as I'm concerned, I wouldn't mind if there was no one else there except the two of us. All that other stuff – the cake, the meringue dress . . . It's just, well, dressing.'

'Cake?' I'm suddenly alarmed that my one excuse to eat something unhealthy in public seems to be going out of the window. 'We've got to have a cake!'

'I was just using that as an example. Anyway, why are you so fixated on this? I didn't have you down as the religious type.'

'I'm not. I just . . .' I decide there's nothing for it but to go with the truth. 'I want to make a big statement to you and how I feel about you, in front of as many people as possible, including, you know, him upstairs. And it might sound a bit girly, but that's kind of how I'd always pictured it.'

Sam puts her diary down on the table, then leans over and kisses me. 'Oh, Edward, that's lovely of you. But I already know how you feel about me. And you've already made a huge statement.' She fingers her engagement ring. 'But our wedding day should be something to be enjoyed. Not endured. Which I'm worried it might be if we go down the traditional route.'

'Yes, but . . .' I start to object, and then stop myself. After all, what Sam's saying makes perfect sense. What's important *is* the two of us, and not some big affair. And thinking about it, I suppose less to organize means we can do it even sooner. With a sigh, I lean over and pick her diary up, flicking through the pages until I find the first available Saturday. 'Well, if that's the case, then we might as well go for the earliest date possible. How about the twenty-fifth?'

'Of April? But that's . . .'

'Three weeks away?' I smile at her, trying to ignore the feeling of panic that's suddenly building up inside me, not only because by suggesting something so soon, I might have given her the perfect excuse to postpone indefinitely or even back out, but also because if she does say yes, then I'll be getting married *in three weeks*. 'Like I said, if we're only having a small do, and not doing any of this stuff . . .' I tap the pile of wedding magazines dismissively. 'Then that shouldn't be a problem.'

'I suppose not . . .' Sam thinks for a second or two, and then puffs air out of her cheeks. 'Works for me.'

'Don't sound so enthusiastic.'

'I'm sorry, Edward. The twenty-fifth would be lovely.' She takes the diary back from me and writes the words REGISTRY and OFFICE in capital letters underneath the date, and then catches sight of my expression. 'Are you disappointed? Not doing the whole church thing?'

'Well, I . . . No. I mean, it's your day, isn't it?'

I smile at her half-heartedly, feeling a little better that at least we've set a date. Trouble is, now there's a different element of doubt in my mind: Why doesn't Sam want a big wedding?

I just hope the reason isn't simply that she doesn't want a big wedding to me.

Wednesday, 8 April

11.52 a.m.

Work's pretty busy this morning. Natasha's keen for us to impress a client we're trying to land, and since – for a change – it's a female client, this means she and I actually have to do some head-hunting, rather than rely solely on Natasha's other specialist 'skills'. I'm so busy, in fact, that I don't get a chance to phone the registry office to check they're free on the twenty-fifth until late morning. Fortunately, there's been a cancellation, although I don't like to ask why that is, and there's a slot available at four o'clock, which I book, even though the registrar informs me that we have to be in and out in fifteen minutes. When he jokes that it will be just like my wedding night, it's all I can do to force out a polite laugh.

6.04 p.m.

I'm in Tesco's with Mrs Barraclough, my stone-deaf eighty-something-years-old ex-upstairs neighbour. Even though I don't live in the flat beneath her any more, I still take Mrs Barraclough shopping every Wednesday, ever since she became too frail to do it on her own, and – more to the point – since the list of old-lady essential items like Vaseline, tissues, and tins of sweets that I used to pick up for her became somewhat embarrassing for me to buy on my own.

I did try and get her to do her regular shop on-line at one point, but seeing as the operation of something as simple as her hearing aid is beyond her, suffice to say it didn't work out. Plus, I suspect she quite likes being driven round Brighton in my Mini, although simply getting her in and out of the passenger seat takes almost as long as the rest of the trip round Tesco's.

To be honest, I like her company too. My parents aren't around any more, and I don't have any aunts or uncles, so she's the nearest I've got to an elderly relative. And what's more, she's thrilled when I tell her that Sam and I are getting married.

'That's wonderful news, Edward,' she says, planting a somewhat spiky kiss on my cheek as we inch our way along the tea and coffee aisle. 'I didn't think you young people got married any more.' There's a pause, as Mrs Barraclough lowers herself slowly down to pick up a packet of her favourite Cadbury's Options hot chocolate off the bottom shelf, and then: 'Samantha's not in the family way, is she?'

'No, Mrs B. Sam's not pregnant.'

'Pardon?' Mrs Barraclough squints at me, not having realized her hearing aid popped out as she bent over.

'We are not having a baby,' I half shout, causing a young couple to look at us strangely.

'Well, congratulations,' she says, popping the earpiece back in.

'Thank you,' I say, peering at the next item on Mrs Barraclough's list, which seems to say either 'toilet water' or 'tonic water' – her spidery handwriting can be somewhat hard to decipher sometimes – but I'm guessing it's the latter, given that the word 'gin' is written underneath it. 'You will come to the wedding, I hope?'

'Of course I will, Edward. Especially if your friend is going to be there.'

'Which friend is that, Mrs B?' I say, teasing her.

'You know,' she says, 'TV Stan.'

Mrs Barraclough is a huge fan of Dan's, and never misses a re-run of *Where There's a Will*. Unfortunately, the other thing she never does is get his name right, which is a source of constant irritation to him – and constant amusement to me – although it's his own fault for introducing himself to her as 'TV's Dan Davis'.

'Of course he will. And I'll make sure he saves the last dance for you.'

Mrs Barraclough chuckles at the thought. 'Will the ceremony be at St Andrew's?' she asks, pointing through the supermarket window at the church opposite.

'Er, no. We're, um, not having a church wedding.'

Mrs Barraclough's face falls. 'Oh.'

'Well, we just . . . I mean, Sam feels . . .' This is a tricky one, since I know Mrs Barraclough goes to St Andrews every Sunday, and I don't want to get into any sort of religious discussion. Plus, to be honest, I still haven't quite got my head round the fact. 'We just wanted to do it sooner rather than later, that's all.'

Mrs Barraclough regards me curiously. 'Are you sure Samantha's not . . .' she lowers her voice, 'with child?'

'Yes. I'm sure.'

'Well, when is it?'

'Two weeks this Saturday.'

'Two weeks this Saturday?' Mrs Barraclough twiddles the knob on her hearing aid again, as if she's unsure she's heard me properly.

'That's right.'

'That *is* rather soon, isn't it?'

For a second, I'm worried she's going to enquire about Sam's reproductive state again, and think about trying to explain, but I'm meeting Dan later, and I'm not sure I've got the time.

'We just didn't want to wait.'

Mrs Barraclough smiles. 'You young people. It's always rush, rush, rush. Back when I was courting, you'd have to be walking out with someone for months before you could even hold hands. Nowadays . . .'

'Sam and I have been dating for quite a while, now, Mrs B.'

'So? You were with that Jane for an awful lot longer, yet you didn't get married to her.'

'Yes, well, she ran off before I had the chance,' I blurt out.

'Pardon?'

'I . . . er . . . said Stan will look forward to that dance.'

'Me too,' says Mrs Barraclough, before realizing that I've just managed to change the subject. 'I'm sorry, Edward,' she says, resting a bony hand on my arm. 'I don't mean to lecture you. It's just that marriage is such a big thing. And some things are worth waiting for.'

I pat the back of her hand, but don't say anything. After all, how can I be rushing into something with someone I've waited all my life for?

7.33 p.m.

I'm in the Admiral Jim with Dan, telling him about Sam's preference for a low-key wedding, and still feeling a little depressed about it. I've already filled him in about my encounter with Jane yesterday morning, although I've decided not to tell him I ended up inviting her to the wedding. Mainly because I can't quite believe it myself.

'Yes, well,' says Dan, brushing some crisp crumbs from the front of his 'iPhone Therefore I Am' T-shirt. 'Lucky escape, if you ask me.'

'What do you mean?'

'It's bad enough that you're getting married in the first place. But having to go through all that church bol-locks – you know: will some joker shout out during the "anyone here know any reason why the two of you shouldn't be wed" bit; are you going to faint; some small baby squealing from the pews so loudly you can't hear yourself think . . . Much better you just go and sign a bit of paper. After all, that's exactly what you'll be doing a few years down the line when you want to get out of it.'

'Very funny, Dan. But . . .'

'But what?'

'She doesn't even want to wear a dress.'

'Really?' Dan leans forwards in his seat. 'Fantastic. Hence the reason she doesn't want to be in a draughty old church, I'll bet.'

It takes a few seconds for me to realize what he's going on about. 'No, Dan, she will be wearing *a* dress. Just not the big meringue number.'

'Oh.' His face falls. 'Right. But I suppose you should be happy. I mean, this is all going to keep the cost down, and therefore leave more to spend on the party afterwards. And besides, I didn't know you were a Jesus-freak. Though now I think of it, those sandals you wear in the summer are a bit . . .'

'I'm not. I mean, I don't *believe*, I don't think. But it means something, doesn't it?'

'Does it?'

'To some people. Haven't you ever gone out with anyone religious?'

He thinks for a moment or two. 'Does shouting out "oh God" in bed count?'

'Dan, please.'

'Sorry, Ed. But if you're not, why are you so bothered?'

I stare into my pint glass. 'I don't know. It's just the

way it's done, isn't it? Registry offices always seem so, well, formal, and a thing like this shouldn't be formal. It's a celebration, after all. And what girl doesn't want a big wedding? So if Sam doesn't see our wedding like that, then maybe it's a reflection on me. Maybe she feels I'm not her ideal partner, and therefore in order not to spoil her *real* big day, she's planning, well, a smaller big day instead.'

I brace myself for Dan's usual long-winded response, but instead, all I get is one word.

'Nah.'

'Nah?'

'It's actually better, if you think about it.'

'How do you work that one out?'

'Less chance of her suffering from PND.'

I sip my beer and wait for Dan to continue, but as usual, he makes me ask.

'What's PND?'

He smiles. 'Post nuptial depression.'

I stare at him, waiting for the explanation, but he just grins maddeningly back.

'Which is?' I almost shout.

'It's quite common, apparently,' says Dan, sagely. 'Most women get depressed afterwards. Even the ones who aren't marrying you.'

'Just try to explain, please, without insulting me.'

Dan looks uncertain for a moment, as if he knows that request is going to be beyond him. 'Think about it. Apparently, most women have been dreaming about their wedding since they were old enough to know what one was. Then there's months of military-style precision planning leading up to the big day itself, where the bride's the centre of attention . . .' He shakes his head. 'And then she wakes up the next day, and she's plain old Mrs Edward Middleton. What's she got to look forward to? Years and years of normal, boring married life. And to you.'

'Sod off!'

'I'm serious. The wedding itself is such a lavish event, of course married life can't possibly live up to it, hence the post nuptial depression.' He helps himself to a handful of crisps from the bag on the bar. 'So like I said, look on the bright side. At least Sam's not going to wake up the next morning and feel depressed. Until she remembers what she's done, of course.'

I stare at him in amazement. 'Where do you get this stuff from?'

'I'm quite widely read, you know,' he says, shoving the crisps into his mouth.

'Really?' I say. Although I suppose that between *Cosmopolitan*, *Heat* and the *Sun*, Dan does pretty much have it covered.

'Yes, really.' He takes a mouthful of beer. 'So you've got nothing to worry about. Besides, at least the registry office option means you can do it sooner rather than later. Which is what you want, isn't it?'

'Registry office?' says Wendy, appearing behind the bar. 'I thought you'd be doing the big church thing.'

'So did he,' says Dan. 'But Sam doesn't want one. And Ed's worried that it means something.'

Wendy shrugs. 'All it means is that Sam wants a registry-office wedding.'

'But why wouldn't she want the whole church experience? I thought that was what all women wanted.'

'And some men, apparently,' says Dan, under his breath.

Wendy shrugs again. 'Not necessarily. Don't worry about it, Edward. And remember, it's Sam's day, not yours. So I'm afraid if she doesn't want a big one—'

'Which she obviously doesn't,' interrupts Dan, 'if she's marrying you.'

'Then what she says goes,' continues Wendy, ignoring him.

As she heads off to serve some other customers, I sigh. 'Maybe Wendy's right,' I say. 'Although . . .'

'Although what?'

'No, nothing.'

'Come on, Ed. Tell your uncle Dan.'

'It's just what you said earlier.'

Dan looks at me blankly. 'Sorry, mate, you'll have to refresh the old memory.'

'Well, Sam and I have lived together for, what, a year now?'

Dan makes the 'how would I know?' face. 'If you say so.'

'So what if she wakes up the next morning expecting to feel different and, well, *doesn't*?'

'Huh?'

'You know – she might expect marriage to make our relationship better. Different, somehow. And apart from the ring on her finger, it won't be. We'll still be in the same flat, doing the same things . . .'

Dan frowns. 'So?'

'So it was easy in the olden days. No one lived together before they were actually married so the first day of married life was the start of a new chapter. A new experience. Some of them hadn't even had sex until the wedding night.'

Dan laughs. 'Yeah, right.'

'I'm serious, Dan. Which is why I need to make sure things *are* different.'

'And how are you going to do that?'

'I don't know. But maybe I was hoping that a big wedding might kick-start all that. As opposed to us just turning up, signing a bit of paper, and going back home again.'

Dan laughs. 'Listen, Ed. It's simple. You think she's going to get bored and leave you after the wedding, then don't get married.'

'But then she might . . .'

'Leave you?' Dan finishes off the last of the crisps, scrunches the packet into a ball and lobs it towards the bin on the other side of the bar, punching the air in celebration when it drops in. 'There, my friend, is the conundrum.'

'So what do I do?'

'Well, like you said, you've just got to make sure you do take it to the next level. Kids, and everything else.'

'What's everything else?'

Dan thinks for a second. 'Just kids, really.'

'Great. Thanks.'

As I put my head in my hands, Dan leans across and nudges me. 'Relationships are all about levels, Ed. There's the superficial level . . .'

'The one yours never get beyond, you mean?'

'Precisely,' says Dan, without a hint of irony. 'Then you start going out with someone, and then they move in. Before you know it, you're engaged, married, and . . . Game over.'

'What's your point?'

'And who initiates all these changes? The women. And why? Because they want babies.'

'It's not as simple as that, surely? I mean, Jane didn't.'

'Yes, but think back. Jane was the one who suggested moving in with you.'

'So she could save on the rent.'

'And then moved out when you didn't want to take things further. And wasn't it Sam who suggested you move in with her?'

'Well, yes, but that was kind of a misunderstanding.'

Dan rolls his eyes. 'That wouldn't be the first time. Or the last. And now Sam's asked you to marry her. Trust me – it's only a matter of time before you hear the patter of tiny feet. Or possibly not so tiny, given how fat you used to be.'

'But how can I tell?'

'I suggest you ask her.'

I let out a short laugh. 'What, go up to Sam and say "Why exactly do you want to get married to me?"'

Dan nods. 'Why not?'

'Well, because . . . because it's just not the done thing, is it?'

'Listen, mate, like you said, Sam asked you, didn't she?'

'Yes, but . . .'

'And why do you think that was?'

'Because she loves me.'

Dan laughs. 'So? I love my car, but I'm hardly going to get down on one knee in front of it, am I?'

'Only because one of your exes might jump into the driver's seat and floor the accelerator while you're there,' suggests Wendy, who's been ear-wigging from the other end of the bar.

Dan sticks his tongue out at her. 'So why change the status quo, unless she's got an ulterior motive?'

'Such as?'

'You're *sure* she's not pregnant?'

'Yes!' I shout, even though I'm starting to feel anything but. 'Dan, people do get married for other reasons, you know.'

'Such as?'

'Well, to demonstrate their commitment to each other – something I wouldn't expect you to understand. And remember, Sam's a lot more straightforward than Jane ever was. I mean, Jane tried to get me to propose to her by dumping me. Sam just came out and said it. And that's refreshing.'

Dan shudders. 'Scary, if you ask me. Maybe she's trying to get her hands on your money.'

'Don't be ridiculous. Besides, I haven't got any left after our little trip to Tiffany's.'

He picks his beer up and takes another mouthful. 'Ed, think about it. Jane also left you because you got fat, stopped caring about what you wore, had dodgy teeth, a naff haircut, and all that stuff, but mainly because you became complacent about you and her. And that's why, in a way, you feeling so insecure about Sam is a good thing.'

'Huh?'

'Because if you're always worried she's going to leave you, then you're going to have to work doubly hard to make sure she doesn't.'

Dan sits back in his seat and looks pleased with himself, as if he's just explained the theory of relativity in a new way, then his face falls as I shake my head in disbelief.

'Yes, but, that's not a good thing, is it? Living life in a constant state of stress?'

He smiles. 'Welcome to marriage. But at least she's focussing on the being married part, not the getting married bit. Which you've got to agree, can only be a good thing.'

'But . . .' I stop talking, because much as I hate to admit it, he has a point. We sit there in silence for a while, before Dan clears his throat.

'Can I ask you something?'

'Sure.'

'Why *do* people get married?'

'Is this a joke?'

'No. I'm serious.'

'Do you mean me and Sam? Or anyone?'

'Well, you and Sam, for starters. I mean, I know you've said she's not eating for two . . .' He scratches his head, as if he can't conceive there'd be another reason. 'Although thinking about it, she's done that ever since I've known her.' One of the things Dan's most impressed about Sam is that she's got a healthy appetite, unlike some of the stick insects he usually dates. 'For example, why did you say yes so quickly? Did you feel you might lose her otherwise?'

I have to wonder where there's a little bit of truth in that because one of the reasons Jane dumped me was my 'inability to commit', apparently. Although it was only my inability to commit to her, as it turned out. 'Not really. I just . . . I mean, we . . . To tell you the truth, I don't know if there's one specific thing. It just kind of seemed right. So when she asked me, I didn't have to think about what my answer would be, you know?'

Dan shakes his head. 'No, I don't know. Explain.'

I stare thoughtfully into my pint glass as I try and put it into words. 'I guess I knew I'd never meet anyone better.'

I daren't look across at Dan, sure he's doing his usual mime of sticking his fingers down his throat as he usually does whenever I'm discussing anything to do with emotions, but when I finally glance up at him, he's gazing at me intently.

'You can take that both ways.'

'No, I mean it in a positive sense. And not just because I was able to measure everything against the relationship I had with Jane.'

'It must have been pretty special, I guess?'

I wait for the punchline, but none comes. 'Er, yes, actually.'

'And how did you feel when she asked? You know, at the precise moment you had to answer. I was reading this thing the other day about people who drown. Apparently there's a lot of struggling, and then right at the point of death, they experience this feeling of calm, almost like euphoria.'

'And?'

'Was it like that?'

I laugh. 'Not at all.'

'Because, it's quite a heavy question, isn't it? I mean, it's all right just going out with someone, but to put them on the spot and ask them if they want to spend the rest of their lives with you. Legally . . .' Dan whistles loudly.

'Why are you so interested, all of a sudden? This better not be for your best-man speech.'

He grins. 'Nah. I'm just curious.'

'Curious? Or interested?'

'What's the difference?'

'Curious suggests you want to know for the hell of it. Interested means you want to know because it's something you're considering yourself.'

Dan makes a face, as if I've just suggested he take all his clothes off and runs up and down the seafront. 'Yeah, right. Dan Davis, get married. A ha ha ha ha ha.'

'Why not?'

'Well, because . . .' splutters Dan. 'For one thing . . .'

'Yes?'

'Er . . .'

'Come on. Is it something you could see yourself doing? One day?'

Dan drains the last of his beer. 'Doubtful.'

'Not even with someone like Polly?'

He winces a little at the mention of her name. 'Someone like Polly? Yes, maybe. But that's never going to happen, is it?'

'Why not?'

'Because there's no one like Polly, and the actual Polly's with someone else now. Besides, even if she wasn't, she might not want . . .'

'You?'

'To get married,' says Dan, as if I've just made the most outrageous suggestion. 'Anyway, it's you we're talking about here.'

'No it isn't. You brought it up.'

'I did, didn't I? Which means I can decide when I want to stop talking about it too.'

'But—'

'Nope.'

'Dan, I—'

'Edward!' He makes the 'talk to the hand' gesture. 'Subject closed.'

'Fine,' I say.

Although by the look on his face when I mentioned Polly's name, I suspect it's anything but.

Thursday, 9 April

7.55 p.m.
Sam's been happily showing the ring to all and sundry, and even wears it to work, which is something I'm pleased about, as it might – *finally* – stop her getting regularly hit on by her clients. I can't blame them, though; it's what I did.

She's also been phoning round various friends and family to check they're free on the twenty-fifth, which I suppose proves to me that she's serious about the wedding going ahead. I've been trying to be more enthusiastic about the registry office too, and while I can't say the idea's exactly growing on me, I can see that I don't have a lot of choice.

Come Thursday evening, I'm in the kitchen, putting the finishing touches to the food we're serving Dan and Madeleine, who – given that they've never met, and since Sam's decided to ask Madeleine to be her maid of honour – we've invited round for dinner this evening to discuss their involvement in our (not so) big day.

Of course, when I say 'putting the finishing touches to', what I really mean is 'putting in the oven', as it's Sam who's been slaving away all afternoon to make some sort of cheese and vegetable bake. I had offered to make my speciality — spaghetti Bolognese — although when I say 'speciality', it's about the only thing I can cook that isn't, well, canned, but as Sam reminded me, Madeleine's a vegetarian.

As to what sort of vegetables I'm baking, I'm not that sure because, to be honest, the only ones I can name come on a round cheese- and tomato-covered base on the rare occasion Sam lets me order us a takeaway Veggie Wedgie from Pizza the Action for dinner but (as she always points out) those aren't 'proper' vegetables anyway. I'd prefer their Meat Treat, but even though (again, according to Sam) the kind of meat you get on a pizza isn't proper meat either, and despite my observation that surely that makes them both as bad as each other so we might as well go the meat route, I rarely get my way.

But whatever it is we're eating, I'm happy. This is the first official 'engagement' Sam and I have had as a couple since we, well, got officially engaged. And the way I see it, the more things we do like this, the more real this whole getting married business becomes.

As the doorbell rings, Sam puts a hand on my arm. 'Try and control Dan this evening, will you? I don't want him making a play for Madeleine and there being atmosphere at the wedding.'

'I'll do my best,' I say, 'but it'll be difficult. After all, she's just his type.'

Sam reaches up and brushes off a piece of cheese from the front of the Spanish bullfighter apron I'm wearing; my Christmas present from her mother. 'How is she his type?'

'She's female,' I say, heading off to answer the door.

8.14 p.m.

Sam, Madeleine and I are sitting in the lounge, waiting for Dan to turn up, while Dan is probably sitting outside in his car so he can be 'fashionably' late. I suspect this for two reasons: firstly because it's what he always does, as he likes to make an entrance, and secondly because I heard what sounded like him noisily parking the Porsche just down the street ten minutes ago.

It's particularly annoying because there's a bottle of champagne chilling in the fridge that I've bought so we can toast our forthcoming nuptials, and which I can't, of course, open until he gets here, so we're sitting without a drink. Madeleine's a bit nervous, and could therefore probably do with one, especially since she's a little bit star-struck at the prospect of meeting Dan. Whether she is *actually* his type, I'm not sure; she's not unattractive, and she's certainly 'blessed in the chest', as Dan would say, which are both plus points, if you excuse the phrase, as far as he's concerned. But besides being a vegetarian, she's also a homoeopath, and if I know him, that's possibly a little too tree-hugging for Dan.

I'm nervous too. Given that Dan's my best man, and Madeleine's going to be Sam's maid of honour, it's important they get on, and to that end, I've already warned him away from getting drunk and making any of his usual loaded 'So do you never put any kind of meat in your mouth?' type observations. It's therefore a relief – when he eventually rings the doorbell, and once I've done that pointless introduction thing where I say, 'Dan, this is Madeleine, Madeleine, this is Dan', stressing their names as if both of them are simple or deaf – that he seems to be on his best behaviour.

'Lovely to meet you, Dan,' says Madeleine, holding out a hand towards him, which he grabs, planting a kiss on her cheek in the same smooth movement.

'Edward,' he scolds, turning towards me, 'you didn't tell me tonight was bring a dish.'

It's a corny line, and out of the corner of my eye I can see Sam groaning, but it seems to have the opposite effect on Madeleine, especially since Dan hasn't let go of her hand yet.

'I'm a big fan,' she says, which immediately sets my alarm bells ringing. Normally that's an incentive for Dan to find out just how big, but instead, he just smiles.

'Thank you. That's nice to hear. So tell me,' he says, 'how did you get the nickname?'

'Nickname?'

'I mean, are you just a bit reckless, or, you know . . .' he circles one finger next to his temple, while sticking his tongue sideways out of his mouth, 'actually loopy?'

Madeleine laughs nervously. 'I'm not sure what you . . .'

'Mad Elaine.' Dan looks puzzled. 'Isn't that how Ed introduced you?'

As Sam and I don't know where to look, there's an awkward silence, made even more awkward by a confused-looking Dan staring at each of us in turn, but then, suddenly, Madeleine bursts out laughing. 'You are funny,' she says, elbowing him playfully in the ribs. 'Sam warned me you were a charmer, but she didn't say you had such a good sense of humour too.'

Dan looks across at me, evidently pleased that Madeleine's laughing, but not quite sure why. 'But . . .'

'Dan,' I say, quickly, 'can I see you in the kitchen for a moment?'

'What? Oh, sure.' He reaches into the Waitrose bag he's carrying and removes a bottle of Perrier. 'I need to put this in the fridge, anyway. Don't go away, *Mad Elaine.*'

As Madeleine erupts into peals of laughter again, he flashes her the famous Dan Davis grin, then follows me as expected.

'What are you playing at?' I whisper, as I pretend to adjust the oven temperature.

'Nothing. Why?'

'Firstly, her name is Madeleine. One word, not a description.'

'But it's pronounced . . .'

'That's because she's French. Or at least, her parents are.'

'Ah.'

'And secondly . . .' I snatch the bottle of Perrier from him. 'Mineral water?'

'Well,' says Dan, gravely, 'I am driving.'

'What for? You live five minutes away.'

'You told me not to get drunk this evening. So I thought if I drove, I'd be more likely to stay sober.'

'Oh. Right.' I immediately feel guilty. 'Sorry. And you're not trying to chat her up?'

Dan sighs. 'Ed, if you think that accusing a woman of being a mentalist is a good way to get into her knickers . . . let's just say it's a miracle you've managed to find one to marry you.'

'Yes, well,' I say, removing the champagne from the fridge, and replacing it with the Perrier. 'It just looked like you were doing, you know, your usual.'

'You said you wanted us to get on, didn't you? So I'm just being friendly.'

'Okay. Point taken. Sorry.'

Dan rests a hand on my arm. 'Apology accepted.'

We head back into the lounge, where Sam and Madeleine are sitting on the sofa. I pop the bottle open, and fill up three of the four glasses on the coffee table.

'Are you sure you won't have one, Dan?'

He takes one look at the bottle, then sits down next to Madeleine, his arm snaking around her waist to give her a squeeze.

'Oh, go on, then,' he says. 'Just the one. I can never resist anything French and bubbly.'

And as Madeleine starts to giggle for the third time this evening, I can already tell it's going to be a long night.

10.42 p.m.
It's getting late, and – apart from one awkward moment, when Madeleine told Dan she was a homoeopath, and Dan replied 'kinky', resulting in me having to whisk him back off into the kitchen to explain that it wasn't some perverse sexual practice – the evening seems to have gone well. Madeleine's been flirting with Dan the whole evening, but true to his word, Dan's nursed the same glass of champagne all night, and so while the rest of us are pleasantly merry, he's in a strangely reflective mood.

We're having coffee, and I'm trying to sneakily eat a few extra After Eights without Sam noticing by slipping them out of their wrappers while still in the box, when Dan suddenly turns to Sam and clears his throat.

'Tell me,' he says, 'why exactly did you ask Edward to marry you?'

This takes me by surprise, especially when Sam glances across at me, meaning I have to stop chewing the latest After Eight she hasn't seen me take and start sucking it instead. And even though I'm embarrassed that Dan's brought it up so brazenly, I nod at her to suggest she should go ahead and answer, although more as a diversionary tactic so I can swallow the contents of my mouth.

'It seemed like the obvious thing to do,' she says, fingering her engagement ring. 'Especially when I found out I was pregnant.'

Thirty seconds later, after Dan's finished whacking me on the back to dislodge the remains of the After Eight I've just inhaled in shock, and it's finally become clear to me that Sam was joking, everyone stops laughing.

'Yes, Sam,' I croak, before guzzling down some of Dan's Perrier. 'Very funny.'

'Seriously, though,' he says, still trying to hide a smile. 'Why *are* you marrying Ed?'

I shoot him a glance, unable to work out why he's doing this. Maybe he thinks he's doing me a favour, trying to put my mind at rest by hearing it from the horse's mouth. Maybe he wants to hear a woman's point of view, so he can understand Polly better. But either way, I'm anxious to change the subject.

'Dan, I hardly think now's the time or the place,' I say, reaching over to refill my water glass.

'Why not?' he says. 'I'd like to hear it.'

In truth, there's a part of me that would like to hear it too. But probably not in front of anyone else. And especially not in front of Dan, particularly given the speech he's going to be delivering in a couple of weeks' time.

'I mean,' he continues, 'when you first met him, he wasn't such a catch, was he? And he was going out with someone else. Although he was the only one in that particular relationship who still believed that.'

'Thank you, Dan.'

'Well . . .' Sam reaches across the table, and grabs my hand. 'That was the thing. I got to know him first, and saw the things he did for other people like Mrs Barraclough, Billy, and – no offence – even you, and I realized what a lovely, decent guy he was, and – again, no offence, Dan – there aren't that many of them around. And when I saw how much he wanted Jane back, how much he obviously cared about her . . .' She smiles, and squeezes my fingers tightly. 'I also knew she'd broken his heart, and saw how much that had hurt him, and so I knew he'd never do the same to me, because he'd never want to inflict that kind of pain on someone else. And then, as the new – or rather, the *old* Edward started to emerge . . . I mean, I fancied him, obviously. But the fact that he was prepared to work so hard, put himself through so much agony, and make so many changes, just to try and win her back, well, I thought to myself: he must really love her to do such a thing. And I remember thinking how lucky she was, and hoping that one day I'd meet someone who felt the same way about me. I just didn't know at the time that I already had.'

I don't know what to say. I've never really heard Sam talk like this before. And I'm not the only one; there's a silence round the table, and I can tell that even number-one cynic Dan is touched, as he shakes his head in admiration.

'Wow.'

Sam's blushing now, and I'm pretty sure I must be too. 'You asked.'

Suddenly, there's a loud sob from Madeleine's end of the table. 'That's beautiful.'

'Which is why it's a shame I can't prove that to you by us having a proper big wedding with all the trimmings,' I say, handing Madeleine a serviette at the same time.

Sam shakes her head. 'You don't need to prove it to me, Edward. Not like that, anyway.'

'Well, maybe I want to,' I say, sounding like a petulant teenager.

'I thought we'd discussed this,' says Sam. 'Is it still that important to you?'

I gaze across the table at her for a moment, then stick my bottom lip out childishly. 'No,' I say, implying the exact opposite.

There's an awkward silence, then Dan taps his fork against the rim of his glass. 'We're still here, by the way.'

'Sorry. So, er, can I get anyone anything?' I say, picking up the After Eight box and handing it round. Despite the number of wrappers still in there, it feels alarmingly light, and I'm hoping I haven't eaten them all.

Madeleine dabs her eyes with the serviette, then looks at her watch. 'No, thank you. Thanks for a lovely evening, but I ought to be going,' she says, getting up from the table. 'It's a school night, and I've got a long walk home.'

Quick as a flash, Dan's out of his chair. 'I ought to get

off too. Hey, Mad Elaine, we should swap details,' he says, adding 'in case we need to discuss wedding stuff,' when he sees me glaring at him.

'Sure,' she says. 'What's the best way to get hold of you?'

Dan, to his credit, doesn't give her his usual 'with both hands' answer. 'Email's probably best. Just use my name at hotmail dot com.'

'Hot male?' says Madeleine. 'I could have probably guessed that last part.'

Dan looks at me awkwardly, as if to say it isn't his fault, so I just roll my eyes. 'I'll give you a lift home if you like,' he says, walking her to the door.

Madeleine hesitates for a moment, then smiles at him. 'Okay, then. Ozzie will be wondering where I am.'

'Who's Ozzie?' says Dan, his face falling suddenly. 'Your boyfriend?'

Madeleine laughs. 'No. My cat.'

'Ah. A cat,' says Dan, and I brace myself, thinking that she's fallen at the final hurdle; Dan has a number of theories about women who own cats, and none of them are complimentary. Instead, he smiles broadly. 'I mean, *aah*. A cat.'

Madeleine takes the arm he's offered her. 'So, Dan, are you an animal lover?'

Dan shrugs. 'I've had no complaints,' he says, winking at me as he walks her out of the door.

Friday, 10 April

8.01 a.m.

I don't hear Sam get up for work this morning, and in fact it's Dan who wakes me, by texting first thing to assure me that despite having to fight off her advances in the car last night, all he did was drop Madeleine off at home. After I've re-read his message three times in disbelief, I lie in bed basking in the things Sam said about me yesterday.

Despite my childish outburst last night, I've realized I've got no choice but to go along with her wishes and make the best of this whole registry office thing, and so have decided I won't mention it again, even though when I pop back for lunch, I catch her reading what looks like one of the wedding magazines I brought home the other day, although she slides it hurriedly underneath a copy of *Health and Fitness* when she hears me come in.

6.53 p.m.

When I get home this evening, Sam's peering intently at her laptop, which is open on the kitchen table in front of her. 'Still working?' I say, nodding towards the screen.

'Just sorting out a few things.' She punches the 'sleep' button, and smiles up at me. 'Speaking of which, here's something you might be interested in.'

I stare at the scrap of paper she's just handed me. 'What's this? A phone number?'

'For Billy. One of my clients works for Shelter. She thinks there might be a place coming up in one of their hostels.'

'Oh. Right.'

Sam frowns at me. 'What's the matter?'

'I don't think Billy has a phone. Or the best phone manner.'

She sighs. 'It's for you, Ed. Seeing as you're so good at giving people rings, why don't you give them one and see if you can't get him in?'

'Ha ha,' I say, leaning down and kissing her. 'Very funny.'

'You'd be doing him a favour.'

As I think about it, I realize that I wouldn't just be doing him a favour, I'd be doing myself one too by saving myself a tenner a week on *Big Issue*s.

'And you think they'd be okay with him? I mean, his dietary requirements are, well, special.'

Sam smiles wryly. We both know I've left the word 'brew' off the end of that sentence. 'It's worth a try, isn't it?'

'Okay. I'll give it a go.'

Whether I can convince Billy to give the hostel a go is another thing entirely.

Saturday, 11 April

9.06 a.m.

I roll over in bed, surprised to see that Sam's already up and pulling on her tracksuit. Groggily, I assume it must be Monday, and have a moment's panic when I see the time.

'Relax,' she says, sitting down on the bed next to me to put her socks on. 'It's Saturday.'

'Oh. Right.' I pull the duvet back over my head, then sit up again suddenly. 'Where are you off to?'

'Client meeting,' says Sam, leaping up from the bed, before disappearing into the bathroom.

'On a Saturday?'

'Sorry, Edward,' she shouts, above the noise of the sink tap. 'Couldn't be avoided.'

'Will you be long?' I say, a little put out. Sam hasn't had a Saturday client since we've been together.

'An air show,' she says, although once I've allowed for the fact that she's talking to me while brushing her teeth, I realize she actually said 'an hour or so'.

'Want me to come and meet you afterwards?'

There's the sound of gargling, and then, after a very ladylike spit, 'No, that's okay. I might just go straight to the gym.'

'I'll come with you,' I say, half-heartedly. 'I could do with the exercise.'

'No, that's fine,' says Sam, quickly. 'Besides, don't you have to meet Dan this morning?'

'Dan? What for?'

She pokes her head through the doorway and raises both eyebrows. 'Our division of labour?'

'Ah. Yes. Of course. I hadn't forgotten,' I say, although in truth, I had. The memory of my and Sam's conversation last night about her organizing everything up to and including the wedding, and me sorting out everything afterwards – which really just includes the reception and the honeymoon – having been dulled a little by the bottle of wine I'd consumed during the course of the evening.

Sam doesn't say anything just lowers one of her eyebrows, then disappears back into the bathroom.

10.02 a.m.
I'm just walking out of the door when my mobile rings. It's Dan.

'Something's just occurred to me,' he says. 'What're you getting married in?'

I look at my watch. 'Fourteen days, four hours and fifty-eight minutes. Why?'

'No, you muppet. I mean, what will you be wearing?'

I shrug, which is a pretty pointless gesture down the phone. 'I don't know. A suit, probably.'

'Which suit?'

'The Paul Smith.'

'But it's black.'

'So?'

Dan sighs loudly into the handset. 'It's a wedding, not a funeral, mate. And in any case, you can't get married in an old suit.'

'Why not? Is it bad luck?'

'Only for those of us who happen to be caught in the same photograph as you.' He sighs again. 'Come on. The Lanes. Now,' he orders, referring to Brighton's trendiest – and most expensive – shopping area.

'Okay, okay.' I pat my wallet gingerly, my credit card still tender from my trip to Tiffany's. 'See you in ten.'

10.51 a.m.
'What're we doing in Moss Bros?' whispers Dan, trying to fit a cummerbund round his 'Bed Taker' T-shirt. 'I thought you weren't doing the traditional dress thing.'

'We're not.' I turn round to face him from where I've been adjusting my cravat in the changing room mirror. 'I just wanted to see what it looked like, that's all.'

'I think the word you're looking for . . .' Dan picks up my top hat from the chair, and places it on his head in a jaunty Daniel Day Lewis in *Gangs Of New York* kind of way. 'Is ridiculous.'

I snatch it back from him. 'Do you mind?'

He grins. 'You'd never get me in one of these penguin suits,' he says, tugging annoyingly on the tails of my jacket. 'Besides, is this really how you want to be dressed in your wedding photos?'

'Well, one of us should at least look like we're getting married. And if it's not going to be Sam . . .'

Dan shakes his head. 'If you feel that strongly about it, why don't you just do it? Show her who's boss. Remember, women are like cars.'

'Huh?'

'You've got to put your foot down every once in a while.'

'Very funny, Dan.'

'I'm serious. It's good for them. Cars *and* women.'

'Sam already knows who's boss, and it's not me. Besides, this is her big day, and I'm afraid what she says goes. So me turning up dressed like this . . .' I sigh loudly, and reluctantly unbutton my waistcoat.

In the mirror, I can see Dan making the 'L for Loser' sign on his forehead with his finger and thumb, although he pulls his hand away when he realizes he's been spotted. 'Well, if you can't be the boss . . .' He walks over to the designer suit rail at the far end of the shop, and selects a dark grey suit with a 'Hugo' label hanging from the jacket. 'Be the *Boss*.'

11.26 a.m.

After a slightly embarrassing incident in the travel agent's, when I ask for a brochure for Lake Como, and

Dan thinks I've said Lake Homo, I'm waiting outside HMV, where Dan is trying to get his money back on the DVD he bought yesterday. After five minutes, he comes back out.

'Everything okay?'

'They wouldn't give me the fiver back, but they eventually let me exchange it,' he says, holding up a small plastic HMV bag. 'I had to threaten them with the trades descriptions act, and everything.'

'What was the problem?'

'Let's just say it didn't quite do what it said on the tin.'

'What didn't?'

'The DVD.'

'I'm sorry, Dan. What DVD?'

'The one I've just exchanged.'

'And what was it?' I ask, patiently.

'Something called *The Birds*.'

'And?'

'It was a horror film.'

'Ye-es?'

'What do you mean, "Ye-es?"'

'I'm sorry, Dan. You've lost me.'

'With a title like that, what would you expect it to be about?'

'Well . . . birds.'

'Precisely. But instead, it's about *actual* birds. And not, you know . . .'

'Women?'

'I know!' says Dan. 'Kind of ruined the mood with my date last night, I can tell you.'

It takes me about two minutes to stop laughing. 'You thought it was a porno?'

'Might have done.' Dan turns away, as if he's looking to cross the road, but in reality he's trying not to let me see he's embarrassed. 'Especially since it was directed by someone called . . .'

'Hitchcock is one word, Dan. Not two.' I shake my head slowly. 'How could you not have heard of it? It's a classic.'

'So? So is *Shaving Ryan's Privates*.'

I manage to compose myself. 'Yes, Dan. You're right. Easy mistake to make. But why on earth did you go to all that trouble for a fiver?'

Dan reaches into his pocket, and removes what looks like a bank statement. 'I had a bit of a shock this morning.'

'What's this?'

He shrugs. 'I never normally open them, to be honest. But what with being unemployed and all that, I thought I'd better check just how healthy the old finances were.'

'And?'

He unfolds the piece of paper, and hands it to me, pointing to a figure at the bottom. 'See for yourself.'

'Six hundred and fifty-two pounds?'

Dan grimaces. 'Exactly. I can't believe that's all I've got left. I mean, I'm hardly extravagant, but . . .'

'Dan.'

'What?'

'This is your credit-card statement,' I hand the piece of paper back to him, 'not your bank statement.'

'Ah.' There's a pause, and then, but brighter this time, 'Ah.'

As I try hard not to laugh again, Dan stuffs the statement back into his pocket, then pretends to be interested in the contents of his HMV bag.

'So, dare I ask what other X-rated "classic" you got in exchange?'

Dan doesn't say anything, but just reaches into the bag, hands me the DVD, then nudges me suggestively.

It's *Fiddler on the Roof*.

1.11 p.m.

Dan's kindly agreed to hide the suit for me until the wedding, so at least I'll have something to surprise Sam with on the day. When I get back to the flat, she's sitting at the kitchen table, talking into her mobile, although she snaps it shut when I walk in through the door.

'How'd it go?'

'Great.' I walk over and kiss her. 'You?'

'Yes. Good.' Sam pulls out the chair next to her, and indicates for me to sit down. 'So?'

'So what?'

'So did you and Dan have any thoughts? About the reception.'

'The reception?' *Damn*. In all the excitement of

buying only my second-ever designer suit, that had completely slipped my mind. 'Of course.'

'And what were those thoughts, exactly?' she asks, when I don't enlighten her further.

'Well, that we'd have one, obviously. And, you know, *after* the ceremony,' I say, although I can't help feeling the word 'ceremony' still seems rather inappropriate, given that we're just going to be signing a bit of paper.

Sam folds her arms. 'And I suppose you want to have it at the Admiral Jim?'

'What?' I look up suddenly, remembering the conversation I'd had with Wendy about precisely that the other day. 'Well, I hadn't thought of that, but now you mention it . . .'

'I was joking, Edward. Over my dead body,' she says, her tone making it plain that it would be the most ridiculous idea in the world. 'You spend enough time in there as it is.'

'Is that a bit of wifely nagging I can hear?'

'You ain't seen nothing yet.' Sam retrieves a large spiral-bound notebook from her rucksack and opens it at a new blank page. 'So, as you were saying . . .'

'Yes, well, I, er . . .' I smile back at her, desperately trying to think of somewhere appropriate, then suddenly realize this might actually be my opportunity to do something on a grander scale – grander at least than the registry office. And in fact, where's the best place for a grand reception in Brighton? 'I thought we might, you know, have it at the Grand.'

'The Grand Hotel?' says Sam, more than a little surprised. 'On the seafront?'

'Why not?'

'But . . .'

'But what?'

'That'll cost a fortune. And you've already . . .' Sam stops talking, and fingers her engagement ring.

'Oh.' I swallow hard. I hadn't thought of that, particularly in the light of the four hundred and twenty-nine pounds I've also just spent on my new suit. 'I mean, so? I can afford it. And you're worth it,' I add, sounding like a bad shampoo advert. 'And seeing as the wedding's going to be so low-key, please let me do something that shows everybody how much I love you.'

Sam puts her notebook down and takes my hand. 'Edward, I know how much you love me. And I love you the same way. Surely that's what's important? Not some big, ostentatious party.'

'Yes, but I want this wedding to be a celebration. Part of it, anyway. And so if we can't do the church thing, then at least let me have this?'

Sam opens her mouth as if to say something, but then evidently thinks better of it. Instead, she just leans over and gives me a hug. 'Okay, then.'

'Great. So don't you worry about it. Dan and I will make the arrangements.'

'Are you sure?'

I kiss her on the forehead. 'Positive. I'll go and speak to the hotel tomorrow.'

'No, I meant about getting Dan involved.'

'Why not? In fact, I'll get him to arrange the whole thing. It'll give him something to do given his current unemployed status, plus hopefully it'll help him get into his best-man role.'

Sam looks a little unsure. 'Here's hoping. And has he arranged anything else? For the stag night, I mean?'

I walk over and open the fridge, on the off-chance that there'll be something unhealthy in there for lunch. 'I don't know. Probably the usual strippers or something.'

'Or something?'

'Yes, you know Dan.'

'Which is exactly what worries me.'

'Don't worry. He's promised he'll look out for me on the night.'

'Hmm,' says Sam. 'The only person Dan ever looks out for is himself. Are you sure it's such a good idea?'

I shut the fridge door again. Everything in there is a little too green for my liking. 'Sam, Dan's not going to let me get into trouble. He knows how important all this is to me.'

'Okay, okay.' Sam turns her attention back to her notebook, and uncaps her pen. 'So have you thought any more about who you want to invite?'

'Well, like I said, Dan's taking care of that. But it's men only, I'm afraid. After all, you wouldn't want me turning up and crashing your hen night, would you?'

'To the *wedding*, Ed. I've done my family, so who else do you want to come?'

'Oh. Right.' I puff out my cheeks while I think for a second or two, then catch sight of my reflection in the window and decide it's not the most attractive of looks. 'Just the usual lot, really.'

Sam raises one eyebrow. 'The usual lot. Which would be?'

'Dan, obviously.'

'Obviously,' says Sam. 'Although he'll already be there, as your best man.'

'Oh, of course. Well, there's Mrs B and Wendy – plus Andy. Assuming she can find someone to mind the Admiral Jim.'

'They're not shutting it in your honour?' Sam smiles. 'What about Natasha?'

'She doesn't know the first thing about running a pub . . . Ah. You mean the wedding. Well, put her down as a provisional, but I better check that with Dan first.' Dan and Natasha had a bit of a thing a couple of years ago. And since she's threatened to cut off his 'thing' if she sees him again, I better tread carefully.

'Good point. And speaking of which, is he bringing anyone?'

'Doubtful. Taking a girl to a wedding would be a little bit too much commitment as far as Dan's concerned.'

Sam sighs. 'I hope he's not going to spend the whole time trying to get off with the bridesmaids. Should I have ugly ones just in case?'

'Might be a plan. Or we can just invite Polly. That should keep him on his best behaviour.'

'Isn't that a bit cruel?'

I'm just about to say that I'm joking, of course, when I stop myself. It's a brilliant idea. Firstly because it's bound to keep him in line for the day, and secondly, because if my suspicions are correct, there's still an awful lot of unfinished business there.

'Actually, no. I see it more as doing him a favour. Then at least he can put it to bed once and for all. Sorry. Bad metaphor. But he just hasn't been right since he tried to get back together with her last year, and maybe this will be a chance to kill or cure.'

'Fine.' Sam adds Polly's name to the rather short list. 'And how about Jane?'

'Jane? My J . . . I mean, my *ex* Jane?'

'Is there any other?'

For a moment, I wonder whether she knows about our coffee the other day, or even that I've already invited her. Maybe Jane just 'happened' to bump into Sam, and has mentioned the fact herself. But surely Sam would have told me. Unless she's testing me.

I know this is one of those questions, where there's an awful lot riding on my choice of answer. I also know that I need to give it some thought, as although my first answer might well be the correct answer, I've got no real way of knowing what the correct answer is until I see Sam's reaction to whatever it is I say.

I suppose an option would be to try and work out what the right answer is and then say the opposite thing, because experience has shown me that more often than not that *is* the correct thing to say. But what on earth is the right answer to 'Do you want to invite your ex-girlfriend to your wedding?' 'Yes' might well mean that of course, why not, you and I have no worries, I'm over her, and we're friends now and that's it – or it might mean that I still need her in my life, and I deem her important enough to want her at what's supposed to be my current girlfriend's big day. 'No', of course, would seem the safer option, although that could be deemed as meaning that I still have feelings for her, and therefore her being at the wedding might give me second thoughts, which I don't want to risk. Trouble is, I don't know if it's actually a trick question, and if so, have I blown it already by not saying 'no' – or 'yes' – immediately?

'Edward?'

'What?'

'Do you want to invite Jane to the wedding?'

'Er . . .'

Sam's staring at me curiously, her pen poised above her notebook, and I know she's going to need an answer. My dilemma is that I can see a problem with both the 'yes' or 'no' options, and as I can't phone a friend, I'm going to have to decide myself. And pretty soon, too.

'Well?'

Quick. Aargh! . . . No, hang on, I've got it.

'What do you think?'

Sam frowns. 'How would I know? She's not my ex-girlfriend, is she?'

'True. But suppose you did have an ex-girlfriend. Like Jane. Not that you'd have an ex-*girl*friend. Or one like Ja— Anyway, what would you do?'

'Ed, it doesn't really matter what I'd do, does it? I'm hardly going to veto your choice of wedding guests. So if you think it's important that your ex is at your wedding just say so. It's okay, honestly.'

I have to admire her dexterity. Straight back at me. And while she doesn't look like she's shaping up for an argument, experience tells me that where women are concerned there's often no warning of the change from normal to nuclear. Well, two can play at that game.

'Why do you think I'd want Jane at my, sorry, *our*, wedding?'

Sam sighs. 'I don't know, Edward. Maybe because you're a nice guy. Maybe because the two of you can still be friends. Or maybe even because you want her to see once and for all that you've moved on.'

Ah. Those are good things, in that they reflect me in a positive light, but they don't quite get me off the hook. It could of course be that *Sam* wants Jane at the wedding for exactly that reason – to show her I'm finally off the market – but she can't of course invite her herself. And then it hits me. A moment of inspiration. An answer that can't possibly be shot down. Hopefully.

'Sam, to be honest, there's only one other person I want at this wedding, and that's you. So if you feel that adding Jane to the guest list is a good thing to do, whatever the reason, then go ahead. But quite frankly, I'd much rather concentrate on more important things. Like how big the cake you're ordering is going to be.'

Sam looks at me for a second, and then breaks into a smile. 'Sorry, Ed. I just wanted you to know it would have been okay.'

'Would it? Really?'

'*Do* you want Jane there?'

And now – I realize – *is* the time to be truthful. Though perhaps not about the fact that I've already invited her. 'Honestly? No.'

Sam smiles again. 'Then of course it would have been.'

'Great' I say, already dreading how on earth I'm going to dis-invite her. 'That's settled, then.'

Because knowing Jane, I've got a sneaking suspicion it won't be easy.

Sunday, 12 April

8.11 p.m.
Sam spends most of the day with Madeleine, leaving me to write out the invitations for the people we want at the town hall, though of course I then have to drive round and hand deliver them, given the fact that we've only got two weeks to go.

'Small and intimate', is how she's describing the ceremony, and while I've got no choice but to let her do it her way, at least we can have a bit of a bigger bash with the reception. Fortunately, the ballroom at the Grand Hotel is free – although sadly not *free* – on the day, so I've booked it, but when I meet Dan in the Admiral Jim to discuss the entertainment, and – once he's stopped sniggering at the word 'ballroom' – tell him what I'm thinking of doing, he makes a face as if he's trodden in something nasty.

'You're sure you want some Scottish country dancing?' he says, enunciating the last three words very carefully. 'I mean, you're going to be the centre of attention, and I've seen you dance . . .'

'Well, what's the alternative? Some bloke called Terry who brings his own stack of multi-coloured flashing lights and tries to get us all to do the actions to YMCA? No thanks. Besides, it'll be fun.'

'Yeah, right – a room full of sweaty people all not knowing whether to stick it in or pull it out at the same time.' He thinks for a moment. 'Come to think of it, that reminds me of this party I went to once . . .'

'Dan, please.'

'Sorry. But can't you think of something a bit more, well, modern?'

'Like what?'

'I dunno. What do people normally do at these things?'

I shrug. 'Get drunk and dance, I think.'

'So hire a proper band.'

'Who?'

'Ed, anyone's got to be better than a bunch of men in tartan skirts trying to get everyone to do the how's-your-father, or whatever those dances are called.'

I look at him disdainfully. 'Can't you pull a few strings and get some of your celebrity mates to do it?'

'Yeah. Sure. I'll just call Take That up and see if they're free.'

'You know Take That?'

'It's perhaps more accurate to say that they know me.'

'Well that's fantastic. Although . . .'

'What?'

'I don't think Sam likes them.'

'Seeing as I very much doubt they'd be interested in playing at the likes of your wedding that's just as well.'

I decide to ignore Dan's 'likes of your' insult. 'Well, who else can we get?'

'Leave it to me,' says Dan, confidently. 'I'll sort something out.'

'Er . . .'

'What?'

'Dan, the only time I'll ever leave anything to you again will be in my will. Which I'm worried you'll be reading sooner rather than later if I let you organize the music.'

'That's not very nice.'

'I'm sorry. It's just that the last time I let you sort something out, I nearly ended up in hospital.'

Dan looks a little offended. 'You're the one who wanted to dye your hair blond for that fancy dress party.'

'Dye it, Dan. Not bleach it. And certainly not with Domestos.'

'Yes, well, the proper stuff was expensive. And besides, this is your wedding. I'm hardly going to do something like that again, am I?'

'You'd better not,' I say, pointing my beer bottle at him. 'Understand something, Dan. This is the most important day of my life – and Sam's, hopefully. So I don't want anything to muck it up. And that includes you and your shenanigans.'

Dan holds his palms up innocently. 'Ed, when have I ever let you down?'

I reach into my pocket, and pretend to take out a piece of paper. 'Do you want a list? I've got places and dates . . .'

He grins. 'Fair enough. But seriously, I should be able to sort something out for the reception. Let's face it, I've got more friends in high places than a stag night on Mount Everest. And speaking of which . . .'

'Ah, yes. I'm glad you brought that up. Before you go any further, I need to talk to you about something.'

Dan's face lights up. 'Is it the strippers?'

'Strippers?'

'For the stag night.' He pats me on the back reassuringly. 'No need, mate. Already in hand. And I have to say, I'm rather enjoying the audition process. There's this one who can shoot a table-tennis ball across the room from her—'

'No, Dan! Not the strippers. It's the speech that I wanted to discuss with you.'

'Speech?' Dan takes a sip of his beer. 'Just thank me for being such a great best man and a brilliant friend and, quite frankly, a fantastic all-round guy, and then you give me those cuff-links, and—'

'No, Dan. The speech you have to give. About Sam and me.'

'*I've* got to give a speech?'

I look at him, not sure if he's joking. 'You do know what you have to do? What the best man's duties are?'

'After I've got you shagged by a stripper, you mean?' Dan laughs, then sees that I'm serious. 'Of course. On the day, all I have to do is say a few choice words about what a small penis you've got, then I get my pick of the bridesmaids. Simple.'

'Have you ever heard a best man's speech before?'

He shudders. 'God no. I've always been far too busy. I tell you, there's a reason why there's the word 'ride' in 'bridesmaid'. Something about weddings just seems to bring out the . . .'

'Dan!' I grab him by the shoulders. 'The speech.'

'Don't worry,' he says, shrugging me off. 'I'll just ad-lib something on the day.'

'No, you won't.' I've heard Dan's ad-libs before, including the time he was being interviewed with some grumpy feminist on GMTV, and he suggested – live – they change the name of the programme to PMTV. 'The speech is the most important part. For example, you have to say how lovely Sam is . . .'

He licks his lips suggestively. 'That won't be a problem.'

'And then you have to, you know, talk about me. And make a few jokes if you must.'

'Relax,' says Dan. 'I've been doing my research.'

'Such as?'

Dan produces a DVD from inside his man-bag. 'Watching this.'

I stare at the copy of *Four Weddings and a Funeral* he's holding like the holy grail. 'Very funny.'

'It is, isn't it? I particularly like the bit where—'

'Dan, back to the speech, please. There are a few taboo subjects.'

He puts the DVD down on the bar, then pulls a small leather-bound notepad out of his pocket. 'Should I be making notes?' he says, uncapping his pen.

'Well, it's just Jane, really.'

'Jane?'

'Yes. I'd rather you didn't mention her, if you don't mind.'

Dan freezes, his pen in mid-air. 'What?'

'Jane. Don't make any references to her.'

'Why not?'

'It's just a bit sensitive, isn't it? Given everything that went on, and all that.'

'But . . .' Dan leafs through several pages in his notepad, where I can worryingly make out several instances of Jane's name in his scrawly handwriting. 'That doesn't leave me anything.'

'Yes it does.'

'Like what? You went out with Jane for ten years, then she dumped you, then you met Sam, who you've been with for, what, eighteen months, and now you're marrying her. So unless you were a particularly promiscuous teenager, which given what I know about your sexual prowess I very much doubt, then the Jane years are the only source of material I've got.'

'It's just that it's going to be my and Sam's special day. And I don't want Jane to figure in the proceedings any more than she will be already.'

Dan looks up in shock. 'You're not thinking of inviting her, are you?'

Ah. 'Of course not,' I say, trying hard to stop myself from blushing. 'I meant, you know, in spirit.'

He grins, mischievously. 'Chance would be a fine thing. What if I didn't refer to her by name?'

I nod. 'That could work. Although what would be better is if you didn't refer to her at all.'

Dan puffs his cheeks out. 'Jesus, Ed. Give me something to go on. I mean, I'm on show here, don't forget.'

'Have you forgotten whose wedding this is? It's not a chance for you to show off in front of everyone. It's an opportunity for you to pay a tribute. To me. And Sam.'

'Yeah, right,' says Dan. 'Next you'll be telling me I don't get to snog Sam's mum, or something.'

'No, you don't. And while we're on the subject of snogging, the last thing I want is for you to turn our wedding into some sort of personal speed-dating session. So no getting off with any of the bridesmaids, or the waitresses, and I especially don't want you taking your clothes off on the dance floor and asking if any of the women want to limbo under your pole.'

'That was once. And I was very very drunk.'

'And seeing as you brought it up earlier – the stag night. No strippers.'

Dan looks as if he can't have heard me correctly. 'No strippers?'

'That's right. I don't think that's the kind of thing that Sam—'

Dan laughs, cutting me off. 'This is your stag night we're talking about, Ed. You need a proper send-off. And

I hardly think Sam is going to have a say in what we — or rather you — get up to. Besides, what she doesn't know won't hurt her.'

'Yes, well, by the sounds of things, that stripper with the table-tennis ball trick might hurt me. And anyway, I don't think it's very appropriate, do you?'

'Of course it's appropriate,' splutters Dan. 'It's your last night of freedom.'

'That we're having a week before the wedding, may I remind you? So it's not, actually.'

'Which might I say is another excellent idea of mine. Gives us both a chance to recover. And you enough time to get a flight home from . . .'

'What?'

'Nothing.' Dan grins. 'Even so, it's still the final chance for you to sow your wild oats. So a trip to the lap-dancing bar is the least we can do. In fact, it's the law. Besides . . .'

I hardly dare ask. 'Besides?'

'I was going to get you a couple. Of strippers, I mean.' Dan nudges me. 'I thought it'd be a chance for you to double the number of women you've ever slept with in one go. Result!'

'Dan, I'm serious. It just wouldn't feel right.'

'You've obviously never met Candy and Bambi. They felt pretty good to me.'

I look at him incredulously. 'How is that the best start to married life? Going and sleeping with another woman—'

'Two other women.'

'Two other women, the week before you promise to be faithful to someone.'

'It's the perfect start. Gets it out of your system.'

'No thank you, Dan. Besides, that'd be the last thing I'd want Sam to find out about just before we exchange our vows.'

'You sure? Once you and Sam tie the knot you won't get another chance. And remember, it's always easier to beg for forgiveness than ask for permission.'

'I'll pass, thanks.'

'Really?' says Dan, incredulously. 'Trust me – you'll thank me afterwards.' He leans back in his chair and knits his fingers behind his head. 'And probably *during*, if you know what I mean.'

'Dan, listen carefully. No lap-dancing. No women stripping at all, in fact. And while we're on the subject of removing clothes, there'll be none of that stripping me naked and handcuffing me to a lamppost rubbish either.'

He looks at me for a second, before opening his notepad again and crossing something off a list. 'Spoil-sport.'

'I'm serious. I just want a nice civilized evening with a few friends.'

Dan yawns exaggeratedly. 'Bor-ing.'

'It's not boring, Dan. It's the way I want it.'

'Okay, okay. And who do you want to invite to this whirlwind of an evening?'

I think about this for a moment. 'Well, there's you, obviously. And me . . .'

'And?'

'Er . . .' The truth is, I don't actually have that many male friends any more. Most of the male halves of the couples Jane and I used to know went with her when we split up, and Sam and I don't really have that many couple-y friends. 'Does Wendy count?'

He shudders. 'This is a stag do, mate, and although Wendy's flat-chested enough to pass as a bloke, the only women there will be ones who'll take their clothes off in exchange for money . . .'

'Or not.'

Dan rolls his eyes. 'And Wendy would have to pay *me* if she wanted to drop her— Ow!' He rubs the back of his head, where a beer mat has just Frisbeed into it.

'Careful what you say in here,' I say, glancing over towards the bar, where Wendy is looking rather pleased with her aim. 'She's got hearing like a bat.'

'Which is kind of appropriate,' whispers Dan. 'Given that she's an old one— Ow!'

'Will you never learn?'

Dan rubs his head again, then glowers back at her. 'Anyway,' he continues, 'back to the stag do. What about Sam's dad?'

'You're joking, aren't you?'

'So . . .' Dan looks down at his notebook. 'It's just the two of us?'

I nod. 'Looks that way.'

'Excellent,' he says. 'Just like old times, before you met the old ball and chain. By the way, I've managed to blag us both a room – or rather, a couple of rooms – at the Grand, so you don't have to worry about getting home late. Or at all.'

'Thanks, Dan, but . . .'

He looks up sharply. 'What now?'

'It's just, well, I haven't spent a night apart from Sam since we moved in together.'

'And you're going to be spending every bloody night with her for the next fifty years, so make the most of it. Besides, you won't be spending the night before the wedding with her, so it'll be a chance for you to get used to it.'

'The night before the wedding? Why ever not?'

'Dunno.' Dan shrugs. 'Ask Sam.'

'Sam?'

He nods. 'She called earlier. Asked if I wouldn't mind putting you up.'

'Whatever for?

'Dunno. Maybe she wants the option of a night's head start, in case she gets cold feet and decides to make a run for it.'

'Very funny,' I say, finding it anything but.

'Relax. It's supposed to be bad luck, I think. So I told her you could stay round at mine. But no funny business,' he adds, wagging a finger at me.

'I think I'll manage to control myself.' I take a mouthful of beer. 'So where are we going? On the stag, I mean.'

Dan taps the side of his nose. 'That's on a need-to-know basis, sunshine.'

'Yes. And I need to know.'

'No way.'

'Why not?' I ask, suspiciously.

'Because I want it to be a surprise.'

'You'd better at least tell Sam, because she's having her hen night the same evening.'

'Good point,' says Dan. 'Don't want to run into her accidentally, and have her spoil the party.'

'Er, what party will she be spoiling, exactly?'

'Oh, nothing,' he says, as innocently as he can muster. 'I've just got a surprise or two up my sleeve.'

'Not like the last time I stayed round at yours and you "surprised" me by replacing my shower gel with that hair-removal cream?'

'Yeah.' Dan laughs at the memory. 'I mean, no.'

'Dan, I've told you, I don't want anything to spoil this wedding. And that includes any practical jokes you might have planned for me on the stag do. I don't want to look ridiculous in the wedding photos.'

Dan stares at me for a second or two, then rips a whole page out of his notepad and crumples it up. 'Don't worry. Nothing's going to happen that you don't want to,' he says, enigmatically. 'Besides, like you said, there's a week between the stag do and the wedding anyway.'

'What's that got to do with it?'

'That's just enough time for your eyebrows to grow back,' he snorts, 'for example.'

'Dan!'

He sighs. 'I can't believe you don't want to spend one of your last nights of freedom looking at naked women. Especially considering you're only ever going to be seeing the one naked woman for the next fifty years. And trust me, you'll only want to see her naked for the first half of that.'

'Would you mind not talking about my fiancée like that?'

Dan grins. 'Sorry, mate. But fifty years. With the same woman?'

'Why do you look at it as a negative thing? As far as I'm concerned, it's time spent with someone I want to be with.'

He picks his beer up, then puts it back down again. 'I'm sorry, Ed. You're right. I guess I'm just a bit jealous, that's all.'

'Jealous?' I'm a little taken aback. It's not like Dan to admit anything like this. And certainly not where I'm concerned. 'Of me?'

'Yeah.' He picks up his bottle again, and pretends to read the label. 'You know. I just wish my expectations were as low as yours.'

'Pardon?'

'Where relationships are concerned. And I don't mean that there's anything wrong with Sam. Quite the opposite. It's just that I always want that *new* feeling. The excitement of finding out what someone's like.'

I don't like to point out that once Dan's done that, he

usually doesn't like what he sees. 'Maybe your expectations are too high. I mean, what's the longest relationship you've had since all that internet stuff happened?' Dan went through a bit of a dry patch last year. Not through choice, but because his ex-girlfriends started writing reviews about him on a website called Slate Your Date. Suffice to say, the reviews weren't exactly making women want to queue up to go out with him.

'I haven't really had any that you'd describe as long, to be honest. I mean, I learnt from that experience. Really I did. And I've been upfront with them all, saying it's not going to be anything serious, that I'm just looking for a fling. But while they say they're okay with that . . .' He sighs. 'I tell you, I used to think I understood women, but not any more. Plus, I'm beginning to worry that they don't understand me, no matter how much I spell things out to them.'

'So, are you going to take anyone to the wedding?'

He scratches his head. 'I hadn't really thought about it. To be honest, I kind of assumed that I might be taking someone *from* the wedding. Maybe even *at* the wedding.'

'Why don't you go with one of your "showbiz pals"?' I say, making the speech-marks sign with my fingers.

'Chance would be a fine thing, seeing as none of them are speaking to me since I got sacked. Besides, most of them are as' – Dan makes the speech-marks sign himself – '"bad" as me. It fucks you up, this life, if you're not careful: people telling you you're great all the time, even when you're not. Maybe that's why

I should get married. Then I'd have someone at home telling me how rotten I was all the time. You know, to balance it out a bit.'

'Thanks, Dan. You paint such a rosy picture of marriage. I can't wait for the twenty-fifth now.'

He frowns. 'The twenty-fifth?'

'That's the wedding date.'

'Ah. Oh yes. Of course.' Dan picks up his pen and makes another entry in his notepad, underlining the numbers 'two' and 'five' three times. 'I'm sorry, Ed. I didn't really mean that you had low expectations. I just meant that marriage is fine for people like you.'

'What's that supposed to mean?'

'Why do you insist on taking everything I say the wrong way?'

'Why do you insist on phrasing everything like an insult?'

'I'm trying to pay you a compliment,' he says exasperatedly. 'This isn't easy for me.'

'What – talking about this kind of thing?'

'No. Paying you a compliment. I just meant I wish I was more like you. More . . . tolerant. Able to accept people for who they are, rather than what I expect them to be.'

'How do you mean?'

'You always seem to be able to see the good in people – however bad they are. I mean, look how long you went out with Jane for.'

'Very funny.'

'Whereas I just see their faults. All of them.'

'Ah.'

I don't quite know what to say. Every now and again, Dan drifts into one of his 'What's it all about?' phases, and I can already see the warning signs. Normally I get him out of them by reminding him it's about the money, fame, flash car, great flat and, of course, the women, but, given his current employment situation and the state of his love life, I've got a feeling that might not work this time.

As I wonder whether I should try to change the subject, Dan stares intently down the neck of his beer bottle. 'I mean, don't take this the wrong way,' he continues, 'but if *you* can find someone to marry then why can't I?'

I'm not sure there's a right way to take that, but I let it pass. 'I'm sure the right person's out there for you somewhere. You've just got to give it a bit of time.'

'Yeah, but I've been out with hundreds of girls. Thousands.' He brightens for a second at the realization, then sighs miserably.

'It's not a numbers game.'

'It isn't?'

'No. It's all about what you're looking for. When Jane dumped me, I was devastated. Not, in retrospect, just because I was losing her, but because I love being with someone, or rather, love being in love with someone. And that's why I'm determined to nail Sam . . .'

'Hur hur.'

'You know what I mean. I love Sam. But I also realize she's about as good as I'm going to get – and I don't mean that in a bad way. I just know it's very unlikely I'll ever meet someone better, more compatible, who I could care about more. And therefore I'm not prepared to let her get away. Besides, I'm ready, you know, and that's what it's all about, because the fact is, sometimes it's all about motivation.'

'Motivation?'

'You told me, when I was trying to win Jane back, to think about what I wanted – what the long-term goal was, if you like – and focus on that from day one. So when I first asked Sam out, I knew I was after something serious: a long-term relationship. Because that's how I've always gone into all my relationships – hoping, wanting, expecting them to go the distance.'

'And?'

'And then luckily, *thankfully*, we fell in love, and that was the best feeling in the world. Whereas you don't give yourself the chance of that ever happening. You just want to get them into bed, and then keep getting them into bed until you get bored. And all the while, you think you're doing them a favour.'

Dan nods in agreement, then stops when he sees my expression. 'Yeah, maybe,' he says, noncommittally. 'But, you know the biggest problem I have?'

I want to say 'your ego', but that's probably not a good idea. 'No. What?'

'The fact that all the women I meet are attracted to me for who I am, then try and change who I am to fit in with their idea of what a boyfriend should be. And that's just not fair. Because what attracted them to me in the first place then becomes what eventually drives us apart.'

'Maybe you need to change your approach?'

Dan looks hopefully up at me. 'How do you mean?'

'Start looking at women differently.'

He picks up my empty pint glass, holds it like a telescope, and squints through the bottom of it. 'What – like this?'

'No, Dan, I'm serious. Whenever you meet someone, think first and foremost whether you could actually have a relationship with her, rather than just relations.'

Dan looks at me as if I've just asked him to learn Chinese. 'I don't know, Ed. I mean, it's not really me, is it?'

'How do you know until you've given it a try?'

He takes a mouthful of beer, savouring it thoughtfully before swallowing it. 'You know, that does occur to me with all of them – whether there could be something more, you know, long term.'

'And what happens?'

He gives a tight-lipped smile. 'I don't know. I guess they just expect me to be TV's Dan Davis when we're out, then mister obedient and normal when it's just the two of us, and to be able to switch between the two of them to order. And I know I can't. So I dump them before they find out.'

'They don't, Dan. They just expect you to be a normal human being who happens to look like Dan Davis. And surely even you can manage that?'

Dan checks his reflection in the mirror behind the bar. 'I guess. But the problem is, I'm just not good at being a "boyfriend".' He makes the speech-marks sign again, but unfortunately, he's still got the bottle of beer in his hand, and ends up spilling some lager onto my trousers. 'And this celebrity thing? I tell you, it's a two-edged sword because it's hard to meet someone who can get past that.'

'Well, maybe you need to go back to your past to someone who knew you before all this.'

Dan scowls at me. 'Don't start all that again, Ed. I'm done with Polly and she's done with me.'

'You're sure about that, are you?'

He shrugs. 'Even if I wasn't, there's nothing I can do about it. She's with someone else now. And I'm hardly likely to split them up just to see whether she and I have a chance again.'

'That's rather unlike you.'

'Yes, well, I've changed, haven't I? Plus I care about her. And I want her to be happy.'

'You see? There you go.'

Dan looks over his shoulder. 'Where?'

'You've admitted you care about someone. Other than yourself, that is. And if you've done that once, you can do it again.'

'Assuming I meet someone like her again. Besides, I've almost forgotten what she's like.'

'You might be able to remind yourself in a couple of weeks.'

'How so?'

'Because I've invited her to the wedding.'

Dan almost drops his beer in shock. 'What?'

'I've invited her.'

'And she's coming?'

I shrug. 'I dunno. She hasn't RSVP'd yet.'

Normally that would be Dan's cue to snigger at the 'arse' part of 'RSVP', but instead, he just turns to look at me. 'With what's his face?' he asks, nervously.

'Well, I had to put plus one on the invitation.'

'Great,' says Dan, sounding as though he means the exact opposite.

'It *is* great. At least you get to see her again. As a friend. And she'll see you, and maybe realize what she's been missing . . .'

'Yeah, right. With her boyfriend there.'

'Assuming she brings him. And look on the bright side. If she does, you'll be able to tell if she's happy or not.'

'Yeah. That's true.' He takes another mouthful of lager. 'Er, how?'

'It's obvious.'

'Can you make it a little more obvious?'

'Look at me and Sam. We're happy. Remember what Jane and I looked like? We weren't.'

'Not that you knew it at the time. Otherwise her dumping you wouldn't have come as such a shock.'

I glare at him. 'Do you have to remind me of that every time?'

Dan nods. 'Just don't want you getting complacent.'

'But you could tell, right?'

Dan nods. 'Oh yeah. Although to be honest, I kind of thought it was just the way you guys were after ten years together.'

'That's what I've been trying to tell you. That's *not* how it should be. Although unfortunately, unless you've been there and recognized it, you won't be able to tell if it's happening to you. I have. And that's why I'll never let it get like that between me and Sam.'

'Yes, well, good luck with that,' says Dan, miserably. 'But that doesn't exactly help me, does it?'

'Yes it does.' I think for an example Dan can relate to. 'Remember when you first got the Porsche, and you drove over that spiked parking thing the wrong way and punctured all your tyres?'

'How could I forget?' says Dan, wincing at the memory. 'It cost me eight hundred quid.'

'But you didn't drive over one of those things again, did you? Because you were able to spot them before-hand.'

'Too right.'

'And that's my point. Surely if anyone knows what a short-term relationship looks like, it's you. And that's why you've got to avoid them from now on. Only go out with women who you think might be goers.'

'Hur hur.'

'No, I mean, in it for the long term.'

'But I don't know what they look like,' wails Dan.

'But you *do* know what they *don't* look like. And surely that's a good start.'

Dan holds his hands up. 'Okay, okay. I promise. No more floozies. Except on your stag night, of course.'

'Dan, for the millionth time. No strippers.'

He re-caps his pen, and slips his notepad into his pocket. 'I'm sorry, Ed, but if you keep on like this, even I won't want to come to your stag night, and I'm the bloody best man – *and* the only other guest. A stag night without breasts – and I don't mean yours – is like, I don't know, an episode of *Close Encounters* without me in it – pointless. You can still *look*, don't forget, so why spoil the fun for the rest of us? Even though the rest of us is only, well . . . me.'

I stare at him for a few seconds, then shake my head resignedly. 'Okay, then. But just the one.'

'Er, two is usually preferable.'

'Strippers, not breasts. And you promise not to let anything happen? To me, that is.'

'Scouts honour,' says Dan, making a weird shape with his fingers, then saluting smartly.

Unfortunately, it's only much later that I remember Dan wasn't, in fact, *in* the scouts.

Tuesday, 14 April

12.56 p.m.

Not a lot happens for the next couple of days. Apart from having to wait for the RSVPs to come in, confirm our Lake Como honeymoon and find out that Dan hasn't done anything about the entertainment for the reception so panic-book something myself, there's actually not that much for me to do. Despite my offer to help, Sam's told me to leave the 'boring wedding stuff' to her, and while I assume she means that the stuff's boring, I'm still a little worried that the wedding might be.

To be honest, for something that's supposed to be not such a big deal, she seems to be spending a lot of time organizing it, and while I can't of course be resentful of this, it means we're not seeing as much of each other as I'd like at the moment. Then again, I'm getting her for the rest of her life, so I suppose I shouldn't complain.

I've decided I'd better come clean about seeing Jane the other day, and possibly about inviting her to the wedding, though, of course, I need to pick my moment. And while I'm aware that the moment probably isn't when

Sam spots her at the registry office, I've been unable to think of a better one. To that end, I've gone for a walk along the seafront to try and work out how best to broach it, although I've taken a diversion via Kemp Town to pick myself up a little something from Muffin To Declare – something I feel is justified given the healthy rocket salad I've just eaten for lunch – when I catch sight of Sam, walking in the opposite direction on the other side of the road.

My first thought, or rather my second, as my first is to swallow quickly the mouthful of muffin I've been chewing and get rid of the rest of the evidence, is that I've been rumbled, but luckily she hasn't seen me. I fall into step behind a tall, impeccably dressed man and, using him as cover, drop the bag containing the rest of the muffin in the nearest bin, and I'm just about to cross over the road and say hello to her when the man I've been shadowing does exactly that.

I jump back onto the pavement, then – as he walks over to where Sam's waiting outside a coffee shop – duck into the nearest doorway, watching as he leans down and kisses her on the cheek, before opening the door for her. I'm just about to follow, but as Sam looks up and down the pavement before walking into the café, I hesitate. I don't feel I can go over and interrupt them, in case he's a new client – Sam often meets new clients at lunchtime – but as far as I'm aware, unless she's decided to adopt the same marketing strategy as Natasha, Sam doesn't greet her new clients with a kiss. In any case, it seems rather inappropriate to meet someone who's potentially interested in losing weight in a place with a huge sign in the window advertising their hand-made speciality cakes and, as I think about it, there's something about the way Sam checked that the coast was clear before going inside that's making me feel a little uncomfortable.

I peer uneasily across the street at the café. It's one I'm never likely to go in to, particularly with Muffin To Declare so close by. And anyway, Sam thinks I never go to Muffin To Declare, because, of course, she thinks I don't eat muffins any more, so she's going to assume I'd have no reason to be in this neck of the woods. While that's not unusual in itself, she usually meets new clients in the café on the seafront, because that's where most of the training takes place.

Almost immediately, I dismiss my fears as ridiculous. Sam's not going to be up to anything – and certainly not so close to the wedding. I feel bad about being suspicious so, with a shake of my head, start walking back to the office, only to stop after a few paces. What if she *is* up to something?

For a second, it occurs to me that maybe I should just pop in and say hello. See if she introduces him to me. But what will that prove? If I was her, and there was something suspicious going on, I'm sure I'd have a cover story worked out for such an eventuality. And what happens if it is all innocent but I, to use Dan's words, 'get the wrong end of the stick' again, and end up making a scene and costing her a client? Not a smart move, particularly since (given my recent jewellery expenditure, and the cost of hiring the Grand ballroom) we could do with all the new clients she can get.

Keeping on the opposite side of the road, I walk back to where I can get a clear view through the coffee-shop window, lurking behind a lamppost while I peer inside, and after a few moments I spot the two of them, sitting at a corner table. Every now and then, Sam glances out of the window, which I can't help but assume is due to nervousness in case she's caught – although I'm feeling pretty nervous that she'll catch me too, as the lamppost's not providing much cover. I'm wondering whether I should move, but don't know how to do it without being seen until, fortunately, a van comes and parks in the space in front of me.

Using the van as cover, I walk along the pavement a little and take up a better position, crouching behind a postbox, while wondering why I feel so uneasy. Am I jealous because he's good-looking? Is there something I don't like about their body language? Is it because she's meeting him in an out-of-the-way place? Or am I simply transferring my own guilty feelings about seeing Jane the other day onto Sam?

I know I'm probably being stupid. Let's face it, there are a hundred and one other reasons why Sam might be meeting him. Okay, maybe not a hundred and one, but at least, well, two that I can think of, although one of those *is* the fact that she's having an affair.

While it's hard to see Sam and her mystery man clearly, given that they're sitting as far away from the window as possible, one thing I can make out is the way Sam leans in towards him as he speaks. What's worse is how every now and then he touches her; not somewhere intimate, but just an occasional hand on the arm. Immediately, I hate him.

From what I've seen so far, it certainly doesn't look like a meeting with a new client, and now I think about it, he doesn't look like he needs a personal trainer in the first place. And then, something happens that really sets my alarm bells ringing. A waitress walks over to their table and sets down a plate of what, to my experienced eye, looks like various slices of cake.

I watch, horrified, as the man picks up a piece, holds it out to Sam, and . . . Noooo! She's taken a bite. The kiss on the cheek I could just about deal with, but this? Sam and I never eat cake together. I turn away in shock, unable to watch any more. I feel cheated – and on more than one front. After all her lecturing, Sam's not only eating something bad for her, but she's doing it with another man.

I can't believe what I've seen, especially after all those things she said about me in front of Dan and Madeleine the other night. There's a strange feeling bubbling up inside me, and it's the one I remember all too well from back when I found out that Jane was having an affair: jealousy.

I pull myself up to my full height, look left and right,

and start to cross the road, mentally rolling my sleeves up, then stop suddenly on the edge of the kerb. This is *Sam*, I tell myself, who's never, in all the time we've known each other, given me any reason to doubt her. And besides, would she have suggested we get married if she'd been having an affair? Of course not.

Unless . . . Unless *he's* married. You do read about these people – or rather, Dan's read about these people, thanks to his regular subscription to *Cosmo*, then told me all about them in admiration – who lead these double lives, even getting married, and bringing up a family, while having another partner stashed away somewhere else.

But not Sam, surely? We live together, so how could she have kept it a secret from me? Unless . . . Being a personal trainer is the perfect cover. Who knows what she's wearing under that tracksuit – her best lingerie, perhaps? And when she disappears off at strange hours in the morning, or comes back home all flushed and perspiring, then heads straight for the shower . . .

Fighting the waves of nausea that are rolling over me, I turn my attention back to the two of them. Sam's on her second slice now, nodding appreciatively as she chews, and I can hardly stand it. Every now and then, in-between bites, she leans back in her chair and laughs loudly at one of his jokes – a little too often for my liking. In fact, given the frequency, Sam seems to think he's some kind of comedian, although I'm not finding any of this in the slightest bit amusing. Does she ever laugh with me like that? I wonder. Or has she been laughing *at* me all this time instead?

I take a few deep breaths, trying to fight a creeping sense of despair, unable to believe it's happening to me again. In hindsight, I can recognize some of the same tell-tale signs from when Jane cheated on me: the unusual Saturday-morning meeting, abruptly ended phone calls, even shutting the laptop quickly when I've walked over to where she's been sitting, but they're hardly proof Sam's having an affair. And anyway, I trust her enough to let her have coffee with whoever she wants. Whenever she wants. And wherever she wants – even somewhere she knows I'm unlikely to catch her. Besides, maybe he's just an ex-client. Or an ex-boyfriend – although I have leafed through her old photo album in a moment of insecurity, and I'm pretty sure he's not one of them.

With the greatest of efforts, I decide not to confront her, so just turn around and start walking back towards my office. The first few steps feel as if I'm wading through quicksand. But I know it's the right thing to do.

And even though I tell myself that's because I've got absolute faith and trust in her, in reality, it's because I'm way too scared to find out if my suspicions are true.

2.13 p.m.
I'm in the office, trying to concentrate on work, but unable to get this lunchtime's events out of my head. When Natasha comes back from lunch, it's about two minutes before I can't help but ask.

'Tell me something, Natasha. What are your views on fidelity?'

Natasha finishes applying her lipstick in the reflection of her monitor and swivels her chair round to face me. 'I beg your pardon?'

'I just wondered, you know, as someone who's, er . . .' this is tricky to word without having something thrown at me, 'been involved with a few other . . . well, *involved* people, what your overall view of the subject was. As a consumer.'

'What? Is it over-rated, you mean?'

'Not really. I was just curious as to whether it was ever . . . acceptable. Cheating.'

Natasha considers this for a moment, then shrugs. 'That's hard for me to answer. Because while most of the men I've gone out with have cheated on their wives to see me – which of course I've accepted – that of course means they're the cheating type, so even if they had left their wives and moved in with me, I'd still have worried what they'd been up to.'

'So, there's a cheating type?' I say, suddenly feeling a bit brighter. As far as I know, Sam's never cheated on anyone. Or not admitted to it, anyway.

Natasha nods. 'Oh yes. Just like there's a faithful type.' She leans back in her chair and crosses her legs. 'There are those who would never do it, because it's just not in their nature. Like you, Edward.'

'Thanks.'

'And then there are those who have had it done to

them, and it makes them feel so utterly horribly bad that they'd never dare do it to someone else, because they know how it feels and would never inflict that on another person.'

'Right. That's me again. In terms of being cheated on.' While I didn't tell Dan back when it happened to me, I'd had to admit it to Natasha. It was hard not to, given that she found me blubbing like a baby in the office one morning. 'By, you know, Jane.'

Natasha stares at me until she's sure I've finished. 'Then there are those people who do it the once, find it's not such a big deal, and realize they're quite happy to do it again. And again.'

'Like Dan, you mean?'

'Oh no.' Natasha laughs. 'Dan's completely different.'

'How so?'

'Because he doesn't think what he's doing is cheating. Even though most women assume because you're sleeping with them, you won't be sleeping with anyone else . . .'

'Sort of like a given?'

'Exactly. But in Dan's mind, he's never made a commitment to these women in the first place. And while for most normal people, sleeping with two different women at the same time wouldn't be on, as far as Dan's concerned, it's just what he does. And that's why he doesn't think it's a problem.'

'So would you forgive a . . . lapse?'

Natasha raises one eyebrow. 'What's brought this on, Edward? Been up to something you shouldn't?'

Even though I'm sitting down, I'm aware that I have to think on my feet. 'Nope. I was just thinking about, er, *Jane*. Whether her cheating on me was my fault. And whether I should have, well, forgiven her.'

Natasha looks at me sympathetically. 'You know, sometimes people tell you that their cheating was your fault. That you drove them to it by your lack of attention – that kind of thing. But as far as I'm concerned, that's rubbish. If someone wasn't paying me enough attention and I still wanted to be with them, then the last thing I'd do would be sleep with someone else.'

'Yes, but I suppose it shows the other person is desired, doesn't it? Like sometimes when we're trying to get one of our candidates a job offer from a particular company, we tell that company that someone else is interested in making them an offer to try and spur them into action.'

'But this isn't the same, is it?'

'Why not?'

'Because our candidates don't actually speak to anyone else. We make it up. Whereas Jane did. Or at least had an oral interview.'

As I shudder at the memory, Natasha smiles. 'Someone who's so unhappy in a relationship that they go and have relations with someone else shouldn't be in that relationship any more, because any normal person would try and fix what was wrong *before* you got to that point, surely? The men I have my affairs with – well, they're different, in that they usually can't leave because of the kids, or the house, or the fact that the wife will take them to the cleaners, which is why they do what they do. But someone like Jane or Dan? What's to stop them heading for the hills?'

Nothing, in Jane's case, obviously. Not even a ten-year relationship. Although as I think about it, it does make me feel a little better. Unless . . . Unless Sam was feeling so frustrated that I hadn't asked her to marry me that she decided to do the asking – maybe even as a drunken mistake, and in turn, those feelings of frustration maybe had already led her to look for someone else. Or maybe she was just starting the affair, while at the same time trying to sound me out as to whether I was ever going to ask her to marry me, hoping my answer would be no, which would give her a reason to leave, and instead, I've – as Dan first thought – mistaken her question for a proposal, in which case she finds herself in a rather awkward situation with me and him – whoever 'him' is. But that still doesn't answer the question as to why she felt the need to start seeing someone else in the first place.

'So all those excuses about women feeling so unloved, or having such low self-esteem that they simply wanted to go and find out whether someone else found them attractive are just that? Excuses?'

Natasha lets out a short laugh. 'That's such rubbish, Edward. Any time a woman wants to feel attractive she just has to undo a couple of buttons on her blouse and walk past a building site. An affair? That's different. Because what you're actually doing is testing what it's like to be with someone else. And don't forget, the fact that you're already with someone means you can dip a toe in the water without the new person having too many expectations.'

'So fundamentally, people have affairs because they're not sure about the relationship they're in, and want to see whether the grass is greener?'

'Sometimes. Or sometimes they just want a little excitement. But also, perversely, they might just want to find out what they really feel about the person they're already with.'

I think back to Dan telling me the same thing while trying to justify his bad dating reputation a while ago, and shake my head slowly. There are times when he and Natasha seem to be singing from the same hymn book.

'And that's . . .okay?'

'Well, not usually if you ask the person who's being cheated on.'

I'm still a little confused. 'But Jane said it was a cry for help,' I say, as the office phone starts ringing. 'To get some attention.'

'Aha!' says Natasha, picking up the receiver. 'And maybe it was. Trouble was, in her case, it was someone else's attention she really wanted.'

As Natasha takes the call, I realize the problem I have is this: if Sam *is* actually having an affair then, according to Natasha – and if I extrapolate from the Jane situation – it might just be to make sure she wants to be with me, and while that's not necessarily okay, I can kind of see how it works.

Jane, on the other hand, was probably testing the water from the security of our situation, in that, having been with me for ten years, she wanted to see what life was like on the outside. And I'm afraid if *that's* what Sam's doing, then in my book, it's just not the done thing.

But the biggest problem I have in all of this, and why I can't work it out, is how I've let this happen. Jane leaving me was such a harsh lesson in how not to be a boyfriend, that I kind of think I know what I'm doing now, as though I've graduated from some kind of intensive course, and I'm determined to remember what I've learned. Plus I've got Dan as a role model in terms of how not to behave.

Plus I know Sam, and she just doesn't give in to temptation. That second biscuit or third glass of wine isn't something she allows herself to have. So why should this be different? Unless . . . Perhaps it *is* the marriage thing. Maybe she does feel someone's said to her, 'Here, these rice cakes are the only kind you're going to be able to have. Ever.' And surely it's natural to want to sample a different type just before you commit to that.

It could, of course, simply be that she and I are coming at it from completely different angles. Even though I'm crazy about her, I'm also so relieved to be settling down with her after my Jane experience that I can't wait for it to happen. But Sam's not the same. She's not had the kind of nightmare loneliness I've experienced, so she's maybe not as desperate as me to be with someone. And if that is true, then maybe she does just need to be sure about what she's doing.

But I do know one thing. If I'm going to challenge her about it, I need to be sure about what she's doing too.

7.01 p.m.

When I get home and flop down on the sofa, I'm a little surprised to see Sam's not in, especially since I don't seem to have received a text from her telling me she's going to be late.

I switch on the TV and flick through the channels in an attempt to stop my imagination running wild, but even a particularly funny episode of *You've Been Framed* doesn't stop me from wondering exactly where she is. I still don't want to believe she's cheating on me, but seeing as I'm unable to come up with any other explanation for what I saw earlier, and of course was too much of a chicken to actually ask her about it when I spoke to her on the phone this afternoon, I don't seem to have any choice. What's more, I can't think how else I can find out what she's been up to. That is, until I switch the TV off and gaze forlornly round the room, and spot Sam's laptop on the dining table. Where she has her email account.

I sit up quickly, wondering whether I shouldn't take a little peek just to put my mind at rest, then get up and walk nonchalantly past the dining table, casually glancing at the laptop screen. Her aquarium screen saver is running, so I 'accidentally' bump against the table in an effort to jog the mouse, but end up just banging my hip painfully.

For some reason, I can't quite bring myself to do it, so head into the kitchen instead and switch on the kettle, wondering why I feel so nervous. After all, I've used Sam's laptop a hundred times – so she's hardly going to be suspicious if she comes in and finds me and, anyway, I'm used to the odd quick 'screen close' from the office. Besides, this should take no more than a few seconds.

I flick the kettle off, then go and sit down at the dining table, grabbing the mouse purposefully and giving it a quick jiggle. Once the fish have disappeared, I click on the Internet Explorer icon, then the Hotmail bookmark, and as the page loads in front of me, take a series of slow, deep breaths, trying to calm what feels like an angry fist thumping the inside of my chest.

Sam's email address is already entered in the log-in box, though for some reason, the 'remember my password' box is unchecked. And while this immediately strikes me as suspicious, it's not a problem, because when I glance up at the photo of Ollie – Sam's recently run-over Collie – on the mantelpiece, I realize I know her password.

Like a cowboy practising his quick-draw skills, I try clicking on the close program button a couple of times, just so I'm sure I can do it if Sam arrives home. Then, and when I can't put it off any longer, I move the cursor to the enter password box, type 'o-l-l-i-e' and hit return.

For some reason, I've shut my eyes, but when I open them again, instead of all of Sam's secrets, there's a message telling me my password's wrong. More than a little frustrated, I try again, concentrating hard on the keyboard to make sure I don't make any mistakes, but despite me actually mouthing the letters as I type them – a bit like Dan does when he reads – I get exactly the same result.

I stare at the screen in astonishment. This can only mean one thing: Sam's changed her password. And if she's changed her password, then that must mean there *are* things she doesn't want me to see.

I stand up and start to pace anxiously round the room. This is worse than I thought, particularly since we're not supposed to have *any* secrets. But as I glare back down at the laptop, I notice a small green light shining back at me from the bottom left-hand corner: the caps lock indicator. Of course! Passwords are case-sensitive – though perhaps not as sensitive as I am at the moment. Reaching over to hit the caps lock button, I type Sam's password again, hit enter, and wait what seems like the longest few seconds of my life until I'm in.

As the front page loads, I almost don't want to look at the screen. What am I going to do if I *do* see something incriminating – confront Sam as soon as she walks through the door? That would mean me admitting I've been reading her email. And even though her 'sin' would be much worse than mine, I can see how that would put me on the back foot.

My hand is shaking slightly as I click on inbox and read anxiously through her new messages, but as far as I can tell, there's nothing out of the ordinary; a couple from her mum, some work ones, one from Madeleine, and the usual spam asking her if she needs some female Viagra.

Guiltily, I click on the mark as unread tab to cover my tracks, then scan quickly through the rest of her inbox, breathing a sigh of relief when I don't see anything incriminating, and I'm just about to switch off when I spot a folder in the list on the left-hand side named 'wedding stuff'. For a moment, I just stare at it. Where's the best place to hide messages from your lover? In a folder about things you've told your fiancé not to worry about, of course.

I'm just about to click on the folder when the doorbell rings, and instinctively I click on close, imagining it's Sam and she's forgotten her key, but when I open the door, my heart still hammering, I see a different person.

'What do you want?' I say, still a little panicked.

'Nice to see you too,' says Dan, peering at me anxiously. 'Everything okay?'

For a moment, I think about not telling him, and then decide I could do with his advice.

'Not really, no,' I say, ushering him inside, then closing the door carefully behind him. 'I think Sam's having an affair.'

'What?' For a moment, Dan can't take this in. 'Sam? An affair?'

I nod. 'Yup.'

'Sam?' repeats Dan. 'An *affair*?'

'Uh-huh.'

'Your Sam?'

'No, Dan. Sam the barman. From *Cheers*.'

Dan looks confused, and I'm reminded that teasing him isn't always as rewarding as you might think, mainly because he thinks irony is a word to describe something made of iron.

'You do mean your Sam, right?' he says, eventually.

'Yes, Dan.'

'Oh. Well, are you sure? I mean, it doesn't sound like Sam. The kind of thing she'd do, I mean.'

'Yes, I'm sure.' I walk over to the dining table and sit back down in front of the laptop. 'Well, I think I am.' I tap the screen in front of me. 'And I was just about to find out before you disturbed me.'

'By Googling it?'

'Nope.' I open Internet Explorer and click on the Hotmail bookmark again. 'By reading her emails.'

Dan leaps across the room and slams the laptop shut, nearly trapping my fingers in the process. 'Bad idea,' he says, hauling me up out of my seat and dragging me towards the door. 'Come on.'

'Where are we going?' I say, unable to find the energy to resist.

'To sort this out, of course,' he says, grabbing my keys from the coffee table, then pushing me out through the front door.

7.59 p.m.

We're in the Admiral Jim, and not, thankfully, off to confront Sam – Dan's idea of 'sorting it out' being – as usual – to talk about it over a beer. I've explained this afternoon's sighting on the way here, and for once, he seems to be taking me seriously.

'Well,' he says, as I reach into my pocket to pay for the drinks he's just ordered. 'The way I see it, there are three things you can do.'

'Which are?' I say, when Dan does his usual trick of not continuing.

'One,' he says, counting them off on his fingers. 'Confront Sam. Two – confront him.'

'And the third one?'

'What third one?'

'You said there were three things I could do. You only mentioned two. What's the third one?'

'Confront Sam.'

'You already said that,' I say, picking up my drink and following him over to a corner table.

'Hang on.' Dan scratches his head. 'You're confusing me, now.'

This happens from time to time, Dan losing track of his own conversation, and usually, it makes me laugh, although I'm struggling to find anything funny at the moment. I sigh, then put my drink down carefully, before collapsing heavily onto a chair. 'Supposing I don't want to confront either of them, what else can I do?'

Dan pulls out the chair opposite and sits down. 'The third thing.'

'Which is?'

Dan shrugs. 'Forget about it.'

'No, come on. What's the third one?'

'No, the third thing *is* to forget about it. Her and him, I mean. So what if she's been playing a little bit of tonsil tennis with someone else. Be the bigger person and let it pass.'

I stare at him incredulously. 'I wish I could, Dan, but we're getting married – and in less than two weeks' time. Besides, I'm not sure that would actually be being the bigger person. In fact, it'd be being the smaller one. And I'm not prepared to do that.'

'So, in that case, you need to find out what's going on.'

'Thanks, Einstein.' I lean forward and stare at my untouched pint. 'And how do I do that, exactly?'

'Like you were going to. Hack into her email account.'

'You mean the thing you just stopped me from doing?'

'Er, yes. Or read her diary. Check her phone. Hire a private detective to follow her. That kind of thing.' Dan clears his throat awkwardly. 'I imagine.'

'But . . .' I slump back in my chair. 'That would suggest I don't trust her.'

'Hello?' Dan reaches over the table and raps twice on the top of my head with his knuckles. 'You don't, remember?'

'No, I do. But maybe it's, you know, *him*. Perhaps he's a former boyfriend, or something, and he's appeared back on the scene, and Sam's just trying to let him down gently.'

'By sneaking around with him behind your back?' Dan laughs. 'That's hardly the actions of a loyal girlfriend.'

'It's exactly what I did with Jane last year. You know, to stop Sam from being hurt.'

'And where did that get you?' Dan grins. 'Oh yes, that's right, she nearly dumped you when she found out, didn't she.'

'All the more reason for her to keep it from me,' I say, weakly.

'All the more reason for her not to, you mean.' Dan gestures towards me with his beer bottle. 'Listen, Ed, if you want my advice, just let it go. Whatever Sam's doing – and it's probably completely innocent – is something she's obviously got to do. If she hasn't told you about it, then there's obviously a reason for that too. And she still wants to marry you, right? I mean, she hasn't started having second thoughts, or said that she's thinking of pulling out?'

'No, but . . .'

'And she's still wearing the ring?'

'Yes, but . . .'

'But nothing. If there's one thing I've learned about women – apart from the fact that they don't like it if you sleep with their sisters – it's that they work in mysterious ways. And trying to understand them? That's like trying to understand how . . .' His face crumples up in concentration. 'Well, how something that's very hard to understand works. You or I for example, we want to get from A to B, we just take the shortest, most direct route. But a woman?' He rolls his eyes. 'She'll go all round the houses, maybe even stopping to buy a pair of shoes on the way, for no other reason apart from the fact that she's a woman. And if you got her to explain why to you, she'd have what she'd think would be a perfectly logical reason, but to us, it just wouldn't make any sense.'

'A bit like you aren't at the moment, then?'

Dan grins. 'My point is, all you can do is let her get on with whatever she's doing, safe in the knowledge that she's going to turn up on the . . . When is it?'

'Tell me why I asked you to be my best man again? The twenty-fifth.'

'That's what I thought. And from that day forwards, you're going to be husband and wife, no questions asked . . . Result.'

As I let what he's said sink in, I realize that this 'no questions asked' lark is the thing I can't really get my head round. Surely the whole point of marriage is that you should have no secrets from each other, and that every-thing should be out in the open, so both of you know what you're getting into: no surprises, and no skeletons in the closet? I mean, fair enough, if there's something from Sam's dim and distant past that she doesn't want to tell me about, and it's over and done with as far as she's concerned, then that kind of thing is okay. But not *this*. Sneaking around with another man doing who-knows-what a couple of weeks before our wedding . . .

And yet, of course I can't just come out and challenge her about it. Because if I'm wrong, and it's all completely innocent, that would show her I didn't trust her. What's worse is, as I think about it, something else occurs to me too. The real issue I have is not that Sam *might* be cheating on me, but *why* she might be. And I'm worried that I know the answer to that.

'Maybe we're silly getting married.'

'What's this? Second thoughts?' Dan raises one eyebrow. 'Remember, better to listen to nagging doubts beforehand, than a nagging wife afterwards.'

'No, Dan. Well, not really. It's just . . .'

'What?'

I take a mouthful of beer. 'It's stupid, really.'

'So is marriage, if you ask me,' says Dan.

'I didn't.'

'Come on.' Dan nods, encouragingly. 'Out with it.'

I lean back and stare up at the ceiling. 'It'll sound ridiculous.'

'So does most of what you say when it comes to women.'

'Do you want to hear it or not?'

'Course I do, Ed.' Dan leans forward and rests his elbows on the table. 'And today would be nice.'

'Sorry. It's, you know, *Sam*. I just worry that maybe she could do better.'

'Do better?' Dan stares at me for a moment or two, then starts to laugh.

'What's so funny?'

'Of course she could! You're playing so far out of your league that . . .' Dan stops talking when he sees the look on my face. 'Sorry, Ed. Just teasing you.'

'Is that what you think too?'

'Don't be ridiculous.' Dan folds his arms. 'Let me tell you something about how women work. The fit ones, they know they can pretty much have any man they want, right?'

'So?'

'So, dummy, that means they don't waste their time waiting for you to make a commitment if they're not sure.'

'Jane did.'

Dan laughs. 'I said the fit ones. And besides, she didn't exactly hang about, did she?'

'What's your point?'

'All I'm saying is, you and Sam have been together for, what, nearly two years now?'

'Something like that,' I mumble, not wanting to admit to Dan that I could probably tell him the precise number of days. If not hours.

'And despite that wobble of yours last year, when you got the wrong end of the stick and assumed you were chucked, it's all been pretty plain sailing.'

'So?'

He sighs. 'So, Eddie-boy, if Sam was going to leave you, she'd have done it by now. But in fact, she's gone the other way entirely, you've moved in together, and she's even asked you to marry her. She's hardly going to do that if she thinks she could do better, is she?'

'I suppose not.'

'And following on from that, she's even less likely to be having an affair, is she? So don't you think you ought to just put these stupid ideas out of your head and have a little faith in her?' He gets up and starts to walk towards the toilets. 'And yourself, for that matter.'

I watch him go, then sit there on my own, staring into my beer, and realize that Dan's right. Marriage is all about trust. If I can't trust her in the crucial period leading up to our wedding, then how can I possibly trust her afterwards? And the last thing I want is to feel like, well, most of Dan's girlfriends probably do, wondering what on earth he's up to all the time. I've got to let her live her own life. Do things her way. And have a little confidence that our relationship is stronger than maybe I'm feeling it is at the moment. After all, *she* wants to marry *me*. And she's seen me at my worst, my most incompetent, and my fattest, plus I'm not rich, or famous, so I've got to accept that she's doing it because of who I am, and the fact that she loves me for – and even in spite of – that.

'Besides,' continues Dan, appearing back in his seat and making me jump, 'why on earth are you getting so worked up about this? Even if she is having a little fling, it's not such a big deal.'

'Dan, it's the biggest deal possible. Imagine if one of your girlfriends – and I use the term loosely – slept with someone else while she was sleeping with you. How would you feel?'

'What – like in a threesome? Well, as long as it was another girl, I wouldn't mind.'

'No, Dan. Another man. And not a threesome.'

Dan laughs. 'That's hardly likely, is it?'

'Oh, sorry. I forgot about the size of your ego. I mean, who'd sleep with anyone else when they could sleep with the great Dan Davis.'

Dan pretends to scratch his nose, whereas in reality he's sticking two fingers up at me. 'It's not that at all. The reason they wouldn't be sleeping with anyone else is that after a night with me they can hardly walk, let alone get up the energy to . . .'

'Dan, please. That's not the point.'

'Yes it is,' he says. 'In fact, maybe it's exactly the point. Tell me something. Is everything all right between you and Sam in that department?'

He holds his beer bottle towards me as if it's a microphone, and I wave it away angrily. 'None of your business!'

'It's just that, well, women are people too,' he says, as if confiding a secret. 'They have needs, desires . . .'

'And Sam's are being met – and satisfied – perfectly well, thank you.'

'You're sure, are you?'

'Perfectly.'

For a moment, I worry that he's going to launch into a Meg Ryan in the diner from *When Harry Met Sally* impersonation. And that's one thing I can do without.

'It's just that, well . . .'

'What?'

'Well, it's one of the reasons, isn't it? Why women have affairs. So if your sex life . . .'

'Just drop it will you.'

'Okay, okay. As long as you're positive.'

'I am.'

Dan leans back in his chair. 'Well, in that case, you've got nothing to worry about, have you?'

'No. I suppose not.' I sip my beer for a few seconds. 'It's just . . .'

'For Christ's sake, Edward. Let it go.'

I stare at him, wondering how I can get across how I'm feeling, and then it occurs to me. 'Okay then. Imagine if Polly had done it to you. How would you feel then?'

Dan gazes back at me for a few seconds, then down at the table, unable to meet my eyes any longer. 'Yes, well, she didn't, did she?'

'You're sure, are you?'

Dan opens his mouth as if to answer, then closes it again. 'Anyway,' he says, eventually, 'that's in the past now.'

'Well, how does even the fact that she's going out with someone else make you feel? And sleeping with them? She's a woman, after all. She's got desires. Needs . . .'

Dan looks as though he wants to tell me where to go, but to his credit, gives it some thought. 'Okay, then. I'd imagine if it *had* happened, then I'd feel pretty bad about it. Like I'd been betrayed. But I suppose, until it's actually happened to you, it's hard to tell.'

I look at him for a moment, and then decide to spill. 'Well, it happened to me. Which is why I *can* tell.'

Dan nearly falls off his chair in surprise. 'What? Sam? When?'

'Of course not,' I say, then realize the irony of that statement. 'With Jane. Just before our last Christmas together.'

'Jane had an affair? You're kidding?' says Dan, before realizing that my expression means I'm not. He leans over and rests a hand on my shoulder. 'Poor guy.'

'Thanks. I . . .'

'Not you. The other bloke.' He grins. 'When? What happened? And more importantly, why didn't you tell me?'

I stare at my beer, wondering if it'd be bad form to drink it down in one. 'Because . . .' I pick the glass up and finish it off anyway. 'Because I was ashamed.'

'Fuck, Ed. It's nothing to be ashamed of. You should have told me. I could have given the guy a slap. Or given Jane one. A, er, slap, obviously.'

'Thanks. I think.'

'Did you catch them at it? You know, in fragrance.'

'In flagrante, Dan. And no, I didn't.'

'Oh,' he says, sounding a little disappointed. 'What did you do?'

'I forgave her. And she promised she'd never do it again. And then she dumped me.'

Dan starts to laugh, and then stops abruptly when I scowl at him. 'Well, at least she was true to her word, I suppose. What exactly happened?'

I shrug, trying to bury the feelings of hurt that are surfacing even now. 'Not much. She snogged some bloke at work, and I found out about it, and . . .'

Dan slams his bottle down on the table. 'She snogged someone?'

'That's right. At some drunken work thing.'

'That's all?'

'What do you mean, "That's all?"'

'Well, I'm sorry, Ed. I know it must have been pretty traumatic at the time, but . . . A drunken snog?'

'Yes, well, it's not just about *what* it was. It's what it *means*. You know "it's the thought that counts", and all that. Which is exactly why I feel so bad about this whole situation. Because if it turns out that Sam is, in fact, seeing someone else, I know exactly how shitty it's going to make me feel. And I fail to see how you could do that – be so cruel, I mean – to anyone you love.' I stop talking, conscious that I'm gabbling.

'That's bollocks,' says Dan.

'It's not bollocks. Until you've experienced it, you can't possibly know what it feels like.'

'Yes, but alcohol makes you do things you wouldn't normally do. Or rather, do people you wouldn't normally do.'

'I didn't think you liked Jane. How come you're defending her?'

'I'm not. I just don't think it's that big a deal, that's all. Although I still can't believe you didn't tell me.'

'I was too embarrassed, all right? I mean, when someone cheats on you, it's not just a reflection on them, it's also a reflection on you. I obviously wasn't enough for her, so she decided to go and look elsewhere.'

'Aha,' says Dan.

'Aha what?' I say, disinterestedly. I'm starting to realize that Dan's observations rarely relate to the real world.

'There you go!'

I sigh. 'Where?'

'You're obviously enough for Sam. Like I said, she asked you to marry her. So why on earth would she be having an affair now?'

'You think?'

'Yes. Of course, after you're married – that's when she might turn to someone else. But not before.'

'Thanks, Dan. That's a comfort.'

'You're welcome,' he says, draining the last of his beer. 'But before you leap to any conclusions, or make any rash accusations, just remember one thing.'

'What?'

'Sam's not Jane.'

And while I know he's right, there's still one thing that troubles me. Despite appearances, I'm still Edward.

Wednesday, 15 April

5.48 p.m.

When I come home to pick my car up to take Mrs Barraclough shopping, Sam's sitting at the dining table, frowning at her laptop.

'Whatcha doing?' I say, as breezily as possible, kissing her on the top of the head while surreptitiously trying to peer at the screen.

'Oh, nothing much,' she says, hitting the minimize button quickly. 'Just a bit of admin.'

'Don't tell me. Wedding stuff?' I try to keep the sarcasm out of my voice, but fail.

Sam gives me a look, and immediately I feel childish. 'If you must know, I'm ordering some more business cards.'

'Oh. Right.' I nod towards the laptop. 'So why the big secret?'

Her eyes flick guiltily towards the screen. 'I was just trying to work out the name thing. You know, to see what looked best.'

'Name thing?' I say, not quite following her. 'What name thing?'

'You know.' Sam swivels round to face me. 'What I'm going to be called. After.'

'After what?'

'The wedding, silly.'

'Mrs Middleton would be a good start.'

'Of course,' she says. 'It's just that, well, Smith's my professional name and I've worked for years to build myself up as a brand.'

'A brand?'

'Yes. "Sam Smith – Personal Trainer".'

'But what's wrong with Sam Middleton? Or even, Sam Smith-Middleton. Or, thinking about it, Middleton-Smith has a good ring.'

'I've already got a good ring,' says Sam, holding her left hand up and wiggling half my life savings in front of my nose. 'I just think I ought to stick with what people are used to. And besides, these business-card people charge by the letter.'

It takes me a second to realize she's joking. 'But you're just talking professionally, right?'

'Oh, yes,' she says. 'And my cheque book, of course. For my bank account.'

'Bank account? I kind of thought we'd have everything in together. You know, as husband and wife.'

Sam turns her attention back to the laptop. 'Well, mine's a business account, don't forget, so I'll need to keep that separate for tax purposes. And besides, the flat's in my name, and it'd be a lot more trouble than it's worth to go about changing the deeds and everything. So it kind of makes sense.'

Not to me, it doesn't. 'Listen, Sam. If you're worried about this wedding . . .'

Sam looks up suddenly. 'Not at all. It's just a big thing for a woman – losing your name. It doesn't change the way I feel about you. But I'm the last of the, well . . .'

'Smiths?' I say, sarcastically. 'I think you'll find there are a few others out there.'

'Not in my family.' Sam smiles. 'Hey – here's an idea. You could always change yours. Then we'd be Mr and Mrs Smith.'

'And feel guilty every time we checked into a hotel?'

Sam takes my hand. 'Edward, whatever my surname is, you'll still be able to call me your wife. Surely that's what's important?'

'Yes, but . . . I'm sorry, Sam. I'm just a bit more traditional than you, I guess. And so you not changing your name . . . It's just not what my impression of being married was going to be like.'

Sam lets go of my hand and folds her arms. 'I thought you were marrying me for me? Not for someone you wanted me to be.'

'That's not what I meant,' I say, conscious that I might be entering dangerous territory. 'Besides, if you don't take my name then what will our kids be called?'

I'm clutching at straws and, as it turns out, they're

extremely short ones, because Sam suddenly looks horrified.

'Kids? Hold on, Edward. We're not even married yet, and you're planning my future as if I've got no say in the matter.'

'I thought you wanted kids?'

'I do. But it doesn't mean I want to have them straight away. And I certainly haven't got as far as thinking about what their names are going to be.'

I open my mouth to reply, but then think better of it. While I know I should be relieved that Sam's just indirectly answered the 'Is she pregnant?' question that everyone else seems to have been asking, I can't help being annoyed at her stance. I don't think I'm being unreasonable, and yet Sam seems to think I'm forcing her into a corner, which makes me wonder whether I'm forcing her into doing something else she doesn't want to do. I know I should sit down with her and discuss this sensibly, but I'm worried where it'll lead, so instead, I just grab my car keys from the table and make for the door.

'I'm late for Mrs B.'

Sam looks up at me. 'We'll talk about this later.'

'I'm meeting Dan later.'

'Dan? I thought we were spending the evening together?'

It's childish, and I know it is, but I can't help myself. 'No can do,' I say, as I slam the door behind me. 'Wedding stuff.'

6.41 p.m.

I'm pushing my trolley into Tesco's when I realize I've left Mrs Barraclough in the car.

'Sorry, Mrs B,' I say, after I've rushed back and opened the car door for her.

'Pardon, Edward?' Mrs Barraclough swings her legs round and places them carefully on the ground, then tries unsuccessfully to get out of the car – a task made somewhat harder by the fact that she's forgotten to undo her seatbelt.

'I'm sorry,' I say again, as we do an awkward little dance where I try and reach across her to press the seat-belt button, then end up having to run round the Mini and get in my side to do it, before unceremoniously pushing her up and out of the car. 'For forgetting you. I'm just a bit distracted.'

'You must have a lot on your mind,' says Mrs Barraclough, handing me her shopping list. 'After all, you are getting married next weekend.'

'I wish I could be that confident,' I say, scanning absent-mindedly through the list.

Mrs Barraclough frowns at me. 'What was that?'

'I said, er, you need a packet of Steradent,' I say, tapping Mrs Barraclough's shopping list, while wondering how on earth I've got to the stage where I'm venting my frustrations to an octogenarian.

I place both her hands on the trolley, then point her in the direction of the supermarket, hoping the gentle slope down towards the door will carry her there at a reasonable speed. Once inside, we take our usual route, starting at the tea and coffee section where, as usual, Mrs Barraclough drops several packets of Options into the trolley, then make our way through the rest of the store as we work systematically through her list.

'Edward, you are a good boy, taking me shopping like this,' she says, tweaking the volume knob on her hearing aid for about the millionth time. 'You must have a hundred other things to be doing.'

'That's okay, Mrs B.'

'I hope young Samantha realizes how lucky she is?'

'I'm the lucky one, Mrs B,' I say, almost automatically.

'Nonsense,' she says, turning the corner as if in slow motion into the toiletries aisle. 'If there's one thing I've learned in life it's that people get what they deserve.'

As Mrs Barraclough selects several lavender-perfumed items from the shelves and drops them into the trolley, I make my way down to the dental section and hunt for the Steradent, thinking about what she's just said. Maybe what's going on *is* what I deserve. Maybe me catching Sam with this other man is repayment for not having told her about seeing Jane the other day. I mean, look what happened to Dan when he went through all that Slate Your Date stuff: if ever anyone needed proof that karma existed, there it is.

Of course, it might not be karma. Sam may simply know I saw Jane – though God knows how – and she's testing me. Or, maybe the reason she's not said anything is because it makes her feel okay about whatever it is she's doing with him. And besides, maybe this is all I can expect. I mean, while I try my hardest, I know I can't possibly be the perfect boyfriend. I certainly wasn't where Jane was concerned, which is probably why she ended up dumping me. So maybe this is the price I have to pay for marrying Sam – a wedding that's not quite how I want it to be, and a wife who, well, might be the same.

I search the shelf in front of me, conscious that Mrs Barraclough is inching along the aisle towards me, but try as I might, I can't seem to locate the Steradent anywhere, and for some reason, find it really upsetting.

'Shit!' I say, under my breath; unfortunately, Mrs Barraclough must have her hearing aid turned up to eleven, because there's a shocked expression on her face.

'I beg your pardon, Edward?'

Immediately I feel guilty. 'I said, where is it?'

'Oh. Can't you see?' Mrs Barraclough points to the relevant section, then lets out a short chuckle. 'It's been right in front of your nose all this time.'

I stare at the shelf, then back at her, wondering whether she's talking metaphorically. 'No, Mrs B, I can't.'

'Here it is,' she says, helping herself to a tube. 'Don't worry, Edward.'

And as we make our way towards the checkout, how I wish I could take her advice.

7.55 p.m.
I'm sitting at the bar in the Admiral Jim, staring miserably into my pint glass for the second time in as many

days, when Dan bangs on the window, making me jump. He takes one look at me, and hurries inside.

'What's up with you now?' he says, putting his notepad down on the bar next to me, then jumping onto the adjacent stool.

'It's a long story.'

'Oh. Okay. Don't bother, then.' He flicks the notepad open, and starts studying the back page, on which he appears to have written what look like several titles for television programmes.

'What are you doing?'

'Nothing.'

'Come on. What are these?'

Dan grins. 'Okay. Your relentless interrogation has broken me. I've spent the afternoon brainstorming.'

'The whole afternoon?'

'Piss off. If you must know, I'm plotting my TV comeback. These are all potential new shows. With me as presenter, of course.'

'What happened to the acting?'

Dan makes a face. 'I'm not sure I was all that good at it, to be honest. Presenting's where my real skill lies. Or rather, it's about the only talent I've got. Well, that's not strictly true. But it's the only one I'll ever get paid for. Actually, that's not strictly true either . . .' He stops talking, then shakes his head, as if to reset it. 'Anyway, presenting's still acting, in a way, so I've been trying to come up with a few ideas. What do you think?'

'Well . . .' I take a look at the page. 'That one's been

done,' I say, pointing to where he's written 'Britain's Got Talent'.

'Not with this kind of talent.'

'Ah. All right, "Survival of the Fittest". What's that all about?'

'Aha,' says Dan. 'Basically, we get a bunch of really fit women – and I mean "fit" in the gorgeous sense – and train them up in various sports. Each week, the one who's the worst gets kicked off, until at the end of the series, you're left with one winner. Who, coincidentally, will actually be the fittest, as well as the, you know . . .'

'Fittest?'

'Precisely. What do you think?'

'I'm not in TV, but I'd watch it.' I point to the next heading, which says 'Mr Righteous'. What's this one?'

'Think *Blind Date*. But for religious people. Although that gives me an idea.'

'Which is?'

'*Blind Date*. But for blind people. Then it would actually *be* blind da— No, that wouldn't work, because blind people don't actually watch a lot of television, do they?'

'No, Dan. What about this next one?'

'Ah. "Get You Back". That's, er, nothing.' Dan shifts uncomfortably on his stool. 'Anyway. You were going to tell me what was up with you?'

I take a deep breath. 'I've just found out that Sam doesn't want to be Mrs Middleton.'

'You're joking?'

'Nope.'

'So the wedding's off? Is this because of the affair? Did she say he was better than you in bed? Because I can give you a few tips, if you want.'

'No! She doesn't want to be Sam Middleton.'

He looks at me as if I've just repeated what I've said, which I suppose to someone with Dan's perceptive ability I probably have. 'Want me to talk to her?'

'What good would that do?'

'Convince her to go through with it. I mean, I can understand her coming to her senses and not wanting to get married to you, but maybe I can talk her round. You know, big you up a bit. So she at least . . .'

'She still wants to marry me,' I say, patiently, 'but she doesn't want to change her name.'

'Why should she? I mean, Samantha's a nice name.'

I realize I have to spell it out for him. 'Her surname, Dan. She still wants to be Sam Smith – after we're married.'

'So what?' Dan shrugs. 'Think yourself lucky. If you get divorced, maybe it'll be the only thing she doesn't take.'

'Dan,' I say, as he chuckles to himself, then, 'Dan!' but louder the second time.

'What?'

'Shut up.'

'Sorry.' He looks up, catches Wendy's eye, and signals for a couple of drinks.

'You two are becoming regulars,' jokes Wendy, walking over and retrieving a bottle of Corona for Dan from the fridge beneath the counter. 'Everything okay, Edward?'

Dan nods towards me. 'Sam doesn't want to change her name.'

'What's wrong with Sa— Ah, sorry,' she says, catching sight of my expression.

'*Professionally*. She says she still wants to run the business as Sam Smith.'

Wendy pops the top off Dan's bottle, inserts a wedge of lime in the neck, and puts it down in front of him. 'That's not such a big deal, surely?'

I glare across the bar at her. 'It might not be to you. But it's traditional, isn't it?'

'So?' She picks up my pint glass and starts to refill it. 'So was being a virgin on your wedding night, but that's not expected any more.'

'Thank goodness,' says Dan. 'Otherwise I'd be responsible for a lot of women never getting married.'

'Honestly, Ed, I wouldn't worry about it. I wouldn't take Andy's surname if we got married.'

'What is it?' sniggers Dan, picking his beer up and leaning out of Wendy's reach. 'House?'

'What it is has nothing to do with it,' snaps Wendy. 'Women are more independent nowadays. We contribute at least half to the marriage, so why should we be the ones to give up our names and identities as well?'

'Steady on, Wendy,' says Dan, 'you'll be burning your bra next. Oh, hang on. You don't need to wear one in the first place.'

Wendy glares at him, no doubt storing up her revenge for a later date. 'Besides, Edward, by the sound of it, it's more to do with branding.'

Dan laughs. 'What – like they do to cows?'

I sigh loudly. 'The annoying thing is, I suppose I can see her point. I mean, why should I expect Sam to give up her name and take mine just because it's what everyone else does?'

Dan gestures towards me with his beer bottle. 'I think you've answered your own question there, mate.'

'Dan, *please*.'

'Sorry. But I suppose you're right. She's agreed to marry you. Why should she make any more sacrifices?'

As Wendy heads off to serve some other customers, struggling to hide a smile as she goes, something more sinister occurs to me. Maybe the reason Sam doesn't want to change her name is to do with the affair she might be having, or rather, because she's planning to carry on her affair after the wedding. Perhaps she hasn't even told him she's getting married, and what's the best way to keep up the pretence? Act as if nothing's changed. But when I repeat my theory to Dan, he shakes his head.

'Doubtful.'

'Why?'

'You're questioning the opinion of someone who's had the number of affairs I've had? Read my lips: Sam's. Not. Cheating. On. You.'

'Sorry, Dan. Silly of me to argue with the master.

But I just can't seem to get past these suspicions of mine.'

Dan puts a hand on my shoulder. 'Do you want me to find out for you?'

'And how would you do that, exactly?'

'I could ask Sam. Subtly, of course.'

The thought of Dan doing anything subtly makes me laugh. 'And how would *you* do that, exactly?'

'Good point.' Dan's face creases up in concentration for a moment or two. 'Or, I could follow her. See where she's going. Tail her in the car. Making sure she didn't see me, of course.'

'You drive a bright orange Porsche convertible. Don't you think she might see you?'

Dan looks at me as if I'm stupid. 'I'd have the roof up, obviously.'

'Obviously.' I shake my head resignedly. 'No, Dan. If she's managed to hide this from me for ages, then I don't think you'll be able to find out. Besides, it's something I need to do for myself.'

'So what are you going to do?'

'I thought I could double-check the signs, for example.'

'Which are?'

'You know. All those hushed phone calls she's been having. Her sneaking out to do "wedding stuff" all the time, but not telling me what "wedding stuff". Her hiding things from me on her computer because they're to do with "the wedding". You've got to admit, it doesn't look good.'

'It doesn't,' agrees Dan. 'Until you factor in the fact that the two of you are, actually, getting married. It could be all about that.'

'Yes, but how much stuff can there be to sort out? It's only a little affair, after all.'

'How do you know? It might be something serious.'

'No, I mean the wedding's only a small affair. And thanks. Unless, of course, she is up to something else entirely . . .'

Dan stares at me for a second or two. 'No, you're right,' he says. 'It does sound a bit suspicious. I'd definitely check it out if I were you.'

I'm a little surprised. 'Oh, you think so now, do you? What about all that "Sam's not cheating on you" stuff you just said?'

'Yeah, well, you've got to be sure, haven't you, and this sounds like the only way to put your mind to rest. I mean, you don't want a little thing like Sam being unfaithful to ruin your big day, do you? Unless you just want to let bygones be bygones.'

'Dan, how can I possibly go through with it if I know she's been seeing someone else?'

He shrugs. 'Maybe you should see someone else too. Even up the score. Maybe even with Candy or Bambi. That way . . .'

'Don't even go there.'

He shrugs again. 'Sorry. But if she is having one final fling, have you considered the possibility you might just be being a little selfish?'

I almost fall off my stool. 'Selfish? How?'

Dan takes a sip of his lager. 'You're marrying her, right? Which means that, unless you get fat and fuck it up again, you'll get her for what, the next fifty or so years?'

'Hopefully.'

'So if she is having an affair, maybe she's just getting it out of her system. You know, so she can settle down and be Mrs Middleton.' He clears his throat. 'Or, er, not. I mean, look at when you gave up smoking. You didn't just stop, did you? Instead, you went out, bought a last packet, smoked them slowly, tenderly, savouring every suck . . .'

'Thanks for the imagery!'

'Sorry, but you know what I mean. So maybe this is just Sam's last cigarette.'

I stare at him, unable – or maybe, unwilling – to believe what he's suggesting. Because while I know this kind of 'logic' makes perfect sense to him, the rest of us don't think like that at all. And while I have to take some comfort in the fact that if she was having an affair, Sam wouldn't just choose some quick fling; she's just not like that – equally, I can't believe she's been seeing someone else for all this time, because surely I'd have known. But then again, I didn't know when Jane did it to me, until she 'accidentally' copied me in on an email to the guy she'd snogged. And suddenly, the realization that because it's happened to me once without me knowing, it might well be happening again, hits me full in the stomach.

'I'm sorry, Dan. I just can't accept that. We're engaged. And there are rules.'

He laughs. 'What. *Rules of engagement*? I'm not sure that's quite what the phrase means.'

'Besides, to keep your metaphor going, Sam doesn't smoke. In fact, she's never smoked. Hates the thought of it.'

'You're sure about that, are you?' says Dan. 'Lots of people do without anyone knowing. You know, do it in the bathroom with the window open, a quick spray of air freshener afterwards, no one's any the wiser . . .'

I try and stop another awful image forming in my mind. 'But . . . Why would she?'

Dan shrugs. 'Maybe just to see what it's like. Or more likely, just to be sure she's making the right decision.'

'Marrying me, you mean.'

He nods. 'Or even, just getting married. Most people only get married because they've lost the will to keep dating. And Sam's not got the longest of dating histories.'

'Well, not compared to you, she hasn't. In fact, no one I know has. And that's even if you add them all together. And include Natasha.'

Dan basks in the glow of what he can't see any other way but as a compliment. 'So you should feel flattered that she thinks seriously enough about marrying you that she's prepared to do this.'

'Flattered is the one thing I don't feel. In fact, quite the opposite. Because she should know, shouldn't she?

After all, I do. And anyway, she asked *me*. Why would she have done that if she wasn't sure?'

Dan frowns. 'I dunno. I suppose because it's not final until the two of you actually say "I do", is it? And you know how it is – you make an offer on a house, go through with the survey and everything, but it's not until you exchange contracts – or in this case rings – that it's legal. A lot of people still look at other houses in the meantime, not because they want to buy them, but because they just want to be sure they've put their offer in on the right one. Some even keep looking at the property pages long after they've bought their house just to make sure they've done the right thing.'

'Yes, but they don't, you know, go and spend the night in them.'

'Well, maybe they should. If it helps them make their minds up.'

I can't quite believe what I'm hearing. 'So you're saying it's okay?'

'No – all I'm saying is, don't jump to conclusions. One – you don't know if Sam's up to anything, so don't start trying to work out why it is she's doing what you don't even know she's doing, and two . . .' Dan stops talking, and scratches his head. 'What was the first one again?'

As he sits there, struggling to remember what he's talking about, I realize I've got a choice. Trust Sam, and let her get on with whatever it is she's doing, or confront her about it, and risk causing damage to our relationship that we might never recover from. And, like I keep telling myself, marriage is all about trust. Isn't it?

'But I can't worry about this for the rest of my life.'

'Which is going to be even longer, seeing as you've given up smoking and all that crap food you used to shovel down your throat like it was going out of fashion.'

I stare thoughtfully into my beer. 'But she might just be marrying me because the old clock is ticking. You know, she just wants babies. Which is another reason not to change her name. So the kids will be . . .' I swallow hard. 'Hers.'

'Do you really think if she wanted to have a baby she'd have it with you? If she wasn't in love with you, I mean.'

'I suppose not,' I say, not quite knowing what Dan's trying to imply.

'And anyway, she's not particularly maternal, is she?'

'Not really,' I say. I've never really seen her around babies. 'Although she's fond enough of Wendy's little one.'

Dan opens his mouth to make a joke, then thinks better of it. 'But she's never offered to babysit, or anything?'

'No.'

'And for the last time, you're sure she's not pregnant?'

I nod, and then stop nodding abruptly. 'Pretty sure.'

'Because that is another reason for getting married. If you've got her, you know . . .'

'Yes, but she'd have told me, wouldn't she?'

'Would she?' Dan nudges me. 'Her dad doesn't have a shotgun, does he?'

I shudder. He does. He's even made a point of showing it to me. 'Christ, Dan, you're supposed to be making me feel better. Not worse.'

'Ed, just stop worrying, will you? You're getting married. To Sam. Who quite frankly is a girl who knocks spots off all – sorry, *both* – of your previous girlfriends. Even that one at college with the really bad acne.' He raises both eyebrows repeatedly in a did-you-see-what-I-did-there? kind of way. 'So *whatever* the reason Sam's agreed to marry you, forget all this registry-office rubbish, won't-change-her-name bollocks, is-she-cheating-on-me? crap, and, instead, grab on to her with both hands and don't let her go. Ever.'

As I let what he's just said sink in, I realize that for once, Dan's advice makes perfect sense to me. But sadly, hearing it and taking it are two completely different things.

'I'm sorry, Dan. You're right. But this is what happens when women leave you. It dents your confidence. I know it's hard for you to imagine, but it took me a long time to get over Jane. Maybe I still haven't. And so every time Sam and I have a wobble, or anything out of the ordinary happens, it's bound to make me feel a little . . . well . . . insecure.'

'Surely you know how she feels about you?' He grabs my shoulder, and gives it a manly shake. 'Especially after that sick-making speech of hers the other night?'

'But that's the thing. When you've been dumped and cheated on, you never want to take that kind of thing for granted again. So I won't know for sure until she actually turns up on the day and says "I do".'

Dan taps his watch. 'Well, thank Christ you've only got ten days' – he looks across at me nervously, and I nod in agreement – 'to go, then – and therefore I've only got ten days of having to listen to you bleating on. Sam's made her decision, so don't worry; it's usually only us blokes who get cold feet. But if you suspect Sam has, then make sure she's got some thermal socks.' He grins, and takes another mouthful of beer. 'Not *actual* thermal socks, of course.'

'Thanks,' I say, flatly. 'I was about to head off to M & S.'

'But remember, women are like sharks. They can sense fear. So whatever you do, don't let her get a whiff of the fact that you think you're not worthy.'

'Why?'

'Because if you believe that, then there's a danger she might start to believe it too.'

'I'm not sure, Dan. I mean, this is commitment we're talking about. And no disrespect, but it's hardly your specialist subject.' I sigh loudly. 'Maybe I need a woman's perspective.'

'Where are you going to get one of those?' huffs Dan.

'I could ask Wendy.'

He smirks. 'I thought you said you needed a woman's perspective?'

Wendy clears her throat, then looks up from where she's been loading the dishwasher not quite three feet away. 'I *can* hear you, you know.'

'Fuck,' whispers Dan. 'How long has she been there?'

'About two minutes.'

'Why didn't you warn me?'

'I didn't know you were going to say something rude about her.'

'Ed, I *always* say something rude about her.'

'What're you two being so secretive about?' says Wendy, standing up and leaning against the other side of the bar.

'Nothing,' says Dan, guiltily.

'I, I mean, *we*, just wanted a woman's perspective on something. Didn't we, Dan?'

'Yeah. That's right,' he says, jumping off his stool and heading towards the toilets. 'So if you know one we can ask . . .'

Wendy picks up a damp beer towel and expertly throws it at him, catching him just behind one ear. He scowls at her, then reaches up to touch the back of his head gingerly, although he seems more worried it might have messed up his hairstyle than actually hurt him.

'Fire away,' she says, turning back to me.

'It's just . . . well, this whole marriage thing. Business. Whatever you want to call it. I was just wondering whether maybe, you know, Sam and I had jumped the gun a bit.'

Wendy frowns. 'Not getting cold feet, are you?'

'Me? No. Not at all. I just meant that – I'm not sure what I meant, really. But I was wondering how soon was, you know, too soon?'

Wendy shrugs. 'When she asked you to marry her, what was your initial reaction?'

'Er . . .' I think for a second. 'I was thrilled. Flattered. Excited. Happy. Ecstatic, even.'

Wendy smiles. 'Then it wasn't too soon, was it?'

'Yes, but . . .' I struggle to find the right way to explain it. 'I was wondering *why* Sam asked me. In the first place.'

She shakes her head 'Possibly because she loves you, and wants to spend the rest of her life with you?'

'Really?'

'*Yes,* really.'

'How do you know?'

'Call it a wild stab in the dark.'

'Who's getting stabbed in the dark?' says Dan nervously, sitting back down at the bar.

Wendy ignores him. 'Edward, a woman doesn't ask anyone that question unless she's absolutely sure she wants to get married. So don't worry.'

'Yes, but how do I know that Sam's serious about marrying *me*?'

Wendy smiles, then pats me on the back of the hand. 'I'm really fond of you, you know, but sometimes you can be a little . . .'

'Thick?' suggests Dan.

'Look who's talking,' I snap back.

'Insecure,' says Wendy. 'Because not only did she ask

you in the first place, but she's set a date. And if she wasn't absolutely one hundred and ten per cent sure she wanted to marry you, that's the last thing she'd have done.'

'Right,' I say. 'Thanks,' trying to ignore the fact that it wasn't Sam who set the date, but me. Besides, setting a date doesn't actually mean anything if you're not planning to turn up.

Friday, 17 April

6.15 p.m.

In spite of all that, I *do* feel a bit better, particularly because, from what I can tell, for the next couple of days, Sam doesn't seem to have any hushed phone calls secretive emails, or – since the only thing my sneaky investigative lunchtime walks past Muffin To Declare have revealed is that they have a new double-white-chocolate muffin, and it's delicious – mysterious meetings. I've apologized to her about my behaviour the other night too because I've decided not to get too hung up on the name issue – after all, I wouldn't change anything else about her, so I might as well extend that to her surname. Besides, I've decided to keep my eye on the prize, and not worry about any of the so-called minor traditions.

I'm also feeling quite chuffed because I've managed to get Billy a place in the Shelter hostel and, although it took a bit of persuading – persuading Billy, I mean, rather than the hostel staff – he seems to be keen to give it a go. Or rather, he hasn't told me where to go. Which I suppose is as much as I can hope for.

When I get home, by the sounds of things, Sam's in the shower. There's a football match on this evening which I'm quite keen to watch, and as far as I know, it doesn't clash with any of her girlie programmes, so I should be okay, particularly since she'll probably fall asleep on me on the sofa anyway. Even so, I'm looking forward to spending the evening with her, but when she finally emerges from the bathroom, kisses me hello, then announces she's going out, I can't help but feel I'm suddenly back to square one.

'Out?' I say, struggling to keep myself from adding the word 'again' to the end of that sentence.

'I won't be long,' says Sam, stuffing her notebook into her bag. 'A couple of hours at most. Back in time for you to have watched your game and made me dinner.'

'Going anywhere nice?' I say, really only interested in the part of her answer that doesn't involve the 'going', 'any' and 'nice' parts of my question.

'Just out for a chat,' she says. 'Last few bits of wedding stuff to sort out.'

'Anyone I know?' I ask, watching her closely for any sign of guilt.

Sam nods distractedly as she picks up some loose change from the table. 'Yup.'

'Do you want to give me a name?' I say, before I've even given her a chance to tell me.

'Calm down, Edward.' Sam stuffs the change into her pocket, then zips up her coat. 'It's just Madeleine.'

'Sorry,' I say, trying to rein in my suspicious mind. 'I'm not checking up on you.' I stop speaking, because we both know that's exactly what it sounds like I'm doing. 'Can I start again? How was your day?'

As Sam shrugs, then proceeds to tell me, I force myself to smile and nod, but I can't help zoning out a little – what Dan would call a 'nonversation' – while I try to work out whether there's anything sinister going on. She's dressed in her usual off-duty uniform of tight-fitting jeans and a plain white T-shirt and, as sexy as I think she looks, it's hardly the gear you'd dress up in to meet a potential lover. Or is it? I mean, if you're off to an assignation, it's not what you're wearing that matters, because you soon won't be wearing anyth . . .

'Edward?'

'Yes?'

'You didn't answer my question.'

Bollocks. Sam's just asked me something and I haven't heard a word of it because I've been too busy letting my imagination run away with me. 'Oh. Er . . . Yes?'

'Yes what?'

'Your question. The answer's yes.'

She narrows her eyes at me. 'So we're having "yes" for dinner, are we? Is this a taste of what married life's going to be like?'

'Sorry, dear.' I grin sheepishly back up at her. 'I . . . er . . . thought you'd asked me if I'd made dinner. Not what I'd made.'

I pick the remote control up and switch on the TV,

congratulating myself on my good recovery, but Sam's having none of it.

'Well, what have you made? And when did this miracle take place, exactly? While I was in the shower?'

'Oh. Right. Actually, when I say "made", what I mean is, I've got all the ingredients.'

'For?'

'I thought I'd surprise you.'

'By cooking something edible for once?' she says, stroking my hair affectionately so I know she's making a joke.

'No. I mean, yes. It's . . . I thought we'd have pasta. In a tomato-ey sauce. With maybe minced meat in it. Oh, and some herbs,' I add, as if that makes all the difference.

'Spaghetti Bolognese.' Sam makes a face. 'That *is* a surprise.'

'It's my speciality,' I say, a little hurt.

'How could I forget?' Sam licks her lips and pats her stomach exaggeratedly. 'I can taste it already. See you in a couple of hours.'

'But . . .' As Sam looks at me expectantly, I shake my head in disgust at myself. What am I playing at? Am I going to feel jumpy every time she leaves the house, even if it's only to get a pint of milk from the corner shop? 'I mean, do you want me to come with you? I could help.'

'I don't think so.' Sam laughs.

I get suddenly suspicious. 'Why not? It's my wedding too.'

'Yes, but it's *my* wedding dress,' she says, producing a surprisingly well-thumbed copy of *What Bride?* from her bag. 'And that's the one thing you're not allowed anywhere near. Apart from me, on the morning before the wedding, of course.'

'I thought you weren't wearing a . . . I mean, didn't want to do the whole dress thing?'

'I don't. But I've got to wear something. Unless you'd prefer me to get married in just my underwear?'

'Well . . .' I smile to myself, picturing the look on Dan's face, then feel suddenly guilty. Even though she doesn't want a big wedding, this kind of stuff might still be important to Sam, and I don't want to sound like I'm interfering. 'I mean, no. Of course not. Sorry.' I glance towards the TV, where the build-up to the football match I've been looking forward to has already started. 'I just thought you might want to spend the evening here. With me. There's a good game on.'

'Ooh,' says Sam. 'As enticing as that sounds . . .'

'We could switch it off,' I suggest, reluctantly. 'There might be something else on the other side.'

'That's okay,' says Sam. 'Besides, I haven't seen Madeleine for a while. And I need to give her her maid of honour present.'

I'm suddenly suspicious again. Sam saw Madeleine on Wednesday, although she doesn't know I know this, because with everything else that's been going on, I'd forgotten to mention that I bumped into Madeleine on the way back from work yesterday, and Madeleine had told me how chuffed she was and how she was going to be the best maid of honour ever. And while at the time I thought that was funny, because, given what I've heard about Madeleine from Dan after he drove her home the other night, she doesn't actually have that much honour, right now, I don't find it amusing at all.

'Can't it wait until tomorrow?' Tomorrow is Sam's hen night. Where, presumably, she'll be seeing Madeleine anyway.

'Er . . . No,' says Sam, matter-of-factly.

'Did you want a lift?' I say, in a desperate attempt to find out where she's really going.

'No thanks,' says Sam, standing on tiptoe to kiss me, before picking her keys up from the coffee table. 'It's just round the corner. You enjoy your game.'

As soon as the door shuts behind her, I'm on my feet. What to do? I could phone Madeleine to check Sam's alibi, of course, but that might seem a little suspicious if she tells Sam I've called. Or I could run after Sam and tell her she's forgotten something – but what? That she's getting married and shouldn't be sneaking around behind my back, perhaps.

Or . . . I could take Dan's advice and follow her. Sam's said she's going just round the corner and, as I peer out through the window, her car's still outside, which means it must be within walking distance. It's twenty-five past six, so presumably, and knowing Sam's penchant for punctuality, she's meeting Madeleine – or whoever – at half past. All I need to do is work out where is within five minutes' walking distance from here.

I know it's dishonest, and I really don't want to do it, but I still can't stop myself from pulling my jacket off the coat rack and heading out after her, promising myself at the same time that if what she says turns out to be true, it'll put an end to all of this nonsense once and for all.

Given that Sam's a faster walker than me, I set my watch for six minutes and start walking, but after only four I've already reached Western Road, and from what I can see, there are approximately ten bars and three cafés that might conceivably be within five minutes of our flat.

I stand there helplessly, wondering where on earth to start, and am on the verge of giving up when I spy Madeleine's car parked just up a side street, outside the Cooper's Arms. Breathing a huge sigh of relief, I tell myself I'm just being stupid, turn round, and start walking back towards my flat – and away from my fears – when it occurs to me I should actually check. I mean, while it looks like Madeleine's car, there are rather a lot of Beetles in Brighton – plus, she might have sold it. Though whether the buyer would have kept the 'Homoeopaths Do It In Small Doses' sticker on the rear windscreen is questionable.

I creep back along the pavement towards the pub, ready to duck behind a lamppost in case Madeleine or Sam come out unexpectedly and catch me, then realize I'd feel a lot better if I had an alibi for being here –

which the Tesco Metro round the corner might well provide me with – so I nip in and buy a tube of sour cream and onion flavoured Pringles. Of course, now I'm running the risk of getting into even more trouble if Sam catches me with a packet of Pringles before dinner, although in my defence, at least I've bought Lites. Better that than be caught following her, I suppose.

Brandishing the Pringles like a relay runner's baton, I hurry back round the corner, relieved to see Madeleine's car hasn't moved, and walk nervously towards the Cooper's Arms. Then I encounter my first real problem. Obviously I can't simply stick my head in through the door and try to spot her in case she spots *me*, but the pub's got these strange little glass windows, most of which are impossible to see through due to a circular ripple effect, so I can't just look through the window either. There is one normal pane – evidently where one of the originals has been broken and replaced by plain glass – but it's a little bit higher than is comfortable for me to reach.

I peer up and down the street, keen to get this sordid incident over and done with, then notice an old wooden crate in the alleyway at the side of the pub. For a second, I think maybe I could use that to stand on, but I don't really want to pick it up because departing drinkers have a habit of using that alleyway as a toilet when the pub's shut.

I stand there for a moment or two considering my options. The most sensible one, of course, is to accept that Sam's telling me the truth and just go home. But if

I do that, I know I'll be wondering for the rest of the evening – and maybe for the rest of my life. I've got to check. But how?

I look up at the pane of glass. It's just above head height, and probably easily reachable if I jump, but, knowing my luck, I'll do it just at the moment Sam's looking up, and she'll see me behaving like some demented jack-in-the-box. And Pringles or not, how on earth would I explain that?

Then I have an idea: the Pringles. Or more specifi-cally, the tube they're in. It's about the right length, and looks pretty sturdy, so maybe if I'm careful I can balance on one foot on the top of it. It's a dilemma, because if it works, I'll be able to see what Sam's up to, but if it does-n't, I'll risk crushing a whole tube of my favourite crisps.

After a moment's consideration, where I can't decide whether the end with the plastic cap will be better at the top or on the ground, I carefully stand the Pringles upside down on the pavement underneath the window and, putting one hand against the wall for support, rest my right foot gingerly on top of the tube. Holding my breath, I gradually increase the downward pressure while wondering, perhaps too late, whether I should nip back into Tesco to exchange them for the full-fat version, in the hope they might be a bit stronger.

Somehow, thankfully, the tube seems to be holding my weight, so I carefully lift my other foot off the ground and, conscious that I need to maintain my weight directly over the tube rather than make any sudden movements, straighten my right leg, using my arms for balance in a Karate Kid–type stance. I'm feeling somewhat precarious, not to mention ridiculous, but luckily it's a dark evening, and the Cooper's Arms is on a side street, so there's not a lot of passing traffic, although I do have to shoo away an old lady who seems to think I'm one of those street performers who pretend to be statues in front of the shopping centre every Saturday.

Slowly, my eyes draw level with the clear pane of glass. It doesn't seem to have been cleaned in a while, and initially I struggle to locate Sam through the grime, but eventually I spot her – fortunately with her back to me – sitting at one of the tables. When I crane my neck to the right, rubbing my forehead accidentally against the dirty glass, I can just about identify Madeleine in the seat next to her, and – thanks to the clean patch of glass I can see through having just used my brow as a squeegee – can even make out that they do seem to be poring over the copy of *What Bride?* Sam showed me earlier.

So there's my proof. I can't help feeling stupid, and not just because I'm balancing on a tube of Pringles outside a pub, but because I've made the mistake of not trusting my fiancée. What was I thinking? If Sam says she's coming out to meet Madeleine, then she's coming out to meet Madeleine.

As I wobble slightly on my perch, I realize that that's all *this* was – a little wobble – and I'm just about to see if I can lower myself back to the pavement without crushing what's now going to be my celebratory tube of Pringles when something occurs to me: neither of them has a drink.

I peer back inside, just in time to see a man – who I assume to be the barman – deposit three glasses of wine on their table. For a moment, I relax again, but then remember the Cooper's Arms isn't the kind of establishment offering table service and, besides, although I know from the other night Madeleine likes a drink, even if that *was* the barman, he surely wouldn't be putting *three* glasses down.

Or be sitting down to join them at their table.

Or be picking up the magazine, then nodding approvingly at something Sam's just shown him.

I get a sudden sinking feeling in my stomach, which sinks even lower when the man looks up from whatever it is he's been reading. Because as his face creases in confusion at the sight of an eye – *my* eye – that evidently belongs to a seven-foot tall man staring in through the pub window, I realize it's a face I recognize from the other day. When it was eating cake with Sam at the café.

Instinctively I duck down – a little too violently for the cardboard tube of wafer-thin potato snacks that's been somewhat miraculously supporting my weight. There's a pop, followed by a sickening crunch – fortunately not my ankle bone – as the tube concertinas, enveloping me in a sour-cream-and-onion-smelling cloud as I hit the ground.

I leap to my feet, then run back round the corner onto Western Road, unable to believe what I've just seen. How could I have been so blind, so stupid, so *ignorant* of the fact that my girlfriend, or rather, my fiancée, is having an affair? And what's more, Madeleine's in on the whole thing.

Dusting the remains of the Pringles off my trousers, I wipe the dirty smear from my forehead, pick a direction at random, and start walking, trying hard not to cry, but feeling angry at the same time. If Sam really is having an affair, then it won't be just my crisps that have been crushed.

It'll be my hopes and dreams for the future.

7.02 p.m.
I'm sitting on the sofa at Dan's flat when his voice comes booming in from the hallway.

'Step away from the stuffed crust.'

As Dan advances towards me, I pick up my can of lager defiantly, then take a couple of quick drags on my Marlboro.

'Leave me alone.'

'Come on, mate, I'm serious. You know those things will kill you.' He's sweating heavily which, coupled with the way he's dressed — in a one-size-too-small-to-show-off-his-muscles white football shirt with 'Davis' and, predictably, '69' printed on the back — means he's probably been out training with Fake Madrid, the celebrity five-a-side football team he plays for.

'So?' I pick up the half-empty packet of cigarettes, childishly stuffing it up my jumper so Dan can't take it.

'I wasn't talking about the cigarettes,' he says, reaching down to grab the Pizza Hut box. 'Do you know how many calories are in one of these?'

I snatch the box back from him, and for a few seconds we engage in a ridiculous tug of war until it rips in two and the pizza falls out – cheese-and pepperoni-side down, of course – onto Dan's expensive rug.

'I don't care,' I say, picking it up and placing it the right way up on the coffee table, much to Dan's disgust. He stares at me for a second or two, then walks over to the kitchen to fetch a wet sponge and some Fairy Liquid.

'What on earth's the matter with you? And more importantly, how did you get in here?'

I reach into my pocket and remove a bunch of keys. 'Your spare set, remember? You gave them to me in case of emergencies.'

'Yeah, but by "emergency" I meant if a woman ever locked me in here and refused to let me go until I'd agreed to go on a second date with her,' he says, kneeling down and dabbing gingerly at the pizza-with-a-slice-missing-shaped stain. 'Not just because you fancied a pizza and a fag. And have you forgotten you're supposed to be getting married next weekend? We don't want you all lardy in your wedding photos.'

'The wedding's off,' I say, slumping back onto the sofa, splashing some lager onto Dan's suede cushions.

Dan pauses, mid-wipe. 'What? Why?'

I shrug. 'Sam seems to have decided that for me.'

'So she finally saw sense, did she?' Dan gets up off the floor and sits down on the sofa. 'I suppose it was only a matter of time. What was it? The prospect of being married to you was just too much for her to . . .'

'No, Dan. My suspicions were right. She's . . .' I swallow hard, almost unable to make myself say the words, 'having an affair.'

For perhaps the first time ever, Dan's actually speechless. 'What?' he says, eventually.

'Sam's ha—'

Dan holds his hand up. 'I didn't mean "what?", exactly. I heard you the first time. Are you sure?'

I nod. 'You know that man I told you about the other day?'

'The one she had coffee with?'

'Yup.'

'The good-looking one?'

'Thanks, Dan. Yes. The good-looking one. Well, I saw him again. With Sam. Tonight. In a pub.'

As I explain this evening's events, leaving out the Pringle-balancing, Dan's eyes widen. 'You must have got the wrong end of the stick,' he says, when I've finished.

'Will you please stop using that phrase. And anyway, how else do you explain all that, then?'

'Er . . .' Dan thinks for a moment or two. Given the

amount of affairs he's had over the years, if anyone could explain it, it's him, and the fact that he can't makes me even more suspicious.

'Exactly.' I pick up another slice of pizza, pull a few rug fibres off it, then take a huge bite, washing it down with a mouthful of lager.

'No.' Dan turns his attention back to his sponging. 'Not Sam. She wouldn't. And besides, even if she would, eating, drinking and smoking yourself into an early grave is hardly going to win her back, is it?'

'I thought you said she wasn't having an affair. So why would I need to win her back?'

Dan frowns. 'Hang on, Ed. You sound like you're trying to catch me out. Surely it's her you should be doing that to?'

I throw the half-eaten slice back onto the table and put my head in my hands. 'What am I going to do, Dan? I can't marry her now.'

'Why ever not?'

'Haven't you been listening? She's having an affair.'

'You don't know that. And even if she was, like I said the other day, maybe it's just one last fling. Something she needs to get out of her system, so she can settle down and be faithful to you.'

I stare at him incredulously. 'Ignoring the fact that it would be so wrong on so many levels, what if it isn't? What if she's been seeing this guy for ages, and wants it to carry on? And why is she seeing him? Is there something I'm not giving her?'

'Hur hur.'

'Dan, please. If ever there was a time I need you not to be smutty, it's now.'

'Sorry, mate.' He clears his throat. 'What proof have you got?'

'Proof? I haven't got any proof. It's just a suspicion. A hunch.'

'What did you see her do?'

'It's not so much what I saw her do.' I swallow hard, still finding it difficult to relive the cake incident, or even say the word. 'It's the fact they were somewhere she knew I wouldn't see them. And then tonight, she told me she was going for a drink with Madeleine. And it turned out it was with Madeleine and *him*.'

Dan raises both eyebrows, and I tell myself that if he makes another reference to threesomes I'll hit him, but instead, he seems to be taking the matter seriously.

'Did you challenge her about it?'

'Yeah, right. Because that's a conversation I want to have the week before my wedding. "Hi, Sam, I've confirmed the DJ for the reception. Oh, and by the way, are you having an affair?"'

'You're having a DJ?' Dan sighs with relief. 'Thank Christ you didn't go for that Scottish stuff. Just make sure they don't play any of that cheesy eighties music you like. Oh, and what about getting him to have some of that foam they use at the clubs in Ibiza? You know – the stuff that makes the women's tops go all see-through.'

'Please try and stop thinking about yourself for five minutes. Weren't you listening earlier? There's not going to be any wedding.'

He puts the sponge down on the coffee table. 'That's a bit drastic, isn't it?'

'Drastic?'

He nods. 'There's too much store put by this fidelity lark, in my opinion.'

I look at him in disbelief. 'I don't want your opinion. I want your help. What am I going to do?'

Dan thinks for a moment. 'I could beat him up for you, if you like.'

For a minute, I do like. But what good would that do? 'He's not the problem. Sam is.'

'Steady on,' says Dan. 'Besides, I'm not sure I could take her. Have you seen her biceps?'

'I didn't mean for you to beat *her* up, Dan.'

As I flop backwards on the sofa and stare miserably up at the ceiling, Dan reaches over and carefully takes the beer can from my hand, like a policeman relieving a potential suicide of his gun.

'Ah. No. Of course. But there's no reason to beat yourself up either. First things first. You need a clear head. Coffee?'

'I don't mind if I do. Thanks.'

'Great,' he says, leaping off the sofa and heading for his bedroom. 'Make me one while you're at it. I'll just grab a quick shower and throw some clothes on, then we'll get this sorted.'

7.41 p.m.

It takes Dan about half an hour to 'throw' his clothes on, which is just as well, as that's how long it takes me to work out how to get the little pods into the flash new Nespresso coffee machine that's replaced the cafetière, and I've just managed to make myself an espresso by the time he reappears.

'Thanks,' he says, taking the cup from me before I've had a chance to drink it, then downing half of it with an exaggerated slurp. 'You not having one?'

I stare at the machine, wondering whether I can be bothered to go through the whole process again. 'I don't need a coffee, Dan. What I need is advice.'

'Okay.' He sits down at the kitchen table, then indicates for me to do the same. 'Fire away.'

'Well, I've changed my mind and decided I'm just going to have to confront Sam, so . . .'

'Whoa!' says Dan, suddenly sitting bolt upright, though that could just be a result of the caffeine hit. 'Steady on there, cowboy. What do you want to be doing a silly thing like that for?'

'How else am I going to find out what she's been up to?'

'Why do you want to find out what she's been up to? And anyway, she might not have been up to anything at all, don't forget.'

'Because we're getting married, Dan. And I can't possibly marry Sam if she's been . . . you know' – I still have difficulty saying the words – 'cheating on me.'

'Okay,' he says. 'But before you do anything rash, think of the consequences. You go up to her – your fiancée – and say, "Hello, sweetheart, I just wanted to check something before we tie the knot next weekend. Are you shagging someone else?" How do you think she's going to react?'

'By telling me the truth, hopefully.'

'The truth. Which is either a) "Yes, I am seeing someone else, and by the way, the wedding's off", or b) "No, of course I'm not, how could you accuse me of such a thing, Edward, and by the way, the wedding's off". Just tell me where the upside is for you in that approach, please.'

'I hadn't thought of it like that.'

Dan sighs. 'Ed, there are some questions you can never ask, especially if you want a relationship to work – "Is it mine?", for example, or "Would you mind if your mother joined us in bed?" – and this is one of those, which is why you've got to let it go. Convince yourself that because she's marrying you, she can't possibly be up to anything. After all, who'd have an affair with someone just before they got married?'

'That Jennifer girl you were shagging last Christmas. Remember?'

'Ah, but that was different. I knew she was getting married. And she wanted me to be her final fling. So everyone was happy.'

'Except for the poor mug she was marrying, you mean.'

Dan rolls his eyes. 'That's the whole point of a final fling. So you get it out of your system. I believe the clue's in the word final. So if that *is* what Sam's doing, then you've got nothing to worry about. Besides, you know Sam. She's not like that. So I'm sure if she is up to something, it's nothing for you to be worried about.'

'But up to *what*?' I whine.

Dan looks a little uncomfortable. 'I don't know. Like I said, I can't understand why anyone would get married in the first place, so asking me what goes through their minds in the couple of weeks before-hand . . .'

'So, if I can't confront her, and I can't let it go, what's the alternative? Sneak around behind her back in an attempt to catch her out?'

Dan nods. 'Yup. That way you avoid any messy con-frontation.'

'But what if she catches me?'

'Make something up. But whatever you do, don't blurt out some half-baked accusation just before your wedding because that's something you won't be able to take back. So if you want my advice, let it go. I know it seems pretty suspicious, but it just can't be an affair. Not Sam. Like I said before, she's not the type.' He drains the rest of his coffee. 'Besides, why does it matter so much to you?'

'Why does it matter so much to me?' I stare at Dan across the table, wondering how on earth he can ask such a thing. 'Because of Jane's affair, of course. Because I felt such a mug at the time, and because the last thing I want to do is to lose Sam the same way.'

Dan puts his cup down on the table. 'Are you sure you don't want one?'

'What good would me having an affair do?' I almost shout. 'Even things up?'

'Steady on,' says Dan, nodding towards the Nespresso machine. 'I was talking about a coffee. Although if you do want one, it had better be decaf.'

As I stare at him, all the fight goes out of me. 'Go on then,' I say, suddenly feeling weary. 'But what am I going to do, Dan?'

Dan selects a brown coffee pod from the rack behind the machine, then puts a clean espresso cup under the spout. 'Well, for starters, don't fuck things up by confronting her. Whatever Sam's up to – and again, that's if she *is* up to anything – she's got her reasons. So as long as she turns up on the twenty-fourth . . .'

'Twenty-*fifth*, Dan.'

'. . . you've got nothing to worry about.'

I get an even sicker feeling in the pit of my stomach. 'And that's another thing. Supposing she doesn't? Turn up, I mean.'

Dan frowns, though possibly because he's struggling to remember how the coffee machine works.

'Why wouldn't she?'

'Duh. The affair, dummy.'

'What affair?' says Dan, clicking the pod into place,

hitting a few buttons at random on the front of the machine, then punching the air in celebration as some coffee miraculously starts to appear in the cup. 'As far as I can see, there's no proof, apart from you accidentally catching her having what's probably an innocent drink with some bloke a couple of times.'

'No, but . . .'

'So, in the absence of any proof, surely the next best thing is to work out whether she'd be *likely* to have one.'

'Huh?'

As coffee starts to overflow onto the granite work surface, Dan peers at the machine anxiously, hunting for an 'off' button, then settles for pulling the plug out of the wall socket. 'That way,' he says, picking the cup up and taking a sip, evidently having forgotten who it was meant to be for, 'maybe we can prove she's not.'

I can't think of anything more original to say, so I just repeat myself.

'Huh?'

Dan looks at me for a second to check I'm okay, and then continues. 'Look at it this way. If you can convince yourself she's got no reason to cheat on you, then surely she isn't cheating on you.'

'Dan, I'm sorry, but I'm not quite getting you.'

'It's simple,' he says, putting his coffee cup down, then jumping up from the table and making for a locked cupboard in the corner of the living room. 'People generally have affairs for two reasons: one – not enough sex in their existing relationship, and two – lack of an emotional connection.'

'That's rather a deep observation for you.'

'Don't take my word for it,' he says, reaching up to remove a key from on top of the mirror above the fireplace, then unlocking the cupboard door. 'Ta-da!'

I peer over his shoulder and into the cupboard, where I can see what look like hundreds of issues of *Cosmo*. What's more, on closer inspection, they appear to have had their covers reinforced with sticky-back plastic, and be carefully filed by date.

'What's that?'

'Only my holy fucking bible,' says Dan, consulting a neatly typed list taped to the inside of the cupboard door. 'Here.' He selects one of the magazines, then hands it carefully to me, as if he's passing over a family heirloom. There's a yellow Post-it note marking one of the pages, so I open it, then stare at the headline.

'"How to Tell if He's a Cheater or a Keeper". What's this?'

'*Cosmo*,' says Dan, reverentially. 'It's taught me everything I know about women.'

'I'm sorry, I'm not quite following you.'

He takes the magazine back from me and points towards the page. 'They often have these quizzes. And this one's most useful if you want to avoid getting caught. You know, find out what they're telling them to look for, then do the opposite. That sort of thing.'

'Now I can see why you've got a subscription. But how does it help me, exactly?'

'Simple. We do the quiz, but as if Sam's the, you know . . .'

'Cheater?'

'Or keeper,' says Dan, encouragingly.

I look at him incredulously. 'You want me to base my decision as to whether to get married in eight days on a *Cosmo quiz*?'

Dan picks his cup up and swallows the rest of his – or rather, *my* – coffee. 'Why not?'

I don't know where to start. 'Because it's *Cosmo*?'

'Which is a very popular magazine with my target market. And therefore representative of you and Sam. Whether you like it or not.'

I stare at the magazine for a second or two, then realize maybe I'm just desperate enough to try it. 'And you think it'll be useful?'

Dan nods sincerely, then picks up a pencil from the desk in the corner. 'It hasn't let me down yet,' he says, sitting at the table.

I sigh, unable to believe I'm even considering it, but then again, I suppose I've got nothing to lose. Or everything, depending on what, if anything, Sam's up to.

'Okay. Knock yourself out.'

'Right.' Dan picks up the magazine and clears his throat. 'How often do you have sex?'

'We *have* started the quiz? This isn't some research you're doing for your speech?'

'Of course.'

'Right. Well, in any case, none of your business.'

'Edward, this is for your own good.'

'Sorry.'

'Is it, A) never, B) once a week, C) 2–3 times, D) 4–6 or E) every day?'

I can't stop myself from blushing. 'Well, er . . .'

'Come on, come on.'

'D.'

Dan arches one eyebrow. 'Really? You lucky bastard.'

'Okay. C. But only because she has to get up early.'

He laughs. 'And you can't?'

'Piss off, Dan.'

'Okay. C it is,' he says, marking the answer down. 'Next question. How often does he tell you he loves you? Though that should be "she", of course.'

'What are my options?'

'Same as before. A) Never, B) once a week, C) . . .'

'Okay. I remember. That would be C again.'

'Great,' says Dan. 'See – this isn't so hard, is it? Next question. When you're out with your friends, do you feel jealous that she pays them a lot more attention than you? I mean, I know that's a little tricky to answer, seeing as you don't have many friends, and everyone always pays the most attention to me.'

'A.'

'I said, when you're out . . .'

'No, Dan. A. Not "eh"?'

'Sorry. A. Right. Next question. Does she sometimes

go out at strange times of the day, and come back home flushed, out of breath, or head straight for the shower?'

'Well, yes, but . . .'

'Oh dear,' says Dan. 'That's not good.'

'Dan, she's a personal trainer. It's her job.'

'Oh. Yeah. Of course.' He nods. 'Good cover story, though.'

'Thanks very much. That's reassuring. Next question?'

'I'm putting E down, am I?'

'Well, I suppose so, but . . .'

Dan shushes me. 'Don't argue with the wisdom of *Cosmo*, Edward.'

'Fine.' I fold my arms. 'E.'

'Great.'

As Dan rattles through the rest of the quiz, I start to feel more and more hopeless. Given the nature of the questions, I can guess what the outcome is going to be, even once we've allowed for Sam's job-related 'infidelities', and besides, a *Cosmo* quiz hardly proves anything – apart from to Dan, of course. Even so, when we've finally finished, I can't help but ask.

'So, go on then. What's my score?'

'*Sam's* score, you mean.'

'Sorry, Dan. Sam's score.'

I lean back in my seat and stare at him while he struggles to work out the scoring system, which seems to be no more complicated than 'Mostly As' or 'Mostly Bs', with the odd bonus question thrown in. Finally he takes a deep breath, and turns to face me. 'Are you ready?'

'As I'll ever be.'

'Okay. 'Mostly Cs': He's . . . I mean, *she's* a keeper. So go ahead and get married next Saturday.' He nudges me. 'I added that last bit myself.'

'Oh really?'

'Really,' he says, setting the magazine triumphantly down on the table. 'So there you go. Nothing to worry about.'

'Says you.'

'Says *Cosmo*,' he points out, stroking the cover a little too affectionately for my liking.

'You'll excuse me if I don't take too much comfort from a magazine that also investigates whether blondes really have more fun,' I say, pointing to an article on the opposite page, titled 'To Dye For'.

Dan shrugs. 'Okay, maybe some of the questions were a bit spurious. But you've got to admit, the overall concept is pretty sound. Sam's not lacking in any department as far as your relationship is concerned. So what possible reason could she have for cheating on you?'

'Well . . .' The funny thing is, as I think it through, I fail to come up with anything. We do have a good time, Sam and I – in all departments. So what possible reason would she have for wanting an affair? Unless . . . 'But what if she *is* just trying to get it out of her system? You know, one last fling?'

Dan walks back over to the cupboard in the corner, slips the copy of *Cosmo* carefully back into its rightful place, then locks the door again. 'Edward, how many times do I have to tell you? Sam's not like that.'

'How do you know?'

'Because . . .' Dan slips the key back into its hiding place, then sits down next to me and puts a supportive arm around my shoulder. 'You know that phrase, "It takes one to know one"?'

'What about it?'

'Well, I'm one. And because of that, I'm pretty sure Sam isn't.'

'Really?'

'Yes, really. I've had lots of affairs. With lots of people. And over the years, I've learned there's a certain type that's happy to cheat on someone – believe me, they're easy to spot. And do you know what? Sam's not one of them.' He nods towards the bathroom. 'So clean yourself up. Go back home. Start getting ready for this wedding of yours. And look forward to spending the rest of your life with her.'

Too exhausted to argue, I haul myself reluctantly out of my seat, trying to convince myself that, maybe, Dan's got a point, but just before I reach the bathroom door, something occurs to me.

'Tell me one thing, Dan, if you're such an expert. What about Jane, eh?'

He walks over and stands next to me. 'What about her?'

'She cheated on me. Then dumped me. And nobody saw that coming, did they?'

Dan sighs, then puts both hands on my shoulders and steers me in through the doorway. 'Ed, I hate to be the one to break it to you, but the only person who didn't see that coming was you.'

8.15 p.m.
When I eventually arrive home, Sam's still not back, which is fine, because it gives me a chance to compose myself, make dinner, and prepare to act as if everything's normal. And while Dan's right, and I shouldn't confront her, I can, of course, do the next best thing, which is give her an opportunity to admit everything to me, because if Sam and I can't be honest with each other, then how on earth can we move forward?

Knowing Sam, if she is up to something, she probably wants to tell me anyway. Maybe she's just looking for the right moment, or the right way to say it. Perhaps it's my fault for not asking. Or at least, not asking the right questions.

I'll be angry, of course, if she has been seeing someone else behind my back. But should I be angry with her or with myself? After all, if she feels the need to see someone else then, despite *Cosmo*, that must only be because she's not getting what she wants from me. And while that might conceivably be her fault for not asking for it clearly enough, I can't help but feel it's also mine for not knowing how to make her happy. After all, Jane was very quick to blame me for her indiscretion. And while Jane was always quick to blame anyone for her mistakes but herself, I could kind of see she had a point.

I could put my foot down, of course. Tell Sam it's got to stop, or the wedding's off. Even give her a few days grace to wind it down. I mean, that's not unreasonable, is it? But then again, do I really want to marry her if she's been seeing someone else? A part of me says yes, of course, like it's an auction, and I'm the last successful bidder. I mean, she's had boyfriends before me, and she's slept with them – I can't deny that, just like she can't deny that I've got a sexual history with Jane and, er . . . well, Jane, mainly – and so I've got to live with that fact. Looking at it clinically, and ignoring the overlap, this is kind of the same thing, and so if I really want to go through with this marriage, then it's also something I've got to live with – as long as it *does* stop. And as long as I'm okay with the reasons why it started in the first place.

But in all of this, the thing that really gets to me is that I thought I'd learned enough from Jane and me to be able to prevent it from happening again. I'm attentive, caring, and probably work harder at being Sam's boyfriend than I do at any other aspect of my life – including my job. To be honest, I can't see what more I can do. So if she is seeing someone else, and we end up splitting up because of it, then I'm going to give up this relationship lark. I obviously just don't understand it.

So that's what I'll do, I decide. Give her the

opportunity to admit what she's been up to, and hope she'll feel comfortable enough to tell me. And what better opportunity than over a large, steaming plate of her favourite dish?

8.48 p.m.

By the time Sam comes in, I've brushed my teeth about five times to make sure there's no trace of either the cigarettes or the alcohol on my breath, and am in the kitchen, ladling spaghetti Bolognese onto a couple of pre-heated plates. I've already set the table with candles, put a flower pinched from next-door's garden in a vase, and opened a bottle of wine – which I can tell from her look of pleasant surprise she appreciates – and after kissing her hello, I direct her to her seat and, trying to hide my nervousness, sit her down.

'So,' I say, sprinkling about half a ton of Parmesan over the mound of pasta on my plate. 'I was thinking. This wedding of ours.'

'What about it?' says Sam, taking the bowl of cheese from me and sprinkling even more over hers.

'It's a good chance for a new start, isn't it? Admit all our little secrets. If there's anything we haven't been, you know . . .' I take a large mouthful of red wine, 'completely honest about.'

Sam stops twirling spaghetti on her fork and looks up at me. 'Oh-kay . . .'

'Because we'd be starting married life afresh, wouldn't we?' I take another gulp of wine, conscious I've finished most of my glass. Sam, on the other hand, has hardly touched hers. 'So it's only fair we should be allowed to own up to anything we haven't been a hundred per cent straight with each other about. Get it out in the open, as it were.'

'Really? I mean, aren't you supposed to let sleeping dogs lie, and all that?' She smiles. 'And I don't mean that in the sense that Dan would.'

Oh no. She does really have something to tell me, or rather, something *not* to tell me. 'No. I, er, think it's healthier this way. So go on. You first.'

'Well . . .' Sam reddens slightly, then stares down at her plate. 'There is something.'

'What?' I say, my voice faltering slightly.

'It's just . . . This.' As Sam starts to push her food nervously around with her fork, I'm getting even more worried. 'I don't like the way you do it.'

'What?' I swallow hard. 'What's wrong with the way I do it?'

Sam shrugs. 'I've had better, to be honest.'

'Better? Better how?'

'You never put enough meat in, for a start.'

'Pardon?'

'And it's never saucy enough for my liking . . .'

'Never saucy enough?' I stare at her in horror for the few uncomfortable seconds to realise that she's not, in fact, talking about my bedtime performance. 'You mean my *spaghetti Bolognese*?'

Sam nods, then pushes her plate away. 'I don't like it.'

'But it's my . . .' I try to stop my voice from faltering. 'Speciality.'

'I'm sorry, Edward. But I've never liked it.'

For a moment, I don't know whether to be relieved or angry. 'You've never said anything. Before, I mean.'

'That's because I knew you liked it, so I didn't want to offend you. Especially since it's your . . . you know.'

'Ah,' I say, definitely landing on the 'relieved' side of the fence. 'Point taken.'

Sam reaches across the table and grabs my hand. 'You're not upset?'

'No,' I say. Of course I am. But in the overall scheme of things, I suppose it's not so bad. 'And there's nothing else?'

She squeezes my fingers tightly. 'There's nothing else, Edward.'

'You're sure?'

'Positive.'

I stare at her, trying to swallow the huge lump in my throat. 'Promise me something, will you?'

'Anything,' says Sam, and the way she says it makes my heart leap.

'Just that you will tell me if there's any other of my . . . *specialities* you don't like?'

'Of course.' Sam lets go of my hand, then stands up and leans over the table to kiss me. 'In fact, why don't you clear up while I go and get ready for bed, and then we can discuss them there?'

As Sam busies herself in the bathroom, I wolf down

a few forkfuls of pasta – I've a feeling I'm going to need the energy – then scrape the contents of her plate into the kitchen bin. As I catch sight of my reflection in the kitchen window, it's a much happier, more relaxed-looking me I see smiling back – and not just because we're about to have sex – though admittedly, that does help. I mean, who in their right mind would go out to meet their lover then come home and have sex with their fiancé? Besides, as Dan pointed out, I've got no choice but to trust her, which means I have to accept that nothing's going on. Especially since I've just given her the opportunity to come clean.

But one thing's painfully obvious to me. The way I feel over a minor thing like Sam not liking my cooking makes me realize that if she was actually having an affair, I'd probably want to kill myself.

Saturday, 18 April

6.59 p.m.
Tonight is my stag do, and I'm a little nervous, particularly because all Dan's told me about the evening's entertainment is that I've got to be at his flat at seven o'clock sharp. And while I've spent most of the day finalizing wedding arrangements with Sam, and almost managed to convince myself that she can't be having an affair, there's still a part of me that needs to know just who this mystery man is that she's been seeing. And just what the 'seeing' has involved.

I'm a minute early when I ring Dan's buzzer, and after a few seconds, he pokes his head anxiously round the door.

'Oh. It's you.'

'Who were you expecting?'

Dan holds up a soggy takeaway bag. 'Sushi delivery. Or rather, re-delivery. I've just had an argument with the company on the phone.'

'Why?'

'Bloody stuff's always cold by the time it gets here.' He looks at his watch. 'Although I don't think they're coming. It's been hours since I called them. Now get out of the way. You're obscuring my abs.'

As Dan throws the door open, I notice he's not wearing a shirt, probably because he's hoping there'll be some paparazzi waiting to snap him.

'Dan, there are no photographers here,' I say, trying unsuccessfully to push past him. 'Besides, does it not occur to you that it might not fit in with your image?'

He takes one last look up and down the street, then gazes down at his perma-tanned stomach, tensing and relaxing his six-pack. 'Why not?'

'Because you're half naked . . .'

'That's the idea, Eddie-boy.'

'. . . and answering the door to a man.'

Dan looks at me for a second. 'Good point. Although it might help my gay fan base. If you were a bit better-looking, that is.'

'Thanks very much.'

'Don't mention it. So,' he says, ushering me inside, 'all ready for your big night?'

'I suppose so.'

'Got your passport?'

'No.' I say, a feeling of mild panic suddenly descending. 'Why?'

'Only kidding! You're so easy.' Dan picks up his T-shirt from the back of a chair and slips it on. There's a logo of a computer screen with a digitized bride and groom on the front, and when I look closer, I can see the words 'Game Over' printed underneath.

I sigh. 'Yes, Dan. Very funny.'

'Wait till you see yours,' he says, then catches sight of my expression. 'What's the matter with you?'

'What do you think?'

Dan rolls his eyes. 'Not this "Sam's having an affair" bollocks again?'

'I can't help it. I mean, I've tried to convince myself she's not, but despite what she said last night, I still can't quite let it go.'

'What about the *Cosmo* quiz?' he says, sounding a little hurt.

'I think you've answered your own question there. Besides, I need some proof.'

'Proof that she's *not* up to anything? That's a little bit harder to get than the other way round. Unless . . .'

'Unless what?'

'Unless you've got a friend who's a genius.'

The feeling of mild panic returns suddenly, and it's a little less mild this time, particularly because Dan's hopping around like he needs the toilet.

'What have you been up to?' I say, regarding him suspiciously.

'Nothing,' says Dan, before breaking into a huge grin, 'apart from finding a way to solve all of your problems.'

'Really? How?'

'I had a suspicion that you weren't convinced. So I've come up with a plan for you to put Sam and this mystery bloke to bed once and for all.'

'Yet again, thanks for the imagery, Dan.'

'Sorry.' He takes me by the shoulders and guides me into his front room. 'But honestly, it's foolproof.'

'What is?'

'My idea.'

'It would have to be if you came up with it,' I say, under my breath. Fortunately, he doesn't hear me.

'Wait there.'

As Dan scampers excitedly off into his bedroom, I sit down heavily on the couch, dreading what's coming next. I've seen Dan's 'foolproof' ideas before, and they usually end up either injuring me, costing me money, or sometimes both.

'Ta-da!'

Dan leaps back in through the doorway, holding what looks like a deflated inflatable woman. Or what's left of one, anyway.

'Er . . .'

'What did I tell you?' says Dan, holding it out towards me, though I'm somewhat reluctant to take it from him, especially if it is what I think it is. 'Genius!'

'I'm not sure I want to touch it.'

'Don't be such a wuss,' he says, lobbing it at me, so I've got no option but to catch it. 'It's particularly lifelike, don't you think? And it was expensive. Made in Scandinavia. Besides, I've only used it a couple of times.'

I drop it onto the cushion next to me in revulsion. 'Thanks for the thought, but I don't see how one of your sloppy-seconds sex-toys is going to help me forget about Sam and her fancy man.'

Dan stares at me for a second, then bursts out laughing. 'No, you muppet. It's a fat suit.'

'A . . . Fat suit?'

Dan does an impression of one of those nodding dogs you see in the back of an old person's car. 'It was made for me for that pilot show we did called *Fat Chance*. I'd put it on and go out on the pull, expecting to be blown off by every woman I spoke to. Trouble was, it turned out that even an overweight Dan Davis was a hit with the lay-deez. So we had to shelve it. They let me keep the suit, though.'

I shake my head, trying not to laugh at the fact that Dan is talking about himself in the third person. 'So how does you dressing up in a fat suit help me, exactly?'

Dan sits down next to me, careful to avoid the pile of latex. 'I don't wear it, Ed. You do.'

'Huh?'

'It's a brilliant plan. Slip this on, wear some baggy clothes, a cap and dark glasses, and you can follow Sam everywhere. Even sit next to her, and she won't be able to tell it's you. Then you can check up on what she's been doing. Sorted.'

As Dan leans smugly back on the sofa, stroking the fat suit in a slightly pervy way, I stare at him in disbelief. 'I know you've got the memory of a goldfish – and one with Alzheimer's – but let's see if you can remember something.'

'Okay. Shoot.'

'If I had a gun, it would be an act of kindness. Do you

remember the circumstances surrounding how I first met Sam?'

Dan nods. 'Of course I do. It was in a café, wasn't it?'

I look at my watch, conscious that this might take a while. 'No, not where, Dan. How.'

He thinks for a moment. 'Er, *Yellow Pages*?'

I nod encouragingly. 'And why had I called her, exactly?'

Dan grins. 'That's easy. Jane had left you because you'd let yourself go, and you misguidedly decided to try and win her back.'

'Correct again,' I say, ignoring his 'misguidedly' jibe. 'And why was that?'

'Why had Jane left you?' Dan scratches his head. 'Where do you want me to start?'

'No, Dan. I mean, what specific aspect of my "letting myself go" did I employ Sam to help me with?'

He frowns. 'Well, you were pretty out of shape, for one thing.'

'Aha,' I say. 'Or rather, nearly. But you're close with shape.'

'Er . . .'

'Fat, Dan. I was fat.'

'Oh yeah.' Dan chuckles. 'You were, weren't you? A right porker.'

'So,' I say, realizing I'm going to have to lead him by the hand through this. 'Sam met me when I was . . .'

'Fat?'

'Exactly. And now, two years later, which for those of

us with memories that actually work beyond the previous day isn't actually that long, you're suggesting the ideal disguise for me in order for Sam not to be able to recognize me is to make myself look . . .'

'Fat.' Dan looks pleased with himself, as if he's just won a cuddly toy at the funfair, then he frowns. 'Ah.'

'Exactly. So it's not such a brilliant plan, is it?'

'Of course it is. I mean, there's no way Sam's going to think it's actually you, is it?' he says, back-pedalling furiously. 'Maybe just someone who looks like you used to look. And what's she going to do? Go across to them and tell them they look like her fiancé once did?'

'She might. Especially if she wants to offer them a business card.'

'All right, then. If you won't wear it to go and check up on Sam, it'll at least stop any future Jane advances.'

'How so?'

'Put it on and go and see her. She'll think you've got fat again, and that'll drive her away once and for all. I tell you, it's a no-brainer.'

'You mean the person who came up with that plan is. Dan, of all the ridiculous ideas you've ever had, this . . .'

His face falls. 'Aren't you at least going to try it on?'

'What for?'

'For me?' he asks, feebly. 'There's a T-shirt and some tracksuit bottoms on the bed that should fit you. I bought them specially.'

I try to ignore how creepy this sounds but, by the look of things, he's actually gone to a bit of an effort, and the last thing I want is for him to be in a mood for the rest of the evening.

'Okay.'

'Excellent.' Dan rubs his hands together. 'Give it a go, and if it really is no good, we'll just have to think of something else.'

Realizing there's no other way out of this, I carry the fat suit into Dan's bedroom, strip down to my boxer shorts, and start to put it on. It feels a little strange once I've wriggled into the over-sized belly, but that's nothing compared to how it actually looks. Ignoring the fact that I've got a better haircut and I'm not wearing glasses, it's the old Edward. The old, fat Edward. Or rather, the old, fat, *single* Edward.

I stand there, staring at my reflection in the mirrored wardrobe, until Dan appears at the bedroom door.

'My God!'

'What?'

'I'm having the strangest feeling of, you know . . .'

'Déjà vu?'

'I knew you were going to say that!'

'Yes, very funny, Dan. Again.' I reach round and try and do up the flapping bits of latex behind my neck, which seem to secure the thing's many chins. 'Gah!'

'What's the matter?'

'I can't get it to fasten properly.'

'Hang on. There's a knack to it.' Dan picks up a felt-tip pen from the table next to his bed and walks round behind me.

'What's that for?'

'I just need it to mark the position of the straps,' he says, drawing what feels like a series of lines on my back, before pulling the fasteners together. 'There.'

As he stands back to admire his handiwork, I inspect my profile in the mirror, struggling a little to breathe. The fat suit feels a little snug, and more than a little warm, and I'm already starting to feel uncomfortable. 'Happy now?'

'Nearly.'

When I turn back round, I'm temporarily blinded by a number of rapid-fire flashes, and when my vision eventually clears, the first thing I see is a smirking Dan sitting on the bed, flicking through a selection of images on his digital camera.

'What the . . . ?'

'You mug. I never thought you'd fall for it.'

'Fall for . . .'

'I was worried about not having enough material for the speech, especially since you vetoed all the juicy Jane stuff, but now . . .' He holds the camera up as if it's a trophy. 'These will come in very handy, thank you.'

'Don't you dare!'

I make a lunge for it, but not surprisingly, the thirty pounds of latex means I'm not as agile as I thought, and I end up almost knocking over one of Dan's expensive hi-fi speakers.

'This isn't funny, Dan.'

'I'll be the judge of that,' he says, easily managing to keep away from my flailing attempt at a rugby tackle.

I try to reach round and undo the straps Dan's just tightened between my shoulder blades, but can't free myself, and eventually just flop down on the bed. 'Okay. I give up. How do I get out of it?'

Dan grins. 'You should have thought about that before you put it on.'

'I'm not joking, Dan. Take it off me.'

'Not until you've tried it out.'

'Dan, I . . .' I pause for a second, then suddenly leap towards him, but he jumps out of reach again.

'I'm serious. I'm not letting you out of it until you've given it a go. In public.'

'Dan!'

'See you at the pub,' he says, side-stepping past me in the doorway, before running out of the flat, me in not-so-close pursuit.

As the door slams shut behind him, I stop to catch my breath, then stare at my reflection in the hall mirror, still shocked that I really used to look this bad, then make an attempt to undo the fastenings again, but with no success – the fat suit's too tight to wriggle out of, and there's no way I can reach the fasteners without help.

I lumber round the flat for a minute or two trying to find a solution, but the only idea I come up with is to use one of Dan's dangerously sharp kitchen knives to cut myself out, but even though they're hardly ever used for cooking, I don't really want to damage either them or the suit. Or myself, for that matter.

With a resigned sigh, I walk back into the bedroom.

There's an extra-large T-shirt on the bed with the words 'Stag Night' printed on the front, although the 't' in 'stag' has been crossed out and replaced with an 'h'. Reluctantly I pull it on, followed by the tracksuit bottoms Dan's left for me, and then my shoes – tying my shoelaces with difficulty – and head for the pub.

7.22 p.m.
I'm in the Admiral Jim, doing my best to ignore Wendy's shrieks of laughter.

'Haven't you got somewhere else to be?' I say. Sam's having her hen night this evening too, and I'd been hoping Wendy might be long gone by now.

'What?' she says. 'And miss this? Besides, we're not meeting until eight.'

'Not in here, I hope?' I say, anxious for Sam not to see me like this.

'Don't worry, Edward. Some place in town. The G-Spot.'

'Never heard of it,' says Dan, who's using the pool table as a barrier to prevent me getting at him.

Wendy laughs. 'You and most men, unfortunately.'

I manage a couple more circuits of the pool table after Dan, then give up, and collapse onto the nearest chair, which almost collapses itself.

'Why did they make it so heavy?'

Dan shrugs. 'Authenticity, I suppose. And given the amount you're sweating, it obviously works.'

'I can't wear it for the rest of the evening.'

'Why not? You wanted me to make sure nothing happened to you, and trust me, as long as you look like that, nothing will.'

'But . . .'

'Besides,' says Dan. 'You remember you told me you wished you could be a bigger person where Sam's affair is concerned?'

'Yes? So what?'

Dan grins, picks up a pool cue, leans over the table, and pokes me in the stomach with it. 'Well, now's your chance.'

9.31 p.m.

I'm sitting in a booth in the Honey Club, one of the many nightclubs just off Brighton seafront. We've just come from the lap-dancing bar round the corner, where Candy and Bambi were certainly as impressive as Dan had made out, even though their attempts to give me a lap dance were somewhat thwarted by the fact that wearing the fat suit, I don't actually seem to have a lap. What was also thwarted was Dan's attempt to chat Candy up, although that was self-inflicted, thanks to his comment about who had the most silicone: me or the two of them, and by 'two of them' I think he was just referring to Candy – which is why we're sitting here somewhat ahead of schedule.

It's still quite early, so there aren't that many people in the club, which is just as well given how self-conscious I'm feeling about how I look. At least I don't have a long embarrassing journey home later, given the rooms at the Grand we've had the good sense to check in to on the way here. I'd have been quite happy to go home to Sam, but Dan's observation that being sick over your fiancée a week before your wedding probably wasn't the smartest of moves convinced me that the hotel option made more sense.

I check the clock on the wall for about the fiftieth time. Dan's been gone for the best part of ten minutes, and I'm peering through the gloom, trying to ignore all the people pointing in my direction and laughing, when I spot him on his way back from the bar. He's carrying two bottles of beer, but when I try and take one from him, he slaps my hand away.

'What are you doing?' he says, squeezing himself into the booth.

I shrug, which sends a ripple effect down through my belly. 'I thought one of those might be for me.'

'Nah. They're both for me. Courtesy of Kelly and Kate over there.' He waves at two women at the bar. 'They're big fans, apparently. And they both wanted to buy me a drink. How could I refuse?'

'Would you like to give me one?'

He smirks. 'Funnily enough, that's just what Kelly said. But I can't. Give you one, I mean. Kelly, on the other hand . . .'

'Dan, please. And why ever not?'

'Don't you think it would be a little bit rude? To give one of them away to you? Seeing as they were presents. Anyway.' Dan nods towards the half-full pint glass on the table in front of me. 'I was about to make a toast.'

'Oh. Right.' I pick my glass up. 'To the end of an era, you mean?'

'Oh,' says Dan, following it with a longer, 'Ohhhh.'

'What?'

'It's just that it *is* the end of an era, isn't it?'

I nod, happily. 'My single life.'

'Not that, dummy. You and me. No more just the two of us. Now that you've got the old ball-and-chain, I mean.'

'What are you talking about?'

'Things change, don't they, when you're married.'

'Not necessarily. Sam and I will still be the same people . . .'

'No. I'm talking about between you and me.' Dan puts both beer bottles down in front of him. 'Before you know it, you'll be preferring nights at home with her indoors to a drink at the Admiral Jim with your old mate Dan. And that's fine, really it is. So don't worry about me . . .'

'Stop being ridiculous,' I say. 'I already prefer nights in with Sam to nights out with you, but we still see each other, don't we? Besides, I've been in one sort of relationship or another pretty much all the time you've known me. Things are hardly going to change between us just because I'm married.'

'You say that now. But wait till the kids come along.

Then the chances of you escaping for a swift one are going to be pretty much zero.'

'You can still come round. You know where we live. And besides, kids will be ages away. And even then, I'm sure they'll love their uncle Dan.'

'Uncle Dan.' He brightens a little. 'They will, won't they?'

'So, tell me something,' I say, feeling like I'm about to give him a 'facts of life' talking to. 'Has this made you think about your own situation at all?'

Dan stares morosely at his beer bottles, as if he can't decide which one to have first, then eventually picks the left-hand one. 'That's what I'm trying to say. You're gaining a wife, but for me, it's like I'm losing a best friend.'

'No, I mean your own situation where women are concerned.'

He glances over at Kelly and Kate, possibly trying to make the same decision as he's just done with his drinks. 'I still like them, if that's what you mean.'

'In terms of you meeting someone. Long term. And maybe settling down yourself.'

'Me?' Dan starts to do a little dance under the table, as if to indicate how footloose and fancy free he is, then stops when he sees I'm being serious. 'With who?'

'Whom.'

Dan frowns. 'She some foreign bird, is she?'

'Who?'

'Hoom. Or whatever you said.'

'Never mind. But seriously, how are you finding the current dating scene?'

He shrugs. 'Fairly quiet, actually.'

'Really?'

'Of course not,' says Dan. 'I'm still having to beat them off with a shitty stick. But there's no one, you know . . .'

'Special.'

As usual, Dan mimes sticking his fingers down his throat at the mention of that word. 'No. So I hope you've lined up someone tasty for me at the wedding.'

As he picks the other beer bottle up and takes a swig, I decide now might be a good time to impart a certain snippet of information.

'Well, as a matter of fact, I have.'

'Really?' Dan stops, mid-swig. 'Who?'

'Polly. I got her RSVP this morning.'

'What about the small matter of what's-his-name?'

'Steve? She's not bringing him.'

'Why not?'

I decide to play my trump card. 'Why would she want to bring someone she's not seeing any more?' I say, using it as a diversionary tactic to snatch Dan's other beer from the table and quickly pour some lager into my glass.

'I'm sorry?' Dan slams his bottle down in shock, nearly missing the edge of the table. 'She's single?'

'I believe so.'

'So she's coming on her own?'

'Yup.'

'You have told her I'll be there?' he says, eyeing me suspiciously.

'I think she'll have assumed that already,' I say, enjoying seeing Dan a little nervous where a woman is concerned.

'And yet, she's still coming . . .' Dan's face goes through a range of expressions, as if he's trying to work out the flavour of a boiled sweet. 'Although that might be because she feels she can't miss your wedding,' he says, eventually. 'Rather than because she wants me back.'

'I'd say that's spot on,' I say, remembering the size of Dan's ego, and realizing what an effort that admission must have been for him. 'But what would you do if she did?'

'Did what?'

'Want you back.'

He picks his beer up and starts to pick distractedly at the label. 'That's hardly likely, is it?'

'Why not? It might be the reason she's coming.'

'Fuck,' says Dan. 'Now I'm going to be spending the whole time worrying about Polly.'

'No you're not,' I correct him. 'You're actually going to be spending the whole time worrying about me and Sam, and ensuring everything goes well from our point of view. Then and only then can you go and do what you have to do with Polly.'

'That's not very fair, is it?' He sniffs.

'Oh, I'm sorry, Dan. I forgot that the only reason Sam and I were getting married was so we could set you up with your ex-girlfriend again.'

He glares at me. 'It's all right for you. You're going to be going to bed next Saturday as a married man, and with the surest guarantee of a shag that evening that anyone could ever have. Me? I'll be doing the home-alone thing. And I'm not referring to that Macaulay Thingummy film. That's going to make for one fun evening, I can tell you.'

'Or, you could look at it this way,' I say. 'Polly finished with you . . .'

'Keep your voice down,' hisses Dan.

'Sorry. You and Polly split up because she thought you were immature. Too self-centred. Too selfish. Well, this is your big chance to show her you've changed.'

After the few seconds it takes to sink in, Dan looks at me as if I'm a genius. 'It is, isn't it?' he says before frowning suddenly. 'How, exactly?'

'By being the perfect best man,' I say. 'By running the show. By giving the world's best speech. By making sure everything goes smoothly, and that everyone – especially Polly – has a great time. That way, she can't help but be won over. Then you can decide how you really feel about her.'

A change comes over Dan's face. 'I can, can't I?'

'Yup.'

'Excellent,' says Dan, draining the last of the beer he's holding, then doing the same with the bottle on the table. 'In fact, that calls for a drink.'

I stare at him for a second or two before realizing that – as usual – that's my cue.

10.18 p.m.

When I get back from the bar and deposit a bottle of beer on the table in front of him, Dan seems not to notice, possibly because he's engrossed in blowing over the top of the one he's currently halfway through drinking, as if he's just discovered it makes a sound when he does.

'What are you so lost in thought about?'

'Me?' Dan drinks a bit more, then blows again, and seems delighted that the note has changed. 'Oh, nothing. Well, something, actually.'

'Come on. Penny for them.'

'Cheapskate.' He blows a couple more times, then puts his bottle down before I can snatch it away from him. 'I was just thinking about this marriage lark.'

'What about it?' I say, wishing he'd stop referring to it as a lark. Particularly because it's been feeling like anything but.

'You know. And why some people do it and some don't. I mean, I know why they do *it*, but marriage. Why they do *that*.'

'Thank you for clarifying that for me, Dan.'

'You're welcome. So, come on then.'

'Come on then what?'

'It's just that . . . I mean, do you think some people just aren't cut out for it? Ever, I mean?'

'You're talking about you, right?'

Dan drains the last of his beer. 'Yeah. Because I can't see the point of giving all this up,' he says, nodding over to where Kelly and Kate are still watching him from the bar, 'just so one woman can take up permanent residence in Davis Villas.'

Pushing my rubber belly to one side, I lean over and move Dan's empty bottle out of arm's reach to stop him from blowing into it again. 'Let me explain something to you. You seem intent on seeing marriage as bad, because you think it'll restrict you from doing whatever – or rather, whoever – you want. For the rest of us – us *normal* people – we want to get married because we've found someone we think it's worth giving all that up for.' As I let what I've said swim through the beer-soaked synapses towards Dan's brain, I hope, *pray*, he'll finally realize that this person needs to be someone who can see through all this celebrity bollocks. Someone who's unaffected by all the glitz and glamour surrounding him. Someone who can help him keep his feet on the ground. And more than ever, I'm convinced it needs to be someone he was interested in before all this started. Someone who he's interested in more than all of it. Someone whose name begins with a 'P', perhaps. And maybe now's the perfect time, given his current unemployed state. 'And they're out there, Dan. Believe me. Even for you.'

'So it's not that I'll never meet the right person?'

'Not at all. Maybe you have already, but you weren't ready for her at the time. But you'll recognize her when she comes,' I say, instantly regretting my choice of words as Dan can't help but snigger.

He shakes his head slowly. 'I mean, I just can't see it. It's like becoming a vegetarian.'

'What is?'

'Me getting married.'

'Huh?'

'You know. Asking me to give up meat. Because I really like meat. And I don't think I could do it.'

'Yes, you could. You just need the motivation.'

'Yeah, but' – Dan searches for an example – 'people usually become vegetarians because they've visited an abattoir, or seen some programme about how badly animals are treated, not because they suddenly decide they like salad so much that they're going to stop eating bacon sandwiches ever again.'

'Maybe you need to visit an abattoir, then. Or start sampling some tastier vegetarian meals, as opposed to this junk food you seem to enjoy . . .'

Dan grins. 'Eating?'

'Or maybe you need to look for that one particularly tasty carrot. Let's face it, if you're looking for a carrot, then they don't come any tastier than Polly.'

There's a pause, and then: 'You mean "carrot" as in "incentive", right?'

'Right, Dan.'

'Maybe, Ed,' he says. 'But I'll tell you. I'm only going to give up meat when *I* decide to.'

'Which might be sooner than you think,' I say, pulling at the neck of the fat suit, which is starting to smell a little suspect.

Not unlike some of Dan's excuses.

12.13 a.m.

I've not often seen Dan under the influence. Normally
when we're out for the evening he likes to stay sober, just
in case he's asked to perform later – and I don't mean in
the acting sense. This evening, however, he's downing his
beer like it's water, which is actually what I feel like drinking, given how much the fat suit is making me sweat.

After what seems like his fiftieth trip to the toilets, and
without question his longest one, so much so that I start
to wonder whether he's actually gone home, Dan sidles
up to me, a lop-sided grin on his face.

'Edward, Edward, Edward,' he says, putting an arm
round my shoulders and handing me a pint glass full of
some strange concoction.

'Dan, Dan, Dan.'

'Dan, Dan–Dan Dan Dan Dan,' he replies, to the *Match
of the Day* tune, then collapses against me in a fit of giggles.

'What's this?' I say, holding the glass up to the light and
peering at the contents, which seem to be settling into
differently coloured layers.

'S'adrink.'

'Really?'

Dan nods. 'S'called a Minesweeper.'

'And what's in it?' I ask, sniffing it suspiciously.

'What isn't in it?'

'Ah. Well, thanks,' I say, not too drunk to be unaware
of the significance of Dan actually buying me a drink.
And what looks like an expensive one too.

'Cheers,' says Dan, picking up his beer bottle and clinking it against my glass, which I take a tentative sip from, although I'm not quite able to identify the flavour.

He flops onto the sofa, beckoning for me to sit down next to him. 'Ed,' he says, putting his hand on my knee and giving it a squeeze, 'can I tell you something?'

'Anything,' I reply, picking his hand up and putting it on his own leg. 'As long as it's not "I love you". Which would still be okay, of course.'

'Nope. S'nothing like that.'

'Well, what, then?' I say, when he doesn't enlighten me, but instead stares wistfully towards Kelly and Kate, who are still standing gamely at the bar trying to make eye contact with him. Unfortunately, given the fact that he can hardly focus on the beer bottle in front of him, it doesn't seem to be working.

'You're my best friend,' he says, or rather, slurs, 'and shall I tell you why that is?'

I look at his blurry expression, and decide not to suggest that it's because he's slept with all his other male friends' girlfriends, so they're not speaking to him any more.

'Please do.'

'Because you've always been there for me.'

I put on a miserable expression. 'So it's not because you like me or anything?'

'There's that too, obviously. Obviously!' he adds, getting louder. 'Keep your chins up. But back when I was having trouble. With, you know . . .'

'Someone's husband? Your eleven-plus?'

'The "P" word.'

'Your penis?'

'No! I've never had trouble with my penis,' he almost shouts, which turns out to be the final straw for Kelly and Kate, who pick up their drinks and walk off to the other end of the club.

'Though it's got you into trouble once or twice. More than once or twice, in fact.'

'Polly,' he stage-whispers, so loudly that Polly can probably hear him, and she doesn't even live in Brighton.

'Oh. Right.'

'Anyway. As I was saying. And that's what's most important. The "L" word.'

'Love?' I say, not sure I want to play this game again.

'No,' says Dan. 'Loyalty. And that's why I'd never sleep with Sam.'

'Apart from the fact that she'd knock your block off if you tried.'

'Well, there's that, too. But that's what it's all about, friendship, loyalty.' He puts his arm around my shoulders. 'I mean. If you don't have that and trust, then what have you got?'

I stare at him for a few seconds before realizing he's waiting for an answer.

'Nothing?'

'Nothing. Thassright. And besides,' he says. 'I owe you.'

'What for?'

'Everything. Y'know. My career.'

I'm starting to wonder just how drunk he is. Forgetting the fact that his career seems to be in the toilet at the moment, normally Dan's ego doesn't allow him to attribute any of his success to anything apart from his talent and his looks. And not necessarily in that order.

'No you don't, Dan.'

'Yes I do,' he insists, rather loudly. 'If you hadn't taken me to that party and introduced me to that producer . . .'

This is true, in a way. Although by 'introduced me to', Dan really means 'got drunk and spilled your drink down her top, which gave me the perfect opportunity to chat her up'.

'Okay, then. Yes you do.'

Dan removes his arm from my shoulders and swivels round to face me. 'So you admit it? S'your fault that Polly and I split up.'

'I'm sorry?'

'So you should be.'

'No, Dan. I'm not actually sorry. I mean, how can that possibly be my fault?'

He jabs a finger into my chest. 'Because I never would have split up with her if it hadn't been for this TV career of mine.'

'Which you owe all to me?'

'Exactly.'

For a moment, I'm sure he's joking, but then I remember one thing about Dan getting drunk, and it's that he usually gets all morose. Normally, I'd let it pass – his logic is hard enough to follow at the best of times, let alone when it's been affected by the best part of a crate of lager – but even given the amount I've had to drink I can see where this is going.

'But that's like me saying that if it wasn't for you not telling me I was getting fat, I never would have lost Jane.'

'S'actly,' says Dan. 'And be loved-up with Sam. For which you owe me big time.'

'You're right,' I say, as sarcastically as I can manage. 'It *is* all my fault. So what can I do to put it right?'

Dan peers intently at me, as if he's willing his eyes to focus, then slaps himself round the face. Twice.

'Help me get her back, of course.'

'What? But I thought you said—'

'Never mind what I said,' he says, suddenly lucid. 'I've come to realize, watching you go through all this wedding bollocks, that this is what I want too. To settle down. To be with someone I love, and who loves me. And not just for this,' he adds, pointing both index fingers at his face.

'Blimey. You must be drunk.'

'Maybe,' says Dan. 'But that doesn't mean I'm not serious. So will you help me or not?'

'Of course I will. But what are you going to do?'

'What you did with Jane. Except I've already done it.'

'Huh?'

'Jane said you were fat, so you lost weight. Polly didn't like what my TV career stood for – now I don't have one. Violas!'

'Voilà, Dan.'

'Whatever.' He taps the side of his nose with his index finger. 'So I'm going to make her an offer she can't refuse.'

I laugh. 'There's a "head in her bed" joke in there somewhere.'

Dan smiles at my reference to *The Godfather*. It's one of his favourite films. Mind you, so is *Bedknobs and Broomsticks*; though not the Disney version, but one set in a house full of Swedish women.

I hold my glass up. 'Well, here's to you and Polly.'

'To me and Polly,' says Dan, raising his bottle towards me. 'And remember. This is supposed to be a stag night.'

'So?'

'So get that down you in one, you big girl's blouse. Assuming . . .'

'Assuming what?'

'That you've got the stomach for it,' says Dan, before collapsing in a fit of giggles.

I smile politely back at him, lift my glass to my lips, and swallow the strange-tasting concoction as instructed, then . . . Well, that's the last thing I remember.

Unfortunately.

Sunday, 19 April

8.31 a.m.
When I wake up, or rather, when I'm woken up by the sound of the bedroom door shutting – Sam doing her best to leave quietly for work again, I imagine – it takes me a few seconds to pluck up the courage to open my eyes. The room's pitch-black, which is a relief as my head is throbbing, but as I reach down to pull the covers back over me with the intention of trying to sleep off as much of this hangover as I can, it's not my duvet I feel, but some unfamiliar sheet-and-blanket combination.

I sit up with a start, which makes my head hurt even more, and fumble for the light switch next to the headboard, but when I can't find it, have to haul myself out of bed and feel my way along the wall until I reach what feels like a pair of curtains, which I throw open, blinking in the sudden glare. And while I'm initially concerned that I don't know where I am, what's even more worrying than the unfamiliar surroundings is the imprint in the other pillow. Because if this isn't my bedroom, then that sure as hell wasn't made by Sam. Plus, as my watch tells me, when I eventually manage to focus on it, it's Sunday. Sam doesn't work on Sundays.

I look anxiously around the room for clues, almost having a heart attack when I spot what appears to be a dead body slumped in the armchair in the corner, only to realize it's last night's discarded fat suit. Given the horrible carpet and the strange curtains hanging over the window, I'm probably in a hotel room – albeit a spinning one – but it's not until I catch sight of the 'Grand Hotel' stationery on the desk next to the door I remember Dan and I were due to stay here last night.

I lower myself gingerly onto the bed and get back under the covers, hoping, *praying*, that my mystery bed-fellow was Dan, having bunked up with me because he'd forgotten his key or, more likely, his room number. Because as horrible as that would have been, it's way preferable to the alternative, which is that I've spent the night with another woman. After all, someone must have helped me out of the fat suit. I only hope they stopped there.

I take some comfort in the fact that I'm still wearing my boxer shorts, but as I think about it, I'm not sure what that proves. I could have put them on after the event, I suppose. Assuming there *was* an event.

There's a glass of water on the bedside table, which I pick up, gulping the contents down thirstily, only to discover as they slide jaggedly down my throat that my contact lenses are in there. As the adrenalin buzz fades and my hangover kicks back in with a vengeance, there's a gentle knocking on the door, so I swivel round and place my feet carefully on the floor, still not a hundred per cent sure which direction is up, and make my way unsteadily to answer it.

'God, you look rough,' says a ridiculously chirpy Dan.

'Please tell me you've just been down for breakfast and you're coming back in?'

'What?' Dan shudders, then pushes in past me and sits on the edge of the bed. 'Why would I be doing that when I've got, er . . . Well, her name's not that important. But she's sleeping it off in my room. Across the hall.'

'Sleeping what off?'

Dan grins. 'Me.'

'Where on earth did you meet her? At the club?'

'Nope. Back here. I was flicking through the room-service brochure and there was a number to call if you wanted someone to turn down your bed. Well, I can't remember the last time that happened to me, so I kind of took it as a challenge . . .' He grins again. 'Anyway, what happened to you last night? I was off having a dance with some tall chick, and next thing I knew, you'd gone.'

'And you didn't think to come and look for me?'

'No. I mean, what trouble could you have gotten into wearing that?' he says, walking over to the chair and giving the fat suit a poke, as if to check it's dead. 'It's like walking around wearing bubble wrap. And I knew you wouldn't be able to get it off.'

'How did I, then?'

'Pardon?'

'How did I get it off?'

Dan stares at the discarded layer of latex, then back at me. 'You crafty old . . .'

'Dan, this isn't something to be proud of. I'm getting married in a week, and I've only gone and slept with someone else.' I collapse backwards on the bed and fold my arms over my eyes. 'It's a disaster.'

'Hold your horses,' says Dan. 'How do you know you slept with anyone?'

'Hello?' I say, nodding towards the fat suit, then jabbing a thumb towards the imprint in the pillow next to mine. 'And I even heard her leave.'

Dan walks over and examines the pillow. 'That's shocking,' he says. 'And without so much as a thank you.'

I lift my head up and look at him in disbelief, wondering whether he knows that's his normal behaviour. 'That's not what I meant.'

'How do you know you had sex with her? Assuming it *was* a her.'

'Very funny, Dan,' I say, dismissing this immediately. While I can't remember anything about last night, surely I'd remember, well, *that*.

'Okay. Let's assume it *was* a girl. Have you checked for physical signs?'

'Huh?'

'You know, *marks*. And I don't mean out of ten carved into the headboard.'

I stand up tentatively. 'What sort of marks?' I say,

pulling the elastic out at the front of my boxer shorts and peering down at my groin.

'Not there, dummy. Scratches on your back, for example. Or on your front.'

'On my front?'

Dan nods. 'Yup. She might have been trying to push you off.'

I march over to the mirror above the desk in the corner to inspect my torso. So far so good – there are no love-bites, or scratches on my front. But when I spin around to inspect my back, I almost fall over in shock: written right across my shoulder blades – and in big blue letters – are what look like the number '3', followed by a backward 'N', then the letters 'A' and 'L', which, when my addled brain manages to work out the mirror image, seems to say 'Jane'. I can't believe it. A week to go till my wedding, and I've gone and got a tattoo of my ex-girl-friend's name across my back.

'Dan . . . what have you done?' I say, falling into the nearby chair in shock, my legs unable to keep me upright. But instead of at least trying to be sympathetic, Dan just bursts out laughing. Very loudly.

I glare up at him as he leans against the wall, struggling for breath. 'You bastard! How could you let me do this? You were supposed to look after me.'

'I'm sorry, Ed,' he gasps. 'Your face . . .'

'My face is the least of my worries,' I say, fighting a sudden urge to punch him in his. 'What am I going to do?'

'Well,' says Dan, eventually regaining his composure, 'you could try a bit of soap and water for a start.'

'What?'

'It's a joke tattoo. Have you noticed how it doesn't hurt?'

'Given the amount I evidently drank last night, everything hurts.'

I get up slowly from the chair and back gingerly towards the mirror. Sure enough, when I lick my finger and reach round under my armpit to rub the edge of the 'J', it starts to come off.

'"I just need to mark the position of the straps,"' says Dan, in a funny voice, before bursting out laughing again. 'Sucker.'

I suppose I might find this funny under different circumstances. But the way I'm feeling at the moment, even a real tattoo of my ex-girlfriend's name would be easier to deal with than what I suspect might have happened.

'Dan, please. Be serious for a moment. This is important.'

He walks over to the bathroom door and pushes it open. 'Chill, Ed. Innocent till proven guilty, remember? Now, how about you wake yourself up with a shower, and I'll meet you down at breakfast. See if we can't work out what really happened.'

8.45 a.m.

I race through the shower – although taking extra care to scrub all traces of Jane's name off my back with one of the hotel's towels – grateful that at least Dan didn't use permanent marker, then pull on last night's clothes, which look somewhat ridiculous now I'm not wearing the fat suit, and head downstairs to breakfast. Dan's nabbed us a table by the window, so I head across the room to join him, moving my chair round to face the room, as the brightness coming from outside is still a little painful.

'So,' I say, once I've downed three double espressos, and force-fed Dan a triple-chocolate muffin in the hope that the sugar will kick-start his memory. 'Can you remember anything? Anything at all?'

He swallows a mouthful of coffee, then scrunches his face up in what looks like concentration, although it could be because he's accidentally shaken some salt into his cup. 'Well,' he says, leaning back and folding his arms behind his head, 'we were at the club. And you were absolutely off your head.'

'Thanks to that cocktail you bought me.'

'Bought you?'

'Yes, you know. You handed me that pint glass and made me down it in one.' I suddenly feel queasy at the memory. 'What was it called? A Minesweeper, or something.'

Dan lets out a short laugh. 'Mate, a Minesweeper isn't a cocktail.'

'It isn't?'

'Nah. It's what you do when you've run out of money at the end of the evening. You just do a quick sweep of the club, and whenever you see any abandoned glasses that have something left in them you shout "mine" – hence the name – and collect them up. Then you pour them all into one pint glass, and get some poor sap to drink it.'

My stomach lurches again. 'That's disgusting.'

'You were keen enough last night.'

I rest my elbows on the table and put my head in my hands. 'It's no wonder I feel so lousy this morning. What happened then?'

'I dunno,' he says, buttering a triangle of toast and cramming it into his mouth. 'It's all a bit of a blur, to be honest. Like I say, I was having a dance, and when I got back to the table, you'd gone.'

'Gone?'

'Yup.'

'You were supposed to look after me. Not abandon me in some nightclub.'

'What are you? Five years old?'

'After that cocktail I was probably just as vulnerable. How could you?'

'Relax. It's not that big a deal.'

'Not that big a deal? How can . . .' I look around at the couples at the adjoining tables, and lower my voice. 'How can sleeping with another woman a week before I'm getting married not be that big a deal?'

Dan holds both palms out towards me. 'Calm down. What happens on tour, stays on tour, if you know what I mean. Sam doesn't ever have to find out. Remember, the first rule of night club is, you don't talk about what happened at the night club.' He makes the 'my lips are sealed' sign. 'Or something like that.'

'But . . . *I* know.'

'Do you?'

'Do I what?'

'Know for sure. If you actually had sex with someone.'

I pick up my fork and stab one of the sausages on my plate, reasoning that I might feel a little less ill if I eat some of the full English breakfast the waitress has just deposited in front of me. 'Dan, I woke up with another woman . . .'

'Person.'

'. . . *woman*, leaving my room, having evidently spent the night in my bed. That's a pretty strong clue, I'd say.'

'Yes, but you don't know if you actually did it, do you? I mean, you've had a shower, so we can't sniff the evidence.'

I put my sausage back down. 'Thanks, Dan.'

'What's the matter with you? If there's no evidence, nothing happened, did it?'

'There *is* evidence. The slamming door. Me mysteriously being out of the fat suit. The second impression in the pillow. *Something* happened. And I can't marry Sam if I've been unfaithful to her.'

'What?' Dan looks up from where he's been trying unsuccessfully to get the lid off a mini pot of strawberry jam. 'Why the hell not?'

I think about trying to explain, then realize that, given

Dan's views on fidelity, I'd probably be wasting my breath. Besides, with the wedding only a week away, I don't have the time. 'I just can't, all right?'

'Okay,' says Dan, putting his coffee cup down reluctantly. 'What do you remember exactly? From this morning, I mean.'

I shrug. 'I don't know. There was a bang, and then I woke up.'

He reaches across the table and nudges me. 'Which is pretty much your sex life from Sam's point of view.'

'A bang from the *door*. This isn't funny.'

'Sorry, mate. Just trying to lighten the mood a little.'

'I don't need the mood lightening. I want last night not to have happened.'

'Did you actually see anyone?'

'No.'

'Well, was there any *physical* evidence?'

I almost don't want to ask. 'What sort of physical evidence?'

'You know. A used condom. Or even a condom wrapper. Or a pair of knickers hanging from the light fitting.'

'Listen, all I know is that I was woken up this morning by the sound of someone leaving my room. And as far as I'm aware, I'd shared my bed with someone. A woman.'

Dan waits until the waitress has filled his coffee cup again, then lowers his voice. 'Listen, Ed, even if you did, you were pretty drunk last night.'

'I know. And that's what probably got me into trouble.'

'Or maybe not.'

'Huh?'

Dan picks up another triangle of toast, and starts buttering it carefully. 'I don't know about you, but I always have to be careful with the amount I have to drink if I want to be sure that big Dan can come out to play.'

'What are you talking about?'

'Just that, you know, you're worried you did something that quite frankly you might not have been able to *physically*. I mean, after a few beers, I'm sort of . . .' He reaches over with his fork and spears the end of my sausage, lifting it off my plate and twisting it so the free end's pointing downwards. 'Honestly, it's like trying to get a Slinky into a letterbox. And you had more than a few beers last night, if you get my meaning.'

I do, although I could also do without his rather graphic depiction. 'So? That doesn't alter the fact that I still spent the night with her.'

'Yes, but there's spending the night, and then . . .' He sticks his tongue into his cheek, and makes it bulge out. 'Spending the night.'

'Dan, the facts, as I see them, are these. At some point last night I must have picked up a woman and asked her back to my hotel room. Forgetting whether or not we had sex for the moment, I obviously wanted to, otherwise I wouldn't have invited her back with me. And like they say, it's the thought that counts.'

'Huh?'

'You know – not only might I have been unfaithful to Sam, but the fact that I wanted to is even more concerning. I mean, does it signify that I'm not as committed to her as I should be? Or was I subconsciously trying to punish her for my suspicions over the last few weeks?'

Dan makes a whooshing sound, ducking as he does so to indicate that what I've just said has gone completely over his head. 'If you want my advice, you'll just forget about it.'

'I can't just forget about it. It obviously means something.'

'It doesn't mean anything. Which is exactly what you're going to tell Sam if she ever finds out about it. Which she won't,' he adds, noticing my sudden look of alarm.

'That may be so. But *I* still need to find out if anything happened. For my own peace of mind, at least.'

Dan puts his coffee down, snatches my key card off the table, and stands up. 'Well, we better check your room, then.'

'Too late, Dan. She left ages ago.'

Dan stuffs a last piece of toast into his mouth, and then chugs back the rest of his coffee. 'No, dummy. Like I said earlier. For evidence.'

9.17 a.m.
We're on our way back up to my room, my head still swimming from both the possibility of what I might have done last night and the amount of alcohol I consumed. I'm having a job putting one foot in front of the

other, but as soon as the lift doors open, Dan starts sprinting down the corridor.

'What's wrong?' I say, breaking into a reluctant trot after him.

'The cleaner,' shouts Dan, pointing towards the far end of the corridor, where one of the hotel staff is pushing a trolley laden with cleaning supplies towards my room. 'Got to stop her tampering with the crime scene.'

'*Alleged* crime,' I say, catching up with him outside my room.

Dan rolls his eyes, then swipes the door open. 'Whatever. Are you sure it wasn't just the cleaner you heard?'

'Not unless she tried to make my bed from underneath the covers.'

Dan grins as he follows me into the room. 'That's my kind of room service. Right, you check the bedroom, I'll do the bathroom.'

'What am I looking for?'

'You've had sex before, right?'

'Of course.'

He makes a face. 'Then I don't have to spell it out for you.'

9.31 a.m.

I've checked everywhere I can think of, looking for anything I can think of, and there's nothing that suggests a night of passion. And even though Dan seems to think that proves something, as far as I'm concerned, all it proves is that there's no evidence. Not for the first time this morning, I sit heavily down on the end of the bed, feeling a little sick, although this time it's nothing to do with my hangover.

'Why the hell did we have to stay in a stupid hotel in the first place?'

'Because it was your stag night.'

'Christ, Dan,' I snap. I'm mad with him, even though I know it's – probably – not his fault. 'Why couldn't you have kept your bloody roving eye on me. I hope she was worth it?'

'Your mystery woman? Well, that's what we're trying to find . . .'

'Not mine, Dan. Yours. The one you abandoned me for.'

Dan stares blankly at me for a few seconds, then turns and races out through the door and across the corridor. 'Bollocks,' he says, fumbling with his key card, before eventually managing to get the light in the lock to turn green. As I follow him inside, he lets out a loud sigh. Even from the doorway, I can see the word 'Bastard' written in red lipstick on the mirror.

'What's all that about?'

'Beats me. Strange behaviour for someone who said she was a fan of the show.' Dan frowns. 'Though I'm guessing that maybe she isn't any more.'

'What did I tell you about sleeping with your groupies?'

Dan looks as if he's giving the question serious thought. 'That I should?' he says, hesitantly.

'So why are you a bastard?' I say, stopping myself from adding the words 'this' and 'time' to the end of that sentence. 'Or don't I want to know?'

'Er, that might be because I promised to bring her breakfast in bed. But then you appeared with this sob story of yours.' He shrugs, then escorts me out along the corridor, and back into the lift. 'Oh well, easy come, easy go. Mind you, it wasn't that easy come, given the amount I'd had to drink . . .'

'Dan, please,' I say stabbing the 'down' button. 'That's too much information.'

'Sorry.'

'So. Back to *me*,' I say, once we're sitting at our breakfast table again. 'What on earth do I tell Sam?'

'Nothing, of course.'

'But that's lying.'

'No it isn't. You don't actually know what happened, do you? So *anything* you say will be a lie.'

'Including nothing.'

'Not necessarily.'

'What am I going to do?' I say, as he waves the waitress over and orders another coffee. 'The minute I get home, Sam's going to be asking me if I had a good time. And the truth is? I don't know.'

Dan reaches over, picks up a leftover piece of toast from the rack on the empty table next door, and sniffs it. 'Okay,' he says, putting it down on his plate and buttering it. 'Turn out your pockets.'

'My pockets? What for?'

'Just do it, will you?'

'Dan, I . . .'

'We're trying to establish whether in fact you met someone last night.'

'She's hardly likely to be in my trouser pocket, is she?'

Dan puts down his butter knife and regards me earnestly across the table.

'Ed. Think this through. This is you we're talking about. Are you seriously telling me you picked someone up for no-strings sex last night?'

'For the millionth time, I don't know.'

'Okay, when was the last time you did something like that?'

'Well, it would be before Sam, obviously. And before Jane. And even Jane and I dated for a few weeks before we . . . you know. And then there was Sally before that. But we didn't even . . .'

Dan holds his hand up. 'Edward. As enjoyable as this trip down the rather short road you call your relationship history is, that's not what I'm getting at. Have you ever picked up a girl for no-strings sex?'

I sit and think for a few more seconds, before Dan can't help himself. 'No, you haven't, have you?' he says. 'So what makes you think you're going to have done it now?'

'I don't know,' I say, rocking anxiously back and forth in my chair. 'I was very drunk.'

'Yes, but . . .' Dan leans across the table, puts both hands on my shoulders, and holds me steady, as if trying to teach an uncoordinated five-year-old to ride a bike. 'Even so, are you telling me you'd have done it without even asking her name?'

'Well, no, obviously.'

'And what did I tell you, about meeting women in bars?'

'I wish it had been "don't".'

'About getting their details?' persists Dan.

'Er . . .' I think back to just after Jane had dumped me, when Dan was trying to pass on some of his pick-up skills. Those single days seem a long time ago – although I can't help worrying they may be reappearing soon. 'Something about getting their email addresses rather than their phone numbers?'

'Bingo,' says Dan, proudly. 'Because?'

'Because . . . that way you've usually got their name, instead of just a scrap of paper with just a number on it, which you can't possibly call, because you can't remember who you're calling.'

'Exactly. So turn out your pockets.'

I stand up and reach into each pocket in turn, but apart from some fluff, my keys, my wallet, and for some reason, a lime tic-tac, there's nothing.

'Maybe I lost it,' I suggest.

'Or maybe you didn't get it in the first place,' he says. 'In both senses of the phrase. Let's turn the clock back to last night.'

'I wish I could.'

'So, you were pretty drunk, right?'

My stomach starts to lurch. 'Don't remind me,' I say.

'And what do you get like when you get drunk?'

I pour myself a coffee from the jug the waitress has just deposited on the table, evidently tired of Dan's repeated requests for a refill. I can already feel this turning into rather a long morning. 'Well, happy, normally. And tired.'

'And do you normally walk round a nightclub and chat up women?'

'Well, seeing as I can't normally walk, no.'

Dan smirks. 'And do you think you could have maybe got up and danced, thus impressing whoever it was with your silky dance-floor moves?'

'Dan, I dance about as well as you do advanced mathematics even when I'm sober. Anyway, you're forgetting something.'

'What?'

'She might have come on to me.'

It takes Dan a good couple of minutes to stop laughing. 'Yeah, right,' he says, eventually.

'It could have happened.'

'Sure. There's you, probably sitting in a corner somewhere, drooling drunk, maybe even nodding off a little, and some woman came over to you and started chatting you up?'

'It's possible, I suppose,' I say, trying to ignore Dan's look of disbelief.

'While you were wearing that fat suit?'

'Some women like a . . . ahem, *larger* gentleman.'

'Tell me, Edward, when Jane left you, and you were *actually* that fat, did anyone ever chat you up?'

'No, but . . . I mean, it would have been a talking point, wouldn't it? Like going out wearing a loud shirt.'

'A talking point?' Dan pours himself a coffee and takes a sip. 'Only if the conversation started with the words "Who ate all the pies?" Either way, you must admit it's looking rather unlikely. And even if it is likely, it certainly doesn't seem you did it on purpose.'

'What difference does that make?'

'If a tree falls over in the forest, and there's no one there to hear it, does it make a sound?'

'What?'

Dan shrugs, as if he's lost his own thread again. 'And another thing. Why do you suppose she didn't stay?'

'What do you mean?'

'The next morning. I mean, I usually can't get rid of them. Why didn't she hang about until you woke up? Ignoring the obvious, of course.'

'You tell me,' I say, not wanting to ask Dan what 'the obvious' is: something rude about my sexual perform-ance, I'll bet. 'Maybe she was embarrassed. Maybe she had to get to work early.'

'On a Sunday? And besides, if you had an early start, you'd hardly be out clubbing until the small hours the previous evening.' He takes another mouthful of coffee. 'Come on, now. You've met someone in a nightclub, and you've gone back with them to their hotel room. Why wouldn't you stay the next morning? At least for breakfast.'

I shrug. 'Maybe she wanted to avoid that embarrassing can't-remember-your-name stuff. Maybe she had to get home.'

'What for?'

I shift awkwardly in my chair. 'I don't know, Dan. You've sneaked away often enough the next morning, so you tell me.'

'She could be married.'

'So?'

'So in that case your secret's safe. Or maybe she knows you — which means you knew her — so she knew the two of you would be embarrassed the next morning. Maybe she knew you were getting married the following week. Maybe . . .' Dan stops talking and looks at me, an expression of horror on his face. 'You don't think it was . . . No. Forget I said it.'

'What?'

'Your mystery woman. There's a chance it could have been . . .' He shudders, and downs the rest of his coffee anxiously. 'No. The thought's too horrible to contemplate.'

'Who?' I grab him by the arm. 'You're scaring me now.'

'Think about it.' He puts his cup down on the table. 'Who's got the most to gain from this wedding not going ahead?'

'The caterers? I mean, they'll get to keep their deposit, while not having to pay for any of the food . . .'

'No, Ed, I mean who doesn't want you to actually get married?'

'Well, I've always had my suspicions that Sam's dad doesn't think I'm good enough for his daughter. But I can't see him doing something like this. You know, getting someone to sleep with me just so I— Ouch!' I reach down and rub my shin, where Dan's just kicked me under the table. 'What did you do that for?'

'Couldn't think of a quicker way to shut you up. Not Sam's dad. No one connected with Sam at all. In fact, someone a little closer to home.'

Maybe it's my hungover brain, but I'm having trouble making out what Dan's on about. Although to be honest, it's not that easy even when I haven't been drinking the night before.

'Er . . .'

'*Jane*, you idiot,' shouts Dan, loudly enough for an old lady at the next-door table to spill her tea.

'Jane?' I stare at him for a second, almost unable to comprehend what he's suggesting. 'My Jane?'

'No, Edward,' sighs Dan, 'I'm talking about Tarzan's girlfriend. Of course your Jane.'

'Why would she do something like this?'

'Why do you think? The old green-eyed monster.'

'Dan, please stop being rude about my ex-girlf—'

'*Jealousy*, Ed. Think about it.' Dan lowers his voice to a conspiratorial whisper. 'She was none too pleased when you told her about the engagement, right?'

'Well, no.'

'So she's obviously suffering from a severe case of the it-should-have-been-me's.'

'Maybe, but—'

'But nothing.' Dan nods smugly. 'There's motive for you, Sherlock.'

I stare at him, open-mouthed. 'So you're suggesting that Jane was so keen to stop this wedding from going ahead she somehow found out where my stag night was going to be, lay in wait in the club until I was too drunk to notice, then took me back to my hotel and' – I swallow hard – 'forced me to have sex with her?'

'Yup.'

'No, I can't believe that,' I say, shaking my head. 'Surely she's at the point now when she just wants me to be happy.'

'From what I could tell, Jane didn't want you to be happy for the ten years the two of you were together. Why do you think she'd want that now?'

'Fair point. But how on earth would she have found out where—' I stop mid-sentence, because Dan is suddenly looking very shifty. 'How could you have?'

He backs his chair away from me. 'Relax. You told me to tell Sam where we'd be, so she didn't rock up and spoil it. I thought it was only sensible to do the same thing with Jane.'

'Christ, Dan. Of all the stupid . . .' I count to ten in an attempt to calm down, but by the time I've got to twenty I still don't feel any better, so take a deep breath. And another. 'Anyway. Assuming she did turn up, I can't really believe that she'd be so . . .'

'Devious?' Dan makes a face. 'Why not? This is the

woman who moved out, took all her furniture with her, and headed off to Nepal without you knowing.'

'Maybe so, but . . .'

'And then she tried to split you and Sam up last year, don't forget. Even though you'd told her the two of you were perfectly happy.'

'But why would she resort to something like this?'

Dan narrows his eyes. 'Probably so she can wait until the "anyone here know any reason why these two should not be joined in holy matrimony" bit, and then burst in and say, "Yes, I do, because the groom slept with me on his stag night." She knows how honest you are, and you won't dare deny it. Job done, I think you'll find. Revenge for that little falling out she and Sam had last year, plus you single again.' Dan sits back in his chair. 'It's the perfect plan. In fact, you've got to admire her cunning.'

'Admire? That's – No, I can't believe it. Even of Jane.'

Dan gazes out of the window as a pretty girl jogs past along the seafront, his head nodding up and down to her rhythm. 'Why not? She knows what you're like when you get drunk, so she knew if she turned up and suggested the two of you go back to your hotel, you'd recognize her, but probably wouldn't see anything wrong with it. Plus you know how she likes to make a scene. Yup, the more I think about it, it's got Jane's fingerprints all over it.' He nods towards my groin. 'So to speak.'

My head is starting to swim again, and not because of

the second fry-up the waitress has just set down on the table in front of me, but because – what if Dan's right? What if this *is* all part of Jane's despicable plan to ruin the wedding?

'But surely she'll realize that's hardly going to win me back?'

'Why not? Even though you might think it'd be a cold day in hell before you'd go back out with her – which incidentally, is a pretty good description of how every day would be if you did – she might be banking on the fact that she'll be there to pick up the pieces – you know, provide you with familiar comfort after Sam's dumped you. At the very least she'll have stopped Sam from getting you. And you know what her competitive streak is like.'

'I'm sorry, Dan. I don't believe she'd do something as low as this.'

'Fine. But unless you want to spend the whole ceremony looking over your shoulder in case Jane appears, you'd better at least cross the possibility off your list.'

'And how do I do that, exactly? By calling her up and saying "Excuse me, Jane, but I was wondering whether we slept together last night, because if we did, I'd rather you didn't mention it to anyone." And what if it *was* her?' I add, my voice sounding more than a little panicky. 'What do I do then?'

'You could always have her killed.'

I look up at Dan, expecting to see him grinning, but he seems deadly serious.

'Don't be ridiculous.'

'Seriously. I know some people. Well, I know some people who know some people. Well, some people who *say* some people they know know some people . . . Anyway, that's not important. Two hundred quid, apparently. And they can make it look like an accident.' He leans over, and rests a hand on my arm. 'In fact, forget the money. It can be my gift to you.'

'You're seriously suggesting you have my ex-girlfriend bumped off as a wedding present?'

Dan shrugs. 'Why not? It's better than that crappy dinner set you want from Habitat. And a bit cheaper too, now I come to think of it.'

'Dan, stop. I just can't believe Jane would do such a thing.'

'I could have her killed anyway,' he says, staring out of the window absent-mindedly, perhaps hoping to spot the jogger on her way back. 'Just to make sure.'

'You are joking, right?'

Dan looks at me for half a second too long before replying. 'Of course.'

'So what do you expect me to do? Just call her up and confront her?'

'I like it,' says Dan, reaching into his pocket for his mobile. 'The direct approach.'

I take the phone, then immediately hand it back to him. Of course I can't call her and ask. Because while Jane might not be calculating enough to pull a stunt like this, she *is* calculating enough to use the fact that I think we might have slept together against me, which is why I need to find out exactly what did happen.

And fast.

11.38 a.m.
Sam's not in by the time I eventually get home, which to be honest, is something of a relief, because I'm so consumed with guilt, and so confused about how I could have let happen what I'm worried happened last night, that I don't have the faintest idea what I'm going to say to her.

And while the combination of how tired I'm feeling plus my massive hangover would normally send me scurrying straight off to bed, I know there's no way I'll be able to sleep with my mind spinning as much as it is. I need to work out a strategy – and quickly – although the best I can come up with as I anxiously pace round the flat is to try and achieve some kind of holding pattern by just not mentioning anything. And even though I've promised Sam that I'll never lie to her again, I manage to convince myself that – using Dan's favourite definition – not telling her anything isn't *actually* lying, but simply 'delaying the truth'. Whatever the truth is.

It's just gone midday, and I'm lying on the sofa with the curtains drawn, trying desperately to remember anything at all, when Sam's key in the lock makes me jump. She looks as though she's been out for a run, and for the first time in I don't know how long, that's exactly where I assume she's been, all thoughts of anything sinister she might have been up to over the past few weeks knocked into oblivion by my own behaviour.

'Look who's home,' she says, smiling at me as she shuts the front door softly behind her.

'Morning.'

'Afternoon, I think you'll find,' says Sam, tapping her watch, then walking over and kissing me gently on the top of my head. 'Bit of a hangover?'

'You could say that,' I mumble, adding, 'How was your hen night?' in a feeble attempt to change the subject.

'Good, thanks. Very civilized. Just a few drinks with the girls.' She fetches a glass of water and packet of paracetamol from the kitchen. 'So,' she says, sitting down next to me. 'Did you have fun?'

'I don't know,' I say, weakly. 'I think so.'

'What did you get up to?'

I take a deep breath, then let it out again. 'To tell you the truth, I can't really remember.'

As soon as the words leave my mouth I realize how implausible they sound and, as I help myself to a couple of paracetamol, I promise myself that at some point I will tell Sam exactly what happened – once I find out what that actually is. But instead of being suspicious, Sam actually looks a little relieved.

'No? Or can't you tell me?' she says, nudging me playfully in the ribs. 'You know, "What happens on tour stays on tour",' she adds, doing a passable impression of Dan.

My first instinct is to blurt everything out. But blurt what out? *I think I might have slept with someone last night, but I don't know who?* Where on earth does that conversation go?

'We just, you know, had a few drinks.'

'Quite a few, by the looks of you,' says Sam, resting a cool hand on my forehead. 'Why don't you go to bed?'

Because that's where all the trouble started. 'No, thanks. I'm probably better staying up and about.'

'And how is Dan feeling today?'

Guilty, hopefully. 'Oh, you know.'

'Well as long as you both had a good time,' says Sam, patting me on the hand, then jumping up from the sofa.

That's the trouble, I want to say, as she heads for the shower. I just don't know.

Monday, 20 April

8.31 a.m.

I'm in the Mini with Billy, driving very carefully along Marine Parade, still feeling a few traces of yesterday's hangover. Although there are a few more pressing things I should be doing, particularly given the weekend's events, today's the day he's due to move into the hostel and, as Sam reminded me first thing this morning, I promised I'd take him there.

He's a little nervous, despite having downed-in-one the can of Special Brew he requested when I offered to buy him breakfast, and is currently chain-smoking a series of suspicious-smelling cigarettes as we slowly weave our way through the usual morning traffic jam. I've asked him not to smoke in the car, so he's obligingly sticking his head out of the window, his roll-up clamped between his lips. This, of course, makes conversation awkward, although this is just as well, seeing as I haven't thought up an appropriate response to the gruff 'If it looks shit, then I'm coming to stay at your gaff instead' comment he greeted me with this morning.

Fortunately, the hostel's a pleasant-looking Regency-style building, just off Marine Parade, and as we pull into the car park, Billy widens his eyes appreciatively.

'You see?' I say, as I switch the engine off. 'You couldn't wish for a less shit-looking place.'

'Maybe.' Billy eyes the hostel suspiciously through the windscreen, then turns round to check that the black bin-bag full of his belongings is still on the back seat. ''S a nice car, this.'

'Thanks.'

'Must've set you back a bob or two?'

'Not really,' I say, conscious Billy's stalling for time. 'I bought it second hand, actually. One lady owner.'

Billy makes a face. 'Why'd they always say that as if it's a good thing?'

I smile back at him, then unbuckle my seatbelt, and climb out of the car. 'Come on. They're expecting you.'

Billy takes a last long drag on his cigarette, then flicks the butt out through the passenger window. 'What if I don't like it?'

'It's not prison, Billy,' I say, walking round and opening his door for him. 'You can come and go as you please.'

Billy laughs as he gets out of the car. 'Unlike what you're getting yourself into next Saturday.'

'Yes, that's very funny,' I say, flatly. 'Good one.'

'Cheer up, Ed. Only pulling yer leg, aren't I?'

Billy reaches into the back of the car and retrieves the bin-bag, then peers nervously at the hostel, but doesn't make a move towards it. We stand there for a second, and strangely, I find myself wondering whether this will be what it's like when – sorry, *if* – Sam and I have kids, and I'm taking them for their first day at school.

'Good luck,' I say, fighting the urge to give him some lunch money, then losing the fight rather quickly.

'You're a good bloke, Ed,' he says, staring at the twenty-pound note I've just stuffed into his hand. 'And ignore me. I reckon you've got a good one there with that Sam.'

'Thanks, Billy.'

He smiles his gap-toothed smile, then takes a step towards me, and for a second I'm worried he's going to hug me, but instead, he jabs a nicotine-stained finger into my chest. 'So whatever you do, don't fuck it up.'

And as I watch him walk towards the hostel door, I can only hope that I haven't already.

9.06 a.m.

I get into work to find emails from a couple of candidates telling me they're accepting the job offers I got them, and while that'll go some way to paying for Sam's engagement ring, I don't feel much like celebrating. There's also a voicemail from Natasha informing me that she'll be out at meetings all morning, which probably means she's gone away for the weekend with someone and they're making a long one of it, but that suits me fine, as it gives me more of a chance to think about what happened. Trouble is, the more I *do* think about it, the more I realize that Dan's right; there's one glaring possibility

I need to get out of the way first. And I so don't want it to be true – because if it turns out that Jane and I did spend the night together, and Sam finds out about it, then it definitely will be – as the T-shirt Dan made me wear on Saturday night said – game over.

12.02 p.m.

With about as much enthusiasm as a child waiting for a dentist's appointment, I'm hanging around outside Jane's office, waiting for her to pop out to the sandwich shop on the corner so I can 'just happen' to be walking by. Unfortunately, what I don't happen to have is any kind of strategy, although I'm hoping I won't need one, and that Jane will kick off the conversation, possibly by saying something like 'long time no see' or even, I suppose, 'you were fantastic on Saturday'. But when she eventually emerges through the revolving doors, there's no such luck.

'Edward,' she says, after a double take once she recognizes who it is that's just rather clumsily bumped into her. 'What are you doing here?'

I try to read her face for any signs of what might have happened between us, or any recognition that we've been intimate, but there's nothing. Then again, Jane was always good at keeping secrets. As I'd found out to my cost in the past.

'I was just, you know, passing.'

'Oh,' she says, a trace of disappointment in her voice. 'Right.'

I stand there awkwardly, knowing what I want to say,

but not knowing how to raise the subject. I can't just come out and say, 'Jane, did we sleep together the other night?', because if we did, she's hardly going to be pleased I can't remember, plus even if we didn't, but I tell Jane I can't remember what happened that evening, she might put two and two together, realize it's the perfect opportunity to split Sam and me up, and insist that we did. I mean, if I can't remember who I spent the night with, then that also means I can't remember who I *didn't* spend the night with. So it might as well have been Jane, if you see what I mean.

And what if she *does* tell me that in fact it was her? How will I ever be able to disprove it? She used to excel at filing away these little snippets of information about someone and bringing them up just when they could cause maximum damage. And like Dan said, what better time to do that than when Sam and I are about to say 'I do', particularly when Jane still hasn't forgiven Sam for 'stealing' me from her?

No, I need to be clever, to find out whether Jane knows I know, or knows I don't know, and draw it out of her. What's the best way to do that? Leading *her* into admitting it.

'So . . .'

'So?'

Ah. It doesn't seem to be working. Mind you, 'So' is hardly the most enticing of opening gambits. 'So even though I *was* just passing, I did want to, you know, talk to you about something.'

Jane raises one eyebrow. 'Oh yes? What?'

Good question. Maybe if I start talking about the stag night in general, then that'll lure it out of her. 'Well, er . . . I wanted to talk to you about Saturday.'

'The wedding's on Saturday, is it?' She smiles. 'I was wondering, seeing as I hadn't received my invitation yet.'

Bollocks. Not only did that not work, but now Jane thinks I've let slip when the wedding is. And while I'd been hoping to avoid her finding out the date so she wouldn't actually come, I can hardly lie to her face. 'Um, yes. And I'm sorry about that. We, er, didn't have your address.'

'Oh. Fine.'

As Jane stands there expectantly, it takes me a few seconds to realize she's waiting for me to hand an invitation over. I put on a show of patting my pockets, then make the 'what an idiot I am' face. 'Would you believe I've forgotten to bring it?'

For a moment, it's quite clear that Jane doesn't believe it. 'Just tell me where it is, then.'

I shrug. 'At home, probably.'

'The *wedding*, Edward. Which church?'

'Ah. We're not actually getting married in a church. It's at the town hall.'

'What time?'

I sigh. In for a penny, in for a pound. 'Four o'clock. So you're still coming?'

'Still coming? Of course. I wouldn't miss it for the world. As long as you're okay with me being there?'

'Well . . .'

'Although I have to say I'm surprised,' she continues. 'I was beginning to think you'd forgotten.'

'Forgotten?'

She nudges me, then lowers her voice. 'About giving me one.'

Ah. Does she mean 'an invitation', or is she talking about the other night? 'Um . . .'

'Oh, and before I forget, I hope you had a nice time?'

'A, er, nice time when?'

'Your stag night, silly.'

Oh *no*. It *was* her. Although she's being extremely polite about it. And while I suddenly feel sick, I still need to keep my wits about me. Damage limitation, and all that.

'Yes, of course.'

'That's good to hear.'

'But it was a one-off, Jane. And you have to understand that it will never happen again. Ever.'

Jane looks at me strangely. 'Unless you get married again, of course.'

Huh? Is she suggesting she'll sleep with me every time I get engaged, or is she just talking about my stag night in general, in terms of having one, rather than, well, having *her*. I still don't have enough information to be sure one way or the other, but I'm conscious I need to tiptoe around the subject.

'You're being very understanding about all of this.'

'Especially after what happened between us?' she says, sarcastically.

I look up sharply. 'Yes. But what happened between us, exactly?'

'Christ, Edward,' she says, suddenly angry. 'Did it mean nothing at all to you?'

I'm at a loss as to what to say. Is Jane talking about the other night, or the previous ten years? I'm aware that there perhaps isn't a right answer to her question, except for not answering at all. But there's a flaw in that plan too, because after a few seconds, Jane starts crying.

'Jane. Please. Don't.' I hand her a tissue from the packet in my pocket I've brought for just such an eventuality, but she waves it away. 'I thought you said you were happy for me?'

'How can I possibly be? I dumped you so you'd go and sort yourself out and come back to me a new man. I didn't think you'd be so heartless to rush out and find yourself a new woman.'

I want to defend myself, but I also don't want things to be bad between me and Jane. And while I don't think we can ever be friends, I certainly don't want to go through life hating her, or worrying that she hates me. I decide on the diplomatic approach.

'It's tough for me too, you know. But I have to accept that maybe I missed my chance with you.'

'But you didn't,' she says, wiping her nose on the back of her hand. 'Or rather, haven't.'

'Yes I have, Jane. I'm with someone else now. And about to marry them. I've moved on.' I smile sympathetically, then reach out and take her hand – unfortunately the one she's just used to wipe her nose. 'And you're going to have to move on too.'

'Well, what if I don't want to?' says Jane, blinking away her tears. 'Especially not after the other day. I knew there was still something between us. And I know you felt it too.'

Bollocks, again. Does she mean in Megabite, and some perception she has that I still have feelings for her, or is she referring to our night together at the hotel? I pull my hand away, and wipe it surreptitiously on my trousers.

'What are you talking about?'

'Don't deny it, Edward.'

'Jane, I . . .' I'm conscious I might be getting myself into trouble, but I just can't come out and ask. I need to get Jane to admit it if it was her. And maybe I can do that by goading her a little bit and making her think that if anything happened, then it didn't mean anything. 'I mean, whatever happened between us, that's in the past. And that's where it has to stay.'

'Oh really?' Jane's expression changes back to her earlier angry one. 'Not necessarily.'

'What do you mean by that?'

'What if I tell Sam exactly what you're like? The kind of things you do.'

Great. Now I'm at bollocks times three. Because now she might be alluding to anything over the ten years she and I were together – and I certainly wasn't the perfect boyfriend then. And while the fact that Jane and I might have slept together the other night is definitely the last thing Sam needs to hear about in the week before our wedding, having a full run-down on just exactly what I'm like over the longer-term is probably not going to be much help to my cause either.

'Why would you do something like that?'

'Why do you think, Edward?' she shouts, then her expression changes, and she forces a smile. 'See you on Saturday,' she says sweetly, before turning around smartly and disappearing back into her building.

I stare at the still-revolving door, unable to believe what's just happened. Not only am I no clearer as to whether Jane was my mystery guest, but I've managed to tell her where and when I'm getting married *and* upset her into the bargain.

1.46 p.m.
When I get back to the office, Natasha's already there, and while I may not have done anything about my own dilemma, at least I can try and help Dan's cause a little. And given the fact that she seems to be in a good mood thanks to the fees those two placements have earned the company this morning, now seems to be as a good a time as any.

'Er, Natasha?' I say, putting the cup of coffee I've bought for myself down in front of her.

She eyes my offering suspiciously. 'What are you after?'

'Nothing,' I say, although we both know the exact opposite is true. 'Nice weekend?'

'Not bad, thanks.'

'Though speaking of weddings, which we weren't, you are going to come, aren't you?'

'Of course, Edward.'

'And are you . . . Bringing anyone?' I ask nervously.

Natasha laughs. 'It's this Saturday, isn't it?'

I swallow hard at the realization of how my feelings towards the day have changed. Two weeks ago, I couldn't wait for it to come. Now, I almost wish it wasn't happening. 'Yup.'

'Then no, probably,' she says, sighing at the prospect of another relationship that's unlikely to last. 'Having him for two consecutive weekends is probably a bit too much.'

'For you?'

'For his wife. Why?'

'It's just that, well . . .' I take a deep breath. 'You do know Dan's coming? And that he's my best man.'

'I assumed as much.'

'Great. But there's one other thing.'

Natasha's face darkens. 'Which is?'

'Well, one of Dan's ex-girlfriends is going to be there.'

'Only one? You can't be inviting that many people.'

'And he's going to try and win her back. Which he can't do if he's going to have one eye on you all the time in case you're coming at him with the knife we use to cut the cake.'

She looks at me levelly. 'Don't worry, Edward. If I

wanted to hurt Dan physically, I'd have done it a long time ago.'

'Oh. Right. Good. Well, that's a relief. I think.'

'So, one of Dan's exes?' Natasha pops the top off the coffee cup and takes a sip. 'This wouldn't be the famous Polly, by any chance?'

'How do you know about her?'

'Dan mentioned her once or twice. "The one that got away." Although when he called out her name in bed one night, *he* nearly didn't.' She smiles to herself at the memory, then shakes her head. 'He'll never go through with it.'

'Why ever not?'

'Because he doesn't really want her back.'

'He does. He said so.'

Natasha sighs. 'How long has he been talking about Polly as "The one that got away", or "His one true love", or "The only person who understands him"? Which, incidentally, if she can, then she's a genius.'

'I dunno. Ever since they split up, I suppose. Why?'

Natasha indicates for me to sit down. 'Don't you see? She's his excuse for behaving the way he does. The fact that he can treat all these women the way he does without any sort of conscience is because Polly's a get-out clause. He tells himself none of them will ever measure up. And so none of them do.'

'That's very, er, astute of you.'

Natasha shrugs. 'I had some therapy once. About why I only ever go for married men.'

'Not for anger management?'

'Why on earth would I need that?' says Natasha, crossly.

'You wouldn't,' I say, quickly. 'And why was it? The married-men thing, I mean.'

She shrugs again. 'It's because I don't want anyone who's able to commit to me, apparently. So I always make sure there's some barrier. That way, I've got an excuse when it goes wrong. It's not my fault, because it would never have worked in the first place.'

'Because they're already married?'

'Exactly. And in a way, that's what Dan's doing. Making sure he's not rejected again, like he was by Polly, by ensuring he's the one who does the rejecting. And always being able to justify it to himself.'

'So why is he preparing to do this, then? Pledge his undying love to her.'

Natasha takes another sip of coffee. 'You think he's serious?'

'I do.'

'Well, in that case, it must be you, Edward,' she says. 'He's finally realized he wants what you've got.'

'That's rubbish.'

'Think about it. While he's always boasted about his many conquests, he's seen you hold down one relationship for the best part of ten years, and then go from that into an even better one. Not only that, you've found someone who's prepared to marry you. How do you think that makes him feel?'

'I hadn't thought of that.'

Natasha smiles. 'Listen. Dan's your best friend, and I'm sure he's really pleased you and Sam are tying the knot but he's probably also a little bit jealous.'

'Jealous?'

'Yes. And there's probably even a small part of him that doesn't want this wedding to go ahead.'

'Because it makes him more aware of his own situation?'

'Exactly. So be aware of that. Because as you know, jealousy can make people do strange things.'

The thing is, I know Natasha's right; jealousy does make people do 'strange things'. After all, I've seen how Jane's behaved ever since she found out about me and Sam. Though when I think about it, given the way Dan abandoned me the other night, I'm not a hundred percent sure Natasha was just referring to his renewed interest in Polly.

Tuesday, 21 April

12.56 p.m.
It's the following lunchtime, and at my insistence, Dan and I have gone out for a jog along the seafront, and while I could do with the workout, I'm hoping more that the exercise will help jog my memory about the events of the other night. I'm also praying that Dan's rec-ollections will have improved over the last forty-eight hours, but I don't hold out much hope. Dan usually has trouble remembering what – or who – he's had for breakfast that day.

'What about the woman you spent that night with?' I say, as we run past the end of the pier. 'She might remember something.'

'That would assume *I* could remember something.'

'What?'

'Who *she* was.'

'Thanks for nothing.' I jog on in silence for a few moments, then grab Dan's arm, stopping him abruptly. 'You don't think someone slipped something into my drink, do you?'

'Like what?'

'You know. That drug that makes you forget what happened the previous evening. Rohypnol, or whatever it's called.'

'Unlikely. In fact, if I was her, I'd have saved it for myself once I'd realized I'd slept with you.' Dan laughs, then sets off again at a slightly faster pace, indicating for me to follow. 'So you might have accidentally slept with someone else. What's the big deal?'

I stare miserably at the pavement in front of me as I run, wondering where to start. For Dan, maybe it's not such a big deal. But for me, it's the complete opposite. The truth is, and despite anything that Sam might have been up to, I feel awful. Terrible, even. And as the wedding approaches, it's only getting worse.

Thinking back, there have been three times I've had reason to feel like this in the last three years: the first was when Jane cheated on me, making me feel worthless, and also repelled that I was touching someone who'd recently been touched by someone else. Then there was the day Jane left me, because it's one thing to be rejected for someone else, but another thing entirely to be rejected because someone would rather be single, or alone, than stay with you. And I remember the heart-wrenching pain of loneliness, and the feeling that if Jane was even experiencing half of that, then things must have been pretty bad for her to have chosen this over the alternative.

And then there was the time last year when I thought

Sam and I were splitting up. Again, it was Jane's fault – sort of – or rather, the fact that I didn't know how to behave towards my ex, while thinking I was doing the right thing by my current girlfriend. And while it was all a misunderstanding, and we actually laugh about it now – well, Sam and Dan laugh, and I pretend to go along with them – it certainly wasn't funny at the time. And ironically, it was because I felt so much more alone, so much emptier and so sick, that it was then I knew I felt way more for Sam than I ever did for Jane, which made me even more determined to get her back. More, even, than I'd been after Jane left, and despite knowing all the hurt I put myself through back then.

But this? It's a hundred times worse than all of those put together. Not only have I let myself down, but I've let Sam down too. And as much as I'd like to be able to blame someone else for this – and Dan's the best candidate – I can't. It's all my fault.

'Dan, you don't understand how it is. Ever since all that stuff last year, I feel bad enough if I forget to call Sam when I've said I would, or if I'm five minutes late home from work. So this – it's a million times more serious.'

Dan spins round to jog backwards in front of me, pressing his thumb onto an imaginary table and grinding it downwards until he sees that I'm not joking. 'Jesus, Ed,' he says, turning back round, then quickly having to leap over a Yorkshire terrier being walked by an old lady. 'Lighten up a bit, will you?'

'What do you mean, lighten up?' I snap.

'Calm down. All I'm saying is maybe you need to affirm your maleness a bit more. And this isn't a bad way to start.'

'By cheating on my fiancée? And what do you mean, "affirm my maleness"?'

'Well, you've got to admit, you're a bit . . .' Dan stops talking as we head down a set of steps. 'I mean, when you're in a relationship, you kind of . . .'

'What?'

'Well, it's just that Jane always . . . And now, Sam obviously . . .'

'Dan, please just spit it out.'

'Wears the trousers. I mean, you're a man, goddam it,' he says, punching me on the shoulder. 'You should be the one in charge. Telling her what to do. Letting her wait if you're late. And if you want to see other women, sleep with them, even, well, that's your right. As a . . .'

'Bastard? Which I'm not.'

Dan grins across at me, then leaps to his left to avoid a pile of dog poo, nearly knocking me into the road in the process. 'Maybe not. But you do need to assert yourself a little bit more. Women like that. Respect it, even. And in fact, some women rather like being, you know, dominated.'

'We're not talking about sex again, are we?' I say, wondering where on earth he gets this stuff from, before guessing it's probably *Cosmo*.

He laughs again. 'No. But you have to be the alpha

male. Because that's what we men do. And if we make a little mistake every now and again, do we get all touchy-feely about it and feel the need to spill our guts? No. We just put it down to experience, forget about it, and move on. After all, that's what our fathers did. And they went through stuff like D-Day.'

I frown at him. 'How old's your dad?'

'Okay. Our grandfathers, then. But my point is, that generation, they did some horrible things. Saw some really yucky stuff. But did they feel the need to come home and tell everyone about it? No. They maintained a stiff upper lip and kept it all buried. Because they were men. And that's what men did. Do.'

'But that was different, Dan. I mean, that was war.'

'And why do you think they call this the battle of the sexes?' He shakes his head. 'Why this need to share everything with Sam? Do you go to the toilet in front of each other?'

'No, of course not.'

'So why air your dirty laundry? People need space, Ed. A few separate things. Their own lives, even. You can't live in someone else's pocket twenty-four seven. And certain stuff, well, you've got to just keep a lid on it. Say you had a hobby, a private interest that you were a little ashamed of . . .'

'I told you, Dan. I haven't played those Queen albums for ages.'

'. . . you'd be embarrassed about it. Want to keep it to yourself, wouldn't you?'

'Maybe.'

'Well, this is like that. You've got to be two individuals. Not just half of a couple. And part of that means keeping a few secrets from each other. Both of you.'

I bristle a little at the 'both of you' part – I'd almost forgotten about whatever it is Sam's been up to in the light of my own indiscretion – and pick the pace up a little in an attempt to shut him up. But even though I'm now breathing heavily, it doesn't seem to faze him. Then again, Dan's often being chased by women, and sometimes their husbands, and likes to keep himself in racing shape for both those reasons.

'Dan, most people live their lives in a different way to you. And after Sam and I nearly split up last year, we promised each other we'd never have any secrets. That we'd do everything out in the open.'

He nudges me, then raises both eyebrows suggestively. 'Kinky.'

'Because that was one of the problems with Jane and me,' I pant. 'We kept everything hidden. And that led to me resenting her even more when I found out what she'd been hiding. Sam and I, we have an understanding.'

Dan grins. 'Well, she's going to have to be very understanding if you tell her you've been unfaithful. Which reminds me.'

'What?'

'Have you actually *been* unfaithful?'

I pull up suddenly, and – after the couple of seconds

it takes him to notice he's running on his own and jog back to where I'm standing – look at him incredulously.

'That's what we've been trying to work out for the past few days.'

'No,' he says, jogging on the spot. 'I mean, have you actually been *unfaithful*?'

'Huh?'

Dan sighs. 'All I'm saying is, and forgetting for a moment the fact that we don't actually know if you had sex at all . . .'

'Which is a pretty major part of it.'

'. . . but say that you did. What is infidelity, exactly?'

'You should know. You've done it often enough.'

'Aha.'

I stare at him for a second or two, hating it when he does this, but knowing from past experience that if I don't say anything, then neither will he, until he's positively jumping from one foot to the other as if his trainers are on fire.

'Aha what?'

'I haven't.'

'Yes you have.'

'Oh no I haven't.'

As Dan turns and runs off again, I feel like I'm at the panto. 'I'm sorry, Dan,' I call after him, before giving chase, 'but if you can remember as far back as a year or so ago and Slate Your Date? I think there are a number of women who would think that, actually, you did. Were. With them. Or rather *to* them.'

'But that's where you're wrong.' Dan slows down to let me catch him up. 'Because infidelity is only infidelity if you've promised to be faithful to someone. I never promised that I would. With any of them.'

'Yes, but, it's kind of implicit, isn't it?'

'Is it?' asks Dan, possibly because he's not sure what 'implicit' means.

'Of course it is. Normally when women agree to sleep with you, they expect something in return.'

Dan grins. 'Not if you're TV's Dan Davis, they don't. In fact, one time there was this one girl hanging around the studio, and . . .'

I hold my hand up to stop him. 'Agree to go out with you, then.'

Dan shakes his head. 'Why does everyone insist on applying labels to things? I mean, what is "going out", exactly? Just because I agree to have a drink with them, or even dinner, and a couple of times, it doesn't mean we're actually girlfriend and boyfriend, does it? And besides, we both know it's just a social convention. A precursor to sex.'

'Not to them it doesn't, apparently, judging by the comments they put on that website.'

'Which I've dealt with,' says Dan, a little tersely. And while this is true, and Dan did start to make some reparations as far as the women he'd wronged were concerned, luckily for him the website eventually closed down. Someone sued it, apparently. And I've got my suspicions as to who that was.

'Anyway,' he says, as we run past a group of primary-school children, 'we're not talking about me here, are we? You're the one who can't keep it in his trousers.'

'Keep your voice down.'

'Sorry,' he says, craning his neck to check out the young teaching assistant. 'I was simply trying to work out whether you'd actually committed a foul. A sin. A fox's paw.'

'Faux pas, Dan.'

'Call it what you will. What I meant was, maybe you and Sam have some sort of agreement whereby this little indiscretion . . .'

'Alleged indiscretion.'

'. . . of yours might be, you know, permissible.'

'We're about to be married. Of course it isn't. Wasn't.'

'No "arrangement" where each of you can go out and have one last fling?'

'No!'

'Shame. But back to my original point. You haven't actually *promised* to be faithful, have you? I mean, I'm no expert, but doesn't that come at the actual ceremony? You know, right after the point you agree to look after her even if she gets some horrible disfiguring disease. Or fat. Which is kind of the same thing.'

'Dan!'

'Okay. Keep what's left of your hair on. I'm just trying to establish whether or not you've got an escape clause. A get-out-of-jail-free card.'

'No, Dan,' I say, patiently. 'Sam and I do not have any

kind of agreement whereby either of us is allowed to sleep with anyone else.'

'Shame.' He jogs on in silence for moment. 'Okay, say you did, in fact, have sex with another woman on your stag night. Let's think a little about the actual definition of infidelity.'

'I think that would be a pretty good one right there,' I say, guiltily.

'Yeah, but surely it's all about intent?'

'Intent? I obviously wanted to have sex with this woman. Why else would I be inviting her back to my room?'

Dan taps the side of his nose with his index finger. 'Not necessarily.'

'What do you mean, "not necessarily"?' I say, sounding like a Dalek as we sprint up the steps to the promenade.

'Well,' continues Dan, puffing slightly, 'say someone took advantage of your drunken state. Although they'd have to have been pretty desperate.'

'What's your point, Dan?'

'You didn't know what you were doing. Which, coincidentally, is pretty much what Jane used to say about your sexual technique.'

I ignore his insult. It's not the first time I've heard it. 'So you're saying that because I was too drunk to know what I was doing, I therefore can't have been unfaithful, because to actually be unfaithful suggests an act of volition. Of consciously wanting to do it,' I add, seeing Dan frown at the word 'volition'.

'Yeah,' says Dan. 'It's like when you see these people on the news forced to rob a bank or smuggle stuff. They're not actually criminals. No one says "They're a nasty piece of work", and condemns them for the rest of their lives.'

I stare at him, so wishing that had some relevance to my actual situation. 'Yes, but this isn't exactly the same thing, is it? I mean, while I might not have actually actively pursued it, I still went through with it. And more importantly, let myself get so drunk where I might have. Or rather, you did.'

'I did what?' says Dan, innocently.

'Let me get so drunk. And then failed to protect me in my hour of need.'

'Hey,' says Dan, holding his hands up as he runs, which makes him look like he's fleeing a gunman. 'It's not my fault if you can't hold your drink . . .'

'A drink you gave me.'

'. . . and then get these urges you can't control.'

'That *you* should have controlled.'

He grins, sheepishly. 'Sorry, mate. I guess I was too busy with my own urges.'

'Anyway. The fact is, I quite possibly slept with some-one else. And no matter whose fault it was, or whatever the circumstances, Sam's going to find it pretty unac-ceptable. *I* find it pretty unacceptable.'

'Then don't tell her.'

'That's your answer to everything, isn't it?'

'It's worked for me up until now.' He grins again. 'Tell her, then. And see how understanding she is.'

'But I can't!'

'Can I?' says Dan, mischievously.

'Piss off, Dan,' I say, at the same time wondering whether that might be my best plan. And if that's true, then I'm really in trouble.

'Anyway,' he says, 'you've got more immediate problems to worry about.'

'Such as?'

'Catching me on this final stretch.'

As he sprints away from me, my knees suddenly feel weak, and I look round for somewhere to sit down. After a few seconds, Dan looks round, expecting me to be following him, then turns and jogs back to the bench I've collapsed onto.

'What's up with you?'

'What you just said.'

'Huh?'

'About catching you. What if I've caught something? Or made her pregnant?'

'Relax,' says Dan. 'Given the amount you used to smoke and drink, you're probably firing blanks anyway. So it's just the old knob-rot you need to worry about.'

'That's comforting, Dan. Thank you very much.' I put my head in my hands and start to rock back and forth, on the verge of bursting into tears. 'But what if I'm not? What if I have got someone pregnant? What if Sam and I get married, and then several years down the line, we get a surprise visit from my child?'

Dan sits down next to me. 'Edward, don't let your imagination run away with you. For a start, and for the millionth time, we don't know that you've had sex with anyone. We also don't know who that person was. We also know she didn't stay around for the morning, which might suggest you weren't able to perform. And even if you could, and you didn't have any protection, there's always the morning after pill.'

'Dan, for the billionth time, that only works if *she* takes it, not if I do. And pregnancy aside, what if I've caught something, and I pass it on to Sam? That's one sure way for her to find out I've slept with someone else.'

'You could always tell her you caught it from a toilet seat.'

'Only if I slept with it.'

'Ed, I've slept with hundreds of women. Thousands, even. And I've never had a single thing. Except for that little rash that turned out to be lipstick allergy, that is.'

'Yes, but you always wear a condom, don't you?'

Dan nods. 'Sometimes two.'

'Two?'

'Yup. Like the Irish say – "to be sure, to be sure". Plus, I don't want to risk it breaking, and have the CIA after me.'

'It's the CSA, Dan. And that's my point. There was no sign of a condom wrapper. And I certainly didn't go out with one in my wallet.'

Dan sighs. 'What have I told you?' he says, pulling his

wallet from his tracksuit pocket and pointing at the well-worn ring shape visible through the leather. 'Don't leave home without it.'

'Even when you're going for a run?'

'Remember.' Dan makes the 'scout's honour' sign again. 'Be prepared.'

As he hauls me up off the bench, then sets off along the promenade, I shake my head in disbelief.

'You're a very sad man,' I say, jogging reluctantly after him.

Although the really sad thing is, it's the one piece of his advice I'm beginning to wish I'd taken.

9.45 p.m.
I have a busy afternoon at work, which quite frankly is fine by me, as it keeps my mind off my current dilemma – or rather, my lack of a solution for it. I've texted Sam that I have to stay late, inventing an after-work interview as an excuse, whereas in reality what I do is spend an hour or three staring out of the office window in the hope that a bright idea will suddenly appear through the glass. In the end, sadly, all I can think of is that I need to arrange what's surely going to be a rather embarrassing appointment with my GP.

By the time I get home, Sam's in bed, and when I slip quietly between the covers, she rolls over and snuggles against me.

'Evening,' she says, her breath on my ear.

'I thought you were asleep.'

'Not yet,' says Sam, inching her hand down my chest and towards my boxer shorts.

I turn my head to kiss her, then all of a sudden, freeze. What if I *have* caught something? I mean, you hear about it happening, especially after unprotected sex, and there were certainly no used condoms floating in the toilet, or ripped foil packets next to the bed, and anyway, chances are that I was so drunk – and according to Dan, any woman who'd have come back to my room with me in that state would have been even drunker – so we probably wouldn't have thought to use one anyway. Which means I can't sleep with Sam until I've had myself tested. Fortunately, I've got the perfect excuse.

'Listen, Sam,' I say, gently moving her hand towards safer territory. 'I was thinking . . .'

'Well, do it quickly, will you?' she says, her fingers resuming their journey downwards.

'No,' I say. 'Wait.'

'Pardon?'

'I mean, I just thought that we might, you know . . . wait.'

Sam stops what she's doing, and even in the dark I can tell she's regarding me quizzically. 'Wait for what?'

'Until we're married. You know, so we can have a proper wedding night.'

'Oh, Edward. There's no need for that.'

'Yes there is,' I say, a little too quickly. 'I mean, we might not be doing the whole church thing, but there's still some other traditions we can maintain. Like this.

And you know, after we're married, I'd like to carry you over the threshold.'

'I'd like you to do that now,' says Sam, provocatively, 'maybe a couple of times.'

'No, I meant . . .' I smile to myself, because I know she knows what I meant. 'I just want us to do some of it *properly*. Traditionally. And it's only for a few days.'

'Really?'

'Really.'

Sam sighs. 'Well, if you're sure . . .'

'I am.'

She nibbles my earlobe gently. 'It'll be a long few days,' she says. 'So it had better be worth it.'

The irony is, I've never wanted her more. And yet, I can't allow myself to act on it because it could ruin everything.

'Can you wait?'

Sam sighs exaggeratedly. 'I suppose so. Although I've never heard of a man turning down sex before.'

And as I roll over, I can't help worrying that that's exactly what I'm afraid of.

Wednesday, 22 April

5.01 p.m.

'So, Edward.' Dr Taylor smiles across her desk at me. She's a kindly, middle-aged woman, which makes all this worse, because it's like talking to my mum. 'What can I do for you?'

I clear my throat awkwardly. 'It's a little embarrassing, really.'

'Come on now. Don't be shy. I've known you since you were so high.' She holds her hand at groin level, which I can't help thinking is rather appropriate.

'Okay. Here goes. I'm, um, worried I might have caught something. You know, down there.' I point towards my trousers. 'And I wanted to get tested. See if I'm all clear. Or, well, not.'

Dr Taylor picks up a clipboard and a pen. 'Have you got any symptoms?'

I swallow hard. 'What kind of symptoms?'

'Itching. Any discharge. A rash or general redness. Trust me, you'd know if you had them.'

I relax a little. Symptoms are the one thing I don't

have. Apart from the redness, of course. But that's just my face, from sitting here and having this conversation. 'No. Nothing like that.'

'But you have had unprotected sex?' she says, writing some notes on the clipboard.

'I'm worried I have. I mean, I think I have. Might have.'

Dr Taylor stops writing and puts her pen down. 'You don't know if you've had unprotected sex?'

'Er, no.'

'Doesn't your partner know?'

'Um, well, I don't know who my partner was. Or even if I had a partner.'

Dr Taylor glances at the clock on the wall. 'Are you sure you're not wasting my time?'

I look grimly across the table at her. 'Actually, I hope I am. If you see what I mean?'

She frowns. 'How can you possibly not know who you did – or didn't – have – or not have – sex with? Unprotected or not. Oh, hang on. Don't tell me. A stag night?'

I nod guiltily. 'Yup.'

Dr Taylor doesn't say anything, but the sound of her snapping on a pair of rubber gloves chills me to the bone.

5.22 p.m.

I've given a blood sample, been inspected, peed into a small plastic container, and even answered a questionnaire about risk factors, although 'going out on the town with Dan Davis' is one that seemed to be missing from Dr Taylor's list.

'Is that it?' I say, pulling up my underwear, relieved it's so far been a lot less intrusive than I'd feared.

Dr Taylor smiles, but without a lot of warmth. 'Not so fast,' she says, advancing towards me while ripping open a small, sterile package, before removing what looks like a cotton bud on steroids. 'I need to take a swab.'

'Oh fine,' I say, assuming she means orally, but as I tilt my head back and open my mouth, Dr Taylor frowns at me. 'No,' she says, 'from inside your penis.'

The coldness of the word makes me jump, but not as much as the coldness of Dr Taylor's hands a few seconds later. Eventually, she drops the swab into a small glass vial and screws the top on.

'All done.'

'How long before I get the test results?' I say, relieved to be zipping up my trousers.

'A couple of weeks should do it,' says Dr Taylor, filling in a few details on the label on the side of the vial.

'A couple of weeks? But . . .'

'Is there a problem with that?'

'Well, when I told you it was 'a' stag night, what I perhaps should have said was that it was *my* stag night.'

'I see. And so you'd be getting married when, exactly?'

'Saturday.'

'This Saturday?'

'That's right. So is there nothing you can tell me straight away?'

Dr Taylor stops what she's doing and looks sternly up at me. 'I take it the person you're getting married to isn't the same person you're worried you had unprotected sex with?'

'Er, no,' I say, reddening even more, which surprises me given the embarrassing afternoon I've had already.

'And so basically you want me to give you the all-clear, otherwise you're going to have some explaining to do on your wedding night.'

I think about trying to explain now, maybe to see how it might wash, but even without saying the words out loud I can tell that as excuses go, 'I was very, very drunk' is a pretty poor one. And, to be honest, I just want to get out of the surgery and back home.

'Well, yes. But it wasn't my fault.'

Dr Taylor sighs, then stands up. 'It never is, Edward,' she says, showing me to the door.

5.40 p.m.
At least Dr Taylor has promised to try and hurry through the results in time for Saturday, but even if they're clear, it still doesn't mean I didn't sleep with someone else – or indeed, get her pregnant. There's only one thing for it in the meantime: I'm going to have to stop trying to find out whether I did, and concentrate on whether I could have – physically. Embarrassingly, I'm going to need some help, which is why I leave the surgery and

head straight for Dan's. When I get there, I find him sitting on his sofa, surrounded by car brochures.

'Don't tell me you're getting rid of the Porsche?'

'I'm thinking about it.'

'What's brought this on?' I say, suddenly concerned. 'I mean, I know you're not working, so if money's a bit tight, I can lend you . . .'

'Don't be ridiculous,' says Dan. 'In fact I've had some good news on that front. You know that list of programmes I showed you the other day? The good old Beeb have only agreed to go ahead and commission a pilot of one of them.'

'Dan, that's excellent news,' I say. 'Which one?'

'The, er . . .' Dan clears his throat, 'that one called "Get You Back".'

'What's that about?'

'Well . . . er . . . we . . . um . . . find people who've been, you know, dumped, and I er . . . well, I sort of help them.'

'Help them what?'

'Get them back. The, er . . . person who dumped them.'

'Get them back in terms of revenge, or . . .' I get a sudden sinking feeling. 'You mean get them back *to go out with*?'

'Yes, you know, I . . .' Dan stares at the floor. 'I help them to sort themselves out. Get in shape. Get a proper haircut. That sort of thing.'

'Where ever did you get that idea from?' I say, sarcastically.

'Do you mind? I mean, I know it's pretty close to home, but they *loved* it. Although . . .'

'Although what?'

'It all depends on a certain someone saying "yes".'

I look at him for a moment, wondering how I can possibly refuse. 'Okay, Dan. Yes.'

He stares back at me looking confused. 'Not you, Ed. Polly. I don't want to do anything that's going to jeopardize my chances with her. And if she doesn't want me to do this TV stuff, then . . .'

'So you'd actually put her above your career?' I say, more than a little impressed.

Dan shrugs. 'We'll see. But if I'm going to have to make some changes, then I might as well start by changing the Porsche.'

'For what?' I say, pointing to the copy of *What Car* on the coffee table.

Dan shrugs. 'I'm thinking of going eco. You know, get one of those hybrids, or something. They're all doing it.'

'Who's "they"?'

'Cameron. Brad. Leo,' says Dan, as if he's on first name terms with them all. 'Or I might even get one of those Smart cars.' He hands me the brochure. 'They even do a sports version.'

I flick through the leaflet. 'What – the Smart RS? That'd be the perfect car for you.'

Dan snatches the brochure back from me, flipping me the finger at the same time. 'Did you want something?'

'Yes,' I say. But when I start to explain where I've been, and what I've got to do, his mouth falls open.

'Hold on. How much of this have you told Sam, exactly?'

'Only that we shouldn't sleep together between now and the wedding night.'

Dan looks at his watch. 'That's three days! I don't get a shag for twenty-four hours and I start to shake. And I don't mean my . . .'

'Thank you for that image, Dan. But what else was I going to do?'

'Haven't you heard of condoms?'

'Yes, of course. But . . .' For the second time in as many hours I feel myself start to redden, more than a little uncomfortable about discussing my sex life with anyone – and Dan in particular, knowing that he'll take the mickey any chance he gets. 'But we don't normally use them. So what am I going to do?'

'You don't normally use them?' Dan stares at me enviously. 'You lucky bastard.'

'Exactly. So if I suddenly introduce them, she's going to get a little suspicious, isn't she?'

'Not necessarily,' says Dan. 'You could always say they're a sex aid. You know – get some of those flavoured ones. Or ribbed – *for her pleasure*. And God knows she probably needs as much of that as she can get seeing as she's in bed with you.'

'If you wouldn't mind not talking about my fiancée like that, please.'

'Or,' continues Dan, warming to his theme, 'tell her you're having a little problem in the early warning department. So you need to start using them so you don't – you know – go off half cocked.'

'This way's much simpler. And Sam thinks it's romantic, too.'

'Romantic?' Dan mimes sticking his fingers down his throat. 'When did you last have sex with her?'

I shrug. 'I'm not sure. Last week, I think.'

'And was it any good? For her, I mean.'

'None of your business!'

'Calm down, Edward. All I'm saying is, say the unthinkable happens, and Sam does end up pulling out of the wedding due to whatever indiscretion you've committed, chances are she's going to dump you, right?'

'Thanks for that particularly cheery observation.'

'But if that is the case, then the last time you slept with her will actually be the last time you sleep with her. Is that how you want to leave it? On that particular note?' He shakes his head. 'Nah, you want to give her a night to remember. Rock her world. Because then, she's always going to remember you as the best she's ever had. Of course, that's only because she hasn't slept with me.'

'Haven't you finished yet?' I say, looking at him incredulously.

Dan winks at me. 'Those are exactly the words you'll want to hear from her.'

'Will you stop joking about this please. We've got

some serious work to do between now and Saturday, including finding out if I, you know . . .'

'Could have got it up? And in both senses of the word.' Dan tries to conceal a smirk. And fails.

'Exactly.'

He scratches his head. 'So how the hell do we go about that, then?'

'Well, in theory it should be quite simple. Like we learned at school for any experiment, all you do is replicate the conditions in a controlled environment, then observe and record the results.'

'Right. Which means?'

'We just do the same thing again, see what happens, and make a note of it.'

Dan nods slowly, then stops nodding abruptly. 'Hang on. What if what happens is I get so drunk I lose track of you and the person you end up going off with? Then you'll be in the same boat all over again. Although this time, that boat will be called *Titanic*.'

'No, Dan. I don't mean that I'm actually going to try and have sex with someone else. That'd be kind of silly, don't you think? Plus you don't have to get drunk as well. Someone has to be the observer, remember.'

'Yeah, but I'm not sure it's the kind of thing I want to observe. And especially not sober, if you know what I mean?'

'Fair enough. But I'll still need you to give me a hand.'

Dan shudders. 'Steady on, Edward. I mean, we're friends, and all that, but . . .'

'Not that kind of a hand, Dan. To help me get drunk. Oh, and I'll need to borrow some of your DVDs. And not the ones of you with your exes, but the proper Danish stuff you keep locked up in your bedroom.'

Dan opens his mouth as if to ask me how I know about that, then thinks better of it. 'Sure. And if that can't get a rise out of you, then we're home and dry.'

'Great. So what time shall I come round?'

'What?' Dan makes a face. 'We're not doing this at my flat.'

'Why not?'

'How many reasons do you want?'

'Okay. Well, Sam's out with a client this evening, so come round at about half seven. With the, ahem, merchandise.'

'Leave it to me,' says Dan. 'I'll get the booze, too. My treat. And don't worry about the DVDs. I'll make sure I bring my favourites.'

'Thanks,' I say, although for some reason, I find the concept of Dan's 'favourites' more than a little unsettling.

6.06 p.m.
By the time I get to Mrs Barraclough's, I'm a little worried to discover that she's not waiting outside as usual. My first thought is that something's happened to her, especially when there's no answer when I ring the doorbell, but when I let myself in with the key she's given me for emergencies, I find her making herself a hot chocolate in the kitchen.

'Hello, Edward,' she says, once she's recovered from the shock of me bursting in.

'Is everything okay?'

'What did you say?'

'I said, is everything . . .' I stop talking, and point to the kitchen table, where Mrs Barraclough's hearing aid is lying next to the newspaper.

'Oh,' she says, picking it up and inserting it into her ear. 'Silly me. No wonder I didn't hear the door.'

'Are you ready to go?' I say, conscious I'm on a bit of a tight schedule.

Mrs Barraclough frowns. 'Didn't you get my message? I left one with that other young lady at your house.'

'Other young lady?'

'Yes. You know. The one who always picks up the telephone when you and Samantha are out. Although I must say, she's never particularly chatty.'

It takes me a moment to work out that Mrs Barraclough is referring to the woman's voice on the BT standard-answer phone message. 'Ah. No. She forgot to give it to me.'

'Never mind. I just rang to say that I didn't need to go shopping today.'

'Oh?'

Mrs Barraclough beams proudly up at me. 'No. I managed to get almost everything I needed locally.'

I smile, and wonder just what 'locally' means to her. After all, Tesco is little more than half a mile down the road. 'What did you do that for?'

'I thought you'd have a few things to do this evening. Seeing as you're getting married on Saturday.'

'That was very thoughtful of you, Mrs B,' I say, deciding not to tell her exactly what it is I've got to do this evening, 'though I don't mind if you still want to go. Honestly.'

'Nonsense,' she says, patting the back of my hand. 'You get yourself off home.'

'I could stay for a cup of tea, if you wanted a bit of company,' I say, nodding tentatively at the pot on the table. I've had Mrs Barraclough's tea before, and given the fact that she always seems to ignore the sell-by date on her milk, 'one lump or two' doesn't always refer to the sugar. 'Or perhaps a hot chocolate?'

'Not at all,' she says. 'We can't have Samantha thinking you've got yourself another woman, can we?'

Not for the first time, I find myself wondering whether Mrs Barraclough's psychic. 'No, Mrs B,' I say, forcing a smile. 'We can't.'

'That's settled, then,' she says.

'If you're sure?'

'Perfectly,' says Mrs Barraclough.

I lean over and give her a peck on the cheek, then make my way towards the door. 'Now are you sure there's nothing you need between now and Saturday?'

Mrs Barraclough walks slowly over to the cupboard in the corner, reaches inside, and removes her last couple of sachets of hot chocolate. 'Well,' she says, 'I could do with a few more Options.'

And as I head back outside and jump into my car, I find myself thinking that she's not the only one.

7.25 p.m.
When Dan rings the doorbell I'm understandably nervous, mainly because despite the fact that I've already warned her he's coming round to help me sort out some 'wedding stuff' – which it is, I suppose – Sam's not left yet. It has occurred to me that a less embarrassing way to have approached this would have been to actually get drunk and try and have sex with Sam, and then if I couldn't, problem solved, but of course I can't, because if it turns out I can actually have sex, then I'm more likely to have caught something, which I don't want to pass on. Still, I'm hoping she won't suspect anything, but unfortunately, Dan's managed to time his arrival just as she's walking out of the door.

'Whatcha got there?' she says, nodding towards the bulging holdall Dan's carrying.

He looks desperately up at me, where I'm frantically mouthing the words *Don't tell her* from just over Sam's shoulder. 'Just, you know, some hardcore Danish porn and an excessive amount of alcohol.'

As my jaw drops Sam grins. 'Yeah, right. Well, you boys have fun,' she says, kissing me goodbye, then slapping Dan on the backside before skipping out through the front door.

'What did you tell her that for?'

'Had to think on my feet, didn't I?' He says, following

me through into the lounge. 'So I decided to bluff. Brazen it out. I knew she'd fall for it.'

'You couldn't think of anything else, you mean.'

'So? It worked, didn't it? Anyway . . .' He sits down on the sofa, and produces a couple of bottles of Harvey's Bristol Cream from his bag. 'Down to business. I worked out that over the course of the evening, you probably consumed the equivalent of these. So all you have to do is get them down you, and—'

'Sherry?'

'Yup.'

'You couldn't have worked it out in a slightly more manly drink, like maybe beer? Or even wine.'

Dan sighs. 'Sherry *is* wine. Just stronger.'

'Cheaper, you mean.' I unscrew the top of one of the bottles and take a tentative swig. It's really quite pleasant, if a little sweet, although whether I can manage the whole bottle, let alone two, we'll have to see.

'How is it?'

'To be honest, a bit sickly.'

'All the better to replicate how you felt after the Minesweeper. Here.' Dan carries the sherry into the kitchen and tips half the bottle's contents into a pint glass. 'Do it the easy way.'

'You mean . . .'

He slides the glass across to me, then helps himself to a Diet Coke from the fridge. 'Down in one.'

'I'm not sure that's a good idea.'

'Do you want to drink it with something?'

'Like what? My nose pinched?' I take a look at the glass of sickly-sweet liquid, and remind myself why I'm doing this. 'To Sam,' I say, picking it up, and clinking it against his can.

'Whatever,' says Dan.

Thirty seconds later, I'm struggling to keep the sherry down, while Dan is filling up my glass again. 'How long before it, you know, kicks in?'

Dan looks at his watch. 'I'd give it about half an hour. Then you can get stuck in,' he says, nodding towards the contents of his holdall. 'Or not, as the case may be.'

7.57 p.m.
'How are you doing?'

'Not great, actually.'

'Great,' says Dan.

'So I suppose I'd better, you know, get in position.'

Dan looks at me strangely for a moment, then shakes his head violently, probably to get rid of the mental image he's just conjured up for himself. 'You mean in the bedroom, right? And not . . .'

'Yes, Dan. In the bedroom.'

I walk over to the table and pick Sam's laptop up, checking the battery's charged.

'Here,' says Dan, handing me a DVD enticingly titled *Danish Delights Volume Two*.

'What was wrong with volume one?'

Dan smiles as he tops my glass up. 'This one's better.'

I decide not to quiz him as to why and, after forcing

down another couple of mouthfuls of sherry, insert the disc into the laptop. The video's set to auto play, and before I can reach the pause button, the usual bad soundtrack starts to emanate from the speakers.

'Right,' says Dan, as I concentrate hard to bring his face into focus. 'Time to try it out. And you might be needing this,' he adds, handing me the holdall. 'There's some extras.'

'Oh. Thanks,' I say, struggling into the bedroom with the holdall and laptop while trying not to spill sherry on the carpet.

'And Ed?'

'What?'

'Close the door, please.'

'Sure. Sorry.'

I shut the door behind me, sit heavily down on the bed, then reach into the bag. There's a selection of magazines in there with titles I can't read, and while initially I think it's because I must be drunk, it's actually because they're in Danish. I start to flick through one of them, gazing at the graphic images, some of which – a bit worryingly – seem to contain animals, but at least I console myself with the fact that the pages aren't stuck together.

After a few minutes, when it's clear the magazines don't seem to be doing anything for me, I dump them on the bed, and decide to turn my attention to the video, but before I can concentrate on the on-screen action, whose plot seems to be loosely based on a group

of naked hikers arriving at an already rather over-pop-
ulated log cabin, there's a knock on the door.

I look around with a start. 'Yes?'

'What's happening?' I can barely hear Dan's voice
through the firmly closed door, mainly due to the various moaning sounds blasting from the laptop's speakers.

'Well, two of the girls are . . .' It takes me a few seconds to understand what he's asking. 'Oh. Hang on.
That wasn't what you meant, was it?' I put the laptop
down and try and concentrate on my groin. As far as I
can tell, there's not so much as a faint stirring, apart
from a slight need to go to the toilet. 'Doesn't seem to
be anything.'

'Are you sure?'

This throws me. How am I going to be sure, exactly?
I glance up to check that the door's still shut, then clumsily undo my trousers and push them – and my boxer
shorts – down past my knees.

As I sit there with my pants around my ankles, the
only thing that starts to rear its head is the futility of the
situation. I've never been much of a one for porn, and
besides, what does this prove, exactly? After all, it's one
thing to look at pictures of perfect-bodied Scandinavians
going at it, and another when there's someone actually
there going at it with you.

Unfortunately, just as I've reached this conclusion, I
hear a commotion from the other side of the bedroom
door, and through my sherry-induced fog I can just about
make out a voice that I think I recognize – especially

once I've turned down the volume of grunting and screaming coming from the laptop – as Sam's.

Even in my inebriated state I know this isn't good, and equally, I'm sure that Dan's ham-fisted efforts to keep her out of the bedroom will probably only make her even more suspicious. Instinctively, I stand bolt upright, then catch sight of my reflection in the full-length mirror on the wardrobe, wondering what Sam will make of things when she inevitably walks in through the bedroom door and spots her fiancé standing next to their bed, knee-deep in hardcore Danish pornography, with his trousers round his ankles. From somewhere inside me, a little voice tells me I need to do something.

Trouble is, I don't know what to do first: attempt to hide the various magazines open on the duvet, or pull my pants back up. And because I can't decide, I end up doing the classic drunk thing of doing neither for a few seconds, then trying to do both at the same time. And of course, because I've got my pants round my ankles, and I'm too drunk to be coordinated, I end up falling over, grabbing the duvet on my way down in a futile attempt to regain my balance.

I lie there on the floor for a while, one of the magazines open and covering my face, not daring to move, especially when I hear the bedroom door opening. Maybe, I tell myself, if I can't see Sam, then she can't see me, although I'm not that drunk to know there is a flaw in that plan. Reluctantly I reach up, remove the magazine, and try and focus my eyes on the upside-down figure in the doorway. Fortunately, it's Dan.

'That was a close one,' he says.

'Did she see . . .'

'Nope.' Dan grins. 'I told her you were trying out a surprise for the wedding. And thinking about it, it's going to be a hell of a surprise. As, hopefully, is this.'

'What?'

'This.' Dan pulls his mobile out of his pocket and snaps a photo of me. 'And I thought the fat suit pictures were good. Oh, and by the way – the mouse is out of the house.'

I hurriedly pull my boxers up and haul myself up onto the bed. 'You better delete that.'

'All in good time, Ed. Now put it away carefully, will you?'

I stare down at the front of my shorts. 'I just have.'

Dan sighs, and points at his precious magazines, which are strewn across the bedroom floor. 'The porn, Edward.'

8.23 p.m.

I'm on my third cup of black coffee, having made myself sick, had a cold shower – to clear my head of the effects of the alcohol rather than the porn – then made myself sick again *in* the shower for good measure, when Dan clears his throat.

'So. No joy, so to speak.'

I shake my head slowly, careful not to make any sudden movements. 'Nope.'

'Excellent,' says Dan, breaking into a huge grin. 'Which proves that even if she tried really hard, you probably weren't. So now we can get on with this wedding bollocks, and not have to worry about whether you did or didn't have sex with another woman.'

'Yes, but it's hardly conclusive proof, is it?' I say, ignoring his pairing of the words 'wedding' and 'bollocks'. 'I mean, looking at dirty magazines, well, it's not quite the same as actually, you know, having someone there, is it?'

'Rubbish,' says Dan, once he's stopped sniggering at my use of the phrase 'dirty magazines'. 'Besides,' he adds, poking the holdall, 'this is the highest quality Danish porn. If it can't get a rise out of you, then I don't know what can. Let's face it, if nothing happened, if you get my drift, then, well, nothing happened.'

'Even so . . .'

'Even so what?'

'Well, it's just . . .' I take another mouthful of coffee, trying to stop the sherry flavour from burping back up, 'we're sort of talking about the mechanics, here, aren't we? And surely, like you always used to tell me, it's more about the motivation.'

Dan sighs. 'What are you going on about now?'

'Fundamentally, whether or not I could have *done* anything, that still doesn't change the fact that I might have asked a woman back to my hotel room.'

'Yes, but if you did, you did it when you were *drunk*,' insists Dan.

'Oh, well that's all right, then. In fact, I'll call the caterers. Maybe they can write it on the cake.'

'Which doesn't count, I meant,' says Dan. 'If you'd have let me finish.'

'But, that's like saying that because Sam and I had had a few drinks before we decided to get married, that doesn't count either.'

'You did?' Dan raises his eyes to the heavens. 'Fantastic. You can get out of it then, and stop worrying about all of this . . .'

'Dan, please, be serious.'

'Only if you will too,' he says, getting up to put the kettle on again.

But the trouble is, I *am* being serious, because I'm worried that – drunk or not – somewhere inside me, there's a person with the capacity to be unfaithful. And the reason I'm worried about it is that in all my time with Jane – the whole ten years – I never strayed once. Didn't even think about it. And while Dan always used to tease me it was because no woman would have been interested in me given how I looked and the size of my beer belly, I'd always thought it was just because I was the faithful type.

And yet now, if I have been unfaithful to Sam, or even just intended to be, I can't help wondering if the closeness of my wedding has got something to do with it. Was I trying to send myself a message to say I'm not ready for it, or even, that Sam's not the person for me? Could it be a cry for help? Or am I simply doing what Dan does all the time, and how he's explained any suspicious behaviour by Sam away – sowing my wild oats one last time?

And if it was just one last fling – something to get out of my system, then is there anything wrong with that? Maybe, in a way, that proves I do want to settle down with Sam, and so I'm doing this to get it over and done with, and closing the door on the single chapter of my life, if you like. But then again, that sounds like the kind of excuse that Dan would use. And if there's one thing I know, it's that when it comes to relationships, I'm certainly not Dan.

'Listen,' he says, sitting back down and placing a fresh cup of coffee in front of me. 'Don't read any more into it than that. You might simply have done it because it was on a plate in front of you.'

'What do you mean?'

'Sometimes, you might have noticed, I sleep with women who aren't, shall we say, my aesthetic equal.'

'I believe the phrase you've used in the past is "as long as she's got a pulse" . . .'

Dan nods, proudly. 'It's like climbing Everest, you know, when people say "because it's there". That's why I sleep with these women, sometimes. Because they're there.'

'But . . .' I struggle to think of a way to say 'I'm not like you', and fail. 'I'm not like you.'

'And you never will be,' says Dan, proudly. 'But think about that last drink of the evening. Your Minesweeper.'

I feel the sherry start to rise in my throat at the memory. 'Thanks for reminding me.'

'Okay. But you weren't particularly thirsty, were you? In fact, you'd probably had enough to drink. And yet you still drank it. Why? Because I put it in front of you. It doesn't mean you were going to cheat on the pint of lager you already had. It doesn't mean you thought any less of that lager. It was just another drink in front of you, so you drank it because that's what drunk people do.'

'What are you trying to say?'

'Just that, any of this subconscious, hidden meaning bollocks is just that – bollocks. Even if you did sleep with someone else, it didn't actually mean anything. You're just trying to convince yourself it did, so you can beat yourself up about it. And have you thought about why *that* might be?'

I know what he's alluding to. Something about Sam cheating on me, and me getting her back, so maybe we'll be quits. But I can't think about that now.

'Dan, please don't confuse the issue. So say it didn't, in fact, mean anything to me. You're forgetting one thing.'

'Which is?'

'That it might actually mean something to Sam.'

'So don't tell her,' says Dan, as if he's stating the most obvious thing in the world.

And this is what Dan just doesn't understand. Keeping something that might mean something from someone you love is just, well, wrong. But when I tell him this, he frowns.

'Why?'

'Because relationships need to be based on honesty. And that's why I'm going to have to tell her once I've found out what it was I actually did.'

'So, you don't actually want the wedding to go ahead?'

'Of course I do.'

'Well, she won't. Once you tell her.'

'But I can't not.'

Dan looks like he wants to pull his hair out. 'You can't . . . What's the opposite of can't not?'

'Look how she reacted when I didn't tell her about the time I saw Jane. And that was one time when nothing actually did happen.'

'Okay. But at least . . .'

'What? Delay the truth a little?' I say, sarcastically.

'Exactly.' Dan sighs. 'Just go through with it, and at some later date, if it does come out, you'll just have to deal with it then. Sure, she'll be mad, but she'll get over it.'

'Yeah. By divorcing me and marrying someone else.' I put my coffee down on the table, and stand up. 'I have to tell her, Dan.'

'Okay. Well, just do me a favour,' he says, grabbing my sleeve and pulling me back down again. 'Promise me you won't tell her anything until you actually know what happened.'

'But—'

'*Promise*, Edward!'

I sigh, then shake the hand Dan's offering me.

'Deal,' I say, realizing that as deals go, it's a pretty big one.

Thursday, 23 April

8.47 a.m.

I'm on my way into work when I spot Billy, with what looks like several dozen *Big Issues* piled up on the pavement next to him. Normally he transports his stock around in a supermarket trolley, but given the fact that there's a red-faced Waitrose employee pushing an empty one past me, I'm guessing he's just been 'asked' to give it back.

'Morning, Billy.'

'Bastard.'

'Nice to see you too,' I say, automatically reaching into my pocket for the obligatory couple of pound coins and handing them over.

'Not you, Ed.' Billy pockets the money gratefully, then hands me a magazine 'Checkout Hitler over there.'

'You had stolen one of his trolleys.'

'I hadn't stolen it,' protests Billy. 'I'd just borrowed it.'

'What for?'

'Moving house, wasn't I?' he mumbles.

'Were you?' I say, disbelievingly, then spot his belongings-stuffed bin-bag behind the pile of magazines. 'What happened to the hostel?'

'Didn't like it.'

'What?' I look at my watch. 'After three days? Why not?'

'My room smelt funny.'

'Really?' Given Billy's own standard of personal hygiene, I find that hard to believe, unless by 'funny' Billy actually means 'clean'. 'So, you're not going back?'

Billy shrugs. 'Doubt it. Besides, I've got everything I need here, haven't I?' he says, nodding down towards his feet, where a four-pack of Special Brew is sitting untouched on top of a pile of dog-eared *Big Issues*.

I sigh. 'It took a lot of work to get you into that place, Billy.'

He reaches down to grab one of the cans of beer. 'Which must have been really tough for you to do from your nice comfortable office.'

'Yes, well, that's not the point, is it? I thought you wanted a roof over your head.'

'So? You thought you wanted that Jane back when she dumped you a while ago, and now you're marrying someone else.'

'That's not the same thing,' I say, wondering whatever possessed me to spill my guts out to everyone who'd listen back then.

'Yeah, well.' Billy tugs open the ring-pull, and slurps half the can down in one. 'Things don't always turn out like you imagined them, do they, Ed?'

And as I make my way to the office, thinking how what's supposed to be the happiest day of my life is currently looking like being the crappiest, I have to concede that he's got a point.

Friday, 24 April

7.11 p.m.
It's the night before the wedding, and in the absence of anywhere else to go, Dan and I are back at the Admiral Jim. I haven't seen much of Sam since Wednesday evening, as she's been running around attending to last-minute wedding stuff, or looking after the various relatives who have been arriving during the course of the day. I'm just hoping I don't have to disappoint them all, especially Sam's dad, who despite his friendly greeting when I picked him up from the airport yesterday, still scares me silly.

Come dinner time, I've said goodbye to Sam, and moved a set of clothes for tomorrow into Dan's flat. Seeing as I've pretty much run out of time in terms of getting to the bottom of what happened on my stag night, I've got a feeling one day's worth is going to be nowhere near enough.

At least I've had my test results back: negative, thankfully, and while that still doesn't put my mind to rest as to whether I might have got someone pregnant despite

Dan's assessment of my, ahem, *potency*, at least it means Sam and I can have a proper wedding night. Assuming we have a wedding, of course.

'What do you want to drink?' says Dan, jumping excitedly onto a stool at the bar.

'I dunno. A Diet Coke, maybe?' I climb wearily up onto the stool next to him. 'I'm not really in the mood to celebrate. Besides, I've got a feeling I might need a clear head tomorrow.'

Dan shrugs. 'Suit yourself. But I'm having one. After all, it's not every day you celebrate your last night of freedom.'

'Dan, it's more likely to be my last night of couple-dom once Sam finds out about what I did.'

He reaches across and ruffles my hair. 'Don't be such a party pooper. Besides, I wasn't talking about yours, I meant mine.'

'Yours?'

Dan nods. 'Yup. Polly, remember?'

'So you're really going to do it?' I say, happy to talk about anything apart from my own predicament. 'Ask Polly if she wants to get back with you?'

'Uh-huh,' he says, shouting his drinks order to Wendy, who appears to be mainlining coffee at the other end of the bar.

'Just remember that assuming the wedding goes ahead, you've got a job to do.'

'I know,' says Dan. 'I just need to work out how to do it.'

'Not that job,' I say, exasperatedly. 'Being my best man, remember?'

'Oh, yeah. That's what I meant too,' says Dan, unconvincingly. 'And like I said, I'm going to be such a brilliant best man that Polly's not going to be able to resist me.'

'Right. Because you've done such a good job of it up until now.'

As Dan looks a little hurt, Wendy walks over and puts a can of Coke and a glass on the bar in front of me, flicking the lager tap open with her other hand. As the tap sputters and emits a couple of globs of foam, Dan sniggers. 'I hope that's not an omen.'

Wendy frowns. 'What for?'

'Ed's wedding night.'

Wendy looks at him disdainfully, then heads off to change the barrel, leaving me to stare miserably at the Coke can.

'What's the matter?' asks Dan.

'I'm not sure I can do it.'

'Not to worry, mate,' he says, picking it up and tugging on the ring pull, then pouring some into my glass. 'That's what I'm here for.'

'Not that, you idiot. I mean marry Sam. Not with all this stuff.'

'Why not?' says Dan, exasperatedly. 'For the billionth time, you don't know whether you actually did anything. And if you think about it, that's a million times better than actually having done something. So you've got nothing to worry about.'

'Except for her and that bloke,' I say, although to be honest, that seems to have faded into the background somewhat given recent developments.

Dan sighs. 'And for the zillionth time, this is Sam we're talking about. There's no way she'd ever cheat on you.'

'That's what I thought about me, and I ended up doing something.'

'Or not,' repeats Dan. 'And even if she has been, you know, just making sure, as long as she turns up tomorrow and says those two little words, then that's all that matters. Just treat it as a blank slate. A new start. For the two of you.'

'That's easy for you to say.'

'But it's not just me, is it? Isn't there some bollocks in the marriage vows about from this day forward?'

'Yes, but . . .'

'Well, there you go. And that's not my words,' he says, jumping off his stool and making his way towards the toilet. 'But *God's*.'

I watch him go, realizing that although he's partly right, I still feel worried about the whole thing. And it's hard to explain, because while I'm sure lots of men get last-night jitters, that's more about whether they're simply doing the right thing. *My* problem is whether I'm doing the right thing under the circumstances – or rather, whether I've already done the wrong thing – and yet, I'm still not sure what those circumstances are. Do I want to get married to Sam? Of course I do. Do I want to get married if she's been cheating on me? That's a harder one to answer. Do I want to get married knowing there's a possibility I've betrayed her? No. But is that only because I'm worried what will happen if I get found out? That's a lot harder to answer.

Not for the first time, I find myself wishing I could take Dan's somewhat shallow approach to these things, and regard it all as water under the bridge. Trouble is, as far as I'm concerned, you can only have so much of that before the foundations get swept away. While Dan might just be able to dismiss this kind of thing with a shrug of his shoulders, and even think that he and Polly have a chance simply because he's prepared to say 'sorry', I'm just not like that. From my point of view, it's worse to be the offender than the offended. But then again, maybe he's right; if I can forgive, or even *ignore* what I think Sam might have been up to, then surely she can do the same where I'm concerned. And if, tomorrow, I promise to be faithful, and maintain that for the rest of our lives together, then isn't that the best anyone can hope for?

But at the same time, I recognize the fundamental flaw in this approach. A year ago, when we nearly split up over a silly misunderstanding, I promised Sam I wouldn't keep any secrets from her, and so what if this mystery woman comes forward – maybe even tomorrow – to announce that she and I spent the night together? How is Sam going to feel then – firstly about the betrayal, and secondly about the secret-keeping? Or what if that happens after a few years? Sam's going to feel that the whole marriage has been based on a lie. And that can't be good.

'Anyway,' continues Dan, leaping back up onto his stool, 'back to me and Polly.'

'So, what are you planning?'

Dan opens his mouth to answer, but then thinks better of it, possibly because Wendy's just reappeared.

'All set, then?' she says, pouring Dan a pint from the now non-spluttering tap. 'No last-minute jitters?'

I'm just about to answer, when Dan interrupts. 'Nope. I've been rehearsing my speech, and everything.'

'Not you, big head.'

Dan laughs. 'We haven't called him that for ages.'

'Not "Big Ed", Dan. She was referring to me.'

He frowns. 'That's what I meant.'

Wendy looks confusedly at the two of us. 'I'm sorry. What exactly are you talking about?'

For a moment, I think about spilling everything to her, but realize I don't actually know where to start, so decide to go for the safer option. 'I was just quizzing Dan about his one true love, but he seems to be a little tongue-tied.'

'Himself? That's one subject he normally doesn't have much trouble talking about.'

'Haven't you got some customers to ignore?' Dan scowls at her. '*Polly*.'

Wendy widens her eyes. 'Polly? Is she back on the scene, then?'

I smile. 'Not yet. But she's going to be at the wedding.
And Dan's determined to get her back.'

'As opposed to getting her on her back?'

'Wendy, please. He's serious.'

'Sorry. But back in what way?' she asks. 'For good?
Am I going to have to buy another hat?'

Dan glances briefly at me. 'You might not be needing
the first one.'

'Pardon?'

'Nothing, Wendy,' I say. 'Get on with it, Dan.'

He shifts uncomfortably on his stool. 'Just, you know,
back. See whether she'll give me a second chance.'

'To do what? Break her heart?'

Dan winces. 'That's all in the past. I've just been thinking about what Ed said. About settling down. I thought
I might give it a try. And Ed's wedding is my beggar-
near-the-cashpoint opportunity.'

Wendy waits for the inevitable punchline, but when
none comes, raises both eyebrows even higher. 'I've a
feeling I might regret asking, but I'm going to have to
get you to explain that one.'

Dan takes a sip of his lager. 'Why do you think beggars
always hang around next to cashpoint machines?' he says,
stifling a burp. 'Because they know you've just got some
money out, so you're going to be feeling more generous.
Polly's going to be sensing the love in the air between Ed
and Sam, so – hopefully – she's going to be feeling the
same. And therefore more likely to send a little bit my way.
Or at least, respond a bit better to my, you know . . .'

'Begging?' I suggest.

'I'm impressed, Dan,' says Wendy. 'But how? More importantly, why?'

'That's just what I was trying to get to the bottom of,' I say. 'And Dan was just going to explain what was so special about Polly, and why it was going to make him change his ways and commit.'

'He was?' This comes from Dan, not Wendy.

'Hang on.' Wendy hurries round to our side of the bar and hops up onto a stool. 'I've got to hear this.'

'So, come on, Dan,' I say. 'Prove to me that you're serious.'

'I don't need to prove it,' he insists. 'I *am* serious.'

'Well, in that case, spill. What is it about Polly that makes her so special?'

'What is it about Sam that makes *her* so special, smart arse?'

'You first.'

'Why?' wails Dan.

'Because I asked first.'

Two minutes later, Wendy and I are still waiting.

'Come on, Dan,' she says. 'There must be something.'

'There's just so much, you know? I'm struggling to put it into some sort of order.'

'We don't need it alphabetically, Dan. Just tell us – I don't know – what it was you first noticed about her, for example.'

As soon as the words have left my mouth, I'm regretting my choice of phrase. Normally, there are two things that Dan first notices about women, and there are no prizes for guessing what those are. But instead of answering in his usual, predictably sexist way, Dan seems to actually be giving it some thought.

Or perhaps not.

'I dunno.'

'Come on. This is the woman who's going to make you forsake all others, so there must be something.'

'Forsake?' says Dan, looking as though he's desperate to talk about something else. 'Is that something rude? I mean, I've always thought it was short for "for fuck's sake", and—'

'Stop avoiding the question.'

Dan looks at me, then at Wendy, and then sighs. 'Okay. It was right here,' he says, pointing to the section of the bar in front of him as if there should be a blue commemorative plaque above it. 'The twenty-third of June, two thousand and two. Around seven fifteen p.m. I was waiting for you, Ed. Do you remember?'

I do actually, mainly because by the time I arrived, Dan was talking to this vision, and ignored me for the rest of the evening as he proceeded to try and get her phone number. Although in his defence, the way she looked that evening, I'd have ignored me too.

'I can't say I do,' I lie. 'Refresh my memory.'

'Well, I was sitting here at the bar, and you were late, and then the door opened, and I looked up, expecting it to be you and Jane, and instead, these two women walked in . . .'

'One of whom was Polly?'

Dan sighs. 'No, Ed. These were just two random women who I'm telling you about to stretch out the story. *Of course* one of them was Polly. And anyway, I must have been sitting here with my mouth wide open, because as they walked past me, Polly smiled at me and asked me if I was catching flies, and I thought she'd said I had something caught in my flies, and . . . Anyway, that's not important.'

'Who was the friend?'

Dan shrugs. 'I can't recall now. But I remember everything about Polly: her smile, what she was wearing, the way she walked . . .'

Wendy raises one eyebrow sceptically. 'Really? What was she wearing, then?'

'Faded-blue jeans, 501s, I think,' says Dan, without hesitation. 'White Adidas trainers. A T-shirt with 'Oasis' written on the front. And she had a blue Umbro sports bag across her shoulder.'

I'm amazed, particularly given Dan's usual powers of recall. It's a bit like watching one of those YouTube clips of a cat playing the piano – you know it's wrong, and you don't quite believe it's real, but you can't help but be fascinated. I'm not the only one; Wendy shakes her head in disbelief.

'Dan Davis, you old softie,' she says. 'I never thought you had it in you. So what was it about Polly that made you fall for her? Her eyes like limpid pools? The way the sunlight tumbled through her hair?'

Dan takes a mouthful of beer, and shakes his head. 'Nope. It was that Umbro bag, actually.'

Wendy and I exchange glances. 'The Umbro bag?' she says.

Dan nods. 'Yup. She had the strap over her shoulder so it ran down between her breasts, pulling her T-shirt so tight I could practically make out the lace pattern on her bra.' He stops talking, and smiles at the memory. 'There are some sights that are just so erotic.'

Wendy shakes her head. 'So that's your romantic "how we met" story? You were staring at her tits, and she accused you of catching flies?'

He nods. 'Well, that's about the size of it. Anyway, I just had to talk to her, but I found myself a little tongue-tied, to be honest. I mean, I didn't know what to say, and I'd never found myself that way with a woman before. It quite threw me. But then she came back over and asked if the stool next to me was free, and I said "No", and she said, "Oh, I'm sorry, are you waiting for some-one?", and I was just about to say "You, and I have been for all my life", and ask her to sit down, when, well, Ed appeared.'

'Which didn't seem to faze you. Judging by how you carried that stool down to the other end of the bar for her.'

Wendy smiles, appreciatively. 'Very gallant of you, Dan.'

I laugh. 'It would have been, if he hadn't then made me stand up for the rest of the night.'

'I got her number, though,' says Dan, the end clearly justifying the means in his eyes.

As Wendy snorts in derision and heads off to serve some other customers, Dan picks up his beer and beckons for me to follow him towards the pool table.

'And just how did you do that?' I say.

'Simple.' Dan slots a pound coin into the slider, releasing the balls noisily. 'You've got to use everything at your disposal. So when I saw the Oasis T-shirt, it was easy.'

'How so?'

'Well, all I had to do was point at her chest, and say "They're fantastic". She got all embarrassed, then when I explained her mistake, and that I was referring to the band . . .' He grins. 'Suddenly, she's on the back foot, and I'm in control. S'easy.'

I pull the triangle out of the slot at the other end of the table, and set the balls up. 'And that's going to work this time, is it?'

'Unless she wears an Oasis T-shirt to your wedding, possibly not.' Dan chalks the end of his cue, places the chalk carefully down on the side of the table, then nods towards the white ball, indicating that I should break. 'Anyway, I was thinking . . .'

'Careful,' I say, leaning down next to him and lining up my shot. 'You know what the doctor said about you trying to do two things at once. And breathing's more important.'

Dan looks at me for a moment, then picks the chalk

back up and touches it to the end of my nose. 'Very funny. This is serious.'

I rub the blue smear off with the back of my hand, then wipe that on Dan's jeans. 'What is?'

'What I was thinking about.'

'Which was?' I ask, automatically.

'My tactics.'

'Tactics?'

'Yeah. I was wondering whether maybe I should invite someone. You know, as my guest.'

'What?' I fire the white ball down towards the other end of the table, then groan as it glances off the side of the pack and into the corner pocket. 'Why?'

'To make Polly jealous, of course.'

'Great idea,' I say. 'Instead of just doing what most normal people would do –talking to her – you want to play games and make her jealous by taking someone else.'

'I thought so too.' Dan retrieves the white ball from the slot and positions it in the 'D'. 'Clever, eh?'

'And what happens then? Either she sees you with another woman and thinks you're off-limits, or you try and chat her up despite having this other woman in tow, and she thinks worse of you for doing that to someone else.'

Dan fires the cue ball down to the other end of the table, and completely misses the ball he's aiming for. 'No, she'll see that I'm still in demand, and that'll make her want me even more.'

'Or she might see that you haven't changed, because you're prepared to drop someone else for her *just like that.*' I click my fingers. 'Which means she might also think you'll be just as prepared to drop *her* for someone else.'

'Ah.'

I put my cue down and lean against the end of the table. 'Dan, don't you think it's about time you started treating Polly decently? If the whole point is that you're trying to win her back by proving how you've changed and what a decent bloke you are now, then why start by trying to play these games of yours?'

'They're not games, Ed,' says Dan crossly, before nodding at the table. 'This is a game. They're tactics. Anyway. You've got two shots.'

'And so do you, Dan. With Polly, I mean. And you're lucky to have them. So don't mess it up. She liked you before, she might well like you again. As long as you change what it is she hasn't been so keen on in the meantime.'

As I say this, I realize the irony of that statement. And Dan knows I'm right, because it's exactly what I did to get Jane back. Even though at the end of it all I decided I didn't *want* her back, it worked.

'So, you're saying I should just go in there and be . . .' Dan picks the chalk up again and rubs it nervously on the end of his cue. 'Myself?'

I smile encouragingly at him. 'Well, maybe not yourself, exactly. More a nicer, less game-playing version. The

Dan she used to go out with, perhaps. Before Mister Celebrity came knocking at your door.'

Dan looks a little confused for a moment. 'Oh. You mean before all this TV stuff happened. Not me actually receiving a visit from someone called . . .'

'Exactly, Dan.' I pick my cue back up and take my shot, and when my ball cannons off one of Dan's and ends up in the opposite pocket to the one I was aiming for, make the 'I meant to do that' face. 'Convince her that maybe you were just going through a phase.'

'Like your "fat" phase?'

I blush a little. 'If you like. But you need to convince her you're in a better place now.'

'The loft apartment?'

'*Mentally*, Dan. And maybe even emotionally.'

'So should I tell her I'm ready for all that long-term commitment stuff?'

I move round the table and take my next shot, rattling the jaws of the pocket with the ball. 'Only if you really are. And only after you've felt her out . . .'

'Hur hur.'

'I mean, found out what she's after. She's just broken up with Steve, after all.'

'Right,' says Dan, nodding at the table to indicate it's still my go. 'So she's going to be vulnerable. Which I can take advantage of . . .'

'Which you absolutely shouldn't take advantage of,' I say, exasperatedly. 'Be her friend, Dan, if she'll let you. And then see what happens from there.'

Dan makes the same face he makes when an ugly fan has sent him a naked photo. 'Her . . . friend?'

I shake my head slowly. 'Dan, relationships are based on friendships.'

'Mine aren't.'

'Which is why you've had so many.'

'Why do you always say that as if it's a bad thing?'

I sigh, then lean over and take my next shot, missing an easy ball into the corner pocket. 'All I'm saying is, if you do get back with Polly, then expect things to be a little different, because after all this time, *she* probably is. And maybe you should find out exactly what her expectations are before you go rushing headlong into it, decide it's not what you want, and like Wendy said, break her heart again.'

Dan winces. 'Ouch. Harsh.'

'But fair, Dan. You don't *want* to hurt her, do you?'

'No, but . . .'

'And it's obvious she still has feelings for you.'

Dan rests his cue against the wall. 'Is it?'

'Of course it is. Just look at the way she reacted when she saw you during all that Slate Your Date stuff. Or the fact she didn't stab you with a fork when the two of you had lunch afterwards. So you owe it to her to make sure it's really what you want.'

He sits down heavily on a chair in the corner. 'You keep saying "what you want". Polly's the "what" in the "what I want". And surely if that's the case, nothing else matters?'

'I'd like to say yes, Dan, but it's not as simple as that. You've got to prove to her you've changed.'

'Right.' Dan picks his beer up, then puts it straight back down again. 'And how do I do that?'

'Well, for one thing, she'd need to stop reading about you in the tabloids, constantly coming out of nightclubs with some groupie on your arm.'

'That's not a problem. Polly doesn't read the tabloids.'

'What I actually meant was that you could stop sleeping with your groupies.'

Dan slumps in his chair, like a five-year-old whose favourite toy has just been confiscated. 'It's just . . . difficult, you know? Particularly because they throw themselves at me. Literally, sometimes, like that one who was hiding on top of the bus stop outside my flat the other week.'

'Yes, but you've *got* to. If you want Polly to take you seriously, that is.'

'But . . . how? I mean, the words "celebrity" and "celibate" might be next to each other in the dictionary, but there's a reason why they're a million miles apart in real life.'

'Remember what you told me a while ago? About giving up smoking?'

Dan frowns. 'Ed, I have trouble remembering what I told you last week.'

'You said to me, the best way to stop smoking is to stop buying cigarettes. And you were right. Remove the temptation, and it's a lot easier.'

'Huh?'

'Well, where do you meet all these women?'

Dan thinks for a moment. 'At nightclubs, obviously.'

'So stop going to them.'

'And at the gym. Or in the street. Or at the super-market. Or when I'm out jogging. And at the hairdressers. And . . .'

I hold up a hand to stop him. 'Maybe you should go out less often. Start shopping on-line.'

Dan puffs his cheeks full of air, then exhales loudly. 'That's easy for you to say, Ed. But one of the reasons I do this is because I like the fringe benefits. The adulation. When you're filming for TV, you don't really get any feed-back, you know. It's just you and a camera. But when I'm out on the street, it's different. People come up to me and tell me they love my work. And sometimes, they want to *show* me how much. And who am I to deny them?'

'But surely all you need to do is exchange a few words, rather than bodily fluids?'

'Fair comment.' Dan grins. 'It's hard, though. Especially because some of them are so attractive.'

'More attractive than Polly?'

'Of course not. But . . .'

'But nothing. Keep your eye on the prize, for God's sake. That way you'll find them easier to resist.'

'So you're saying I should' – Dan clears his throat, then lowers his voice – 'lay off the women for a while. Instead of laying them, that is.' He smiles at his own joke. 'Did you see what I did there?'

'Yes, but it's Polly you should be worried about seeing what you did. And if you're going to be plastered all over the papers, make sure it's for the right reasons.'

'The right reasons. Sure. Will do.' He takes a mouthful of beer. 'Which would be what, exactly?'

I sigh exasperatedly. 'I don't know. But anything's better than being photographed sticking your tongue down some half-dressed teenager's throat.'

'She was sixteen, for the gazillionth time. That's one of the *legal* teens.'

'Just.'

'That day, in fact,' says Dan, as if that makes it any better. 'Which was why she asked for a birthday kiss. How was I to know that there was a pap from the *Sun* there?'

'That's not the point. Why don't you do some charity work, or something?'

'Charity work. Right.' He picks his cue up again, leans over the table, and narrows his eyes in concentration. 'Maybe I could start my own. The Dan Davis Foundation. For fallen young women. I could give them a bed for the night, and . . .'

'Be serious. Imagine how Polly will feel if she opens the paper one day and sees a picture of you doing something good.'

Dan makes a face I don't see very often – of comprehension – and stands back up again. 'You know, that's not a bad idea,' he says, chalking the tip of his cue.

'You've got to convince her you've changed. And

she's not going to know that just by looking at you, is she?'

'Not unless I get as fat as you were. But then again, that wouldn't be a good thing. So what do I say if she asks me about it? You know, the womanizing.'

'For one thing, you tell her you've stopped. And for another, tell her you were only doing it to fill a hole . . .'

'Hur hur.'

'Dan, please. In your life. Where Polly used to be.'

'Oh yeah. Right. And?'

As he looks expectantly up at me, I realize this is what I need to make Dan understand. Polly dumped him because he was turning into something she didn't like; someone she didn't know any more – just like Jane did to me. Because that's what women do, I've learned – go as far as their breaking point, and once they've reached that, it's incredibly hard to convince them to come back from it. But what I can't work out how to tell him, and what I suspect he feels himself, is that she might not want to be TV's Dan Davis's girlfriend, or certainly not the Dan Davis he's become.

'And you've got to convince her that she should give you a chance to prove that you've changed.'

'So, should I tell her that all these women didn't mean a thing?'

'Yes. And no. Because that would make you out as a heartless shag-monster. Which is not something to be proud of,' I add, as a grin spreads across his face. 'Just be honest. Tell her how you feel. There's nothing more flattering than hearing that someone wants you more than anything else in the world, so that's what you've got to concentrate on. Show her on the day that you're courteous, helpful, witty, and, above all else, don't try and snog anyone else.'

'Apart from Sam, right?'

'*Especially* Sam.'

Dan sighs. 'I'm not sure, Ed. I mean, this is all a bit outside my comfort zone.'

'Can't you just accept it's where you need to be?'

Dan looks at me as if I've just made the most outrageous suggestion. 'This is women we're talking about, Ed. Who knows more about them than me?'

'Well, a woman, for one,' I say, waving Wendy over.

Dan looks round to see who I'm gesticulating to, then grabs my hand. 'What are you doing?'

'Like I said the other day, we need a woman's perspective.'

'And like *I* said the other day, if that's the case, why are you asking Wendy?'

'Dan, she's hardly going to help you if you insult her all the time. And don't you think this silly feud of yours has gone far enough? It's childish.'

'She started it.'

'See what I mean? And in actual fact, you started it, by sleeping with her flatmate then never calling her again, I seem to recall. Now be nice.'

'What can I get you?' says Wendy, arriving at the table. 'Another Coke, Ed? Some manners, Dan?'

'No, thanks,' I say, patting the seat of the stool next to me. 'We, I mean *Dan*, needs a bit of advice.'

Wendy looks at Dan suspiciously, then sits down reluctantly. 'About what?'

'Women,' says Dan, although only after I've poked him with the blunt end of my pool cue.

As Wendy bursts out laughing, Dan turns to me. 'You see, I told you it was a mistake,' he says, throwing his cue onto the table and making for the toilets.

I chase after him, and guide him back to where Wendy's sitting. 'Wendy, be serious for a minute, please. Dan needs help.'

'Of the "professional" variety,' says Wendy, struggling for breath.

'Please, Wendy. This is your chance to save all woman-kind. You can spare them all from any future hurt.'

She stops laughing abruptly. 'How?' she says, suddenly interested.

'By telling Dan what it is he needs to change about himself to win back Polly.'

Wendy considers this for a second or two. 'How about everything?'

'Which is what he's prepared to do. Aren't you, Dan?'

'What? Oh. Yes. Of course. Whatever it takes,' says Dan, through gritted teeth.

I nod encouragingly. 'I mean, how did Andy convince you he was the one for you?'

'Getting me pregnant was a good start,' says Wendy, only half joking.

Dan frowns. 'Yes, but Polly's hardly going to let me get close enough to . . . Ah. You weren't being serious.'

'Jesus, Dan. For someone who's been out with as many women as you have, you don't actually know a lot about how we really work.'

'Which is why I need your help,' pleads Dan.

Wendy looks at him levelly for a moment or two. 'Okay. Well, as far as we're concerned, you need to let us know you're interested in us. Does Polly have any idea?'

'I dunno.'

'When was the last time you saw her?'

Dan shrugs. 'About a year ago. I went to say sorry. For the way I treated her.'

'And?'

'And nothing. We had lunch, she had a boyfriend. So I left it at that.'

'And you haven't seen her since?'

Dan shakes his head. 'What was the point? She was with someone else, and I didn't want to do anything to jeopardize her happiness.'

Wendy makes a face that could mean she's either surprised or impressed, either of which would be a rarity as far as she and Dan are concerned. 'That was very caring of you, Dan. And now?'

'She's coming to old numb nuts' wedding tomorrow,' he says, nodding towards me. 'On her own. Which would indicate she's single again. So how do I, you know, get her interested?'

'You need to make her feel like she's the only girl in the world,' says Wendy. 'For you, I mean.'

'Right.' Dan nods thoughtfully. 'So, if I tell her that I could have any woman I wanted, but in fact I want her, she's bound to be a pushover?'

Wendy stares at him in disbelief. 'Quite the opposite. I mean, she has to feel that as far as you're concerned, there aren't any other women in the world.'

'But there are.'

'No there aren't.'

'But . . . Ow.'

'Sorry, Dan,' I say, as he scowls at me for poking him with my cue again, although with the pointy end this time. 'But I'm supposed to be getting married tomorrow afternoon, and I didn't want to be late.'

'Think about it,' says Wendy. 'The moment you let someone know you're interested in them, it's really flattering, and they look at you in a new light. So for you to be telling them that not only are you interested in them, but you're prepared to forsake everyone else . . .'

'And how do I do that, exactly?'

Wendy shrugs. 'Make a big gesture, maybe.'

'But I am making a big gesture. By giving up all other women.'

'What I mean is, make a big gesture that she'll appreciate.'

'Well, if she doesn't appreciate something like that, then . . . Ow.'

As Dan recoils from where Wendy's hit him this time,

she smiles. 'Dan, Polly doesn't want to think you're making some sort of sacrifice by being with her, or you're doing her a favour. She needs you to make her feel you're lucky to have her. Not the other way round.'

Dan inches out of arm's – and cue's – reach, and thinks about this for a second or two. 'So, let me get this straight. In order to convince her I'm worth taking a chance on, I've actually got to get her to believe I think she's the only girl in the world for me.'

I sit down next to Wendy. 'By Jove, I think he's got it.'

'But isn't that rather, well, desperate?'

Wendy nods. 'Of course it is. We need to see you're helpless. Because then we know we've got you where we want you. Desperate, Dan.'

'Very funny.'

'She doesn't want to be holding the tiger by the tail,' continues Wendy. 'In fact, *she* should be the tiger. And she wants to see you value her highly, and appreciate the sacrifice *she's* making.'

Dan makes a face. 'What sacrifice is she making, exactly?'

Wendy raises one eyebrow. 'Where do you want me to start? And this is all the more important because you've got history. I mean, you ran out on her once before, don't forget.'

'Yes, well that was a mistake.'

'You know that now,' I say. 'And actually, telling her that might just give you a chance to win her back.'

'No, an *actual* mistake,' says Dan. 'I think I might have

got the wrong end of the stick, and by the time I realized that, it was too late.' He puts an arm round my shoulder. 'You see, Ed? It happens to the best of us. Anyway, thank you, Wendy. I'll give what you've said some thought.'

Wendy peers back at him, unused to this kind of reaction. 'You're, er, welcome,' she says, jumping off her stool and making her way back towards the bar.

As Dan watches her go, I nudge him out of the way, then walk round to where the white ball is and lean down to line up my next shot. 'And just remember how lucky you are.'

'Lucky?' Dan stares at me across the table. 'How do you mean, lucky?'

'Not everyone gets a second chance. This is yours. So don't mess it up.'

'I won't. I've been to a thousand auditions. I know what to do.'

'But was the part ever this important?'

As Dan sniggers at the word 'part', I draw my cue back, then hit the white ball down towards the far end of the table, where the eight-ball is perched precariously over the pocket.

'Missed,' says Dan.

'Not so fast,' I say, as the cue ball bounces off the far cushion, does the same off the one closest to me, before making its way back towards where I was originally aiming. 'I think I might get it on the rebound.'

And as the eight-ball drops into the pocket, I can tell that Dan is hoping for the same thing tomorrow.

Saturday, 25 April

6.21 a.m.

When I wake up on Dan's sofa after a restless night's sleep, the first thing I think about is the goodbye kiss Sam planted on my lips yesterday, and wonder whether the next thing she'll plant on me will be a right hook. I still haven't worked out how, when, or even what to tell her, but with the two of us due at the registry office in just under ten hours, I'd better think of something, and fast.

My gut feeling is that I am going to have to come clean before the wedding, but when I think about what her reaction is likely to be, my other gut feeling is extreme nausea.

7.44 a.m.

I'm on my second cup of coffee, staring at the hand-written notice Dan Sellotaped to his bedroom door last night that says 'keep out', wondering when's safe to wake him. To be honest, I'm tempted to let him have a lie in because while he's the last person to need any beauty sleep, what he is going to need if he wants to win Polly back are his wits about him this afternoon. Even if the wedding turns into a disaster, there might as well be one happy ending today.

11.12 a.m.

Dan and I are back in the Admiral Jim for something to calm our nerves. On his insistence, we've called in at the local oriental supermarket on the way here to try and find some "Thai cheese" Dan's heard is good for relaxation, despite me and the chap behind the counter insisting that Dan must mean Tai Chi.

In spite of this amusing interlude, I'm still not sure I can go through with the wedding, and Dan is trying to help in his own way, but as usual, Dan's way isn't mine.

'Listen,' he says, sitting down at the bar next to me. 'If you want my advice, just put it down to experience. Brush it under the carpet and move on. If anything happened at all, it was a mistake, that's all. An accident, even.'

'That's easy for you to say. You weren't the one driving.'

'No,' says Dan. 'But neither were you, by the sound of things.'

'Don't you see? That makes it worse.'

By the look on his face, Dan evidently doesn't think so. 'I still don't see why you're so hung up about it.'

'Because I don't want to hurt Sam.'

'So don't. By not telling her.' Dan waves to Wendy, and indicates our empty glasses. 'Besides, remember you're worried about something you're not actually sure you did.'

'Yes, but what if I *did*, and she finds out.'

'Finds out? You haven't been able to, and you were there. And if you couldn't, how's Sam ever going to?'

'How's Sam ever going to what?' asks Wendy, materializing behind the bar with a bottle of champagne and a couple of glasses.

As I start to blush furiously, Dan grins at her. 'Just a surprise Ed's thinking about giving Sam later.'

'Ooh, lovely,' says Wendy, popping the cork out of the bottle and pouring us both a drink. 'Girls love surprises.'

'Not this kind, they don't,' whispers Dan.

'But don't you understand?' I say, once Wendy's out of earshot. 'These things always have a way of coming out. Far better that I tell her about it now, rather than have it look like I was trying to keep it from her. I mean, what happens if someone announces it at the wedding?'

'Trust me. Anyone who's slept with you is hardly going to want to boast about it. And certainly not in public.'

I stare at him, tight-lipped. 'And that's supposed to make me feel better, is it?'

'Listen,' says Dan. 'If – and it's a big "if" – there *was* someone else, chances are, whoever this person was was as drunk as you, so there's a good chance she doesn't remember it either. Or maybe she's embarrassed because she got off with some fat bloke – I mean, let's face it, she was out of there so quickly the next morning you'd have thought the fire alarm had gone off.'

'What's your point, Dan?'

'And so she probably wants to forget about it too. Which makes two of you. Problem solved.'

'I'm sorry. I simply can't risk Sam finding out from someone else.'

Dan sighs. 'So tell her then. I mean, you didn't dump Jane when she did the dirty on you, did you? So maybe Sam will be the same.'

I stare at him for a second, wondering whether to explain that Jane had already decided we were finished the moment she snogged someone else. And although she'd defended her actions, telling me they were just a cry for attention, in reality, as Natasha pointed out, they were a cry for attention from someone else. The reason I hadn't dumped her there and then wasn't anything to do with how much I wanted to be with her, but just how much I didn't want to be on my own.

And the problem with my current situation, given that the roles are reversed, is this: because however much Sam might love me – at the moment, at least – I know she doesn't have a problem being on her own. Which is why I'm so scared to tell her.

'I *can't*. I just know if I tell Sam what happened, she'll leave me. But equally, I can't not tell her.' I put my head in my hands. 'What am I going to do?'

Dan swivels round to face me. 'You're forgetting

something. The one simple reason why you can't tell her what happened.'

'Which is?'

'You. Don't. Know,' he says, punctuating each word with a poke in my chest. 'Or rather, you can't remember.'

'But how can I remember?'

Dan thinks for a moment. 'You could always try some of that hypnosis bollocks.'

'Does it work?'

Dan nods. 'I tried it once. The guy took me back to my childhood.'

'That can't have taken long.'

'I'm serious. Tell you what, I'll give it a go if you like. I think I can remember what he did.'

'Just listening to you talk about your career is usually enough to send me to sleep. And besides, the last time I dozed off in front of you, you drew a moustache on my face with a permanent marker. So there's no way.'

'Suit yourself.' Dan smiles to himself at the memory. 'But just bear in mind if you do spill your guts to her, then the only woman you'll be seeing every night is the receptionist at whatever hotel you end up having to go and live in when Sam kicks you out.'

I pick my glass up, get it halfway to my mouth, then put it straight back down again. 'Dan, you're a genius,' I say, grabbing his head with both hands and planting a kiss on his forehead.

For a second he doesn't know how to react, torn between being flattered that I've complimented him on his intelligence – although he obviously can't work out why – and the fact that I've just done something that is way off the scale on his gay-o-meter.

'What?'

'You're a genius.'

'I am?'

'Yes. What if we ask the receptionist? At the Grand.'

'To hypnotize you?' Dan frowns. 'Why would she be any better at it than me?'

'No, dummy. If she saw anything. That night, I mean.' I jump off my stool, convinced I've sussed it. 'There must have been someone on duty that night. And I'm bound to have walked past reception.'

'Or stumbled. Or been carried.'

'Even better. Because that would have been more noticeable.' I leap off my stool, then head towards the door. 'Come on.'

Dan gazes longingly at his half-full champagne glass, then climbs reluctantly down from his stool. 'We don't have a lot of time, you know.'

I stride purposefully back to the bar, grab his arm, then physically drag him towards the doorway, ignoring Wendy's enquiring shout from the other side of the pub.

'Which is exactly why we need to get a move on.'

11.31 a.m.
As Dan and I walk up to the Grand Hotel's front desk, the bored-looking receptionist glances up from her computer screen.

'Hello, gentlemen,' she says, in an Eastern European accent. 'Can I help you?'

I nudge Dan. 'Recognize her?' I whisper.

'Nope. You?'

'Dan, if I could remember anyone from that fateful evening, we wouldn't be here now.'

'Not to worry.' Dan beams at her, as if turning on a switch. 'Well, hello, Lenka,' he says, his eyes lingering longer than necessary on where her name badge is pinned to her ample chest. 'How are you today?'

Lenka eyes him suspiciously. 'Fine.'

'Lenka,' he says. 'That's a pretty name. Where are you from?'

'Krakow,' says Lenka, curtly.

Dan raises one eyebrow. 'Crack off?' he says, repeating Lenka's Polish pronunciation. 'That's not a very nice thing to say. Although I wouldn't mind cracking one o—'

'Dan! Behave. She's from *Poland*.'

Lenka looks at the two of us levelly, then glances up at the security camera on the wall above her head for reassurance. 'Do you want a room?'

'That's very forward of you, Lenka,' says Dan. 'I mean, we've only just met.'

I shush him. 'No, thank you. Just some information,' I say, sounding like someone from a bad cops and robbers movie. 'Do you recognize us?'

Lenka peers at each of us in turn, then points at Dan. 'Yes. You do look familiar.'

'Yes, well, a lot of people say that. You might have seen me on TV.'

'No,' says Lenka, shaking her head to emphasize her point. 'I do not have a TV.'

Dan looks aghast, as if Lenka's just admitted to being a devil-worshipper. 'If you did, Lenka, you'd know that I'm famous.'

Lenka peers at him again. 'What is your name?'

'Dan. Dan Davis.'

Lenka shrugs. 'Well, Dandan Davis, I have never heard of you.'

Dan forces a smile. 'And does that say more about me or you, do you think?'

I hold a hand up to interrupt the two of them. 'Lenka. Please. Were you working here last weekend?'

Lenka nods. 'Yes. I do all the weekends. The late shifts. From midnight till midday. Why?'

My heart starts to beat a little faster. Half an hour later, and we'd have missed her. Finally, I seem to be getting some luck.

'And do you recognize me?'

'He's not on TV like me,' clarifies Dan, as Lenka peers across the counter at me. 'He stayed here last Saturday night. We both did.'

'I am sorry,' says Lenka, after a moment or two. 'But no.'

'Are you sure?'

She shrugs again. 'We have a lot of guests.'

I stare back at her in disbelief, willing her to remember something, *anything*, that'll help me out, but she just gazes

blankly at me, and I'm just about to give up, when Dan
has an idea.

'Do your drunk face.'

'What?'

'Do your drunk face.'

'I don't have a drunk face.'

'Go on.' He nudges me. 'Make that face you make
when you've had too many drinks. You know, with the
lolling tongue. And the dopey expression. And . . .' He
dashes across to the sofa in the corner and grabs one of
the cushions. 'Stick this up your jumper.'

'What? Don't be ridiculous.'

'Do you want to get to the bottom of this or not?
She's only going to recognize you if you actually look
like you did that night. Which was drunk. And fat.'

I start to laugh at the ridiculousness of what Dan's just
suggested, but then think I'm desperate enough to try just
about anything. Wordlessly I snatch the cushion from him
and stuff it underneath my jumper, then turn back to
Lenka, relax my features, then push my tongue out slightly.
But as Dan tries hard to stifle a grin, Lenka suddenly smiles.

'I do remember,' she says. 'You stayed here last Saturday.'

'Told you!' says Dan.

'You also told her. A few moments ago.'

'Ah. Sorry.'

'Did you see me coming in that evening, Lenka? After
midnight, I mean?'

Lenka nods solemnly. 'Yes. You were very drunk.'

I swallow hard as I pull the cushion out from my

jumper. 'And was I, you know, with someone? When I came back in, I mean.'

'With someone?'

'Yes. You know. A girl.'

Dan clears his throat. 'Or a bloke. Got to cover all the bases after all.'

'I think so,' says Lenka. 'Yes, it was a girl, I believe.'

My legs suddenly feel wobbly, and I lean heavily against the counter. This is great. And isn't, at the same time.

'Do you recall what she looked like? Can you describe her face, for example?'

Lenka thinks for a moment. 'It is hard to say. I remember it was pretty . . .'

'There you go,' says Dan, proudly. 'Couldn't have been Jane, then. And good on you.'

I look at him incredulously. 'What do you mean, "good on you"? It's not something to congratulate me about, you know.'

Dan does his usual trick of opening his mouth as if to say something then deciding against it. 'You're right, Ed. Do go on, Lenka.'

She smiles back at him. 'As I was saying, I remember it was pretty hard to *see* her face.'

'Why was that?' I ask.

Lenka shrugs. 'Because, how do you say, your face was stuck to it.'

'I'm sorry?'

Lenka smiles. 'You kept trying to kiss her. And she was trying to get you into the lift.'

I get a sudden sinking feeling as any chance that it might just have been a good Samaritan helping me back to my room start to disappear.

'And would you recognize this girl if you saw her again? I need to find out if she was a . . . Friend.'

Lenka shakes her head. 'I do not know. There are lots of girls who come back here at night with our guests. And they are not all friends of the guests. You understand?'

As Dan starts to snigger, I get a terrible feeling in the pit of my stomach. Surely it can't have been worse than I'd thought, and I'd brought a prostitute back? But no. I certainly wasn't missing any money the following morning, and surely if I was paying for it, then, well, I'd have paid for it – unless I *was* too drunk to perform. But then again, as far as I know, prostitutes are paid by the hour, and not on a 'no in, no fee' basis. So it can't have been. Even completely paralytic, it's not the kind of thing I'd do. Unless . . . Unless I didn't do it. I glower across at Dan, who seems to be trying blatantly to stare down Lenka's blouse.

'A word, mate.'

Dan breaks away reluctantly, and follows me over to the sofa by the fireplace. 'What?'

'I'm going to ask you a question, and I'm only going to ask it once, and I want a straight answer. Not one of your jokes, or trying to avoid the issue.'

'Okay.' He looks a little alarmed. 'Fire away.'

'Is there any chance that you might have paid for a woman to have sex with me that night?'

Dan stares at me, and when he doesn't answer immediately, I start to feel even more worried.

'Well?'

'I'm thinking. I mean, I was very drunk too, don't
forget.'

'I'm waiting.'

After a few seconds, Dan shakes his head. 'It's hardly
likely, is it? I mean, prostitutes are expensive, aren't they?'

'Are they?'

Dan blushes. 'Allegedly.'

I scowl at him, realizing it *is* pretty unlikely that a man
who hasn't bought me a drink for as long as I can
remember would have put his hand in his pocket for
something like this.

'You're sure?'

'As I can be.'

'Well, that's it, then,' I say, staring miserably down at
my shoes. 'Game over.'

Dan puts a consoling arm round my shoulder, and
gives me a squeeze. 'Come on,' he says, escorting me past
a bemused Lenka and out of the reception area. 'You've
done your best. Now it's time to get ready.'

But as I follow him through the hotel door, I don't
know what I'm going back to get ready for.

1.01 p.m.

I'm sitting back in Dan's flat, wearing my new Boss suit,
but despite the fact that it *isn't* black, I'm still feeling as
though I'm off to a funeral instead of a wedding.

'Cheer up, mate.' Dan finishes adjusting his tie in the mirror above his pebble flame-effect fireplace. 'Remember, it's supposed to be bride and *groom*, not gloom.'

'Very funny, Dan.' I slump back on the sofa. 'I just wish there was something more I could do.'

He sighs. 'Ed, no one could have tried harder. Really. And the amount of remorse you've shown when you still don't actually know you've done anything to be ashamed of.' He smiles, and turns back to the mirror. 'Anyway. Just put a brave face on it, and give me a hand, will you?'

'With what?'

Dan walks over towards his huge flat-screen TV, and opens the cupboard underneath it. 'I need to erase these.'

'What are they?'

'They're my video collection. Of me and my exes. After all, the only video I want Polly to see is the wedding one. And speaking of which, I know it's normal for me to stand on your right, but I'm worried the photographer won't get my best side, so . . .'

As Dan drones on, I stare at the collection of alphabetically ordered discs, then a flashbulb goes off above my head. 'What did you say?'

'I said I want the camera to capture my—'

'Camera.' I jump out of my seat excitedly. 'Exactly.'

'What?'

'There'll be a *video*,' I say, as if it's the answer to life, the universe, and everything.

'I know,' he says, turning back to the mirror. 'Why do

you think I'm spending so much time trying to get this bloody tie right?'

'No. At the hotel.'

'The hotel?'

'Yes. There'll be a security video. Of that night. And so all we have to do is get hold of it and—' I stop talking, as judging by the look on Dan's face, for once, he's ahead of me. I peer anxiously at my watch; sadly there's not enough time to let him savour the moment. 'Come on. We've still got three hours before we need to be at the registry office. That should be long enough.'

Dan picks his keys up and follows me towards the door. 'So how do we, you know, get it?'

I shrug. 'We could try just going in and asking.'

Dan shakes his head. 'Nah. There are rules about that kind of thing.'

'How would you know?'

He lowers his voice, despite the fact that no one's in earshot. 'You remember that exposé in the *Daily Mail* last year? Me and that pole dancer? The one I sued them over.'

'What about it?' A picture of a naked Dan had appeared under a headline which read 'Soap Star Gives Pole Dance of His Own'. He was quite proud of it, actually. Though more because the pixellation of his private parts had made him look particularly well-endowed.

'I found out a few things after the court case. The good news is that they're required by law to keep the recordings for thirty days now. Trouble is, they're also required by law not to show them to anyone.'

'So what do we do?'

'We're just going to have to steal it, aren't we?' he says, putting on his best Sean Connery accent.

I look at him in disbelief. 'I don't think we've actually got enough time to get arrested and out on bail.'

''S'all right,' says Dan. 'I've got a plan.'

1.17 p.m.

When we walk back into the hotel, Lenka is nowhere to be seen, which Dan is more than a little relieved about, given what he's planning. He strides confidently up to the front desk and clears his throat, and when Lenka's replacement looks up, she does a double take.

'Can I help you?' says the girl, whose name badge identifies her as Lucy.

'You can. Although it's rather sensitive, actually.'

Dazzled by the full Dan Davis smile, Lucy starts to blush. 'You're him, aren't you? From the telly?'

Dan looks round to see if anyone else has heard her, and by the look on his face, is disappointed that no one has. 'Well, yes.'

'So what can I do for you, Mr Davis?'

'*Dan*, please.'

'Sorry. Dan.' Lucy giggles, then shakes the hand he's offering her. 'I'm Lucy. Although my friends call me Luce.'

'That's good to hear.' Dan winks at me, and looks like

he wants to respond in his normal fashion, but a sharp nudge in the back from me prevents that. 'Listen,' he says. 'I'll be here for the Middleton wedding reception this afternoon, where incidentally, I'm the best man – although I probably don't need to tell you that. So I just wanted to check on how we're going to keep the paparazzi out. Is it possible to speak with your head of security?'

'We don't have one,' says Lucy, unable to stop staring at him. 'But if you wait a few minutes, the assistant manager will be back from his lunch break, and—'

'I'd like to, really I would,' says Dan, taking Lucy by the hand and leading her round from behind the desk, then peering up at the security camera on the wall. 'But I'm in a bit of a hurry. And if you could help me out, I'd consider it a personal favour.'

Lucy gazes up at him, and then looks nervously back at the front desk. 'I'm not really supposed to leave—'

'I know. But I won't take up too much of your time. All we need to do is check what areas are covered by the CCTV so we know where the paps might be hiding. I'd be very grateful,' he says, smoothing down the lapels on her jacket with his fingers, managing to brush his knuckles against her breasts at the same time. 'Besides, no one needs to know. It'll be our little secret.'

It's an impressive thing to witness: Dan in full-on flirt mode, and even though for a moment I'm worried Lucy's going to say 'no', if Dan suspects this he doesn't let on. After all, he's not used to having that word said to him. Particularly by a woman.

'Okay,' she says. 'Follow me.'

As Dan gives me the thumbs-up behind her back, Lucy leads us out of reception and along a corridor, until we reach a door with the word 'security' written on it. 'Here it is,' she says, producing a bunch of keys from her pocket, then looking embarrassed when the door turns out to be unlocked already.

I follow the two of them inside. There's a bank of television monitors above the desk on the far wall, all showing views of various floors, corridors and function rooms, as well as – of course – the reception area.

'Good, good,' says Dan, pretending to inspect the equipment, his other hand casually stroking the small of Lucy's back. 'And these are all being recorded?'

Lucy nods. 'We keep the old ones here,' she says, pointing to a large shelf, where there are several labelled disks filed – not unlike Dan's collection – by date. Although I imagine the content is a little different.

Quick as a flash, Dan reaches up and selects one from the shelf – the one from last Saturday – as if by random. 'And what happens to these recordings afterwards?' he asks, examining it for a few seconds, before slipping it back onto the shelf so it protrudes slightly from the rest.

Lucy seems to forget I'm here, and edges towards him. 'Oh, they're deleted. Eventually, I mean.'

'Really? That's fascinating. And is there a camera in here? This room, I mean?'

Lucy starts to blush again. 'No. Why?'

'Why? Well, because . . .' Dan suddenly stops talking, then grabs Lucy, spinning her round so her back's facing the shelf, and starts to kiss her. She resists for a second, and then, like you see in those old nineteen-forties films, melts into his arms. I'm about to turn away in embarrassment when I realize what he's doing – or rather, why he's doing it, especially when he opens his eyes, glares at me, and with his free hand – and I don't want to think about where the other one is – points frantically towards the shelf.

After a moment's hesitation I reach up, grab the disk, and slip it into my jacket pocket, then give him the thumbs-up to indicate that he can put Lucy back down now, but he doesn't seem to want to, and instead, waves me out of the room.

To be honest, even if I didn't have a movie to watch, I'd be keen to get out of there.

2.07 p.m.

By the time Dan eventually gets back, proudly announcing he's just 'taken one for the team', I'm none the wiser. I've managed to find the section that features what looks like me staggering in through reception, and while the recording's a little bit fuzzy, there does seem to be a girl holding me up. The only trouble is, thanks to the bulk of the fat suit, I can't see enough of her to identify who it is. The worrying thing is that I do seem very keen to get back to my room with her, but then again, I also seem to be having such a job coordinating my limbs when I'm upright it's doubtful I'd be able to do anything horizontally either.

'So, where does this leave us?' says Dan, fast-forwarding and rewinding through the section a couple of times, which has the effect of making me look like I'm doing a very drunken hokey-cokey.

I shrug. 'I dunno. I suppose if it proves one thing, then it's that I did go back to my hotel room with a woman.'

'Yeah, but she could have just been helping you up there. It might have been a member of staff.'

'Lenka would have said. No, the evidence is there. And I'm just going to have to tell Sam what I know. Or at least, what I've seen.'

Dan looks at his watch, then sighs. 'I suppose it's now or never. Although . . .'

'What?'

He makes a face. 'I'd still recommend never.'

2.33 p.m.
It feels funny knocking on the door to my flat – well, Sam's flat, as it's going to be again soon. I haven't quite worked out what I'm going to say, although the truth – or at least, as much as I know of it – seems like my only option. It's occurred to me that I could use whatever Sam's been doing to try and soften the blow, but the downside to that approach is that if Sam hasn't been doing anything, then it'll make my situation even worse. Above all, I know I need to keep calm, but when the door's answered – not by Sam, but by the same man I've

seen with Sam in the café, the pub, and in my night-mares – any sense of that goes out of the window.

'Oh no,' he says, his face draining of all colour. 'You're not supposed to be here.'

'I could say the same thing to you,' I say, instantly hating the familiarity in his tone, then – despite Dan trying to hang on to me – I barge past him and into the front room. 'Sam? Sam!'

'Edward?' As Sam emerges from the bedroom, I'm too angry to notice the beautiful wedding dress she's wearing. 'What are you doing here?'

'Surprise.'

'Ah.' Sam glances guiltily across at her mystery man. 'I guess our secret's out.'

'It certainly is,' I say, a little taken aback at her flippancy.

Sam smiles at me. 'Well, you'd have found out soon enough anyway. Edward, this is Patrick.'

Sam's mystery man – sorry, *Patrick* – advances towards me and sticks out his hand, and I automatically shake it, which rather makes my idea of punching him in the face seem a bit out of place.

'Edward,' he says, 'it's so nice to finally meet you.'

Sam walks over and loops an arm round his waist. 'Patrick's the reason you haven't seen much of me over the last few weeks.'

And there it is: the revelation. *Confession*, even – but I can't think how to respond. Suddenly, my anger and desire to hit Patrick disappears.

I collapse onto the sofa as if my plug's been pulled out. None of this makes sense, because despite the gravity of the situation, Patrick is smiling, Sam is too – although she's also looking a little sheepish – and even Dan is sitting in the armchair in the corner with a great big grin on his face. A grin that speaks a thousand words.

'You knew about all this?'

Dan nods. 'That's right, Eddy-boy. And there have been times when it's been tough to keep it a secret, I can tell you.'

My head starts spinning, unable to take any of this in. For the last few weeks, not only has my fiancée been cheating on me, but my best friend has known all about it too. And for some insane reason, they're all talking as if it's no big deal.

Patrick smiles. 'Your fiancée's been a hard woman to satisfy, I can tell you.'

Dan starts to snigger, and this immediately makes me annoyed again. So much so that I leap up off the sofa and walk menacingly across to where he's sitting.

'How could you?'

'I'm sorry, mate. But you've got to admit that was quite funny. Although if you can manage to do it, how hard can it—'

Dan stops speaking, possibly because I've grabbed him by both lapels and hoisted him out of his chair.

'Easy, mate,' he says, putting his hands on my shoulders in an attempt to calm me down. 'This is Armani.'

I let him go, unable to believe that with all that's going

on, the thing he seems to be most worried about his suit, then turn back to look at Sam.

'I think you've got some explaining to do.'

Sam grins nervously. 'Guilty as charged. Though in my defence, it is all your fault.'

'My fault?' My legs nearly go out from under me, and I lean against the wall for support. It's the Jane scenario all over again. Except . . . It's *Sam*. I take a couple of deep breaths as she continues.

'I mean,' she says, 'I always wanted a little affair . . .'

'What?'

'. . . but everything you said kind of got me thinking. About wanting a larger one. You know, doing it properly. And then a client of mine recommended Patrick.'

'Recommended?' I'm stunned. Not only that Sam's suggesting her infidelity was my idea, but also by the fact that anyone would recommend someone to do it with.

'That's right. And after I met him and told him what I wanted to do, it kind of just grew.'

I shake my head to get rid of the horrible image that's forming in my mind. 'Spare me the details, please.'

'You don't mind, do you?'

'Mind?' I don't know where to start. 'What is there to mind? The fact that you've been doing it behind my back, and with him?' I jab a thumb in Patrick's direction, then sit back down on the sofa and put my head in my hands. 'And the fact that Dan knew all about it.'

Sam comes and sits down next to me. 'But I thought this was what you wanted?'

'So . . . You're doing this for me?'

'Well, not *just* for you, I suppose. When Patrick got involved, I started to get excited about doing it for the first time in my life. But I was pretty sure you wouldn't object. Especially since it was your idea in the first place.'

'My idea?' I stare at her incredulously, unable to believe how this can all be my fault and my idea. But then again, Jane told me it was my fault that she had an affair, so maybe Sam's right. Perhaps somehow I've led her to believe it'd be okay, or maybe even a good thing. All of a sudden, the shame of the situation knocks what's left of the wind completely out of me. 'Who else knows about this?'

Sam shrugs. 'Everyone. At least, everyone who's going to be there.'

'Where?'

Sam rolls her eyes. 'At the wedding, silly.'

'At the . . .' I stare at her in disbelief. 'You still want to go through with it?'

'Why wouldn't I?' Sam rests a hand on my arm, and I'm too shell-shocked to pull away. 'Otherwise all of Patrick's efforts will have been wasted. As will the money I've paid him.'

'You had to *pay* him?'

'Of course.'

Patrick laughs, then walks round behind the sofa and puts his hands on Sam's shoulders. 'You wouldn't expect me to do her for nothing, would you?'

As Patrick and Sam seem to be having a joke at my expense, I can feel my anger start to rise again. But surprisingly, it's Dan who twigs what's wrong with me.

'And wedding planners don't come cheap,' he says, getting up out of his chair.

'Huh?'

'I mean,' continues Dan, 'how on earth was Sam going to organize the big wedding she knew you wanted on her own, and in such a short space of time? I tell you, Patrick's been a godsend. Plus it's been tough keeping the wool pulled over your eyes.'

Not for the first time, I can't think of anything to say, so I just repeat myself.

'Huh?'

Dan looks at his watch, then hauls me up off the sofa, and I'm still too stunned to resist. 'So we better go off and get you ready. Especially if we're going to get you to the church on time.'

'The . . . *church*?'

'That's right,' says Dan, leading me towards the front door. 'Besides, Sam's got to finish getting ready too. For your surprise big church wedding.'

As Dan almost shouts these last four words, and I take in just what it is Sam's wearing, I finally seem to be getting it, although my immense relief at the fact that Sam isn't having an affair is tempered a little by the fact that, at least if she had been, I might have felt a little less guilty about my own misdemeanour.

Sam walks over and kisses me, which makes me feel

even worse. 'I mean, after you got me this lovely ring, I didn't know what to get you. So I got you, well, *this*.'

I stare at her in disbelief. 'I feel like such a fool. How could I have missed it?'

'I'm sorry, Edward. I know we promised not to have any secrets from each other. And I promise I won't keep anything from you ever again. But I wanted to surprise you.'

Dan laughs. 'And it looks like you have. Come on, Ed,' he says, putting one hand on the door handle.

While there's a big part of me that's tempted to follow him, I force myself to stay where I am, knowing this is my moment. And while it's something I'm worried – especially now – is going to absolutely crush Sam, there's no way I can back out of it.

'You're right, Sam. We should always be honest with each other. And if that's the case, then there's something I've got to tell you.'

Over Sam's shoulder, I can see Dan frantically shaking his head, but I'm determined to ignore him, as I can't possibly marry Sam this afternoon – especially in a church – without her knowing. But before I get a chance, she reaches up and puts a finger on my lips.

'No, Edward, there's something else I have to tell you first. Or rather, I have to apologize. For not trusting you.'

'What? When?'

'On your stag night.'

Oh crap. Talk about teeing it up. 'Sam, I . . .'

She nods, then takes my hand. 'I mean, I know Dan

promised to look after you, but . . . well, he has enough problems looking after himself sometimes.'

'Don't mind me,' says Dan, looking a little affronted.

'I'm sorry, Dan. It's not that I didn't trust you either, but I know how you can get . . . distracted. So I thought Edward might need some help.'

I look down at her quizzically. 'What kind of help?'

'You know. To get back to your hotel room. Safely. And, well . . .' She starts to blush. 'On your own.'

'Because you didn't trust me?'

'No, because I didn't want anything to happen to you — and there is a difference. So when I eventually found you . . .'

'What do you mean, "found me"?'

Sam grips my hand even tighter. 'I came to look for you. In the club.'

Oh even crapper. That means she'll have seen what I did. But hang on. If she did, and she still wants to get married . . .

'Anyway, like I suspected, you were asleep in the corner, while Dan was off having a snog with what looked like some bloke in a dress.'

I look over at Dan, who's hopping uncomfortably from one foot to the other. 'Yes, well, appearances can be deceptive,' he says. 'Although now I think about it, she did have a very big Adam's apple.'

'Women don't have Adam's apples,' says Patrick.

'This one did,' says Dan, defensively. 'She was just big-boned. At least, she would have been, had—'

'She actually been a woman?' suggests Patrick.

'So, anyway,' continues Sam. 'I thought I'd better try and get you back to your room safely. And then, by the time I got you undressed, and got that fat suit off you – thanks, Dan – and into bed, well, I thought I might as well stay.'

'To check up on me?'

'I didn't want you to choke on your own vomit, for one thing.'

Dan lets out a short laugh. 'And they say romance is dead.'

'So why didn't you hang around? The next morning, I mean.'

Sam looks at me imploringly. 'Because Patrick and I had to go and meet the vicar. Plus, I felt guilty that you might think I didn't trust you to behave yourself. And that's no basis for getting married, is it?'

Dan frowns. 'Meeting the vicar?'

I ignore him while I struggle to process this new information, which as far as I can tell is all good. Not only is my girlfriend, my *fiancée*, not having an affair, but it turns out that neither am I. For a moment, I wonder whether I should apologize for my behaviour over the past couple of weeks, and tell her what I've been worried about. But what would be the point?

'No, Sam,' I say. 'It isn't.'

She smiles at me again. 'Now, what was it you wanted to tell me?'

'Nothing. Or at least, it'll keep. Until after the wedding, in any case.'

'So you do still want to get married to me. After all this?'

I take her in my arms, my heart feeling as if it's about to burst. 'Of course. If you still want to marry *me*, that is?'

Sam nods. 'You don't think I'd get all dressed up like this for just anyone, do you?'

As I try hard to swallow the lump in my throat, Patrick clears his. 'You may now kiss the bride.'

So – being careful not to crumple her wedding dress, while trying to ignore Dan, who's miming sticking his fingers down his throat – I do.

3.49 p.m.

We're in Dan's Porsche, driving towards the church and, while I'm conscious that maybe I should be feeling a little anxious, to be honest, after the events of the past few weeks, relief is my overpowering emotion. And funnily enough, it's Dan who seems to be the nervous one.

'I never thought this day would come,' he says, rounding a corner at, unusually for Dan, well within the speed limit.

'I know it seemed unlikely after everything that went on. And by the way, I still haven't quite forgiven you for not telling me.'

He grins guiltily. 'Yes, well, it kind of seemed like the perfect distraction. All the time you were worried about Sam cheating on you, there was no way you'd suspect what she was really up to. And besides, I wasn't talking about you, Ed. I mean me. Settling down. With Polly.'

'Oh. Sorry. Silly of me to think that you might be thinking of someone else rather than yourself for once in your life.'

'Whereas you, well, I always thought you'd get married. No question of that. Even though for a long time it looked like it might be to Jane.'

I start to laugh, then it suddenly catches in my throat. 'Bollocks.'

'What?' says Dan. 'Don't tell me you've remembered something else you've forgotten to tell Sam.'

'No. It's Jane.'

'Where?' says Dan, instinctively ducking down behind the wheel.

'No – not here, dummy. What if she turns up and ruins everything?'

'Why would she do that?'

'Because I invited her, for one thing.'

'What?' Dan slams the brakes on and screeches to a stop. 'Why?'

Once I've explained the circumstances, Dan rolls his eyes. 'So what? Even if she does turn up, what's she going to do?'

'I dunno. But she could spoil it all by making a scene. Or by saying something nasty to Sam.' I slap myself on the forehead. 'Why am I so stupid?'

Dan looks at me as if he's considering answering that question, before common sense gets the better of him.

'Ed,' he says, putting the car into gear again and setting off, 'I don't think she's going to come.'

'Why not? Because she doesn't want to see me happy? Because it'd be too much for her to see me getting married to someone else? Maybe because she's worried Sam will kick her arse again.'

'No,' says Dan, calmly. 'Because you invited her to the registry office, and we're going to the church, remember? And you're safe there. She's not allowed on holy ground.'

I stare at him for a second or two as what he's just said sinks in, then grab him by the shoulder and shake him violently, nearly causing him to swerve into the oncoming traffic. 'Dan, you're still a genius,' I say. 'I could kiss you.'

'Well, don't,' he says, shrugging me off.

We drive in silence the rest of the way to the church, both lost in our own thoughts. Eventually, Dan nudges me.

'What's the matter with you now?'

I sigh. 'I don't know. I mean, it *is* the happiest day of my life, but what's strange is that I feel like crying.'

Dan shakes his head, but with a smile on his face. 'You big girl's blouse,' he says, pulling the Porsche into a space outside the church that – fittingly for Dan – has 'Pick Up Zone' written on it. 'Well, here we are,' he announces, climbing out of the car. 'The end of an era.'

'You mean you and me, right?'

Dan laughs, then points to my Mini, which is parked

along the street with 'Just Married' written on the rear windscreen, and a number of Special Brew cans tied with string to the back – courtesy of Billy, no doubt. 'Of course,' he says, blipping the Porsche shut, before escorting me along the path towards the church.

I take a deep breath, then peer nervously in through the church door. Sam's parents are there – fortunately without anything resembling a shotgun – along with various relatives and friends I half recognize from Sam's photo albums. Wendy and Andy are sitting near the door, a pushchair in the aisle next to them, obviously ready to make their escape if the crying gets too much – their baby's, I mean, not mine – and even Natasha seems to have brought someone.

As my eyes grow accustomed to the gloom, I spot Polly, sitting by herself at the end of one of the pews. She looks gorgeous – not as gorgeous as Sam, of course – but as I start to walk inside, Dan stops me.

'Wait a second.'

'What?'

Dan swallows hard, and actually looks a little vulnerable. 'I just wanted to say . . .'

Before he can continue, I turn round and give him a hug, and – for once – he doesn't push me away, or question my sexuality.

'Good luck?'

He takes a deep breath, then fixes me with that famous Dan Davis grin, although I've got a feeling it's more for his benefit than mine. 'Edward,' he says, making one final adjustment to his already impeccably styled hair, 'how many times have I told you? Luck has nothing to do with it.'

And for the first time in my life, I think that maybe – just maybe – he might be talking about me.

Acknowledgements

Thanks, yet again, to Patrick Walsh, Jake Smith-Bosanquet, Alex Christofi, and the team at Conville & Walsh. To Maxine Hitchcock, Libby Yevtushenko, Emma Harrow, Emma Lowth, and everyone else at Simon & Schuster. To my parents, Frank and Sheila Dunn, my brother Ewan, my sister Clare, and of course Tina, for your continuing love and support. To Tony Heywood, Lawrence Davison, Chris Raby, and John Lennard, without whom I'd have to make it all up. And finally, to the Board. You know who you are . . .